CAPSIZED

BRIDGET E. BAKER

For Jesse

I think about you every day
Pieces of you are in every book
The pain never really goes away
But I'd never trade the time we had
I never regret loving you
Not for one second

PROLOGUE

My childhood isn't chock full of happy memories. In fact, it's not even somewhat full of them.

I now know that my parents adopted Jesse and me when we were already several years old. Someone, probably an alpha of some variety, erased our earlier memories.

But one memory stands out, like a lit bulb in a room full of burned out lights.

I'm small, wearing shoes that close with Velcro, and Mom has bought me a kite. It's shaped like a butterfly, with long, trailing tails that flutter in the breeze. "You must hold it tightly," she says. "You can't let go of this string. Okay?"

I nod.

Jesse stands behind me, his kite clutched in his slightly larger, but still not very big, hands. He chose a big green snake kite, because it wasn't *girly*, like mine. But it's ugly, and I'm glad I picked the pretty monarch.

Dad takes Jesse's kite from him gently and spreads it out wide. Then he places a black stick inside tiny, clever pockets to keep it spread out. Mom does the same thing to mine, and then they jog together down the beach, the kites rising up into the air behind them, like magic.

They go up, up, up, and my legs pump, trying to catch up with them. "I wanna hold it! Let me, please? Please!"

Jesse's clamoring for his kite as well, now that they're flying.

Mom passes mine to me with a smile.

Dad hands the string attached to the snake to Jesse. "But remember," Dad says. "You have to hold on tightly to the string. If you let go—"

"It'll fly away," I say. "Mom said already."

"Actually." Mom crouches down between Jesse and me, both of us intent on our kite strings, unwilling to lose them. "When you release a kite, it might fly up higher for a bit, but it won't fly away for very long. What I said was that you'd lose it, and it might even break, because without tension in the line, it'll fall to the ground."

I blink. "I don't understand. Why would it fall?" I unloop the string on my kite carefully, giving it more length, and watch intently as it sails higher and higher and higher.

Dad drops onto the sand next to us. "Life is funny like that. You can give a kite a lot of rope, and as you do, it flies higher and higher. But once it's no longer tethered, as soon as it comes completely untied, it doesn't soar higher anymore. It crashes to the ground."

"Why?" Jesse asks.

"Being securely linked to the ground allows it to soar," Dad says. "It needs an anchor to stay aloft."

"Do we need anchors?" I ask.

"We aren't kites," Mom says. "But that's a good

question. Like kites, people need anchors, too. Your dad and I will keep you safe while you sail up to great heights. That's our job."

But not long after our trip to the beach, Mom and Dad—our anchors, our safety against the buffeting winds of life—died.

Our strings were cut.

We should have crashed to the earth.

Broken.

Useless.

But I found another anchor. Jesse stepped up, keeping me tied to the earth, allowing me to fly high, strong, and true. Just like that kite, I need something to keep me steady, to keep me strong. He anchored me to everything that mattered. He allowed me to soar.

Until one day, that string was cut, too.

What Mom and Dad failed to explain that day at the beach is that, unlike kites, sometimes when people hit the ground, they don't just break.

They go BOOM.

ANCIENT EGYPT

Sneaking in through a window gracefully is much, much harder than I expected it to be. I hop up onto the sill easily enough, but then my boot gets stuck and I swear under my breath.

"Where in the world have you been?" Shu's eyes shine like lanterns as he Binds me in place, but his fury almost eclipses the light created by his Lifting.

"It's late," I say. "I was hoping you'd be asleep."

"Asleep?! Have you lost your mind?"

I'm not sure there's a great answer for that question.

"Tefnut was pacing for more than an hour. I finally sent her down to the common room to start asking questions, even though we don't want to draw any attention to who we are or why we're here."

"I'm fine," I say. "I was always fine."

"How were we supposed to know that, when you darted off?"

Pretty sure half the building can hear him right now.

"Aren't you curious what questions she's asking?"

Not really.

"I'll tell you. She's asking about any notable *arrests* or *executions*." Shu clenches his fists. "I should never have gone along with this. I should have told Father—"

I flex my abilities and pop his Binding, finally shoving through the opening and collapsing into a heap on the floor of our rented room. "Have you ever been in love, Shu?"

His mouth drops open and his shoulders droop. "Excuse me?"

I look up at him, trying not to look too idiotic when I ask, "If you have been in love before, how did you know you *were* in love?"

He sinks to his knees next to me and takes my hand in his. "You're not in love, Sekhmet. You can't be. You don't even *know* Alexander, I promise."

"But have *you* been in love?" I blink at him.

He sighs. "Yes, I have."

"You were? Why didn't it work out?"

"How do you know that it didn't?"

"I haven't met her," I say. "Or him."

He laughs. "It was a woman, and it didn't end well."

Dad and Mother. Shu and some woman I've never heard anything about. "Why didn't you ever tell me about it?"

"I already answered that—it ended poorly."

"But at some point it was going well enough for you to love her, so why didn't I meet her then?"

He rolls his eyes. "It happened before you were born, cub."

I don't like knowing that Shu had a whole life, experiences, and apparently some epic love, before I was even born. It almost feels like I don't really know him at all. I suppose I can be important to him and he to me without us knowing every single thing about one another. "Fine. Well, I'm not saying I'm in love. That would clearly get me mocked. But maybe I understand how people *could* be."

Shu releases my hand and leans back against the wall under the window. "Please, please, please tell me the person you like isn't Alexander." His eyes bore into mine.

"Uh."

"Sekhmet! His mother wants *to kill* our father. Did you forget that part?"

I swallow.

"Our father tinkered, magically, with him *in the womb*."

"I know." I fold my arms. "But he's not a monster. He's. . ." I can't exactly describe what he is. He's bold. He's unexpected. "He's good without being oppressive. He's strong without being dominating. With him, there's a new surprise with every breath."

Shu yanks me up to my feet. "Oh, no, no, no. We need to head back home this very minute."

I pull myself free and back slowly toward the wall. "I don't want to go home yet." The words surprise even me. I should race home. I should put as much distance as I possibly can between me and Alexander. Tonight. Right now. But for some reason, I know I won't do that. I can't.

"Tell me you didn't talk to him. Tell me he doesn't know we're here or who you are." Shu's eyebrows draw together. "Please, Sekhmet, tell me that much, at least."

"I can tell you whatever you'd like to hear," I say.

He groans. "What possessed you to race away? Why would you risk yourself like that? Do you know what would have happened if—"

"If what?" I realize I'm shouting and force my voice

down. "If someone attacked me? I'm not made of glass. I don't shatter. I can siphon *anyone*. I can Lift *anything*. I can tear down people's very wills and make them do as I wish." I straighten my shoulders. "It's borderline absurd that Dad has me guarded so carefully, when I could probably kill every one of my guards without blinking."

Shu swallows. "Perhaps he wasn't worried about the safety of your body."

Huh? Is Shu saying that I'm not capable of making my own decisions? My nostrils flare with fury until I consider that it's Shu saying this. He loves me, I know he does, and he wants what's best for me.

Which means he might be right.

I do feel more mixed up than I've ever been. "It's not like I'm betraying Dad," I say. "It's just that I had an idea. Last night I happened to bump into Alexander, kind of like the last time." Okay, that's a total lie, but it's not a harmful one. "He recognized me, even through my disguise." And that part's true.

"How could he possibly have done that?"

"I might have accidentally mentioned Gordion." I bite my lip.

Shu throws his hands into the air. "Sekhmet! I can't believe I have to say this—"

"I didn't mention I was there," I say. "I'm not an idiot. I just mentioned that he sliced the knot, when they've been disseminating the story that—"

"He solved it." He exhales slowly. "What idea could you have that would possibly justify the risk in what you've already done? Do I need to remind you that his mother wants to *kill* our father? That she probably wants to kill you, too?"

"I haven't *done* anything," I say. "I talked to him. So what?"

"So he only knows that you're the same woman he met in Gordion?" Shu arches his eyebrow.

"Maybe he figured out that I'm Ra's child. Is that a crime?"

"You told him who you really are?" Shu's eyes are wide. "How could you possibly have been that careless?"

Selfish would have been a better accusation for him to level at me. "I don't know how his mother feels, but he doesn't hate me," I say. "And he doesn't even think that his mother hates Dad either. He says that she *loved* him."

"Since you've never been in love, I'll share a little secret with you. Loving a brother or a father is simpler than loving someone romantically. When you're talking about romantic love, love and hate aren't opposites—they're the closest feelings in the world. And love can flip to hate in a second—which makes love almost as dangerous as hate."

I think about my mother. About my feelings for her —and hers for me. I love her. I miss her. But there's more to it. I think, even when you're dealing with non-romantic love, Shu may have a point. But I can't acknowledge that right now—he's trying to bundle me off and if I know one thing, it's this.

I can't leave. Not yet.

"I had another idea the second I ran away from him, but this time, I came to talk to you about it. That's progress, right?"

Shu scowls. "Is asking for approval before you smash a priceless vase progress?"

Once he hears my idea, he may change his mind. "I can plant an idea in his head, Shu, a lie. I can tell him the only way to successfully kill Dad."

"Why in the world would you do that?" Shu shakes his head. "It's like the world has turned on its head."

I smile. "Not a real secret, dummy. There *is* no secret way to kill him, but if I convince Alexander there is. . ."

"Then he'll tell his mom, and they'll believe the act we're putting on when they 'conquer' Egypt," Shu says. For the first time since he caught me sneaking into the room, the panic fades from his features. His mouth drops open, just slightly, and his eyes focus miles away from me. But after considering it slowly, thoughtfully, he still shakes his head sharply. "No, it's too risky. You're clearly attached to Apophis, whatever you say. I'd even venture to call you obsessed. Seeing him again will only make things worse, even if you've managed to fabricate a somewhat compelling reason to justify it."

"It may be the only way this escape plan really works," I whisper. "Do you really think Isis and Apophis will buy Dad's defeat without a sell job?"

"Wasn't that the point of the Gordian knot?" Shu frowns.

His failure to see my point infuriates me, and I wonder what my real motivation is. For the first time in my life, I'm not sure whether I want to leave Egypt with Dad at all.

I can't seem to think straight where Alexander is concerned.

Shu huffs. "Let me think about it."

The sound of footsteps in the hallway outside the door draws our attention and Shu's voice drops to a whisper. "Not a word of this to Tefnut. She would *never* understand. Tell her you wanted to meet people and move around and lament that you're never, ever alone. She'll understand that. Tell her you wanted to go shopping, or that you wanted to flirt with guys. I don't care what excuses you make, as long as you don't breathe a word about making contact with Alexander or revealing who you are. And promise me you won't go near him again without telling me *first*."

I nod.

"You must get my approval. Swear it, or I'll Bind your hands and toss you in a barrel."

"A barrel?" I can't help my incredulous tone.

"A barrel," he insists. "One that stinks."

I sigh. "Fine."

It takes me all morning and into the afternoon to convince my older brother that it's a good idea for me to see Alexander again, but he finally comes around. The lure of tricking Isis and Apophis is just too tempting. And as much as it pains me with my newly found half-sister, I heed his advice with Tefnut. He knows her better than I do.

"Apophis is receiving tribute from nobles in the surrounding areas today," she says with a satisfied smile.

Shu's head whips toward mine.

"Are you going?" I ask. "It would give you the chance to evaluate him."

Shu licks his lips and swallows.

"Isn't that why we came? Shouldn't someone go?" Tefnut asks.

"You should absolutely go," Shu says. He spends the next few minutes going over various ideas for Tefnut's alias. "You'll need some kind of impressive gift." He folds his arms and looks pointedly at me.

"What am I supposed to do about that?" I ask.

"Magic something for me," Tefnut says. "A chest with gold. A box of jewels. Something easy to carry."

I consider fashioning something obnoxious, annoyed by her authoritarian tone.

"Oh, don't be crabby. Tefnut meant to say *please*." Shu hip-bumps her.

"Right." To my shock, my older sister actually bobs her head in a peremptory curtsy. "Of course I did. If you'd be so kind as to—" She flutters her hands. "—whip something up. That would help me maintain my cover. Then we could report back to Father that one of us has seen him face-to-face."

It's too much. I'm going to tell her. I open my mouth to do it.

Shu wraps one arm around me. "I think the easiest thing would be a small case of jewels." He clears his throat. "A handful of rocks would be a great base for her to use." He looks at Tefnut expectantly.

She jumps. "I should get them. Of course. I'll be right back." She ducks out.

And I shove away from Shu. "Why does she get to go? I thought we agreed—"

He claps his hand over my mouth. "Are you insane? We said we wouldn't tell her. You can change your appearance and go yourself as another petitioner. Then Tefnut won't know *and* she'll be busy while you leave."

Shu's brilliant. Why didn't I trust him? I'm an idiot.

It doesn't take me long to use a bit of energy to turn the rocks into jewels. "How long will these remain like this?" Tefnut asks skeptically. "Is there any chance they'll change back before I hand them over?"

How does she know so little about assimilation? "They won't change back. Altering their state slightly, from one mineral to another, that's basic shaping. They're actually the gems they appear to be now."

Her mouth drops open. "You're saying that you could turn the entire world into diamonds and rubies?"

I shrug. "Theoretically, I suppose I could. But things have value for their rarity. So if I started doing that, before too long, no one would want it anymore. Plus, the energy that kind of wide-scale transformation would require. . . It would be unbelievable."

"That's a good object lesson for all of us," Shu says. "So many of the things we care about are *transitory*." He glares at me. "Family is what really matters—something that lasts."

Oh, please. I don't need the reminder that Dad matters more than Alexander. I couldn't forget that we're enemies if I wanted to. . . Which I kind of do. After Tefnut leaves, I start casting about for something else I could take as our tribute. He must know what I'm doing, but Shu ducks out of the room instead of helping. "Hey, where are you going?"

He's gone for a moment, and then re-enters in a heavily embroidered red robe, with a conical hat. I can't help my laugh. "What are you doing?"

"I'm your manservant, clearly, Roxana, daughter of Oxyartes."

"Who in the world is that?"

Shu grunts. "You can't very well go as Neser, and I doubt you mean to go as a lion and allow me to do the talking?"

"Who's Roxana? Or Oxyartes? What an odd name."

"We're Sogdian," he says. "Imhotep brought back a load of clothing from there—which is where I got this robe and hat—when he went last month. I brought it along in case we needed more disguises. The Sogdians used a number of unique healing techniques he'd never seen." Shu sighs. "I can almost guarantee Alexander hasn't been there, since even Dad hasn't been in the last few decades."

"Fine," I say.

"Copy my clothing and give yourself a darker complexion, deep brown eyes, and long black hair."

"You're bossy."

"And your tribute will be silk. They have loads of it, apparently."

I blink. "Silk?"

"Floating a trunk of it along behind us will be easy enough."

"Or we can use a horse for that. We don't want to look like paupers."

"Don't we?" he asks. "You merely need to get close enough to ask for a private audience, no?"

I didn't exactly tell Shu how I left things. I'm fairly certain Alexander will be interested in speaking to me again, but I'm not sure quite how he'll react. "It might be best if I don't let on that I am whom I actually am until we're alone." I bite my fingernail. "All I need to do is convince him that I'm a reputable source of information. Tell me everything you know about Imhotep's visit, and I'll wrap my story around that."

Moments later, with our backstory coordinated, my appearance modified, and some silk magicked out of linen, we're approaching the palace. There's already a long line running down the main street. I don't see Tefnut, so hopefully she's almost to the front. Even if she spots us, she'll never recognize us. I've completely altered my appearance, as well as Shu's. He's massive, and I'm small and sultry. I practice my pout.

"What are you doing?" He frowns.

I stop. "Nothing."

"You should've looked less. . ." Shu shrugs. "Less *everything*."

"I need to catch his attention, don't I?"

Shu rolls his eyes.

My nerves are a jangly, bouncy, jumbled up mess, but as we wait, and wait, and wait, they settle.

And annoyance sets in. "How long does he think it's appropriate to make us all wait out here?" I hiss.

"Remember who you are," Shu says. "You're unlikely to be annoyed with Alexander *the Great*."

He's right. If I'm going to sell this, I need to think and talk and act like Roxana would. He's already proven a little too canny for me.

Hours later, we finally approach the front. If the sun's already close to setting, I worry he might turn us away. Could he? Panic grips me. What if he's tired of making small talk with local envoys and accepting gifts of goats and fruit baskets and he sends us away? I shift our trunk slightly so that it's obvious we aren't bringing a box full of dates or a crate of chickens.

Thankfully, we're next in line. Surely they'd have sent us home already if they meant to, wouldn't they? It suddenly occurs to me that he might not be greeting all these people. He may be fobbing us off on some kind of regent. It's a real drag, not being who I am. I'm unaccustomed to having to wait for things and hope for the best.

"Listen to me." Shu's voice is low and urgent. "You're not to spend more time than strictly necessary. You're to stick to what we planned. Promise?"

I nod.

"By ma'at and all that is holy, I swear that if Father ever finds out that I helped with this, I'll be lucky if all he does is string me up by my toes and chuck scorpions at me. For a week." He keeps muttering after that, but I don't pay him much attention.

Shu's just being Shu.

That's why I love him, after all. Even knowing full well that Dad will be furious, he's right here, prepping me and giving me advice. I hug him tightly. His eyes fly wide at first, but then he hugs me back. When I don't immediately release him, he pries my arms off. "You can't be hugging your guard." But the smile he suppresses on his lips shows in his eyes.

"I love you, Shu."

He straightens next to me.

"Names and positions?" The gruff guard ahead of us barks.

I realize for the first time that I don't know any Sogdian at all. I hope they don't try to verify any of that, because if they happen to have any Sogdians in residence, I'm in trouble. I answer in Greek. "Roxana, daughter of Oxyartes, noblewoman of Sogdia. I bring the finest silk for the noble Alexander."

The man glances over me quickly, and then studies Shu as though he's a viper before finally waving us through the doorway.

I've met Alexander twice. The first time he approached a man and woman standing alone in a street. He was surrounded by his men, probably travel weary, and irritable. He was riding Bucephalus, a Reaper alpha, and he looked impressive. The second time, he was safe and at ease in his own room. Dressed down. Informal. Off guard.

But I've never approached him like this—like most everyone in the world must see him.

We walk slowly down an ornate hallway, decorated with murals and tall pedestals adorned with vases full of long-stemmed, fragrant lily blossoms. Men stand at attention in long lines, leading up to the raised platform on which rests a solid, heavy wooden throne.

And on that throne, in a resplendent purple chiton, rests Alexander. His shoulders are broad. His eyes electric. His powerful arms rest lightly on his knees. A massive sword hilt protrudes between his shoulders.

His well-muscled shoulders rise and fall gently with each breath, and I can't look away.

He's magnificent in every way. His face is so beautiful it's almost painful. His skin glows—a deep golden color. His vibrant, ice-blue eyes pierce the crowd as they scan. They pass over me at first, then reverse and pause briefly. I smile at him coyly, which is exactly the opposite of what I'd normally do.

His lips compress with displeasure and his eyes move on.

My heart races—is he looking for me? That possibility didn't occur to me, but it should have. Whatever he felt for me before, now that he knows who I am, he'll surely want another discussion at best, and to put a sword through my heart at worst.

There's no world in which we are enemies.

A shiver runs through me as I remember him saying the words.

Words he can't possibly mean.

We're enemies in every world, probably in every time. We're eternally and fundamentally at odds and have been since birth. Maybe before. He says his mother loved and lost. My father says Isis is a crazed lunatic. The truth, as with most things, probably rests somewhere between those two—but it's not up to me to puzzle it out.

Whatever my motivations in coming originally, whatever my unhealthy obsession, I have one goal now: to strike a deal based on a lie I must convince him to believe.

It's time for me to figure out how to lie effectively around him. I square my shoulders and swallow slowly. A man with a long, sharp nose and curly hair announces me in a nasal voice. Coming from him, 'Roxana' sounds brittle and shrill, and the way he quirks his lip makes it clear how he feels about Sogdia.

"Silk?" Alexander lifts one eyebrow. "Isn't that a kind of fabric? Sogdia is quite far from here."

"News of your power and virility travels far and wide, my lord." I try the pout I practiced, hoping that Alexander reacts differently than Shu did.

"His *Majesty*," the curly-haired man intones nasally.

I bob a curtsy. "Of course. Pardon me, your majesty."

Alexander's eyes are dancing when I meet them again.

"Why have you come so far?" he asks.

"I'm hoping to strike a bargain that may benefit both of us." I shrug.

"What type of bargain?"

"It would be easier to discuss in private." In spite of my attempt to be bold, the last few words come out as barely more than a whisper.

"A private audience?" The curly-haired man scoffs. "His Royal Majesty, Alexander the Great, does not have time—"

Alexander cuts him off. "Why do you need to speak to me privately?"

"I have sensitive information to barter."

"You'll leave your man behind?" He glances behind me, his eyes hardening as he examines Shu.

I turn around and notice my brother's massive frame is taut. Animosity rolls off him in waves. "I'll leave him here," I say softly.

Shu shakes his head. "She will not."

"Do you often give your mistress orders?" Alexander stands.

"Incessantly," I mutter.

"You can come too," Alexander says. "I'm not afraid."

My eyes widen.

"I'm sure no one will mind a short break." Alexander turns to the nasal man. "Pass refreshments around to all those who are yet waiting."

A loud cheer goes up behind me.

He gestures toward an open doorway and begins to descend the stairs toward it.

Instead of walking the long way around the raised platform to follow him out, I walk up the stairs, placing myself far above him.

Alexander looks back at me over his shoulder and beams. "I knew it."

"Pardon me," I say. "My Greek is imperfect, and I am afraid I do not understand. What did you know?"

There's no way he'll buy that, but I must be more convincing than I thought, because Alexander simply frowns and says, "Never mind."

Shu tsks behind me.

The anteroom behind the throne room is quite a bit smaller and occupied by far fewer people. Two men follow us out. One has long, shaggy black hair and nearly black eyes. When he glances my way, I can *feel* his presence, like a hand pressed against my cheek. I strongly suspect I've only seen him in horse form before now.

The other man is so beautiful that he'd very nearly make a stunning woman if he didn't have such a mascu-line, warrior's build. They take up positions on either side of Alexander, both with their arms crossed, swords on their backs.

"Bucephalus, I assume." I stare pointedly at the man with shaggy black hair.

He scowls.

"It's impressive what you've done for Alexander's armies, especially before he took the throne. Not many supras have ever been willing to submit to someone and also attack at the same time, but no Reapers at all, unless I'm mistaken."

Bucephalus' lip curls.

I shake my head. "You mistake my words as hostile. I merely mean to compliment you."

Uncertainty sneaks across his face, and his eyes dart toward Alexander.

I'm surprised he's remained silent.

"And you must be Hephaestion," I say. "Alexander's dearest and oldest friend."

Unlike Bucephalus, he smiles at me. "You're very well spoken for a Sogdian. You've come a long way."

"We're quite far apart," I admit. "I'm trying to bridge a very deep divide by coming here and speaking to you."

"I wasn't aware that we were at war with Sogdia," Hephaestion says.

"You aren't," I say. "But I admit, I may have come here under false pretenses, though my intentions are pure." I glance at Alexander.

He locks eyes with me, and a smile creeps onto his face. "I was right."

"Right about what?" Bucephalus' head is whipping between my face and Alexander's, clearly not a fan of being left out.

"The two of you will leave us." Alexander's voice is low.

"She came, just as you said she would," Hephaestion says. "I'm more impressed than you said I'd be."

"Wait, who is she? Why did she come? What does she want?" Bucephalus tosses his head almost exactly as an irritated horse would. "Surely we mustn't leave while there are two of them to one of you."

Shu shakes his head. "I won't leave *Roxana* alone."

Alexander waves his hand through the air. "Hephaestion, Bucephalus, go. I'll be fine." His voice is low, and it sparks a fresh memory. Alexander's arms around me. His lips pressed against mine. I practically shake with *want* of it. "You can go too, Shu," I whisper. "He won't harm me."

Shu's hands fist at his sides.

"Shu?" Hephaestion freezes. "I've seen him before. This can't be Shu."

"Think about it," Alexander says.

"Oh." Hephaestion sighs. "Right."

So he really does know everything about who I am. That knowledge disappoints me, for some reason.

"We must go, now," Shu says. "If he's told—"

"Only my dearest friend." Alexander steps closer, his voice pleading. "I swear it on my mother's life. On my hope of an afterlife."

Shu swallows, the same vein in his temple throbbing in his massive, hulking form that always throbs. He finally drags his eyes away from Alexander and turns to me. "Are you sure?"

The corner of my mouth inches upward. "Am I sure I can protect myself if he attacks me? That I can siphon every single person in this entire palace until there's nothing left but dust and despair?" I laugh then. "Yes, brother dearest. I'm absolutely, villainously positive."

Alexander's laugher shakes the foundations.

Hephaestion joins him.

Bucephalus swears under his breath and grabs Hephaestion's arm. "You're going to tell me who she is the second we're outside."

"I'll wait just through here." Shu points at the door into the throne room. "Shout and I'll return."

I incline my head slightly as he disappears.

And then the entire room narrows to one thing.

Alexander. His shining hair. His broad shoulders. His slanted brow and angular jaw. And his eyes, oh, his eyes. "You came back."

"I have a proposal," I say.

"I accept." He steps toward me.

My hands spread as I stumble backward inelegantly. "No, stop, just listen."

"You came, and you wanted to speak to me." His stride is too long. His arms too brawny. He's standing less than a handbreadth away from me now, and his smell floods my senses—heady, bright, overpowering. Surprisingly sweet, like lilies and sandalwood.

"I came to negotiate." I look upward until our eyes meet, and then I forget every single thing I meant to say.

His head lowers slowly. His eyes drop from mine to my mouth, and a shudder runs through me, starting in my toes and racing toward my center. His mouth has almost reached mine when I manage to press my fingers against it.

"No. I can't."

"You can't what?" His lips smile against my fingers, his eyes pleading with me. "You can't be saying you can't kiss me. You did it well enough last night."

"I can't breathe with you this close." I close my eyes.

He kisses my fingers and the world warps around me.

I try to step backward again, but his arms circle my waist. "I knew you would come."

"You didn't search for me," I whisper.

His smile broadens. "I didn't want to scare you off."

"I'm not afraid of you," I say.

"That's one of the things I like best about you." His breath fans across my face.

My heart thunders in my chest.

"One of the many things." He releases my waist on one side and uses that hand to tug on my elbow, shifting my fingers downward and away from his mouth. "One of the many things." His head dips again, and this time I don't stop him. His mouth covers mine, stealing my opposition. Quieting my fear. Supplanting my resistance.

Eliminating every single thought in my head.

His arms. His mouth. His warm strength. It's my entire world.

It's everything.

And for the first time in my life, I surrender entirely. My arms wind around his waist, sliding across the fabric of his chiton. My fingers graze the planes of his stomach through the thin fabric, and I wish even that wasn't between us. A shiver races up my spine. His lips press harder, hungrily. Like he'll never tire of kissing me.

A rumble starts in my throat.

As a pit of desire opens inside of my body, the rumble expands and suddenly, *I'm purring*.

How embarrassing.

I stumble backward, bright color staining my cheeks.

Alexander's beaming. "Did you—were you—"

"Shut up," I say.

If he asks me whether I was purring, I'll. . .

"You said you came to make a deal." He crosses his arms, his eyes scanning my current form. "I'd be happy to hear you out, now that you've *properly* greeted me."

His smirk is absolutely infuriating. "But I'd strongly prefer to see you as you really are."

I arch one eyebrow. "This form is nicer than mine. You should appreciate it."

"I respectfully but strongly disagree."

I roll my eyes. "You're pretty demanding."

He bites his lip, his eyes dipping again to my mouth. "That surprises you, does it? You didn't seem to mind my demands a moment ago."

Heat floods my face again. "My offer is this. I'll tell you how to defeat my father."

He inhales sharply. "You said he was considering surrendering."

"Would that satisfy your mother?"

His lips press together.

"We both know it wouldn't. She'd question his motives, and as soon as we settled elsewhere, she'd urge you to follow us."

"You know her better than I expected."

"I think my father knows her quite well," I say. "While I know her not at all."

"She'd like you, I think," he says.

"I doubt that very much."

"You might be surprised."

I don't bother telling him that my dad is wonderful. It seems pointless.

"Why would you betray your own father?" He leans against the wall next to him, and it looks like a calculated shift, like he wants me to think he's relaxed. I doubt he's ever really relaxed while negotiating something.

"Because of what I stand to gain in return."

His eyes flash.

"You'll betray your mother."

He shakes his head. "I can't do that."

Something inside me contracts at his words, at how easily he dismisses my request out of hand. "You don't even know what I'm asking."

"My relationship with my mother is. . .complicated." He sighs. "She's not perfect—far from it. But I believe she loves me as much as she's capable, and I believe she'd raze the world to the ground for me if I but asked. I can't betray her, not in any way."

"Nor could I ever truly betray my father. Our relationship is utterly uncomplicated. I *adore* him."

He blinks. "Then why—"

"I'll tell you how to defeat him—if you swear to tell your mother that you killed him. . .when truly, you let us go."

"Why would you even want that?" His head is cocked sideways, like a panther listening for telltale signs of prey.

"I was honest from the start. My father is weary, as am I. We're tired of ruling, but even you and your mother must admit we've done a good job of it. Our people are prosperous and well cared for."

He shrugs.

"We want to leave it all, but our departure would create a vacuum. One that unscrupulous people might take advantage of, unless someone new immediately replaced us. This does two things. First, it satisfies your mother so we can move on without her following us, and secondly, it ensures that our people will continue in prosperity and peace."

"You don't think she'll hear rumors when you set up another empire elsewhere?"

I shake my head. "We plan to disappear. Live a quiet life."

He frowns. "You could never live a quiet life. You're

like a lodestone. The world reorients itself around you."

"Hello, cart. Wagon. Nice to meet you."

His laugh is part snort. "It's harder for me. I do it consciously. You do it as easily as you breathe. You can't ever disappear."

"You know me so little and yet you have no faith in me at all."

He's suddenly right next to me, his hand pressed against my cheek. "I know you better than anyone else ever could. We're two of a kind, you and I."

I shake my head, but his hand doesn't move, his fingers cupping the curve of my jaw.

"I've always known you, I think. Your father, my mother. It might sound insane, but it feels like fate had plans for us all along. We've been on a crash course since before our births."

There's truth in what he says—our parents should have known. Perhaps Isis did. Perhaps she's been waiting on me to come to him all this time. "Crash?"

His smile is mirth filled. "Not all crashes are bad."

"Really?"

His mouth crashes into mine to prove his point, and my heart reacts instantly. My belly tightens. My body leans into his. His lips move against mine. "This is the crash I've waited for my entire life."

But I can't let him distract me, no matter how tempting the distraction. I promised Shu. "Will you do it?" I don't pull back. I'm not sure I want to see his face. I know I don't want any more space between us.

"Do what? Attack your father and take him down?"

I pull away then. "Spare his life, if I make him vulnerable. Tell your mother that he's been vanquished."

"Lie to her." His voice is flat. His hands tighten on

my waist almost to the point of pain. "You want me to betray the one person who would never betray me."

"I imagine there are others who would never betray you." I Lift his hands away gently, reminding him who I am. I straighten. "Because if you don't agree. . ." I let the threat drift.

"You'll eradicate us?" His eyes dance. "You'll siphon us down to nothing but dust and despair?"

I frown. "You should be afraid of me. You should be shaking, really. I could do just that."

"I'll never be afraid of you. There's no world in which we're enemies." His face hovers above mine. "I've seen your real face. I see your heart, Sekhmet. *I know you.*"

"You know nothing about me."

His next words are a mere whisper. "I've tasted you. I've listened to you. I've *seen* you."

I can't call it a lie. It feels too true. "But will you do it?"

"Perhaps I'm not as good a son as I've said. Perhaps my biggest objection with granting your request is something else entirely." He bites his lip.

"What?"

"Have you considered that if I do what you ask, I'll never see you again?"

I close my eyes. "You'll never see me again either way."

"That's what you want?" he asks softly. "For me to defeat your father and lie to my mother?"

I nod.

"Then I'll do it." But his heart looks broken.

Mine feels battered.

I remind myself that I barely know him.

"Swear that you'll tell her he's dead, but then spare him instead."

"I swear it on heaven above and hell beneath, on my mother's life and on my afterlife."

It's enough. "Time hasn't passed without a toll. In the last few years, Dad hasn't been able to use his powers at dusk or dawn," I whisper. "You can defeat him then, if you're fast enough. He'll try to flee as either timeframe approaches, and he's not without protection from his commanders at any time. It's not going to be easy, but if you immobilize him with the help of Bucephalus—he's terrified of alphas, especially supras. Dad's father was a supra and held him, abused him, and used him, for decades."

Alexander nods sharply.

"Please don't tell anyone about that, not even your mother."

He nods again.

I turn to leave.

His arm catches mine. "It's not part of our deal, but I'd like to see you again."

"You don't believe in love," I whisper. "So what's the point?"

The corner of his mouth turns upward. "Maybe you'll make a believer out of me yet."

He's wrong about that—but he might be right about something else. I do think that maybe we were destined from the beginning to crash. I just hope the world can withstand the fallout.

EARTH

"I don't want ramen," I complain. "It's all we ever eat, and I'm pretty sure it's bad for growing brains."

"My brain is done growing." Jesse smirks. "And I'm not the one who eats like an army of teenage boys."

"But you *are* a teenage boy," I snap.

"Only for one more year."

"You eat a lot too," I say. "That's my point."

He's right, though. It's the sheer volume of calories that I consume that keeps us from eating better than we do. We can buy four packages of ramen for a dollar at Wal-Mart—the next cheapest meal we can make, spaghetti, still costs four to five times as much.

"Chin up. I sprung for frozen vegetables this time." Jesse plonks the bowl down in front of me.

Bright, slightly spongy green beans, wrinkly peas, and blocky carrot chunks swim around in my salad bowl. It's pathetic that I'm so excited about the addition of a bag of frozen veggies, but it's still true. I'm heartily sick of ramen, but even that doesn't stop me from digging in.

It's not fair for me to growl and bark at Jesse. Our boring diet isn't his fault. "Thanks." I stuff a huge bite of noodles in my mouth and begin to chew.

"See?" His crooked grin always improves my day. "Nothing is as bad with a full stomach."

I'm a long way from being full, but with every bite, I'm less hangry.

"Maybe tomorrow we can hit McDonald's and see if they've added anything to the value menu," he says.

French fries are my weakness. Jesse knows me well. A smile creeps onto my face. "We could probably do that."

He walks across the room and turns on the television. "Seven o'clock. Almost forgot."

Ensnared comes on at seven. "She's going to get roasted for sure," I say.

"They can't roast her," Jesse argues. "She may be surrounded by dragons, but she's the main character. The one thing that's a given is that she'll survive."

"But what if they *did* kill her off?" I shrug. "It would be a real plot twist, to eliminate the main character."

"It's the middle of the season?" He rolls his eyes. "Besides, remember that big author who did that? That dystopian story that ended with her *dying*? Oh man, fans were ticked."

I laugh. "We should get a new library card."

"Saturday," he says. "We can go then."

A small twinge in the back of my mind distracts me. We can't go Saturday. . .we can't, but I'm not sure why. "Are you sure we don't have other plans?"

Jesse frowns. "Like what?"

The theme song on the television reminds me that the show is starting. But it's an episode I've seen. "I thought Thursday night was a new one."

Jesse glances my direction, his eyebrows raised. "It is new."

I shake my head. "I've seen this."

The corner of his mouth quirks up. "You best friends with the network president or something? How could you have seen it already?"

I blink. The golden dragon's about to incinerate someone, even though Eliza jumps in front of them. It singes the hair on her arms.

"Are you okay?" Jesse asks, still staring at me. "You seem strange today. Off, somehow."

I turn my attention to him, and I notice a dozen tiny details that aren't quite right. His hair's a little too stiff, like it's frozen in place. His smile's a little too perfectly crooked. His teeth are pristine, even though he's just eaten a bowl of noodles—not a speck of food stuck anywhere. And his eyes are wrong. I can't quite figure out what about them is off, but they're not like they should be. "Are *you* alright?" I lean toward him, studying the features I know so well, and notice more discrepancies.

His deep blue eyes are just a little too dark.

The shoulders that have always carried me through the problems in our lives are a little too beefy—not quite thin enough.

And his eyebrows should be a bit bushier.

As if my thoughts could somehow change reality, his eyes lighten. A fleck of green something pops into existence over his right incisor, and his frame thins slightly. His hair softens up. His eyebrows bush out.

I try to swallow, but I can't.

"You're white as a ghost. Are you sure you're okay?" Jesse's eyes narrow.

As if *I'm* the problem.

I reach out to touch him and he flinches.

Jesse has never flinched when I reached for him before.

Never.

I can't breathe either. They're small things—tiny, inconsequential inconsistencies, but they add up to something more. Like the world is warped or buckled. Something that should feel right, that should feel safe, that should feel like home—our old, patched bean bag chairs, our painted spool table, our dingy, scuffed floors. . .

It's all wrong.

This all feels foreign, somehow.

We aren't safe here.

"I'm your brother," Jesse-who-is-not-Jesse says. "I love you."

I try again to swallow, but my throat is still strangely blocked. I can barely force out any words. "Something isn't right," I say. "Something about you feels wrong."

He tilts his head exactly like Jesse would tilt his head. "Of course it does. Because I'm dead."

Memories punch into me then—Jesse crumpled on the pavement. Jesse, surrounded in a growing pool of blood. Jesse's lifeless body.

And then.

Jesse's cold, white corpse on a rolling table.

The world shatters all around me, and becomes white and black and dark and light all at once. The only thing that remains is the not-Jesse. "If you died, then how are you here?" My voice wobbles. My knees are weak. "If you died, how are you talking to me?"

"You couldn't accept my death." His eyes are sad. He steps toward me. "You made me up. You created—" He gestures at himself. "—this. You made me what I am, so that you could pretend."

Horror slips into the cracks between my body and my soul and wraps around my heart. "No." I shake my head. "You're not dead. You're alive. I saved you."

His laugh is exactly the same as Jesse's. It's spot on. For one second, I believe that he's fine. That this was all some kind of misunderstanding. "You can't save someone who's already dead, Alora. You know that."

And then the entire world goes blank.

I don't even care.

Because if he's gone, nothing else matters.

❀   3   ❀

EARTH

I have never in my life slept in a bed this large, or with blankets this soft. I rub my bleary eyes and wonder for a split second where I am.

Then I sit straight up in bed and begin to scream.

Because Jesse's dead.

"Alora?"

I'm in a vast room they showed me to in Buckingham palace. I know it now. The heavy wooden door across the way opens a crack. The person whose head pokes through has dark hair and bright blue eyes. My screaming stops immediately.

Because it's Jesse.

I leap from the bed and race across the room, heedless of the fact that I'm wearing a stupidly long and bulky nightgown. I don't even recall putting it on. I should have paid more attention to my bizarre apparel because I trip over it and nearly faceplant into the plush carpet.

My big brother catches me before I hit the ground. "What's wrong?"

Filtered early-morning sunlight streams through the

windows on either side of the huge canopy bed behind me. It's enough light for me to see the concern in his perfectly normal, familiar eyes. "I'm not sure. I wasn't here—I'm not sure quite where I was—but you were —" I choke and can't quite finish.

"I was what?" His arms around me are strong. He smells exactly like he always does. Like puppies, and fresh-cut grass, and M&Ms.

"You were—you argued with me. You—"

He laughs. "That's hardly new."

I shake my head and lean against his chest. "You were dead, J. You were arguing with me, telling me that you were dead, and then you were just. . . gone." I choke again.

He chuckles.

"I fail to see anything funny about this."

He drags me across the room to a sitting area next to the bed. He gently presses me down into a wingback chair and sits in the one right next to it, taking one of my hands in his. "You had a nightmare." His half grin is wry.

"I had—was that what it was? A nightmare?"

"Your entire life has been one hundred percent waking life, either here or on Terra, or on Erra, or on Rra, but now that's all gone. For once in your life— your brain literally shut off. When that happens to normal people, we *dream*."

"You're saying that every night your worst fears come true?" My eyes widen. "Why would you ever go to sleep?"

His voice is deep and practically bristling with humor. "Not every night. I frequently dream that I have a pet dragon, or that I fly. But sometimes, yeah, my worst fears haunt me. And sometimes I dream about having cotton candy hands." He wiggles his fingers in front of my face. "The brain is a strange place and it crams all sorts of things we experience into our subconscious. They all come out and frolic while we're sleeping."

"Surely you can control it, somewhat?"

He shakes his head. "Not really. It's all kind of random."

"That sounds miserable."

"Well, you don't need to worry about that particular nightmare." He stands up. "I'm alive, if not entirely well. No dead Jesses to mourn today."

I stand up too. "I feel like this nightgown is going to figure into my next nightmare." I frown as my memories from last night catch up. The maid who showed me to this room insisted that the wardrobe was full of all the garments I might need. Unfortunately, they're all bizarrely Victorian.

"If you're going to use it in a nightmare," Jesse says, "you should don that nightcap as well." He points.

I follow his finger and cringe at the hideous white monstrosity sitting on the nightstand near the bed. "What was the point of those?"

"To control your bedhead, maybe?" He quirks an eyebrow at me.

I glance in the mirror above the heavy wooden dresser a dozen feet ahead of me, noticing the snarl of mess my hair has become, probably from tossing and turning through a horrible nightmare. Jesse might have a point, but I'd rather endure bedhead for a year than wear that odd white cap. "I'd better shower. I assume there's a list of people for me to meet and a dozen problems to deal with?"

Jesse shrugs. "No idea. Your screaming woke me up, and I raced right over. But I'll bet if you show your face outside, you'll quickly find out."

"Shower first," I say.

"Good plan. I'm assuming you don't want to face the world looking like a muppet." He wraps one arm around my shoulders and squeezes again before he ducks out.

While I shower, my mind races. Kahn is gone. Even thinking those few words makes my heart contract. I thought he'd argue when I asked him to go. I thought he'd refuse. I thought he'd fight for me. But any passion and enthusiasm he had for me back in Egypt hasn't made its way to modern day Earth. That much is clear.

Ra is awake. That causes my heart to race for entirely different reasons. I wonder whether it's a mistake to have freed him. But I long to see him as well.

It's all very confusing.

At least the soap, shampoo, and conditioner in the marble shower are the best I've ever used. I smell like the faintest, lightest rose in all of England when I step out and towel off with a pristine white towel so fluffy that a Persian cat would weep with envy. If cats can weep. I'm not sure they can.

And lucky for me, my recollection of the bizarre clothing must have been specific to the nighttime options. The walk-in closet has dozens of different outfits ranging from power suits to sweater sets to sheath dresses. After rummaging around in a few draw-ers, I even manage to find a pair of slacks and a plain blue silk blouse. It seems suitable for a day of. . . I don't know quite what.

I can always come back and put on a sheath dress with a back-stitched suit coat if I need to take out an army of accountants later. Or some black leather boots and a camouflage jacket if another army threatens us. How strange my life has become. I'm about to exit the room, braced for whatever tasks will urgently demand my attention, when my eyes fall on the ancient golden collar I left on the top of the dresser. The stones are bright red—filled to the brim by the energy siphoned from the collapse of Rra.

I don't want to touch it.

It doesn't go with my outfit.

Actually, it doesn't really go with any outfit designed since about 300 BCE, probably.

I grab it and latch the heavy thing around my neck anyway. No telling what issues may arise, and I'd rather be gassed up and ready to go than grasping for straws. Or siphoning baby puppies or something. Ugh.

The second I emerge, people do almost appear out of the woodwork. Mrs. Connor is the first—she runs the daily details of the palace, from food to house-keeping and 'more,' whatever that means.

"Did you find everything to your liking?" Her dark brows slant across her deep eyes, and her hand is poised with a pen over a pad of paper, as if she's taking my order at an IHOP.

"Uh, well, the nightgowns were a little. . .dated."

"Modern sleepwear." She jots something down.

I'm terrified what her definition of modern might be. "Otherwise, everything was great."

"We should talk about your schedule," she says, still looking at her notepad. "Do you want to be woken up? If so, when?" She glances up at me.

"Um, I think I can set an alarm on my phone."

Her eyebrows climb her forehead.

"Or maybe not, I don't know. What's a good time? Eight?"

"In the morning?"

Good grief, does she think I want to wake up at eight at night? "Uh, yes?"

She bobs her head as if I'm making very little sense.

"What time did the er, well, when did the queen wake up? Usually? Or, you know, the king?"

She frowns.

This whole thing is beyond bizarre. I bet she hates me.

"Most Divine." Am-Heh says in loud, clear English. He and Mehen are standing at attention at the end of the hallway, looking blessedly normal. Until they both bow deeply, in tandem.

"Most Divine?" Mrs. Connor freezes.

"Alora!" Jesse strides down the hall toward me easily, and I've never been happier to see him.

The other half a dozen people I don't know, following behind Mrs. Connor and myself, glance back and forth between Mehen and Am-Heh and me.

"We need to talk about security," a man in a black suit with a black tie and an earpiece says.

"I handle the protection," Mehen says in heavily accented English, practically jogging toward us, seemingly desperate to position himself between me and the usurper.

"Perhaps you could work together," I suggest.

The next few hours quickly devolve into a sort of free-fall of administrative tasks that I forget as quickly as they're brought to my attention and addressed. I spend as much time telling people who's in charge of what as I do dealing with actual issues. We're lucky that the Followers of Isis aren't attacking us imminently. We'd be totally unprepared to deal with anything—my advisors are actually arguing over who has jurisdiction over preparing my breakfast.

I've nearly sorted who's in charge of the various sub-categories (Administration: John. Housing, personnel, and dietary issues: Mrs. Connor. Security: Mehen. Military: Am-Heh.) when a very tall man with a fuzzy black top hat pushes through the conference room door.

"Who's that?" Mehen asks in Egyptian.

I shrug. "I don't know these people any better than you."

Mehen's eyes light up and the man floats into the air, his feet dangling.

He splutters and kicks, his dark brown eyes wide. "Put me down!"

At least he didn't wet his pants. I might have done that, if someone flung me up in the air.

"Mehen, it's fine. Release him and let's see what sent him in here so quickly."

"I'm Captain Riggins." The man brushes the lapels of his coat down and shakes himself a bit. "I've come to report something alarming." He glances around the room, his eyes finally stopping on me—probably because I'm the only woman in the room. Or, perhaps he recognizes me from the videos Isis circulated about how I'm public enemy number one.

"Well?" I lift my eyebrows. "What is it?" I've been expecting more alarming news all day. Ra is burning capitals. The Followers of Isis are storming cities. Elephant shifters are stampeding. Who knows?

"It's my understanding that you recently freed us from Rra." He bows deeply. "For that you have my gratitude."

So he's a shifter. "Uh, you're welcome."

"I saw your face clearly, just as my Rra consciousness rejoined my body here on Earth."

And that's why he recognized me. "Okay."

"My wife and children crossed over too—we're all hyena shifters."

Interesting, but hardly alarming.

"You saved us all." He bows again.

Get on with it, dude.

"But only my son and I can shift."

"Excuse me?"

"My wife and our two daughters are alive." He tosses his hands in the air. "They even have their memories of our time on Rra intact, but they can't shift. Not here."

I blink. How can that be? Rra and Ā were both destroyed. All the women should have their powers restored. "The women of Terra and Erra can use their powers?" I glance around the room. I've seen Rosalinde heal. I've seen women's eyes light up on video clips. I assume they can.

Heads bob.

"Why wouldn't the Renders and Reapers be able to use their power?" I translate for Mehen and Am-Heh, hoping they'll be able to shed some light, but they look as shocked and confused as I am.

"Is it the same for all the people who have transitioned from Rra?" I look around the room.

No one seems to know. "I'm going to task you with finding that out, Captain Riggins." I'm not sure who else to ask. "Can you handle that task?"

He salutes and bows again before leaving.

"As far as alarming information goes, it's strange, but at least the sky isn't actively falling. Nothing is burning. Lack of power is hardly different than where they were yesterday, last month, or last year. It could be much worse.

"Alora," Jesse says.

I startle. He hasn't asked for anything all day. "Yeah?" I'd almost forgotten he was here, he's been so quiet. I study his face, searching for weakness or exhaustion. But his face has good color, and he looks hale and strong. I breathe out easily.

"Hear me out. I've been thinking about this. Someone mentioned, one of those guys." He points at the men in black who are communicating with Am-Heh as best they can about the Buckingham palace security protocols. "Dad's here."

Ra? For a brief moment I straighten and look around, casting about to see whether I can sense him. Which is insane. Jesse doesn't even think of him as his father. He must mean Duncan. Duh. "We brought him with us, yes."

"I'd like to see him. Talk to him."

So he can tell Jesse how he thinks my saving his life caused the demise of Terra? How I tore the whole thing down because I saved him? No thanks. But how can I tell him no? I can't. I sigh. "Alright."

"Would you at least consider freeing him?"

I wish I'd freed him yesterday, before he could talk to my brother. "I'll consider it."

He beams. It's worth it, for that smile. I'd do most anything to see him happy. He hasn't had enough happiness in his life—in large part thanks to me.

Within the hour, we've worked out enough that I'm able to break away for a moment to take Jesse to see Duncan.

Of course, the second I stand up, Mehen is on me like white on snow. "Where are you going?"

I explain we're going to see Duncan—and that I might release him. It hardly seems necessary, with Rra and Ā both dissolved, to keep him locked up. I mean, Isis may still want to take me out, but they're not going to be able to keep me from doing whatever they hoped they'd prevent with the prison world. That ship has sailed.

"You should release him immediately," Mehen says. "If you harbor any affection for him, tell him to run far and hide well."

That's not at all what I expected him to say. "Why?"

Am-Heh, also clearly listening in the second I switched to Egyptian, cuts off his conversation and marches across the room. "I agree. You should release him immediately."

"You both think I should free him? He threatened me. He came with an army to attack me." This seems like quite a significant about-face.

"He failed." Mehen shrugs. "He has no power now, but when Ra comes, he will kill him for the attempt."

I almost choke. "When Ra comes?"

"I've felt him," Mehen says. "He's awake."

I can't believe what I'm hearing. "You've *felt* him?"

"He calls us," Am-Heh says. "We both feel the summons pulsing just beneath our skin." He presses his fisted hand to his chest.

"Why haven't the two of you answered?" Jesse asks.

Am-Heh's eyes are so earnest. "We were tasked to care for Sekhmet. There's nothing he'd place above that."

That's a little weird, but also almost touching. "You really think he's gathering his minions? That he's definitely alive?"

"He'll arrive here soon," Mehen says. "When he does, he will eliminate anyone who has harmed you in any way. He'll surely consider what Duncan did to be a terrible betrayal."

A shiver runs up my spine. "He'd kill him for it? Just like that?" Most of me is horrified, but part of me. . .likes it? The idea that someone in the world, other than Jesse, would be incensed that I'd been betrayed.

Would be upset enough to defend me, even if it means killing people.

Am-Heh nods. "He will not find it acceptable that your mortal father here in this new life would not have protected you. He'll be heartily displeased."

I think about their assessment as Jesse and I travel down to the holding cell they prepared for Duncan when we transitioned here. They don't doubt that a man who awoke from a two-thousand-plus-year nap, a man who knows nothing of the modern world, a man whom *I* likely trapped in that prison, will show up here at any time to help me. That he'll be coming as my ally. I wish I was as positive that his reaction and actions on Ā were sincere.

Duncan looks somewhat more excited to see me than I expected when John opens the small door, but his tone when he speaks is as flat as I knew it would be. "You did it. You ruined everything."

"You don't know that," I say. "The world may be a better place now."

"They were right." He slumps dejectedly onto the wooden chair in the corner of his small room. "I should have killed you."

John's hands clench at his sides, but it's Jesse who explodes. "You shut your mouth. She has spent every minute of the last few weeks trying to fix this mess alone. You should thank her for saving billions of worthless humans at great personal cost."

Duncan's eyes widen. "Jesse?"

"And most of all, you should be thanking her for coming down here to free your unworthy self. Now get out before I change her mind."

Duncan stands up stiffly.

Jesse points. "Now."

This isn't going the way I worried it might. "You

know I love you son, but every time I look at you, it just reminds me of the horrible things she's done. You shouldn't even be here."

Jesse's lip curls, and then he punches Duncan in the nose.

When our father stumbles out of the room and staggers down the hall, guards falling in behind and in front of him, I expect to feel something. I should feel. . .empty, sad, angry, or elated.

I only feel numb.

Too much has happened in too short a period. I don't know what to make of anything anymore. Is he right? Did I do all this? Did I ruin the world? Have I unleashed a great evil? One that even I won't be able to contain? Mehen and Am-Heh seem so positive that Ra will have no issues integrating.

I don't know why it surprises me that they're right behind me, even now. Perhaps it's because they let Jesse and me handle Duncan. "Why do you think Ra will adjust so well to modern life? You two can't even speak English yet."

Am-Heh scoffs. "I speak it good already."

"Well. You speak it well."

He rolls his eyes. My three-thousand-year-old uncle rolls his eyes at me, but I notice that he switches back to Egyptian readily enough. "Nuances come. But your father has always been adept at managing people. Other than his unfathomable power, it's his greatest strength. That won't have changed."

"He can't manage people he can't communicate with."

"His assimilation is not limited to energy," Mehen says. "He can also assimilate information in a very similar way."

I head back to the conference room, gesturing for them to follow. "What does that mean?"

"Each Lifter has an aptitude," Mehen says. "Mine is fine control." He waves his hand and his eyes light up, and dust motes from both sides of the hallway lift up and begin to dance intricately. "I can sustain this all day. It would exhaust most Lifters within moments if they could manage it at all."

I don't quite understand. "And my aptitude within Lifting—"

His laugh is rough. "You're an anomaly. You can do all things well, but your greatest strength likely lies in your tremendous capacity. You can Lift mountains."

"But what does that have to do—"

"Your father is an anomaly among Assimilators in that he doesn't need to touch a human or organism in order to siphon it, but that's not his aptitude." Mehen looks a little too smug.

But I do need the information. "You're saying Assimilators have certain things they're very good at?"

"Exactly," he says. "And your father's has always been his ability to use his energy to help others integrate ideas and concepts."

"What does that mean?"

"You can't have missed the fact that he gathers followers easily." He scrunches his nose. "His talent is a difficult thing to explain. When he's here, he can show you."

"What about me? Do I have an aptitude within assimilation?"

He stops just outside the door to the conference room and pins me with a gaze. "What do you recall about your time in Egypt? You don't remember your aptitude?"

I shrug. "Making disguises?"

He laughs. "You're thinking of Anat."

"Okay, then what?"

"You make constructs," Mehen says. "You don't recall?"

Am-Heh's eyes light up. "They're marvels!" He claps his hands. "Once you made me a lightning bug. It followed me for days."

I did what?

"Never mind," Mehen says. "Listen, your father can use a tiny amount of energy, funnel it through the mind of someone who understands engineering and structures, and, voila. Ra then understands them."

"He can what?" It sounds like he's saying he can steal someone's knowledge.

"The same principle applies to funneling the knowledge of a language," Am-Heh says. "He learned tribal languages in a moment, using his assimilation of information."

"What happened to the people he. . . funneled?" I almost cringe as I ask.

"Nothing." Mehen and Am-Heh both laugh. "They were fine."

"And he can take that information and give it to others?" I could have spared Jesse the two years of Spanish he muddled his way through. "Because that I would like to learn."

"You don't need to learn languages," Am-Heh points out.

"That must be the way you're able to speak so many languages," Mehen says. "You must have put some kind of aspect of that information assimilation into the spell that created Terra. Something that allows you to comprehend every language spoken by the humans trapped."

Bizarre. I shove my way through the door and walk

back into the conference room where things have not slowed down a bit. The multitudinous power struggles that were taking place when we left are all still raging inside. At least a tea cart has arrived and people are taking a break to grab something to eat and drink between arguments.

Jesse and I devour a couple of scones, and John hands me a cup of tea. "You need to make sure you take breaks. Even if they're only for a few moments."

"There are too many things to do." I blow on the liquid in my steaming cup.

He sits down next to me and puts a hand on my knee. "There will always be too many things to do." John's not wrong about that.

"I should probably start looking for my dad." I fill him in on the things Mehen and Am-Heh have been telling me. "Even with his affinity, he must be really adrift right about now. The world has marched along for two millennia while he was stuck in Ā. And now he's awake, but he's powerless, alone, and he's trapped who knows where." My heart goes out to him. By all accounts, it appears his own daughter locked him up, and now that he's free, he won't know anyone or how anything works.

A woman in a bright blue business suit pokes her head through the door. "Um, your Most Divine?"

Oh my word, this cannot be catching on. "Please just call me Alora."

She grimaces, though whether from the informality or the ridiculousness of saying 'Most Divine,' I don't know. "Uh, Alora?"

"Yes?"

"I think you might want to turn on the television."

"The television?" I ask stupidly.

She points to a giant screen on the far wall.

Someone, I'm not sure who, clicks a button, and it blares to life.

"Channel one hundred and forty-seven," the same woman prompts.

As soon as the channel is changed, I understand why she asked us to turn it on. "—this footage from just outside Cairo shows a man emerging entirely unscathed from the utter destruction of the Pyramid of Khufu, the largest of the Pyramids of Giza."

An enormous pyramid explodes and then what remains of it begins to crumble as a small figure moves away from it and toward the screen.

"Egyptian military personnel first suspected a violent terrorist attack on the oldest of the seven wonders of the world, the only one to remain largely intact. . .until today. It was the tallest manmade structure on Earth for over four thousand years. Military leaders were inclined to offer no forgiveness to the man responsible for destroying it, but as they approached the figure, it became clear he didn't work for any other government, nor had he intentionally destroyed the amazing site."

"What's going on?" Jesse whispers.

I forget sometimes that not everyone can comprehend every language. I wish this channel wasn't in Egyptian. "The Pyramid of Khufu was just destroyed, and one man walked away from the decimation. Alone."

Jesse's eyebrows rise.

"It must be him."

"And as always, we have the scoop for you!" The tinny speakers on the television blare uninterrupted. Mehen and Am-Heh stare intently, clearly understanding most of what's being said in spite of the modernization of the Egyptian language from the one they're accustomed to speaking.

"In fact, the man did not ruin the pyramid, but instead freed himself from it. As the entire world must surely know by now, until recently, we were all held in some version of a prison world that was created many thousand years ago. The first segment was for telekinetics and went by the name Terra. The second was Erra, for elementals. The third was for Renders and Reapers, and went by Rra. And finally, the last world, inhabited by the fewest people, was called Ā, for those who can siphon energy and use it for other things, otherwise known as Assimilators. For simplicity, the Followers of Isis and Amun, the people on Earth who knew of the existence of these linked prison worlds, referred to them as TERRA, an acronym for the words telekinetic, elemental, render/reaper, and assimilator. Now that the entire Terra structure has been destroyed, the man known as Amun-Ra and formerly worshiped as a deity in ancient Egypt has returned!"

After a lot of applause and shouting, the screen pans back to the same speaker.

"How would you like to meet him?"

Their applause is even louder, and the entire audience stands up to shout. When I think it can't possibly get any louder, the screen cuts to a bizarre commercial I don't understand, but at least it gives me time to process what I've seen, and catch Jesse and John up to speed on what's being said.

And then, when I've barely even explained that they're claiming Ra is there, he's on the screen. Sitting in a wooden chair, his hair neatly combed, wearing a modern-day suit, with faint smile lines framing his eyes. His body lines are relaxed, his posture confident.

The talk show host, a bald man with a round face, beams. "How do you like Cairo, your majesty?"

Ra shrugs. "The buildings are taller than I remember." The side of his mouth turns up in the exact same way Jesse's does.

"I'll bet they are," the man says, "but what about the cars and electricity? Is it frightening, after being asleep for so many years, the number of things that have changed?"

"I'd be deeply disappointed if nothing had changed," Ra says. "I have a keen sense of expectation for the human spirit, and I expected that we would flourish, even when removed from our natural abilities."

"But it still must be quite a shock." The man leans toward him conspiratorially.

"Not as much as you might think. I've been keeping up to speed on the modernization of the world. It's nothing short of miraculous, the way that humanity has harnessed the power of science to bridge the gap created by the displacement of magic." Ra beams. "To finally experience firsthand all the things I've read about has been exciting. Very exciting."

"But now the magic is back in full force," the man says. "I imagine you're pleased."

"I'm delighted to be free." Ra chuckles and the audience laughs with him. "I'm sure many of you are wondering what exactly it all means."

"I'll admit that I'm reeling a bit." He leans toward Ra yet again, steeples his hands, and drops his voice. "Can you tell me a little bit about the framework of magic that controls this world? I think I'm not the only person who's confused."

Ra launches into an explanation of the various

types of power that exist. Telekinetic, healing powers, elemental magic, shifting, and finally, assimilation.

"That's what you can do, is it not?" The man's brows draw together. "You can take the energy of one thing and transform it into something else entirely?"

"It is." Ra's smile is quite modest.

"It's the rarest type of power?"

Dad nods again.

"What exactly can you do with this life force energy, once you've assimilated it?"

Ra spreads his hands wide. "The better question is, what can I *not* do?"

The talk show host beams at him. "I feel like a demonstration of some kind must be in order. What do you think?" The audience explodes, clapping and hollering.

I lean toward the television, completely unsure what to expect, and I realize I'm not the only one. Jesse's eyes are intent. John's attention is rapt. Only Mehen and Am-Heh appear unfazed.

"My understanding is that you now have such amazing technology that anything I might do on a television screen cannot be trusted." Ra tilts his head. "How could I possibly impress anyone in this new and modern age of special effects and digital modifications?"

"A parlor trick, then," the talk show host says. "A show of good faith."

"The best part of assimilation is the healing it can provide in a broken world," Ra says. "For instance, you have lost your hair."

The talk show host's eyes widen. He sits back. "I have."

"Would you like to have it back?"

The man guffaws, and then slaps his knees. "Of course I would!"

"It's not something a Healer could do, as it's not an illness or an injury, but an Assimilator?" Ra leans toward him slightly, and lifts his hand, running it down the front of the man's bald head.

Hair sprouts and grows, dark and thick and full. The man's face transforms—fear, excitement, and wonder playing across his features in quick succession. "How—"

Ra drops his hand, his work done. "I think you will find that a great many things that were not possible before, now are."

The talk show host runs his hand through his hair slowly and turns to face the cameras with a beatific smile on his face. "Amun-Ra, ladies and gentlemen. The man worshipped as a god for millennia in ages past is just as powerful today. I think I may safely say that his reappearance is the best thing I've seen yet."

The applause must be deafening onsite.

"I'm sure you're a very busy man, and we won't try to keep you." The talk show host chuckles. "But I'd like to ask you one last question before we end your segment. Now that you're finally free, now that the world is restored, what do you plan to do?"

"My first order of business is to reconnect with my most beloved daughter. I hear that Sekhmet now uses the moniker 'Alora,' and that she has recently accepted the position as Queen of England. My only firm plans right now center on reaching her as quickly as possible."

"Ra, the God of the Sun, a family man." The talk show host whistles and runs his hand through his hair again. "You're welcome on my show any time, and I think I speak for everyone on Earth when I say that I look forward to watching what you can do."

They cut to another bizarre commercial break.

Jesse's eyes are wide. Actually, as I look around the room, every single face in the room reflects the same kind of shock and borderline horror—John, Mrs. Connor, even Martin. Only Am-Heh and Mehen are grinning like idiots.

A moment later, when the phone on the long conference table rings, I'm shocked yet again. The man in the grey suit answers and extends the receiver toward me. "It's for you. He says he's your dad."

The little thrill that runs through my entire body leaves me standing dumbly for one beat. Then another.

"Alora?" Jesse prompts.

I finally manage to free my feet. I cross the room and take the receiver. "Hello?"

"Sekhmet!" Ra's voice sounds larger than life, even routed through the weak microphone.

"I just saw you on television."

"I recorded that segment hours ago," he says. "The imbeciles promised they'd figure out how to get you on the phone right away, but it's taken them hours. I'm unimpressed."

I snort. Of course he is. I still can't believe he's so. . . modern. "You look like you're doing just fine," I say. "The transition back to Earth must not have been too hard." I wonder whether he's been assimilating information from many people. Or, even worse, life force.

"I can't wait to see you. Should I come to you? Or would you rather join me here?"

I hardly know what to say. I can't ask him to figure out modern-day travel, but I don't want to fly to Egypt either.

"How about I come to you? My advisors tell me it

won't be difficult, assuming your government welcomes us."

"Which we will," I say.

"Perfect. Then I hope to break my fast with you in the morning."

And then he hangs up.

ANCIENT EGYPT

Dad never raises his voice. He's always utterly calm, and the more upset he gets, the quieter he becomes. Usually.

But not today, apparently.

"You did what?" he roars.

"I told you this was a terrible idea," Shu mutters.

I hiss right back. "You were on board by the time I did it."

Shu ducks out the door before Dad can round on him. I don't really blame him. He did warn me.

"You're telling me you *spoke* with Apophis? You stood right across from him?" Dad's voice is quieter, but he's shaking, visibly.

"Dad, stop. I'm strong. I'm not easy to break."

His shoulders slump then, and he closes the space between us, wrapping me in his arms. "You're not. I know that, but you are the most precious thing in my life, and the idea of that monstrous barbarian—"

I shove back, putting some space between us. "He's not monstrous, and he's definitely not a barbarian.

That's what we went to confirm, and Tefnut and Shu will both tell you that—"

Dad's hands tighten on my shoulders. "His mother—"

"His mother hates you. She wants to destroy us. She's plagued you, and you've been unable or unwilling to destroy her, so we concocted this entire plan." He's finally calmed down enough to listen to me. That's good. "I know it seems like I was hasty, and I know hearing about it is upsetting, but Dad, the meeting was a *good* one. I convinced Apophis that I was the daughter of a noble who wants to trade information about you. He agreed to spare my father in the future if my information is good."

Although his lips are tightly compressed, Dad listens as I explain that I called myself Roxana. That I made up a fake vulnerability. That I told Alexander that Dad masqueraded as his commander, Darius, and that he went to battle himself, leading his own troops in each fight. I told him of the final deal I demanded, that he lie to his own mother and spare Ra's life.

"Why would he agree to that? What reason could this Roxana even give for wanting that? Keeping a man she'd betrayed alive?"

This is the hardest part of the whole task. I want to just tell Dad that I like Alexander. I want to tell him that I trust him, and that we want the same things. We both want his mother to calm down and be happy. We all want freedom for us.

In my entire life, I've never lied to my dad about anything more important than whether I ate my leeks. Not once. I always tell him exactly what I feel and think and want. I open my mouth to lie, and I can't quite do it. I'm about to tell him everything, confess my admiration for Alexander, my trust in his word, when the door swings open again.

"If your daughter was one whit less remarkable, she'd never have pulled the whole thing off. She convinced him that her religious beliefs compelled her to spare as many of her people as she could, but that she couldn't be responsible for your death. It took some back and forth, but Apophis agreed, and I think he meant it."

"And if he didn't?" Dad lifts one eyebrow. "If he kills me instead?"

We all laugh then, at the idea that even Apophis, a celebrated conqueror with command of the elements and great strength in telekinetics, could end the God of the Sun.

"I still can't believe he bought it," Shu says. "That he thinks Ra can't siphon or shape energy at dawn or dusk."

"People often believe what they wish to be true," Dad says. "It's one of humanity's greatest failings. Instead of seeing the world around us as it is, we see it as we wish it existed. We color reality with broad strokes of hope and desire and miss the stark danger lying in wait in front of us."

"But in this case, he won't be hurt," I say. "The deception based on his own hope will benefit all of us."

"And perhaps provide his mother some peace," Dad whispers.

I wonder whether there's more truth to Alexander's version of events than I believed—and whether Dad was the great love that broke her somehow. Dad never mentioned a great love of her to me, but maybe he doesn't tell me everything.

That's a sad thought, but I don't have grounds on which to be upset, since I just sat here while Shu lied to him epically on my behalf. And at the end of the day, I'm not even sure I'm entitled to know every detail of my dad's history and experiences. He loves me, and that's enough.

After Shu has left, after we've eaten dinner, after Dad appears to be utterly calm and accepting of our rash decision, after I think the turbulent storm is behind us, Dad leans in close. He presses a kiss to my brow. "Do you truly wish to do this?"

"Do what?" My heart races. What does he know? What has he seen? Did he know we were lying?

"This is the only home you've ever known. Isis has her reasons for wanting to see me uprooted, punished, or even dead. But she can't touch us here—she must know it. We've gone to great lengths to prepare to give her the delusion of triumph, and with this newest idea of yours and Shu's, we may even succeed."

I swallow and meet his eyes. Nothing but concern, love, and trust. It pains me, the honesty in his face. I vow then and there never to lie to him again, even if it's for us and our future.

"Are you sure you're willing to leave your home? Are you sure you want to go out into the world?"

I think about the safety I had here, the home he created for me, for us, and I realize how blessed I truly am. Mother may have left, she may even hate both Dad and me, but I have one parent who would do anything for me—who has done everything. But we're essentially chained here, serving the people of the civilization he's created.

"I do," I say. "I want us to be free to travel and explore." And I want my dad to be free of the never-ending and exhausting petitions and demands and issues. I want to free him from his past and finally let him live a life with me. "It's all I want."

❧ 5 ❧

ANCIENT EGYPT

Ptah droned on and on, during what felt like an interminable trip to Gordion. He covered topics like the beautiful symmetry connecting design to completion. The most effective way to create blueprints and take measurements so that your final product matches your vision. He talked about his many, many visions and all the forethought that went into each and every project he made. . . over three hundred and eighty-five years of life. I was lucky enough to hear about all the details and the transitions and the unexpected changes that cropped up with each new creation. At first it was kind of interesting, like the issues he had with the first temple he built to Dad. But by the eighth, the twentieth, the *fiftieth* story that sounded like a new variation of the same thing, I couldn't make myself focus anymore. I started forgetting what he said as he said it. I appreciated his zeal for creating something that lasts—buildings that people live and worship and work in—but egads, in such a long life, it didn't feel like he'd *grown* at all.

But in the midst of all his droning on and on, one thing he said stuck with me.

"Nothing prepares you for the slap in the face when your plans are brought to life."

At first, I only noticed it, remembered it, because I thought about how greatly I'd enjoy slapping him in the face. But now that I look back on his sentiment, I realize that he was right.

He may not have had a lot of insight, but he got that one thing right.

It's one thing to make a plan. You work out details. You lay the preliminary structures. You anticipate every thing that might happen and prepare contingencies. But it's totally different to watch the plan go into effect. The butterflies swarming in my belly confirm the true difference.

The best laid plans can still fall apart, with little warning and no time to change your actions.

Reality often doesn't conform to your desires.

Now that it's finally time for Dad to go to battle, a battle he's planning to lose spectacularly, a battle not far from here, in Tyre, I'm afraid.

"Don't go," I whisper.

Dad spins around, his eyes brightening and widening. "Why ever not?" He steps toward me, his thick, lushly embroidered clothing wrinkling and flattening. "What's wrong?"

A single tear runs down my cheek. "What if Apophis fooled me? What if he doesn't spare you?"

The smile that splits Dad's face reassures me. "Then I'll siphon him to dust."

I press my hand against his cheek. "Don't do that either."

"I think you like this conqueror." His lips twist with humor. "I think he made an impression on you."

"He did," I admit. "I do admire him, and I don't want him harmed at all if you can help it."

Dad leans a little closer. "I won't harm him." He presses one finger against my nose. "But I can't say I like you having any feelings for him at all. His mother is. . ." He shudders.

But again, he doesn't finish that train of thought. I'd like to press, but he's too observant not to notice that I'm more interested than I should be.

"I'm still concerned," I say. "About Shu. About Am-Heh. About Aha—I mean Bastet." Now I'm the one who struggles to use the right name. "About all your warriors. They aren't as invulnerable as you."

"Bastet was the first to volunteer," Dad says. "I think she's excited to be back to warring."

Just in time to retire. Surprisingly, all of Dad's lieutenants have opted to come with us. It's hard not to love my father, I suppose, but I thought many of them would want to stay in the world that worshiped and revered them.

"I'm going to come," I say.

Dad straightens then, his eyes sobering immediately. "We've been through this."

I lift my hand. "I know, I know, and I'm not arguing about that again. I had an idea of a way I can come that you might approve."

He frowns.

Instead of trying to convince him, I decide to show him. "Look!" I crook my finger and a small sparrowhawk hops up on the windowsill and chirps, its dark eyes alert.

"What am I looking at?" Dad asks. "A tiny bird?"

"It's me." I close my eyes and focus.

The sparrowhawk's eyes don't pan very broadly. Instead, they focus on very precise things at any given time. When Dad moves, I follow his movement carefully, and then I launch, propelling my tiny, feathered frame at his shoulder.

He backs away and lifts his right hand as if to siphon me. I squawk in a friendly way and land on his shoulder. Then I brush my beak against his face. "Caw!"

"This is. . .you?" He frowns, his entire face so very large from this angle.

I bob my beak up and down.

The corners of his mouth turn upward in a grin. "Wonderful." He extends one finger and runs it down the feathers of my neck and back. "Absolutely stunning. Your best construct yet."

I pull away from controlling the sparrowhawk and allow it to go into automatic operations, relying on its avian instincts to guide it. "In this way, I won't be at risk, but I'll be there with you and Shu, to see what's happening."

"I'll bring this little bird along," Dad says, "on one condition."

"Okay."

"You swear that no matter what happens, you will physically remain here, in Memphis."

I purse my lips.

"It's the best I'll do," he says. "I'm all for allowing my baby girl her freedom, but I won't risk your safety in the process."

Stuck here in my cage, but at least I can watch. "Fine."

When Am-Heh, Bastet, Shu, Horus, Tefnut, Ammit, Mehen, Ptah, and Imhotep leave the capital, gathering Dad's forces to cut off Alexander's supply lines, I'm flying alongside the army, incognito, as just one more feathered voyeur. Only Dad and Shu know who I am, but I imagine the others will figure it out. After a while, I grow bored of nothing but riding and chatting, and land on Shu's shoulder.

"I can't say I've ever seen a hawk land on any soldier's arm." Shu smirks. "You're going to start some rumors."

I tuck my head under my wing and set it to sleep. I can always check in later. Dozens of check-ins come and go without much news. Until, suddenly, days later, I'm jolted awake.

"Sekhmet!" The cry is an echo in the back of my brain, and I immediately seize control of the hawk's senses. I launch from Shu's shoulder and wheel through the air, taking in the activity below. Down near the mouth of the Pinarus river and the town of Issus, forces have gathered. Dad's shouting something. Shu's intent on his words and I wheel lower, too. Troops salute me as I pass, which means even Dad's non-commanders know there's something special about this particular hawk. I wonder whether they know it's me, or whether they believe it's somehow an extension of Dad. I imagine that either way, it will soon become a new feather in the cap of Dad's powers. I can already see new statues being carved to worship Ra, featuring the head of a falcon or some such ridiculous thing.

Just as Dad said he would, he's positioned his troops inopportunely, between the mouth of the Pinarus River and the Gulf of Issus, limiting his options when Alexander finally brings his troops to bear. It's hard for me to watch the carnage that follows. A large contingent of Dad's cavalry attacks the flank of Alexander's troops, and it's clear to see that Bastet is helping them along, but that Bucephalus is close to her equal.

The Nubians attack next, and I'm not sure how far

Dad plans to push things before he lets Alexander surge. The Lifters hang back, hurling projectiles, as the shock troops, the Renders, clash. Fangs, claws, feathers, and fur fly, and I spin higher and higher, questioning our path more and more. Is our freedom worth this carnage? Was there a better way?

People will fight—over everything. Over nothing at all. I have to cling to the hope that we're creating a more peaceful world by bowing out, by letting Alexander and his poor, embittered mother take over in our place. A short-term loss for a long-term gain.

Luckily, I don't have very long to fret—Alexander, riding the brilliant and terrifying beast form of Bucephalus, the largest and finest black stallion I've ever seen, charges directly at Dad's central command, their shining red feathers flying outward from their shimmering metal helmets, their arms and shoulders curved forward, eagerly facing down the devil of their nightmares. He's not alone—he's surrounded by his loyal Companions. It's a good name for his inner circle that shows an egality of mind I admire. They charge at my father in unison, Alexander surging farthest ahead at the front of the charge. Just as we planned, Dad runs. The sun is beginning its descent, which means Alexander has done exactly as we expected. He circumspectly took a beating, luring my dad's forces inward, delaying, and waiting for the perfect time to chase down Darius, whom he knows to secretly be Ra.

I dive toward my dad, soaring alongside him as he escapes at the back of the battlefield. Meanwhile, Alexander and his men thunder along after us, intent on the real power behind the army, eager to end things once and for all.

What if I was wrong? What if Alexander was playing me? What if I'm a fool? He could have seen through my ruse. Dad's incredibly powerful, but he does have real vulnerabilities. If he's unconscious, he can't siphon. If he can't siphon, he can be killed. If he's killed because I trusted the wrong person, because I lied to my dad about how much information I shared, I'll never forgive myself.

I'll never recover from that mistake.

I know it's my fault this is all happening, and now that the time is finally here, I worry that my tiny avian heart will give out and I'll miss it all. Shu's at the back of the charge, bringing up the rear, and I bank along next to him, my powerful but small wings beating furiously.

Keep him safe, I want to say, but all that emerges is a strangled sounding caw and a shriek.

"Don't distract me," Shu says.

He's right, of course. He's always right.

Dad pulls up short, ducking into a copse of trees that he probably knew was there all along, and wheels around, his lieutenants circling him unsteadily, Imhotep jostling Mehen for the closest position at his right side. His personal bodyguard and his healer are both ready to save the man who doesn't need saving, the man Alexander believes he can slay.

I perch on a limb that's a little too small and it bows slightly, bouncing and swaying in spite of the lack of wind. But I want to be high enough that I don't attract notice and I can see the entire clearing.

Alexander yanks sharply on the reins and Bucephalus slides to a dramatic stop at the edge of the treeline. "Your people certainly seem devoted," Alexander shouts. "That's a surprise, given the vicious stories I've heard."

Dad's expression doesn't change, but I wish Alexander's first words weren't an insult. "You've come for me." Dad's voice is low and urgent, but it carries. Probably used a bit of magic to work that.

"Of course I have. Even the most terrifying creature must eventually be vanquished." Alexander smiles, his gorgeous teeth sparkling, his arms taut with muscle. My heart contracts just a bit at the realization that if this works as planned, I'll never see him again.

"And am I so terrifying?" At the sound of Dad's voice, my feathered head swivels again. I wish I'd chosen a creature with a more panoramic view. Sitting calmly, on a plain brown horse, even flanked by his most powerful warriors, Dad doesn't seem too terrifying.

He looks old.

Weary.

And resigned.

He's playing his part perfectly, I have no doubt, but I also wonder whether there isn't a strong helping of truth in his behavior. He's been ruling for thousands of years. It's not easy, ruling. Perhaps at the beginning there's excitement and glory in conquering, but in the adjudication, and the planning, and the day-to-day minutiae of managing? I think it's worn on him greatly.

He might want this even more than I do.

"You appear to have maneuvered us into a very unfavorable position." Dad glances nervously at the setting sun. "What exactly do you want?"

"Your head on a platter," Alexander says. "Nothing less will satisfy my mother. I imagine you know that."

Dad's perfectly choreographed act stumbles then—he blinks quickly, and glances up at me. But then he's back on his game, and he smiles. "My head? And even now, with your troops at your side, and mine here by me, do you think that's a real possibility?"

"I think the only way we'll know is for us to fight.

Here and now. I challenge you to personal combat. A duel between would-be rulers."

"You think it's fair for such a young man to fight one so old?" Dad raises one eyebrow.

Alexander shrugs. "I can't return you to your former glory. That's beyond my power."

Dad's laugh is barely contained fury wrapped in outrage. "I wasn't worried the scales were tipped in your favor."

"Then you shouldn't object." Alexander slides off his horse and unsheathes his enormous broadsword. "I'm willing to fight you with or without the use of magic."

"You're willing to fight me. . .and allow the use of magic?" Dad can't keep the humor out of his voice.

"If you'll agree to do it right now, right here, and to send all your warriors away, save one. Whomever you trust the most may stay." Alexander believes me, utterly and completely.

"And which one companion will you keep by your side?" Dad's eyes cut to the left. "The Reaper, the one who can force my will?"

"Of course not," Alexander says. "Just as I'm sure you won't keep your Render. Watching a battle of supra willpower would certainly be entertaining, but I don't think it's appropriate for today. I think the real test stands between you and me."

Dad inclines his head slightly. "I'll keep my son, Shu."

"And I, my dearest friend, Hephaestion."

Imhotep and Mehen are the first to shout, the first to argue, not being privy to the plan Dad and Shu and I made—and even Tefnut chimes in to express her displeasure. I hadn't thought her very vested in Dad's well-being, so it would make me smile if I wasn't stuck with a beak. But in the end, he sends them all away with a simple gesture of his hand. "Wait beyond the dunes, near the seashore."

Those few words, a handful of furtive glances, and they slink away. Slowly, but they go.

And the sun continues to sink.

Alexander and Dad watch it together—one with delight, the other with trepidation.

"I think if we're doing this, we should begin," Shu says. I can tell by the vibration of his tone that he's worried our plan won't work. He's worried that Hephaestion might be able to overpower him, or that Alexander has somehow deceived us.

I share his concerns, but it's too late now.

Dad doesn't wait. He unsheathes his slim, narrow blade and lunges for Alexander. He may appear much older than Isis' fresh, young son, but he moves like a man of five and twenty.

The two of them do not fight similarly. Dad dances, almost, moving in and out in perfect balance and harmony. He curves and bends, twists and turns, and advances and yields in equal measure. He watches and modifies his reactions to Alexander's.

Isis' son, on the other side of the scale, attacks like a beast. He growls, he charges, he grunts, and he lunges. His eyes shine. His muscles bulge and contract. He shoots forward like a comet, and then bangs on Dad's blade like the strikes of lightning against a jet-black sky.

On at least a half dozen instances, I'm positive Dad's blade will crack with the force of his furious blows. Dad must be using energy to reinforce it—it's the only explanation for its endurance. Luckily, there's no way for Alexander to know that, and slowly, as we planned, Dad visibly weakens. His balanced defenses falter. His steps slow. His blade barely blocks the punishing hacks and lobs from Alexander.

Until the killing stroke comes. Alexander's broadsword arcs downward with the fury of a molested hive of hornets, about to separate Dad's neck from his body.

I've miscalculated. I was wrong about Alexander, his motivations, his trustworthiness, and my own judgment. I dive from the branch, flying and falling in equal measure, desperate to do something—anything—to stop Alexander from killing Dad, and to prevent Dad from siphoning Alexander into ash.

One of them is about to die, and I can't fathom losing either one.

I scream, the call erupting from between the sides of my sharp beak, and my claws extend as I bank toward the two combatants.

But Alexander, at the last moment, pulls up short, and I veer away.

Shu and Hephaestion both exhale loudly.

"Darius, do you accede? Have I defeated you?" This time, Alexander's voice is low, controlled, and quiet, like Dad's usually is. "Will you yield?"

Dad's hands release his blade and come up to his neck, his fingers finding only smooth skin—Alexander's sword less than an inch away. "I yield to you, son of Isis, and I will go one step further. You clearly know my true identity, and you clearly know what's at stake here. If you will tell me why you spared me, I will agree to vacate Egypt as well. You can waltz in and take Memphis, and the rest of Egypt at once."

Alexander smiles. "And deny us future battles like this one?" He shakes his head. "I'll release you now, and I'll report to my mother that I was able to defeat you.

I'll tell her that you're a worthy adversary, but that I think I can conquer you in the end. It'll be enough."

I circle overhead, confused and lost. Why did he not honor the terms of the bargain we struck? Why's he releasing my dad and telling his mother that Dad's still alive? Why isn't he doing what he came to do—pronouncing his win and 'killing' my father?

As Shu approaches, Alexander offers his hand to Dad.

Dad declines it, standing on his own. "You're not what I expected," Dad says. "Nothing like the boy I last saw at the age of ten."

Alexander backs away. "A lot of growth happens in a child's adolescence. I hope a lot more growth yet lies ahead of me."

"I hope you're right," Dad says. "And I look forward to meeting you again, perhaps under more advantageous circumstances for me." He glances once at the sun, now dipping out of sight.

"I'll allow your troops a clean retreat," Alexander says. "If they depart immediately."

Dad nods, and he and Shu circle back, rejoining his lieutenants. I land on a larger branch that's closer to Alexander and Hephaestion.

"That didn't go as planned," Hephaestion says. "Weren't you supposed to kill him? Hadn't we decided?"

"I couldn't do it." Alexander sighs.

"But you could have done as she asked," Hephaestion says. "You could have accepted his terms and let him retreat."

His eyes light up, then. I tilt my head so I can see his face a little more clearly.

"Why didn't you?"

"My only play was to change the rules of the game."

Alexander's whisper is so soft that I can barely make out his words.

I hop one limb lower, and neither of them even so much as glance my way.

"What does that mean?" Hephaestion asks.

"You're the only one who knows why I started all this madness." He sighs.

"Your mother."

"I had to find a way to escape her ambition and control, and if I could bring her some peace in the process, if not actual joy, well, even better."

"She's not someone who finds joy in anything," Hephaestion says.

Alexander shakes his head.

"But I don't understand what you meant about changing the game."

"I started the assault on Ra for Mother. . .and for me. I had to change the world we lived in or die trying. She made it impossible to do anything else." Alexander wipes his blade on a rag. "I knew I'd die in the effort, I knew Ra would destroy me, but I couldn't listen to another moment of Mother's ranting, or go over another one of her impossible plans."

"Okay."

"But now I've met *her*."

A shiver runs up my spine and my feathers fluff. I hop down one more limb, startling a lark. Luckily the men still pay no attention to the bird life around them. They should, really. Reapers and Renders are everywhere.

"And if I'd done as she asked, if I'd allowed her father to escape while lying to my mother. . ." Alexander's hands clench on the hilt of his now-pristine blade. Is he upset that I asked him to lie?

"You'd never see her again."

My tiny bird heart races.

"Although I'm not free of my mother, the world has changed. My goals have shifted," Alexander says. "In fact, it feels like I've found something worth fighting for, and facing that terrifying man is my only play to see her again."

"So you broke your promise to her. . . for her?" Hephaestion cringes.

"Not the best beginning, perhaps, but then I've always been excellent at disappointing the women in my life who matter most."

"At least you know one thing," Hephaestion says.

"What's that?" Alexander sheathes his sword.

"She wasn't lying."

"How do you figure?"

"Her father would have destroyed you. Did you see his distaste? His revulsion?"

Alexander laughs. "Which means the great Ra really can be defeated, and now that I know how, I can't bring myself to use the knowledge. Mother really can't catch a break."

I hadn't considered that an attempt at laughing in bird form would emerge as a strangled sounding squawk. Both men pivot immediately, narrowing their eyes at me. I bolt immediately, but it's too late. An arrow hits me square in my chest and my beautiful construct disintegrates, dumping me back in my body with a disorienting wrench.

I should be reeling from the quick pace, or worrying about Dad and Shu.

But all I can do is hold his words against my heart, repeating them again and again. *But now I've met her.*

And I've met him. And he's right. It has changed everything.

❧ 6 ❧

EARTH

Time really crawls by when you're jumping at every single sound. Every door that opens. Every plane that flies overhead. Every unfamiliar deep voice. They all cause my brain to seize up and my heart to flatline, even if only for a moment.

It feels like I've been waiting to see my father, in person, for my entire life.

Duncan was never my father, not really.

Neither was my adoptive father.

They may have loved me in their own way, but neither of them were really *right*, and we all felt it. It's probably the reason I don't even blame them. It's not a puzzle piece's fault that it's the wrong shape to hug the adjoining piece. It just doesn't *go*.

That's how my parents have always felt. A little off. A bad fit.

But now Ra's coming—he said so—and I've given up pretending that I'm indifferent. Every cell in my body buzzes with anticipation. I want to see him, yes. I want someone to take over, absolutely. But also. . .I have unreasonably high hopes that once he's here in

74

person and can use the stupid energy fizzing in the stones around my neck, he can heal Jesse.

After all, if anyone can do it, it's Ra, right? He can finally set right the greatest wrong in my entire life. He can set my heart at ease. I know it's unfair, to pin that responsibility on him. I know it's optimistic, hoping that he can heal something that no one else thinks can *be* repaired, but in every single memory of him, in every single experience from this lifetime, he's been infallible. He's been larger than life.

That's what I need.

Someone to save me, for once.

I'm so tired of saving everyone and everything else.

"—the migration continues," the clerk drones on. "And people are ignoring property laws, disregarding the sacred laws of His Majesty's—erm—your Majesty's Commonwealth. It's as if they feel the old rules no longer apply."

"I'm sorry, are you saying that people are leaving their homes and finding abandoned ones, or sequestering themselves into new housing based on. . .their magical abilities?"

The man's lips compress and he nods slightly.

"Everywhere?"

He shakes his head. "No, not everywhere, but in many, many more instances than anyone could have anticipated. Especially among those we are calling Reapers and Renders. They seem to want to live in herds or mobs or packs."

I laugh. "Let me guess. You're Earth Called?"

He frowns.

"Your complete disdain for any desire to live in close proximity to those who *feel* and *smell* and *act* like family gave you away." I shrug. "You clearly don't get it."

"Actually, I've been identified as a Lifter, albeit without much strength." He scowls furiously. It must stink to have been a fairly high-born aristocrat and then, when the world is upended, to find yourself near the bottom of the pile.

"Well, I appreciate the reports you're taking. Obviously one of the keys to making this work is prevention of conflict, and our best method to do that is to ease the new. . .desires of our citizens into some semblance of compatibility with the old ways."

"You might need to translate that." Jesse's words are practically a snicker.

"Make sure *someone* present owns the new buildings, or if no one who's living there does, try and track down the new people and obtain their permission for the herds or packs or mobs. I think that even with things changing rapidly, property laws must be upheld."

"For tax purposes, if nothing else," the clerk says.

I hate this. Hate, hate, hate. I groan. "Right. Yes. Assemble some kind of team and make a presentation to me tomorrow on how we can restructure some existing government organization to address this sort of thing—property transfers and communes based on magical affinity."

He gulps and looks around the room in desperation. No one offers a speck of support, so he finally bows and leaves.

Next impossible task? What will it be?

"Most Divine?"

My eye twitches. "Can we make a sign? CALL ME ALORA!" I drop my voice and try to remove the irritation. I really should try not to make anyone cower. "Please."

The man clears his throat. "Your Honorable Alora."

Oh, good grief. "What can I help you with?" I scan

the room and realize it's someone I spoke with yesterday. I liked him. "Captain Riggins, right? Hyena shifter?"

He nods.

"Do you have an update?"

He licks his lips. That doesn't seem promising.

"Well, what is it?"

"We spent the majority of yesterday and more time this morning locating other Renders. Most of the Reapers refused to speak with us, but it appears that all those with whom we spoke were in the same circumstance as us. Since the forced shift on Rra, none of the females have had the ability to shift, or any of the powers that accompany it."

"No additional strength, eyesight, ferocity, or hearing?"

He shakes his head tightly.

"Well, that's concerning," I say. "It should all have been restored with the eradication of Rra, as it was with Erra and Terra." I tap my lip. "I'll look into it. Please do let me know immediately if you discover more information or even have any hunches."

He bows and marches out.

"Could it be that some part of Rra remains?" John asks. "Perhaps you didn't drain it entirely."

I shake my head. "I can't sense any part of it."

"Do you recall anything about how it was created?" Jesse asks.

Mehen and Am-Heh interrupt before I can answer, badgering me to explain what's going on. They really need to learn English faster. Maybe when Ra comes, he can, like, assimilate the language and customs into their brains. That would be nice.

"Have you recalled how Terra came to be?" Mehen seconds Jesse's question once he's up to speed.

I shake my head, but answer in English. "I'm recovering more memories every time I sleep, on some kind of expedited, past-life-reboot, but so far I haven't remembered anything very helpful or relevant." Color rises in my cheeks as I think about my past few memories. All of them revolve around Kahn, who hasn't even bothered to reach out since I had him escorted away. I haven't even had a message from him since I destroyed the world, to his mind. I wonder if he hates me now.

The opening of a door bumps me out of my head.

"It's almost time for the press conference," the Prime Minister says expectantly.

I'm wearing slacks and a white blouse. "Can I go like this?"

She grimaces. "Well."

"How much time do we have?" John asks.

"We should hurry."

It's downright impressive how much four women are able to do in a forty-minute period. Before I can even offer to Bind it, they tuck my unruly hair into a clean French twist. My eyebrows are plucked and tasteful makeup applied. My clothes are changed four times, tucked and pinned, and finally, I'm shoved into elegant heels, which I refuse to wear, and then shoved into somewhat less elegant flats.

"Ready?" The Prime Minister's voice is more urgent this time, but as she takes in my red sheath dress with navy piping and immaculately crafted navy flats, her expression softens. "Much, much improved."

"What exactly are we doing?" I seem to always be about three steps behind.

"The people in the Commonwealth need to be notified of the transition of power—"

"I'm not entirely clear about what is happening," I

say. "Maybe you can enlighten me so I don't look like an idiot."

"We have all voted—the House of Lords, the House of Commons, and the Minister—to create a new position. It will be known as the Supreme Prime Minister. That's you. Once elected, you'll remain in power for a period of five years, at which point we may re-elect you, or not. I'll remain in office, as will the King, but we all answer to you."

"And that means?"

"That you're our new sovereign in every sense of the term. An elected Supreme Prime Minister, based in large part on your ability to protect our nation's and our citizens' interests in these turbulent times."

I swallow. "You're still sure you want to do this? You really want an American orphan ruling the entire UK?"

Her smile is bitter. "We don't feel, in light of your recent eradication of the world you called Terra, that we have any better options."

I lean close enough to whisper. "You can be the new supreme chancellor, or whatever. I don't mind. In fact, I don't really want to have anything to do with this."

"Are you trying to back out?" Am-Heh's voice is deep.

The Prime Minister startles.

"Of course I am," I answer in Egyptian.

"New world, new rules, same Sekhmet."

I push past them both and walk down the hall toward the press room. "Oh, fine."

The press conference isn't as bad as I worried it might be. A very kind woman in a blue business suit introduces me and asks me questions about my upbringing, which I try to skim past. She moves along to my likes and dislikes, which I mostly outright fabricate, since I've had zero time for hobbies. Then she calls for the Prime Minister to announce to an empty room and a blinking camera that a new position has been created. She's pretty eloquent at explaining that it's a position that will keep the UK both strong and safe.

"Most of you, unless you've been hiding under a rock, have already seen footage of Alora Benson, erstwhile savior of London Proper over the past few days, as rogue forces from a group known as Isis have attacked citizens and her supporters alike, but in case you've missed it, here are a few clips."

The red blinking light stops on the camera and the Prime Minister takes a sip of water. "They're showing a few of my favorite shots now, taken by citizens' cameras on rooftops and down alleyways."

I blink.

The camerawoman points and begins silently counting down on her fingers. A moment later, the light starts blinking again.

Without missing a beat, the Prime Minister chimes in. "Always focused entirely on the safety and prosperity of our citizens, your Parliament and I worked in close contact with the King and voted, unanimously, to create a new position. A Supreme Prime Minister. A job for someone who has the power to keep us safe."

She inclines her head toward me.

"All of us, over the last few turbulent weeks, have discovered that a world we didn't realize existed is very much real. We have powers we don't know how to control, largely, and powers we don't understand. The world around us is changing quickly, but one thing we do know is that the woman responsible for restoring all this magic to our world is also the only woman on Earth who possesses each and every power."

My jaw drops. I didn't even know she knew that detail.

"Sitting before you is Alora Benson, previously called Sekhmet, the daughter of Ra. She has the power to Lift, or control things telekinetically. She's also Fire Called, and she's a Render who can shift into an alpha lioness. And finally, in the most rare ability of all, she's an Assimilator, which means that, like her father Ra, she can transform the energy from one thing or one person into something else. You witnessed that ability in action when she stopped the aggression from the followers of Isis, and she has agreed to use her immeasurable powers to keep us all safe. We couldn't be more delighted to welcome her as our new Supreme Prime Minister, and we welcome you all to attend a ceremony that will take place in three days' time on the grounds of Buckingham Palace."

Okay, that was a bit much.

As soon as the camera light shuts off, I open my mouth to ream her for springing some kind of ceremony on me.

"Sekhmet!"

The voice I've waited all day to hear, only it's so black in this room, and my eyes are so blinded from the camera floodlights, that I can't tell where it originated. I blink and blink and rub my eyes.

"You spoke truth. Your people have welcomed me impressively." The familiar, deep cadence is exactly what I recall from my memories of Egypt and from Ā. I can't see him yet, but he must be standing in the doorway I came through myself.

I stand and pivot on my heel and move toward him as fast as I can manage. When he finally comes into view, he looks exactly as he did on the Egyptian talk show. Modern. Understated. Confident. Healthy and strong and classically handsome.

I should pull up short and address him as a Supreme Prime Minister would. Or I could treat him the way I treat Duncan—cold and aloof. Distrustful.

Except I can't bring myself to do either of those things. This man—he's my father. Now that he's here, it's even more clear than ever before. Instead of slowing down, I speed up. . . and leap into his arms. "Dad." I bury my face in his shoulder, like I always have. He smells exactly as I remember, which should be impossible. How could the same scents from Ancient Egypt still cling to him now? How could he not have changed in thousands of years?

Because he's a force of nature.

Any doubt I had at my decision to save him, at my eradication of Ā, fades. Now that he's here, he can take over. He can be the Supreme Chancellor of everything and I can retire before I've even been ceremonially recognized. Surely they'll be keen to trade the actual God of the Sun for his inept, confused teenage daughter.

Thank goodness.

"I wish you'd arrived an hour ago." I finally release him and step back enough to see his face. "You could have done that dumb press conference."

"You did an admirable job." The lines of his face are as powerful and timeless as ever, but with his hair cut short and wearing a black suit, he looks. . .different. Still commanding, still magnificent, but contained, somehow. "I was quite proud."

His words bring me back to the moment. "Wait, you saw it?"

"I caught the end," he says, and I realize that he's speaking in flawless English.

"How are you speaking English?"

"It's the national language here, is it not?" He smiles. "I always advocate for using the native language of the people in each community."

I'm just not used to anyone else being able to do that.

"We have many things to discuss, now that we're finally reunited." His smile is warm—open. He drops an arm around my shoulder and all the latent stress, the never-ending fear that I've been lugging around. . .dissipates.

Just like that.

Is that what it means to have a father?

I haven't felt this way since. . .well, not in thousands of years, I imagine.

It's nice. Really nice.

"Alora?"

John's voice is tentative, but there's a hint of excitement. He knows who's standing next to me. Everyone must know, or they'd never have allowed him to pass. I shift a little and Ra drops his arm, moving enough so that he can face John.

"Dad, this is John Rochester, a very close Fire Called friend of mine. He has been with me every step of the way, from the day Jesse was killed."

Ra's eyes widen, but he smiles easily, offering his hand to John as though he's a local businessman, familiar with all the norms and customs. "Nice to meet you, John. I'll be sure to repay every single thing done for my daughter in my absence."

John takes his hand. "That's unnecessary. Everything I did, I did for Alora, not for any kind of payment. Serving her is its own reward."

Ra's smile broadens. "I like him," he says in Egyptian.

Mehen pokes his head out from behind John, pushing his way through the doorway. "He's been kissing her, too," he mutters. "Still like him?"

To my utter shock, Ra laughs. "Maybe even more than before."

Clearly some things I remember about Ra are not going to translate perfectly to the modern day, but I roll with it. I can figure out why he's a fan of me kissing John later. I can ask where he procured the knowledge of shaking hands, and how he managed to travel here so quickly, eventually. But for now. . .

Jesse's hovering behind everyone else in the doorway.

Ra's other child—the sick one.

All the fear and stress I've been carrying around slams right back into me. This is the moment I've longed for, and also the moment I've dreaded. Now that Ra is here, in person, on Earth, he can examine Jesse. The man who can restore someone's lost hair with the wave of a hand can tell me whether Jesse can be saved.

Or whether—I can't even think the words.

"Dad, this is Shu. He goes by Jesse now." I wave him forward, and his steps are small. He's nervous, I realize. I've been marinating in recollected memories from my past life, but as far as I know, Jesse hasn't recovered any. He's been lucky just to regain memories from his time on Earth.

My heart contracts at all that he's lost. How afraid he must be—and how hopeful.

"I know you've only been here for moments."

"It's okay." Ra smiles.

Am-Heh follows Jesse through the doorway, Martin just behind him. "Ra knew that healing Shu would be your first request. He knew it was your greatest priority. It's his fondest wish as well."

So they spoke on his way in? Probably during my press conference.

"Have you already met Jesse, then?"

Ra shakes his head and steps toward Jesse at once, his powerful arms wrapping around my big brother and squeezing him tightly. "Son."

I should watch as he examines him. I should do as I did in those old memories and examine his heart myself, but the thought of seeing it broken or splintered. . .

"Sekhmet, why don't you go and change clothes?" Ra glances over his shoulder. "Give your brother and me a few moments alone."

Relief washes over me. He'll take his time. He'll examine things carefully.

"Yes. Right."

"Could someone show us to a smaller room? And give us some space?" Ra looks around.

Everyone clamors to help him at the same time.

For the first time since my arrival, I'm not the center of attention, and I love it. I duck out and make it halfway down the hall before John catches up to me. "Your dad—Ra—he's. . ." He shakes his head. "I don't even know what to say about him. I was worried he'd decapitate me or something, but instead he seems to, well, he seems to *like* me."

I freeze.

John shifts slightly until he's facing me, his eyes studying mine. "Are you alright?"

"He has to be able to fix him, right?"

His face falls. "I'm sure."

But he isn't. It's clear that he's lying. Even if he knew Ra, we all know that Jesse's situation is beyond weird. He *died*, and then I brought him back, but from Terra. At best, he has a hole in his soul. At worst. . .

"They call him the God of the Sun, Alora. If anyone can—"

"No, I know." If *anyone* can. Meaning, even Ra probably can't save him. My hands tremble. My stomach ties in knots. A million memories flash through my mind. Jesse blowing bubbles for me when I was tiny. Jesse giving me his cookie when I'd eaten mine and greedily wanted another. Jesse threatening bullies who mocked me. Jesse laughing, his head thrown back. Jesse's eyes squinted up in his smile. Jesse's incredulous look. The feel of safety when his arms are wrapped around me.

Ra may be the father of my soul. He may be recognizable to me, even here, even now.

But Jesse is my heart. If I could save only one person in this entire world, it would be him.

Over and over.

Forever.

And my last hope of saving him is talking to him right now. Evaluating his injury and looking for a cure.

I sink to my knees and clasp my hands in front of me. And I pray. I beg God, if he or she really exists in any form, on any plane or sphere. "Please, oh real and most divine God. Please let him be okay. Please let Ra heal Jesse. I can't lose him. I'll do anything, I'll give anything, I'll be anything at all, if only you spare him."

Tears roll down my cheeks.

The world in front of me blurs.

Sounds around me lose their meaning.

"Sekhmet."

Ra's voice penetrates the desperation crowding around me. Suddenly, as quickly as my entire world crumpled, it sharpens. To one person—to one place—

to one moment. Ra's standing at the other end of the hallway, his face serious, his eyes sad.

No.

No, he can't be saying what I think he is. He can't.

"Sekhmet, I have news."

He steps sideways, and Jesse's standing behind him. Smiling at me. Healthy. Whole. He runs down the hall toward me.

And I sprint toward him.

He picks me up and swings me around. "I feel amazing, Alora!"

And now, for the first time since that night at the movie theater, so do I.

7

ANCIENT EGYPT

I don't spend a lot of time gazing into mirrors. Most people can't—mirrors are expensive and hard to come by—but I could. Anat says the reason Dad has been given so many mirrors over the years is that he admired the very first one ever created. It was a tremendous invention at the time, almost two thousand years ago, a round, hammered, and polished plate of bronze, so smooth that one's reflection could clearly be seen on its surface.

Since then, Earth Called all over the empire have tried to create the most perfect version of it and gift it to Dad to gain his favor. Our palace is practically littered with them.

But I prefer to check my appearance in the smooth surface of the calmest parts of the Nile, or sometimes in the reflection pool outside my room, or really anywhere else. Bronze mirrors, no matter how carefully created, always show an image that's a little distorted from reality. The dissonance sometimes turns my stomach.

Today, the face staring back at me only reminds me

of where I'm headed. It doesn't make me sick, but I am jittery.

"He knows you're a lion." Shu's voice carries clearly from near the doorway. "The second you shift, he'll immediately recognize you."

"Since he's seen my lion before, he definitely would."

"Wait, when has he seen your lion form?" Shu's frowning when he reaches my side.

Drat. I forgot that I didn't tell him that. "Uh, actually, he hasn't. I got confused."

"Sekhmet." He crosses his arms.

"I didn't exactly bump into him last time." I straighten. "I might have been spying on him. . .in lion form."

The streaming curses that pour from his mouth are inventive.

I Lift a quill and ink to my side and make note of two or three words I've never heard before.

"What are you doing?" He bows his head to read what I've scrawled on the edge of a papyrus scroll. "Sekhmet! Have you taken leave of your senses?"

I tuck the scroll into my belt so he can't try to take it away. "Listen, I'm not a child. You don't need to read me bedtime stories or tuck me in. You can ease up a bit on the protective older brother bit."

He exhales gustily, but stops chastening me. "The shimmering golden hair is a little much." Shu leans against the open window. "What's your name this time?"

I run my hand over the shining mass of my wheaten hair. "Despina." When I grin, the corners of my mouth turn up to reveal perfect, shining white teeth. "Daughter of a Spartan merchant who can't read well enough to handle the negotiations for supplies to Alexander's army on his own."

I've met Alexander three times. All three times, I've worn a different face. This fourth will be different in several ways. For once I'll be facing him as one of his own people—a Greek. He won't expect that. For another, I'll be quite beautiful—I've always been plain or furry or even homely. Even as Roxana, I was unique looking, but not quite beautiful.

This time, I'll be *trying* to catch his attention.

I'm equal parts horrified and excited to discover how he'll respond.

"It's not lost on me that you're going as someone nice to look at. Don't think Dad won't notice, either."

I pull on my own energy reserve a bit and wipe my false appearance, returning to Sekhmet once again. "He thinks I'm going as Roxana again, obviously, to demand that Alexander explain why he reneged on our bargain."

"Why *aren't* you going as Roxana?" Shu's lip twists. "Wouldn't that be much simpler?"

This is the part I can't explain because I don't quite understand it myself. It's not simply about being beautiful. It's more than that. "It's not about what's simple." My voice is quiet. Unsteady. I straighten my shoulders. "It's. . .I can't explain why I need to look different, why I don't want him to spot me immediately."

Shu groans. "I can. You're flirting. This is some kind of game you're playing. Some twisted version of cat and mouse, only I'm not sure who's the cat and who's the mouse."

"Look, Dad said—"

"Why Father agreed that you should see him again, after he failed to honor his end of the bargain last time, is beyond me."

"He honored his end. He verified that our lie about Dad's vulnerability was true, and then he *didn't* kill him."

"But he didn't tell Isis that he'd killed him, so we still aren't free."

"Think about it." I've thought of nothing else. "He must have realized she wouldn't have accepted it, not without a body, and that's something he won't be able to provide, since as you mentioned, he didn't really kill Dad."

Shu steps toward me, his face stopping inches from mine. "Tell Dad whatever you want, but don't lie to me, and don't lie to yourself. Something is going on between you and Apophis, and denying it means it'll come back to bite you."

"Fine, I like him," I admit, "but if you think—"

"You like whom?" Dad's voice carries from the doorway.

Shu and I both freeze.

"Ptah," Shu says quickly, his face utterly serious.

Dad frowns. "Fine, don't tell me. I know that was a terrible idea, and I promise I won't ever try to meddle in your love life again. I'll puzzle out this new guy eventually though, one way or another." He gestures toward the window. "Are the two of you ready to go? The entire entourage is waiting on you."

"Dad, we decided it would just be me and Shu," I say. "Remember? Too many people will make it hard for us to slide in unnoticed, and if we want to talk to him about why he didn't complete our bargain—"

"Just until you're close," Dad says. "You can't begrudge me that much. You're powerful, but even you have to sleep, cub. Even you must eat. Splitting your focus leaves you exposed."

I don't bother arguing. I simply hug him and count

my blessings that he's not insisting on coming himself, perhaps disguised as my maid or something equally ridiculous. If he had any skill at constructs, he'd be sending a tiny spy with me. Luckily, he's never had a knack with things like that.

"Guard her with your life," Dad says.

Shu nods. "Always."

"You two are so ridiculous," I say. "I'll be fine—I don't need a guard at all."

A few days of boring riding later, I'm certainly glad Shu's along, at least. "With as much power as you have, isn't there some way you can, I don't know, magic us there?"

"Where is there, exactly?" I arch one eyebrow. "Part of our job is figuring out where the heck Alexander even is right now."

"He's running a siege on Tyre," Shu says. "Duh."

"Is he? Yesterday the reports said Parmenion's commanding that siege."

"Send some of your little carrier pigeons out or something," Shu says.

I laugh. "My constructs are a little harder to manage than just sending a carrier pigeon."

"How do they work, then?"

"You really want to know?"

Shu gestures at the rolling hills in front of us. "Did you have something better to do?"

He's got a point there. "It's like I take a tiny little piece of my soul and I wrap energy around it."

"That sounds. . .horrifying."

I can't help my smile. "It feels beautiful to me, like I'm giving wings to my spirit somehow, but it's also a little exhausting. I don't think I could do more than one, and certainly maintaining more than two simple ones at once would be beyond my ability."

"So when that bird was following us, you could see and hear everything it saw and heard?" Shu's forehead crinkles up. "How can you control it and also do anything at all in real life?"

"That one was always an actual sparrow hawk," I say. "I found it, wounded and dying after an attack by a caracal. Having a living entity to tie my energy to makes it much, much easier. Like, watch." I cast out with my senses and locate a dragonfly. I tug gently on its energy and draw it to me, where it circles my palm slowly.

The ears of my horse swivel, clearly sensing that something is going on. I pat his shoulder. "It's okay boy. Nothing dangerous here." I turn my attention back to Shu. "So, I've pulled this dragonfly into my realm of influence as you can see, drawing it with a tendril of energy."

"Like leaving cheese for a mouse."

I shake my head. "Not exactly, but I can't think of a better analogy right now." I move my hand back and forth, and the dragonfly shifts with me. "You can see he's already attenuated to me. And then I reach out like this. . ." I spin a tiny filament of energy from deep inside and wrap it around the dragonfly once, then twice, and then a third time. "Now he's bound to me."

"I didn't see anything. What did you do?" He frowns.

"I wrapped a bit of magic around him," I say. "It bound him to me."

"And that's it?" Shu asks. "Now he's your slave?"

I snort. "I wish it was that easy. I still have to decide what powers I'd like him to have, and what I want him *be* and to *do*."

"What does that mean, what you want him to 'be'?"

"A dragonfly would hardly be any use at all. They

can't fly far. They have no strength or dexterity. They're not fearsome, and they can't communicate with others. Their vision isn't very helpful either, what with all those tiny eyes. My brain can't comprehend much of the data his tiny brain collects. So instead of keeping him as he is, I'd reshape him into something more useful." I think for a moment of my options. We're bored, traveling to unknown places, for an unknown length of time. I decide to make something entertaining and cute. I funnel more energy into the dragonfly, expanding, strengthening, and reconfiguring until. . . "As you can see." In place of the dragonfly resting on my palm, I'm now holding a small, orange-striped cat.

Shu exhales softly. "It's feline. The bug is now a cat."

I can't help my smile. "Exactly. And I can control its actions. I can let it be what I've made it, a cat, and it will behave as it ought in most circumstances, or I can take more control and become the driving force behind its actions."

"But how?" Shu shifts his horse closer, eyes intent on my new pet.

"It requires a somewhat steady influx of power," I say, "but it's not overwhelming and I'm accustomed to it. I stream tiny bits of energy into it as needed. The more it does, and the further the end construct is from the original host, the more power it requires."

"Fascinating," he says. "Truly. Amazing."

I shrug. "Dad thinks so too, and Anat. Neither of them can manage it."

"Where did you get the idea?"

"Dad wouldn't let me have a pet, remember?"

"That bird—"

"When it flew away, I was so sad, I asked for a pet of my own. Dad said pets become a weak spot—something our enemies can use to manipulate us." I roll my eyes. "So I made my own. Dad was horrified at first."

"And now he thinks it's amazing."

I shrug. "Something like that, or at least he hasn't tried to stop me. He said it's not in him to go against my very nature, but it's not quite as cool as a pet, since it doesn't really have its own personality."

"Yeah, it's sort of like. . .petting your own hand." Shu peers at the cat. "Does it take a lot of energy to keep it alive?"

"Not really, no. Barely a trickle once I've made it. But the more action and activity I press upon it, the more independent thought and movement I endow it with, the more energy it pulls, obviously."

"Most Divine." One of Dad's guards has broken off from the group and trotted up beside us, a Wind Called, I think. "The main encampment is not far from here. They're flying the Imperial flag."

"I don't understand," Shu says. "So he's really not laying siege to Tyre?"

The soldier salutes. "The Emperor, Alexander, is encamped further in—not far from here."

"Why isn't he with Parmenion, I wonder," I say.

"Perhaps he's less focused on the military strategy and more focused on. . .other matters." Shu's lip twitches.

I think about swatting him.

"What would you like us to do?" Dad's soldier is utterly earnest.

"I'd like you to make camp behind that copse of trees," I say. "Keep wearing your disguises, and look like the convoy traveling with a wealthy merchant. Stick to the story. Speak in Greek, as we discussed."

The soldier looks a little uncomfortable, but he doesn't argue. He salutes and moves away.

"Dad's not going to like this," Shu says, "when they report back, which they will. He wanted them in camp with you, close enough to do something. He only agreed that we'd approach Apophis in a pair."

"I'm in less danger as the daughter of a merchant, with you as the merchant," I say. "Any extra troops will only draw attention to us."

"I didn't say it didn't make sense." Shu shrugs. "Only that he's not going to like it."

"Ready for the transformation?" I don't give him time to object. I tug a bit of energy and remake my brother into my 'father,' a tall, Spartan man.

"I always feel naked in these stupid robes," Shu says. "I wish the Spartans were a little more modest."

"Just be happy I didn't make you fat." I smirk. "Merchants aren't known for their generally athletic physiques. This could be much more entertaining for me."

He sighs. "I can feel the wrinkles and see the grey hair."

"Oh, I didn't realize that you wanted to be conscripted the second you stepped foot into camp." I arch one eyebrow. "You worry too much about how you look."

"Says the woman dressed in finery and sporting a rather ornate hairdo." Shu's new, deep brown eyes scan my attire. "You *want* to attract his attention."

"I'm trying something different," I say. "He'll be expecting someone low, someone humble, someone homely. It's what I've always done. Sometimes the best way to hide is to stand out."

"Sure," Shu says. "Sure it is."

I ignore him and urge my horse forward. He's eager to move after the long days of plodding walks and takes off at a lively trot, but my newly created cat hisses and digs his claws into his back. I hadn't contemplated that, and my gelding bucks and then surges forward at a canter before I can calm him down. Luckily he doesn't dislodge the cat. I only just made it. I would hate to watch it be squashed.

Shu scrambles to catch up, he and his mount both breathing heavily when they finally pull up alongside us. "You need to calm down, or he'll spot you immediately. Or worse, one of his men will decide you're a threat and spear you."

"Please. Like you'd allow that."

"He knows I'm a Lifter. I've been with you every time. He'll be watching for that."

Shu's right, and I force myself to calm down. But nothing prepares me for the tingling in my limbs and the unsettled state of my stomach as we approach. Why do I feel like this, nearly sick? What's wrong with me? My heart whams in my chest. My fingers shake.

"You're excited to see him," Shu whispers. "It's normal."

I startle.

"But try to remember that it's only a crush. You barely know him."

He's right. Of course he's right. And Alexander even said I'm a game to him. I need to remember that. Our disguise gets us past the guards to the encampment, and they direct us to stake out a spot on the far left.

"Speak to Ollivargas about a meeting with the camp steward," the guard says. "He'll be the one who makes all supply decisions."

"Thanks," I say. "We appreciate it."

But Ollivargas is not especially helpful—he barely even glances up at us. "The next available appointment with Lichearnus isn't for almost two weeks."

It hadn't occurred to me that it would be so difficult to get an audience with someone close to Alexander. It should have, but it didn't. We slink back to our
small corner of camp where our horses are tied to a
stake in the ground, and Shu offers me a handful of
jerky. My mind whirls in tiny circles while I chew and
chew and chew. "This is gross."

"Hardtack and jerky are easy to travel with, but
they don't taste great, Most Divine." Shu's eyes sparkle.

"Excuse me?"

"Soldiers are lucky to have them, you know. They
wouldn't turn their noses up at any of it."

"Good thing I'm not a soldier."

"What's the plan?" Shu says. "Will we be waiting
here for two weeks?"

I cross my arms. "Yes. Yes, we will."

"Dad is not going to—"

"Unless you have another idea—"

"And even an audience with the supply master isn't
the same thing as meeting with Alexander."

I clench my fists. "I know that. Believe me, I know.
Give me some time to think of something better." I
toss the remaining jerky at him and march away from
camp, my dumb orange cat trailing after me like a dog
would.

Shu immediately follows as well. "You aren't being
safe."

"Oh, please. You sound like Dad."

"I take that as a compliment."

"It wasn't meant as one."

My brother's smile only annoys me more, which is
probably why I'm paying no attention to the dragonfly-
cat I made. And that's probably why he pounces on a
chicken scratching around in the ashes from last night's
campfire.

"Hey!" a soldier shouts. "Is that your cat?"

The chicken's now squawking loudly.

I snag control and force the cat to freeze, calling out to it to cover my connection. "Dragon! Here, kitty." He releases the chicken and bounds back to my side. "Sorry."

"It injured my chicken," the soldier says.

A man next to him chucks him on the shoulder. "Guess I know what we're having for dinner, eh?"

The soldier shoots one more pointed look my way and turns to pick up his bird.

"You need to pay more attention to your creature," Shu hisses. "Or maybe just let it go."

"I can hardly do that here," I whisper, "with all these people looking." But if the cat can wander into someone else's camp and wreak havoc. . . "Why don't you get us settled, and I'll take a walk out of camp to dispose of him."

Shu narrows his eyes. "You're going to walk out of camp alone, in broad daylight, with a cat, and then return empty handed?"

I gesture around us. "No one's paying attention, and it's not like they'll find a carcass."

My brother's stare grows even more pointed. "You had an idea. That's your sneaky voice."

Sometimes it's really irritating when someone knows you too well. I don't even bother telling him it's not true.

He walks back toward the area we've claimed and points at the bench he Bound in place out of a few logs. "Sit. Tell me the truth."

"I can go for a walk, figure out where Alexander is, and then send the cat bounding over as an excuse."

He blinks and waits, as if he's expecting more.

"That's all I've got."

"That's not much of a plan." He raises one eyebrow. "I mean. It's barely even an idea. It could just as easily attract the wrong attention, and do I really need to point out that you don't know where he is? This camp is massive, or hadn't you noticed?"

I drop my voice to a whisper. "I'm not plotting an assassination. I'm not trying to coordinate a five-pronged attack. Simple is fine. I just want—"

"You think he'll recognize you." Shu leans back and crosses his arms over his chest. "You think you have some special connection with him, don't you?"

My hands clench at my sides. "Don't be ridiculous."

A smile spreads across the old, weathered face he's wearing. Even disguised, his grin is familiar. Even when he looks like someone else, I know exactly what he's feeling. "It *is* ridiculous, and it's also what you think is going to happen. Isn't it?"

I stand up and walk away, but Shu won't leave it alone. He strolls along behind me, much more agile than a man of his age should be.

"Do you even know what power you're supposed to have?" Shu quirks one wizened, white eyebrow.

I shush him. "Geez. What's with you? Trying to draw attention to us, *Dad*?"

He rolls his eyes. "Do you take after me or your mother? There aren't many Lifters, after all."

"Fire Called is even rarer," I hiss. "And lions are worse. So, we decided on Lifting, remember?"

At least his baiting keeps me from fretting. I wonder how much of that was his plan. He's known from the beginning that we're here more as a way for me to see Alexander than anything else. He touches my arm and I freeze, listening.

"—right now, yeah. Remember?" a tall woman asks.

Her companion smacks his forehead. "Of course.

He's displaying the new methods he's been employing so our pods can try them out."

Displaying new methods? It must be Alexander, right? Or at least one of his commanders. Without another word, Shu and I drop into step behind the man and woman and try not to draw attention as we follow the soldiers streaming toward the center of camp.

As we move, our progress slows and it's clear something big is happening. There's a raised platform Bound in place and masses of people are jammed into every open space. With very little fanfare—no announcement, no preamble—Alexander leaps up to the platform. He doesn't even have to raise his voice, because everyone falls silent.

The second I see his face, my knees go weak. Which is idiotic. I hate it.

And I kind of love it.

"I'm happy to see my pod leaders here." He smiles warmly.

My stomach flip flops, along with a million other stomachs here, I'm sure. That's a sobering reminder.

"For centuries, the various groups in our societies have worked separately. Renders attack together. Lifters attack together. Elementals attack in their respective specialties. But that's not the only way. As most of you know, my dear friend Bucephalus and I have changed things. I put a Reaper at the head of my cavalry with tremendous success. People say Reapers are all afraid of their own shadows, too shy to attack. I think it's safe to say that we've disproven that old wives' tale."

Plenty of people in the audience chuckle, which makes me wonder how many shifters are listening.

"I can manipulate all four elements *and* I can Lift, and I'm living proof that putting our strengths together can create combinations beyond our imagining. I've been working on new ways to use powers in tandem to take our enemy by surprise." The sparkle goes out of his eyes and his tone drops. "We will soon be facing an enemy that none have ever conquered. The Egyptians worship Ra as a god. They say he cannot be defeated." He pauses, and it's like the world itself is taking a breath. "I say that they don't know what they don't know! I say that he isn't a God. He's barely a man!"

The gathered warriors cheer and shout and throw their arms into the air. I suppose they'd have to be pretty confident in Alexander in order to march on Memphis.

"This guy's a real piece of work," Shu mutters in Egyptian.

I swat his arm.

"Today I'm going to teach you something new—something we'll be using in the upcoming confrontation to defeat Ra in his own country. We will show him that we're bringing the best warriors in the world!"

While his gathered soldiers cheer, Alexander gestures slightly. Soldiers swarm the stage carrying different sizes and shapes. Sacks of something small and heavy. Bales of straw. Crates that appear to be full of fruit. The last man leads two sheep behind him that bleat and stomp.

"I'm going to show you a few of the things that you can do if you work together instead of staying segregated, and when I'm done, I'm going to ask you all a favor."

Murmurs abound, but they're all about the same thing—what 'favor' would their commander ask for? Wouldn't he just order what he wants? Shu's quirked eyebrow tells me that he's wondering the same thing.

I'm not sure how long Dad would remain in charge if he 'asked his people nicely' to do things for him.

"I'm going to demonstrate a new combination each morning," he says. "And we're going to start with the simplest today, a combination of Lifting and Ice." He lifts one hand and curls his fingers, crafting a spear of ice from the water in the air—a feat not many Ice Called can manage. It's lucky for him we're close to the coast, or he'd never have been able to do it either. It would have been more like a toothpick, unless he had a bucket of water handy. "Most of you have seen this. Ice Called fight in formation, and they craft projectile weapons. Otherwise, ice is somewhat useless in battle. Freezing opponents typically takes too much effort and yields too little gain." He smiles, then his gorgeous eyes light up, casting a pale blue light around him. "But when combined. . ."

He Lifts a dozen figs from a crate and Binds them in the air in front of him, hovering over the gathered crowd. "I'm only Lifting them so that you can all see. It would be just as effective were I to have left them in the crate." He Lifts a handful of pebbles from the small sacks, and he flings them at the fruit.

They lodge with small squishing sounds, juice dripping on people below the suspended figs.

Most of the audience laughs.

"You've all seen this kind of attack before. It's effective, but it's something we've done for centuries. With properly-used shields and with well-placed Healers, the effects of projectile attacks are relatively easy to mitigate. Remove stones. Heal the damage, keep moving." His smile is almost diabolical. "But not this time."

He Lifts another round of figs. Then with a twist of his fingers, he freezes them. "From that, they would quickly thaw. They would not die. . .but now." He Lifts and flings another round of stones, only this time, the figs shatter, the shards pelting the people below them ominously.

"I know what you're thinking, my Ice Called friends. Freezing an entire person would be too exhausting. It's not sustainable." He meets the gaze of many of the gathered soldiers. "But you could freeze just their arms, if you don't have an appetite for violence, or just their heads if you do." He shrugs. "I need these armies incapacitated so they'll surrender. Either way, effectively defeating them *saves* lives. You need to keep that in mind." He Lifts the sheep next, and people scramble to move away from the space below where they're hovering. "And before you think I'm being wasteful, these sheep will be eaten for dinner tonight." He twists his fingers, freezing the sheep's heads.

I can't watch. I stuff my face against Shu's shoulder. But at the last second, I can't *not* see it, either. I peek around, horrified, as his stones shatter the sheep heads, just like the figs. "Minimal expenditure of energy, maximum damage." The carcasses drop.

I shudder with equal parts revulsion and admiration.

"I have dozens of new methods, many more lethal than this, many just as hard to counter. But they'll only succeed if you work together—if you're willing to bridge the gap that has separated elementals from telekinetics. Renders from Reapers. Shifters from elementals. Our segregations are deep-seated and long-held. Bridging them won't be easy, so I'm asking you to *volunteer* to join a new pod. I'm asking you to choose to make new friends among people you've been taught to dislike. And then I want each of us to partner with other soldiers of compatible strength so that we can maximize the effectiveness of our upcoming assaults." He gestures and Bucephalus trots up on the stage, his mane and tail rippling, his neck curved. Alexander leaps to his back. "If I can become dear friends with a Reaper, and if he can trust me enough to fight beside me, you can bridge these meaningless gaps too, for the betterment of all mankind."

8

ANCIENT EGYPT

After the presentation, Alexander's commanders are a little overwhelmed with the sheer number of volunteers. It seems like the perfect time to strike. Or, you know, sneak.

I begin weaving between the soldiers clamoring for their leaders, asking to be placed with a match in a compatible pod. I'll give Alexander this much—he knows how to motivate people. Now, whether they actually manage to work together, that's another issue.

"Despina," Shu hisses.

I'm impressed he remembered to use the right name. I follow his line of sight and see that Alexander has been held up by a leader of some kind of pod—I'm guessing Fire Called by the emblem on his robe.

Time to loose the hound of war—er, kitty of distraction.

I send the little orange-striped cat bouncing past two dozen people and then run chasing after him. "Wait," I call in Greek. "Dragon, stop!"

"Cats don't follow orders, idiot." One man kicks at the cat and spits at me.

I don't Lift him and smash his face in the dirt. I consider my restraint a small miracle.

Shu isn't quite as restrained as I am. I barely see the light shining from his eyes before the man goes sprawling. "Have a little respect for a lady of Sparta." His accent is perfect. I'm proud.

And he looks so old that when the guy comes up swinging, he pauses, taken aback by his age. "If you weren't ancient, I'd knock you on your backside."

"You and what pod?" Shu jokes, in rather poor taste to my mind, since his friends are now striding up to his side.

I throw my hands wide and bat my eyes. "Don't be upset with my father. He spoils me, but he's a good man, and a wealthy one too."

The soldier brushes the dirt from his robes and crosses his arms, staring pointedly at the stain above his hip. "You don't say."

"I am not paying anyone—"

Before Shu can cause a fight I'll have to finish—or that will have me scrambling to find a Healer after—I press two gold coins into the man's hands. "Sorry for the misunderstanding."

By the time I glance back at where Alexander just was, the location close, my cat nearly there. . . he's gone. And now because my brother was unable to just swallow the kind of insults women deal with daily, I'm also out two gold coins.

Male pride, I swear.

I still love him, but gods help me. If men could spend a week as a woman, we'd have a much more orderly and sensible world.

"We'd better be going," I say.

"So soon?" The deep voice behind me sets the hairs on my arm on edge.

I turn slowly, my hands already trembling.

It's Alexander, holding my cat. "What kind of lady travels with a cat?"

I curl my fingers and 'call' Dragon over, seizing control of his brain. He scratches Alexander forcefully when he leaps across the two paces separating us, jumping into my arms and purring. "Who said I was a lady?"

"Your father, I thought." Alexander lifts one eyebrow.

"Right." I bat my eyes. "Of course he did. And I am." I stroke Dragon's head. "And you are?" I can barely ask that question with a straight face, as if I didn't just witness his entire presentation and know exactly who he is. But I want to know what he'll say.

"I'm a soldier," he says.

The men around us don't give him away by laughing, but they don't wander away either. They're curious.

"I think that perhaps, in a war encampment, it should be *me* asking the questions. What brings a lady of Sparta, dressed in embroidered finery, to a camp in the middle of nowhere?"

"You're on your way to join Parmenion, I presume? In his siege of Tyre?"

Alexander laughs. "He won't need my help. Tyre is crumpling as we speak. It's poorly defended, the whole encampment not well thought out."

I lift my eyebrows. "Oh is it?" Ptah designed it himself. "I had heard quite the opposite, that the city was remarkably split between an island and an inland village, and that most of the people evacuated, leaving you entirely unable to capture the forces that are protected on the island fortress."

Alexander steps closer, his lips compressing. "You're

remarkably well informed for a lady of Sparta." He turns toward Shu. "And who are you, sir?"

"Horek Kilmarnis, oil and wine merchant." He looks around camp slowly. "I thought that, with a lengthy siege before you, your men might welcome an influx of oil for the making of bread, and wine for warmth during the long nights."

Alexander's lip twitches. I wish I knew what he was thinking. "A lady who travels into open war with her cat, and her elderly father, an eager merchant." He shakes his head. "I can't decide which part is the most absurd."

"My father never had a son," I say. "I wasn't inclined to pursue a life of war or athletics, but he developed my mind, and while he can't read and write and keep tallies, I'm quite adept." I shrug. "The cat I can't explain. He's always been an oddity, and he never leaves my side."

Alexander's smile broadens. "You don't say." He almost looks like he suspects me of something, but my Greek is flawless and my slight Spartan accent is perfect, I'm quite sure. This time, he has no reason to doubt my story. I look and sound exactly as I'm representing myself to be.

I came all this way to see him, but now that I'm standing in front of him, I'm twitchy and nervous somehow. My heart's racing, and I have no idea what to say. "I'm sure you're quite busy," I finally say, "but we'd love to meet with one of the men in charge of supplies."

His mouth is bemused and his eyes dance. "So you do know who I am."

I incline my head. "Of course, your majesty. How could I not know?"

"Then why don't you come with me? I'm about to

eat supper. You and your father can join me and we can discuss timing and the volume you're able to provide."

I duck my head. "I wouldn't dream of imposing on you like that."

"Wouldn't it be better for you to work with me directly?"

I cock one hip and slide my hand down Dragon's sleek fur. After a short pause, I say, "I'm sure your time is precious, and surely there's someone else we could work with to negotiate the terms."

"I think I can judge what best befits my time." A note of annoyance has wormed its way in. Alexander never likes being told no.

I'm not going to lie. I'm a little annoyed he's asking this gorgeous woman to eat with him. It appears to be his normal behavior, since none of his men have so much as batted an eye. They haven't even ribbed him for it.

So much for thinking I'm special.

"I'm not sure any man knows what's in his best interest." I shrug. "Either way, we can't possibly come with you to dinner. But we're camped over there." I gesture. "Out near the far edge. We were unable to get an appointment sooner than two weeks hence, but if your agents find a time that's sooner, that would be wonderful." I incline my head again and begin edging back toward Shu.

"You haven't even told me your name," Alexander says.

I set Dragon down, sure that I'm keeping enough of a hold on him that he'll stay near me. "Despina, sire." I have to force my feet to work again and keep moving away from him, when I'm torn. Half of me wants to escape, and the other half wants to race toward him and throw my arms around his neck.

In the end, it's likely my irritation at his warm welcome of some Spartan woman that keeps me moving away.

"Despina." His voice is soft, like he's testing the word for something. "Despina!" This time his voice is louder. Urgent. "I'd love to introduce you to a dear friend of mine."

When I glance over my shoulder this time, Shu is rolling his eyes behind me.

Alexander's gesturing forcefully. "I have an idea. I think my friend can help us." But no one is coming. I'm not sure who he has in mind. "He doesn't normally handle our purchasing," Alexander is saying, "but he takes an active interest in wine." When no one reacts, Alexander frowns, and then he bellows. "Bucephalus! Get over here."

His Reaper friend has clearly shifted out of his horse form, and he walks toward us briskly. I suppose I shouldn't be surprised by his long black hair, his deep brown eyes, or his broad shoulders. "Yes, sire? What can I help with?"

"I'd like to introduce you to a wine merchant and his charming daughter. They've traveled quite some way, and for some reason are reluctant to join me for dinner." Alexander crosses his arms.

"Oh." Bucephalus scans Shu's wizened face and then stops on mine. "Oh!" He nods, understanding dawning, and I realize what Alexander is really asking him to do at about the same time Bucephalus does, I think.

How dare he ask his friend to *force* me to eat dinner with him!

Bucephalus looks just as surprised, his eyes wide, his body tense. "Are you sure?" he whispers.

Alexander's lip curls up very slightly, and he nods.

"Alright." Bucephalus' facial features focus, his gaze honing in on me.

That's when I feel it. The push.

It's strong. Stronger than I've felt before, if I'm being honest. And Bastet spent a lot of hours training me to resist the overtures of another supra, so this isn't new. But Bucephalus comes as close as anyone ever has to overpowering me. When I still don't back down, he flexes one last time, the push strengthening.

Resistance is a complete reflex, drilled into me over years of practice, and so is my next reaction. I slap him back pretty hard with my own push.

Alexander's friend stumbles, his expression shifting into one of abject horror.

Well, shoot.

He steps in front of Alexander and draws his sword, his free arm to his temple.

About a thousand soldiers all around us do the same thing.

"Who are you?" Bucephalus asks. "And what do you want with Alexander?"

Shu swears under his breath next to me.

"I'm Despina of Sparta," I insist.

It's a struggle, but Alexander finally shoves Bucephalus to the side and jogs toward me, his smile broad. "I knew it."

And that's when it hits me—he never meant to force some poor girl to have dinner with him against her will.

He knew.

This time I'm the one swearing under my breath.

"Stand down," Alexander shouts. "All of you. I'm fine. This was part of a. . .a game. It's merely a ruse. Please don't worry. Carry on."

Bucephalus is trailing Alexander like an unpaid merchant. "Sire, I don't think—"

But Hephaestion's laughing as he jogs toward us. "She came?"

And finally understanding dawns on Bucephalus. The two of them work together to convince the other soldiers to resume their duties and back away.

I don't bother arguing further. "What gave me away?"

"Your brother doesn't move like an old man," Alexander says.

Shu splutters. "You have got to be—"

"The cat was suspicious as hell," Alexander continues. "But the real clincher for me was when you handled all the interactions, and your allegedly illiterate father said almost nothing." He shrugs. "Not many Spartan fathers would bring their daughter to my camp, but even fewer would let her negotiate for them, regardless of whether they needed her to pen the agreement."

I clench my hands. "Was it really necessary—"

Alexander takes one last step, closing the space between us, and clasps my hand with his.

My brain quits working. Just, snap, like that, all words gone.

"I'm sorry about Bucephalus. I should have been more confident, but can you imagine my horror if it turned out my guess was wrong, and some manipulative Spartan woman successfully wormed her way into a dinner invite? I'd be stuck talking to her all night."

His words are a balm to my irrational jealousy. "Well, at least the terrible Spartan woman isn't too bad to look at." I arch one eyebrow.

"The beautiful ones are the hardest to deal with."

Alexander smiles. "Besides, it's your soul that calls to me. Always."

I shake his hand away, remembering why I'm here. "You broke the terms of our deal."

He's still smiling, his happiness never faltering. "Come to dinner, *Despina*. You can yell at me as much as you'd like then."

"Why should I eat dinner with you? You're attacking my people, you're raiding outlying villages and laying siege to Tyre—all of it unnecessary, all of it senseless. And you're working on ways to inflict maximum damage." I cling to my sense of outrage as if I'll drown without it.

His eyes spark, all icy fire. "Of course I'm doing those things." He shakes his head. "Do you really think my mother would have bought that *Darius* went down easily? Without new and earth-changing methods of warfare?" He shakes his head. "Your plan was too simple. It would never have satisfied her—would never have been enough."

He doesn't confess that he wanted to see me again —I'm not sure whether I like that, or whether it annoys me. "My plan was fine, and you screwed it up."

"What's done is done," Alexander says. "Now, come to dinner."

I shake my head. "I meant it when I said that I came to do business. Not oil and wine, obviously, but I'm not here to fraternize. I'm here to—"

Alexander drops down and wraps his arms around my legs, standing quickly and dumping my body over his muscular shoulder.

I shriek and thump against his back with both fists. Dragon's agitated, circling my legs and hissing.

Shu, my own brother, just laughs. "Why haven't I ever thought of that when she's being pig-headed?" He trails along after Alexander as if he didn't just pick me up like a child.

I stop shrieking and clench my hands. "I could Lift you upside down and paddle your bottom," I threaten. "I could force you to put me down, and then make you sing a children's song at the top of your lungs. Naked."

Alexander laughs.

"I should do all those things and more."

He swats my backside. Swats it. "Hush, woman. If you'd been sensible before, you'd be walking alongside me to my tent for dinner right now."

In all my life, no one has ever treated me like this. No one, ever. They'd never have dared.

Maybe that's why I love it so much.

I'm starting to get a little lightheaded when he finally lowers me from his shoulder to the ground gently. "Now. We're here. Are you going to walk inside calmly, or am I going to have to ask my soldiers to prepare for battle?" He quirks one eyebrow, his arms still resting on either side of my waist.

Shu's not laughing, but his eyes are sparkling.

"I'll walk inside."

Alexander's eyes never leave mine. "Just you and me? Or does your *father* need to come along?"

I glance back at Shu—he shrugs.

"Just you and me. But he can stand outside in case I need help."

Shu nods and takes up a silent position next to Alexander's guards. Surprisingly, they allow him to take the place closest to the open tent flap. And then I duck inside.

His tent looks about like I'd expect. A pile of furs. A few chairs. A table and desk, all covered with papers and drawings, letters and plans. I'm looking around when Alexander takes my hand. "Drop it."

I blink. The light is low in here—does he think I picked something up I shouldn't have? "I haven't touched anything."

His fingers interlace in mine, and his voice is soft. "This fake front. Drop it, please."

Ah. "But it's quite nice." I pull my fingers away and spin in a circle. "It's a definite improvement, trust me."

He snorts. "It's not."

Something inside me, something I don't understand, unfurls, releasing feelings I can't properly identify. "Okay."

For most of my life, it's been hard for me to know whether anyone really cares about *me*, whether anyone really values *me*. They're so in awe of (or sometimes terrified of) my father, or of my powers, that I'm not sure they even contemplate me as a person. But for the first time outside of my family, it feels like someone truly does.

So I unwind the carefully constructed modification to my appearance, and I stand in front of Alexander. . .as myself.

He swallows slowly, the muscles in his neck working. His eyes travel from my feet upward slowly, stopping on my face, our eyes meeting with a zing I can't quite explain. I shudder.

"You feel it too."

I shrug. "Feel what?"

Only a small space separated us before—I didn't really think we could get much closer, but I was wrong. When he steps into my space, his breath mixes with mine. Heat from his powerful body rolls over me, his scent filling my nose, his energy flooding my entire being. My heart races, gallops, and then sprints. The hairs on my arms stand up.

And then I shift, ever so slightly, toward him.

As if he was waiting on that, as if he was requesting permission, he exhales, his breath painting me his. And then his mouth comes down over mine, claiming me, stamping me, branding me. His lips sear mine, his body blocks out everything else.

This time my movement toward him isn't slight. It's seismic. I cling to him like dew to a fig leaf. I curl around him as though I'll wither if left alone. He rewards my fervor with a groan.

The thrill that races through my body in response to that sound is the most exciting thing I've ever experienced.

I want to hear it again.

And again.

And then again.

Until nothing else makes sense. I dig my fingers into his shoulders, and he moans. And it's even better the second time. Even so, I'm utterly unprepared when his tongue touches mine. His tongue! I should hate it, but instead, it's me who makes a sound of approval.

Then he jumps, tugging me sideways, and squeaks in alarm. "What—"

It's Dragon, brushing against his leg.

"What's with the cat?" He shivers. "That threw me for a minute. I mean, I know Egyptians are weird about their cats, with all the Renders who take feline forms, but you have a pet who never leaves your side? Really?"

I shift my fingers and Dragon shifts. I lift my hand and he stands up on his back two legs. "Dragon's less of a pet, and more of a useful tool."

Alexander's arms tighten around me, but his eyebrows draw together. "I don't understand."

I giggle. "He's, well, Shu didn't get it either. I'm

guessing your mother doesn't make. . .Dad calls them constructs."

At the mention of Ra, Alexander stiffens and steps back. I want to swear, but that doesn't seem like it would be very encouraging either, so I keep quiet.

"What exactly is a construct?" He crouches down, intent on Dragon.

"It's. . ." I sigh. "It might be easier if I show you."

He drops to his backside and gestures for Dragon to crawl up on him. "Are you saying this isn't really a cat?"

I shrug. "Not really, no. Watch." I focus on poor little Dragon. . .and release his energy. The fur and teeth and feline attitude evaporate in a puff of fur.

Alexander scrambles backward so fast he looks like a crab fleeing an enthusiastic gull. "What in the—"

I can't help my tiny chuckle. I extend my hand and call my dragonfly friend over. He lights on my finger. "I created him to show Shu, actually. I just forgot to extinguish him."

"You *made* a cat out of thin air?"

I shake my head. "Not thin air. I made him from this. Another, smaller life force." I lift my finger. "Dragon."

He blinks repeatedly. "The cat is that bug?"

"Should I remake him?"

He finally peels his eyes away from the dragonfly and looks at me. "*Can* you do that?"

"Of course."

"Then, uh, yes. Do it."

I tug a little more power from my reservoir and work it carefully to shape a new Dragon—slightly larger. A little more aggressive. A little more powerful. Dragon plus. And suddenly he's squirming in my arms, a heavier version of the prior Dragon, ready to find something to attack. I set him on the floor. He rubs against my leg once, and then heads past Alexander toward the center of the tent to see what he might find.

"Can you control it?"

I nod. "And if I focus, I can also see through his eyes."

"Remarkable. Mother would be desperate to learn that trick."

"I'm not sure if I could help her. Father and Anat can't replicate them. They said it's my special talent—apparently all Assimilators have something they're quite adept at doing."

"Mother's is containment spell construction," Alexander says. "She can create the most elaborate spells to prevent someone from doing something, or even from moving. It's remarkable."

I file that information away. I'm sure Dad already knew, but all of this is new to me. Sometimes I feel like the person who knows the least in all the world. I'm sure Alexander would blame Dad. He'd probably say that Dad keeps me in the dark, but protection isn't the same as control. "Anat's special ability is—"

"Appearance modification, in herself and others." Alexander's smile is a little smug. "Mother knows most of your dad's supporters. She's prepared me. But it seems that Anat has taught you well."

"You saw through my disguise quickly enough."

"Not really," Alexander says. "If you'd behaved as most women would, I'd have ambled right past double quick. Your disguise was perfect. Your soul just shines a little too brightly for something like that to work."

I roll my eyes. "Oh, please. I'm sure you say that to every girl you meet."

"Ah, yes, the shining soul line. It's a good one." He

bites his lip, taking my hand at the same time. "Sekhmet, you must know that you're the most remarkable person I've ever met, no contest. I wish—"

My heart skips a beat. "What do you wish?"

"I wish you'd stay with me. Don't go back to Egypt. Don't—"

"Don't go back to my father. Is that what you're asking?" I sigh. "He'll come for me, Alexander. He'll always come for me."

His fingers tighten on mine. "But you're *spectacular*," he says. "You're the one person who can truly defeat him."

My jaw drops.

"Yes." His fingers trace the curve of my brow, running down my cheek, tracing along my jaw slowly, so slowly. "I know you lied."

I drag a breath into my lungs. "Wait."

"Did you really think I'd believe that Ra can't assimilate or shape energy at twilight or dawn?" His laughter, usually so warm and bright, is brittle. Dry. "At first I was angry that you thought I'd believe that. But then I considered. If you and Ra were in on this together—why would you make up such a preposterous story?"

I can't bring myself to say anything.

"He really is tired. He wants out—and he thinks that if you can convince me to believe this preposterous tale, Mother and I will let you both walk away. It's not even a bad story."

"You saw through it."

"You're a terrible liar," Alexander says, "but your heart is good. That's plain as the day is long. That's why I 'tested' your story, risking my own life to see whether Ra would strike me down. To see whether it was a trap."

My head's shaking so much I can't quite stop it. "It wasn't a trap. I didn't want to harm you—the opposite."

"I know." His lip twitches and his eyes drop to my mouth. "But I couldn't do it. I couldn't *defeat* Ra, not in the moment I realized he meant to let me."

"Why?" My words are barely a whisper. "Why?"

"I needed to see you again," he says. "I couldn't let you escape. I couldn't let that be the end of our story."

Our story.

My heart races again, thundering in my chest. It's so loud he must be able to hear it, to feel it. He must know how I feel. "I'm here, like you wanted."

"But you won't stay." He inhales deeply, his chest swelling impressively, brushing against the front of my tunic.

"I *can't* stay," I practically wail. "You know why."

The words almost feel dragged from him. "I don't." His fingers brush against my mouth. "By all the gods, I don't know why you can't stay. And the more time I spend with you, the less I can remember about all the things I've learned about life, love, and the universe. Sometimes I'm so distracted thinking of the exact color of gold in your eyes that I miss things my men tell me." His breath fans over my face. "Day and night, night and day, I burn for you."

But if I stay here, I break my dad's heart. And he won't betray his mother either. I should never have come.

Shu was right.

Touching him is bliss. Feeling his hands against my body is divine. Hearing his voice is ecstasy.

And it's also the most exquisite torture.

"I can't stay," I say. "I have to leave right away. I came to beg you. Abandon Tyre. You'll never defeat us there. Come to Memphis, defeat Ra according to our bargain, and then report to your mother that Darius—Ra—has been vanquished." My voice wobbles. "Let us—let me—go."

There's an eternity in his eyes. "What if I can't do that?"

"You have to do it," I say. "Promise me that this time you'll honor our bargain. This time, you can't betray me."

"What if I really did defeat him? Would you ever forgive me?"

I think about the Alexander I saw up on the stage—confidence, grace, control, ingenuity, and strength. But I also know my dad. "You can't ever defeat him," I say. "Not in any world. Not ever."

"But you'll never win either, not as long as you're with him." Alexander's eyes are sad. "I hope that one day you'll see that, too. There's more to him than you understand. More evil that you don't yet comprehend. When you do see it, when that day comes, I'll be here, Sekhmet. I'll welcome you a thousand times over."

"Your mother would never accept me."

"Oh, she would." Alexander snaps his mouth closed, as if he knows that the very idea of betraying my own father is unfathomable. "But you won't even try. You'd rather run away."

"It's not running. It's an escape, but you can't understand the distinction." I shake my head, profoundly sad. "Once you've ruled for a few decades, maybe then."

"I'll wait as long as it takes for you to understand."

"No, we're talking about you understanding why I want to leave, why Ra and I both want—"

"Okay."

He's infuriating. I stomp.

"I promise you that I'll never betray you. And beyond that, I promise that I'll pretend to defeat your father—in his guise as Darius—and I'll lie to my mother about it so she'll finally give up." He pauses. "If that's really what you want."

My eyes can't seem to stop staring at him. He's the most beautiful man I've ever seen. All hard planes and golden hues, his azure eyes the only spot of cool color.

What do I want? Do I want to escape? Do I want to leave everything Dad has created and see new lands?

I thought I wanted that.

But now I *yearn*. . .

For something I can never have. I yearn to be with someone I can't ever be with. Someone who is fundamentally at odds with everything I care about, everything I love. "It is what I want."

Some of the hardest steps I've ever taken are the ones that take me out of Alexander's tent. I'm walking past Shu, who falls in next to me, jabbering about my disguise, when I realize that I've left Dragon in Alexander's tent.

Even with my mind splitting focus between Shu's tantrum and Dragon, I'm able to restore my disguise as Despina, but then I'm so distracted that I place my hand in Shu's and let him drag me to our horses.

Because Alexander drops to his knees in front of me and stares me right in the eyes. "You said you're sure. You said you want to leave with your father, but you also left just a bit of yourself here, didn't you?" His smile is absolutely breathtaking. "It would be a lie not to admit that fact makes me deliriously happy. It gives me hope I probably shouldn't have."

He picks me up and places me on his lap, his heavy hand running down my body from my head to my tail. I've never given cats enough credit—there are a lot of pleasure receptors embedded in their fur. The purring happens almost automatically as he continues petting me. But it's not just an automatic response. Being near him makes me hum inside—a little like a purr—and not only because I'm a lion shifter. It's more than that.

When he asked me to stay. . .I was tempted. It wasn't as impossible a thought as it should have been.

And that scares me.

How could I even consider leaving my dad? How could I ever contemplate betraying him? For any reason at all?

I can't.

Which is why I absolutely can't think about Alexander anymore, except as an escape hatch for me and Dad and Shu that doesn't involve making Dad kill his ex-girlfriend, or whatever Isis is.

"Are you listening to me right now? Sekhmet?" Alexander's hands lift me up, curling around my midsection behind my front legs and bringing me to eye level.

I'm vaguely aware that Shu's helping me mount our horses. "Time to go," he says. "You kicked the anthill in a big way. It'll be a miracle if we aren't swarmed." There do seem to be a lot of soldiers milling around.

"If you can hear me," Alexander says, "there's something I've been thinking about a lot. It's about a past conversation we had. I wanted to clear something up."

"Mraow." It's all I can manage to make Dragon say.

"Is it you?" He squints at me and tilts his head sideways. "Show me something, a sign, if it is."

I scratch his forearm.

He laughs. "Alright, I get it."

I lick the place I scratched.

"A cat is the perfect alternative form for you, you know." He chuckles. "Look, Little Miss Claws, I know

I told you before that I don't believe in being in love. I don't—I never have. I've never seen any evidence of its goodness, only of its destruction. But the thing is, since you argued so strenuously for it, I've been thinking about. . ."

"Sire!" Shouting from outside the tent snaps Alexander's head outward.

"What is it?" He stands up, setting me on the floor, and his best friend strides through the doorway.

I hiss in frustration. Alexander might be right. The cat form isn't a bad one.

"Your mother is here—in the camp. Headed your way." Hephaestion's eyes are wide, his hands trembling slightly.

I've never met Isis, but his reaction seems a little dramatic. She's Alexander's mother. How much of a threat could she be?

"Son," a silky female voice says. The flap of the tent opens and the woman who strolls through—I've always wondered why no one ever provided a proper description of her. Is she tall? Short? Thin? Fat? Dark? Light? No one ever says. And now that I think about it, as an Assimilator, she can look pretty much any way she chooses at any point. So banal physical descriptions are likely useless.

But now that I've seen her, I finally *understand*. She's not tall or short or dark or light. She's all the air in the room. She's all the salt in the ocean. She's all the light in the sky. All the blackness of the darkest night.

She's everything—she's *intense*.

But even that word isn't strong enough.

Her black hair flows down her back like the ripples of a river. Her golden skin shimmers as if it's been dusted with metallic powder. Her deep eyes practically shine as they spear Alexander. "What's this I hear about some Spartan woman?" She arches one black eyebrow, her midnight blue eyes sparking. "I haven't met her, and already I don't approve. You certainly can't develop feelings for her until she's been thoroughly vetted."

I slink away from him, ducking under the blankets of his bed. I'm worried she might light me on fire or something equally horrible. Who knows what someone like that would do to a stray cat?

"Well? Is it true?"

"Why are you here, Mother?"

"Answer my question first." She frowns.

"You expect me to believe that you traveled out here because of a rumor that was sparked merely an hour ago?"

She laughs. "Of course not, darling. I was already on my way here to tell you that Tyre is ripe for an offensive attack. You can destroy it in a day if you go now. Parmenion needed a little. . .incentive. . .of course, but he's finally done what was necessary to prepare it. You can crush it like a gourd—the inland town and the island fortifications, both at once."

"But Mother—"

"Imagine my surprise when, upon my arrival, I hear that you're tangled up with some minor merchant's daughter—gorgeous, apparently, but a *nobody*."

"Mother—"

"I know what you're going to say—that it's none of my business with whom you *tangle*, but trust me. You'll be glad later—"

"Mother." Alexander's tone is thunderous. "You barged into my tent, uninvited and unwelcome, and you're certainly not being useful. I could have been doing anything when you came in, by the way, including *tangling*."

She freezes and gulps. "But you weren't."

"Which doesn't render your interference acceptable." This time his tone is quiet, but the fury infused in it nearly crackles. "You made me a vow never to interfere with my methods or my plans. Not ever. You swore."

She licks her lips.

"You've broken that promise. Over and over and over." He sighs. "But you will not break it again. You will gather your things, whatever and whomever you brought with you, and you will go. And you will not come again without my express invitation." His next words are so quiet I can barely hear them, even with my feline ears. "Or I'll stop my attack and return home, never to wage war on your behalf again."

She reaches toward him, her hand outstretched. "Alexander, you know I only want what's best for you."

His belly laugh always surprises me, but this time more than ever before. "I know one part of what you said is true—*you want*. That's all I know. You never seem to be satisfied. I made you a promise, and I'll keep it. I'm pursuing your *eternal* enemy, but you need to uphold your end and let me live my life, free of your interference when it's not specifically requested."

Her hands fist on the material of her robes. "Yes." She spins on her heel and heads for the entrance.

I poke my head out to see if she's gone.

"What is that?" She spins, lightning quick, and races toward me, crouching down low. "What is this? It's not a cat."

If cats could swear, Dragon would be swearing up a storm. How can she tell I'm not really a cat? She grabs the scruff of my neck, and I twist around, sinking all my claws into her flesh as deeply as I can. She flings me across the tent, and I slam into the back of the chair.

"Mother!"

"That's got the stench of an Assimilator on it," she says. "It's spying somehow. I don't know how, but that must have been sent by Ra." She flings her hand toward me, and then everything goes black.

9

EARTH

I burst upward from the bed, pressing my hands to my throat, and drag in a labored breath. My hands run up my throat and over my cheeks. No whiskers. No fur. I'm not a cat.

But it felt so real, powering Dragon, with Alexander staring into my feline eyes.

I shake my head to dispel it. That was thousands of years ago. I'm still me, still here, in the present, and my dad has returned. Another thrill runs down the length of my body. Jesse is healed. The world is right again—except it still feels off. Perhaps because the more I dream, the more ancient memories I recover, the more I feel tied to Alexander—to Kahn—in ways I can't even really explain. Who cares if I saw him a few times back then? Who cares if I felt drawn to him?

It was a crush.

I might not have known it then, but I'm wise enough and jaded enough now to recognize it for what it was. Sure, I felt like we were connected, but I was naive. I hadn't seen enough of the world around me, so sheltered by Ra that any flirtation felt real.

Even now, the words don't ring quite true in my brain.

I was naive then, yes. I was optimistic and hopeful and shiny and bright. All those things are true, but even in my very critical, very modern life, I've never felt the way I do around Alexander.

Except around Kahn.

The man I sent away.

Even then, he did as I asked. He left. He didn't throw a melodramatic fit or shove his way into my life. I'm connected to him in a way I don't entirely understand, and yet he respects my space, my power, and my choices. Even in the modern world, that's unique. It's something special.

A rapping on the door has me checking: I'm wearing pants.

Phew.

I walk across the thick, padded carpet of my new bedroom. It's still surreal, this ruling-a-country thing. I kind of felt like, once they got to know me, they'd take it back. I mean, without any threats looming, and now with the appearance of my much more capable and intimidating father, they'll surely want a review of their decision.

They'll change their collective minds.

I wouldn't even put up a fight.

Part of me is searching for the exit more often than not, looking for an escape route. The other part of me is constantly shocked when someone in power looks to *me* for an answer. When they turn toward me to make decisions on important issues, it feels *wrong*. After a lifetime of hiding, a lifetime of trying desperately (and failing) to blend in, it's not natural for me to stand up, much less stand out.

I yank the door open.

I wasn't expecting John to be standing on the other side. His bright, golden brown eyes are warm, welcoming. "Morning."

He left the 'good' off, probably out of habit, but for the first time in a long time, it really *is* a good morning. I'm not alone. I'm not flailing around, desperately hoping for a solution. My problems are past tense. My fears are laid to rest. I should be delighted.

I *am* delighted.

"Morning." I force a smile. "Jesse? Ra?"

"They're eating together in the ridiculously large and fancy breakfast room—I think it's called the Morning Room or something. Ra's sampling all the British food and comparing it to stuff from Egypt. It's pretty entertaining watching his face as he tries things." John leans a bit closer. "Though I'm pretty sure the kitchen staff is messing with him. I haven't seen them prepare haggis any other morning—it's more of a Scottish thing—but they brought it out to him as if they ate it regularly."

"And?"

John shakes his head. "I think you'd be better off seeing some of this yourself."

"Give me a moment to change."

He steps inside my personal space in a smooth and surprisingly quick movement, his hands dropping on either side of my hips. "Don't change much. I like you the way you are." He moves toward me slowly, clearly planning to kiss me.

I bring one hand up to my mouth—thinking for the first time of the surety that I've got morning breath. "Oh." I expect him to be upset or hurt that I blocked him, but his sideways grin tells me he knows why.

"Sorry." He shrugs. "We have plenty of time for that, now that—well." John probably doesn't want to mention my dad in the context of kissing me, and I can't blame him for that.

"How late did you two stay up talking after Jesse and I went to bed last night?" Color stains John's cheeks. I'm guessing that means he was up late, trying to secure Ra's approval. I think he might have a bit of a hero-worship thing going with my dad. "He's not perfect, you know."

"Actually, I don't know that at all. My dad is sort of the gold standard for imperfect, but Ra?" He sighs. "He's funny. Smart—no, brilliant. He's powerful, but it's understated. Like, if you didn't *know* what he could do, you'd never guess. And he manages people so perfectly, encouraging them to do better. Every minute I spend with him, I learn something new."

I'm kind of losing my happy glow as I listen to him gush about my dad. "Uh, but it's not like you need his approval or anything. He's my 'dad,' but not really." I'm still not entirely sure how I feel about him, and I can't quite recall everything that went down in the past yet. "I'm reserving judgment until all my memories have returned. Maybe you should do the same."

John's eyes brighten and he clenches his fists. "He's offered to help me."

Wait. Help with what? "Huh?"

"Never mind."

"Look, I'm going to change, but can you wait here? Walk me to breakfast?"

"Of course."

I think about his words as I browse my options, running my hand over both the brighter and the more conservative color choices lined up in my closet. Ra has offered to 'help' John, but help him with what? It's something he didn't feel comfortable explaining right off, which either means I won't approve or that it's embarrassing.

I wonder which.

I put on one of the outfits prepared for me by my new wardrobe coordinators. I brush a speck of lint from the black slacks and tuck in my blue silk blouse. My hair's a mess, but it's a snap now for me to Bind it back into a perfectly smooth bun without thinking. Some things about this new world are amazing. I slide into black flats and open the door. "Ready?"

John snaps to attention, smiling at me broadly. "Of course. You look great."

"I have a wardrobe coordinator now, to *help* me." I tilt my head. "It feels a little silly, honestly, that a person's entire job is helping me choose clothing that I can choose for myself."

John swallows and starts walking, effectively dragging me along behind him so he can hear what I'm saying.

"I've been thinking of nixing that job." I have to take a step and a half to match one of his regular ones. "I'm not sure I need that kind of help."

"Totally your call," he says, "although, keep in mind that it's someone's method of supporting themselves. It's kind of important for people to have something worthwhile to do, to have a purpose in life."

"Sure," I say. "But if their purpose isn't worthwhile, wouldn't it be better for them to move on and find something that is?"

"I suppose," he says.

"What exactly is my dad doing for you?" I arch one eyebrow. "In the way of help, I mean. Is it useful? Something you need?"

He coughs.

"Come on, John." I stop. "Before I walk in there

and greet someone I barely know, tell me what you asked him to do."

"He healed Jesse," John says. "He's done nothing but help you."

"What does that have to do with—"

"A house cat can't marry a lion." John's whispering and staring down at his feet.

Marry? What's he talking about? I think about my dream with Dragon. Did he somehow—what is—

"Look, I know this is the kind of thing that will get your back up, but he's not wrong. I'm closer to a housecat than a tiger."

Finally understanding permeates. "I'm sorry, did you and Ra stay up late talking about *me*? And whether you're worthy to—" I can't quite choke out the word *marry*. "Whether you and I should be dating?" I think about Mehen and Am-Heh insisting that Ra wouldn't find Kahn appropriate. Does he think he's entitled to *approve or disprove* men I want to date?

I swear under my breath. I yank John's arm and drag him the last dozen feet into the breakfast room—correction. The Morning Room. I shove him forward, and he steps another two paces.

Every eye in the room locks on me.

Half a dozen attendants. Am-Heh. Jesse. Ra. And Imhotep, whose skin is just as deep, whose jaw is just as strong, and whose eyes are just as fierce as they were in my memories. "Imhotep!" I smile. How could I not? "Welcome. It's wonderful to see you. I'm sure my dear friend Martin would be absolutely delighted to speak with you—to learn from you."

"We've already been introduced, Most Divine. He's a very gifted prospect."

Prospect. I refuse to consider how that word would make Martin feel, although to Imhotep, that's what most every healer in the world is—a prospective student. "Wonderful." I spin on my heel, turning to face my dad, my anger resurging. "But you." I point.

Ra's eyes widen.

"I'm glad you're alive, but don't make me regret it." The heat of righteous indignation floods my chest. "How dare you compare my *boyfriend* to a housecat! He's a tiger if ever I knew one. And I have known them. Dozens. But that's not even the point." I march across the room to the table where Ra's sitting next to Jesse.

He stands calmly, confident, not even looking chagrined. "I'm not sure where this anger is coming from. I don't recall likening John Rochester to any animal at all. As I'm sure you know, he's an elemental, not a shifter."

I slam my hand on the solid wood table, causing the tablecloth to bunch and the glasses to rattle. "Don't be cute with me. You told John you'd *help* him be worthy of me." I clench my hands at my sides and a tiny flame appears in front of me, flickering and rolling.

"You might be the one who needs the help," Am-Heh mutters, "getting your powers under control."

My head snaps his direction. "Is that so?" The flame doubles in size. I create four more, two on either side. "Are you offering your help?" My nostrils flare. I'm not sure why I'm quite so angry—and a memory of a toddler shrieking, his fists and feet pounding on the tile floor of Perry's when his macaroni and cheese was 'too yellow,' surfaces.

Am I overreacting?

The fires wink out, and I modulate my tone. "Having a father is. . .new."

"It shouldn't be new," Ra says. "You have a father

here, do you not?" He glances toward Jesse for confirmation.

Jesse shrugs. "Not really. I mean, one of them left us. One of them died. Strictly speaking, I had one on Terra, but Alora? Not so much."

I think about Martin, and how sad he'd be to hear that I had no father. "I had father figures," I say. "It's not like you're that special."

Ra's eyebrow twitches. That's the only sign that he's displeased, but Am-Heh shifts nervously. Imhotep gulps air.

"Look, let's focus. Why did you tell John that you'd help him? And help him with what?"

"He's a simple elemental," Ra says.

As if that explains anything at all.

"I offered to help him maximize his abilities," Am-Heh says. "It was really all my fault."

John clears his throat. "Your father merely mentioned that once Am-Heh was done, we might explore the possibility that I might be able to do *more*."

"What does that mean, more?" My fury is coming back. I'm beginning to wonder from the set of Ra's mouth whether he's filled with the same—but over the thought that I didn't have any support from a father figure. He may be more like me than I realized.

"More." Ra spreads his hands. "All things yearn for more, is that not so?" He glances around the room. "Squirrels accumulate and save for the coming winter. The artist dreams of creating a work of art that all will speak of. The hunter dreams of taking down a bear. A farmer imagines that one day he might become a warrior, bringing fame and good fortune to his kin."

"Dad." I pin him down. "What exactly did you offer to do?"

He sighs. "His mother was a fire elemental, but his

father, this Devlin, Lifts. I noticed something strange about him when we met, a feeling that something about his power was. . . incomplete?" He shrugs. I wondered whether we might persuade that ability to manifest."

"That's not how it works." I shake my head.

Ra points at Jesse. "That's not how that works, either." His voice drops to a lower decibel. "Things are always changing, cub, and only when we change them."

"What life force are you using for all these plans?" I narrow my eyes. "I can't have you sacrificing housecats to transform my boyfriend into a tiger."

Ra's laughter is loud, full, and totally assured. "No, you definitely can't have that." He circles the table and slowly approaches me, watching me for any signs of anger or upset.

All he sees is confusion and doubt, I'm sure.

But those don't stop him. He steps closer and closer until his arms can wrap around me. Then he pulls me tight. "I'm still me, cub. The same person you've always known. I won't enter hell in order to secure heaven. The world doesn't work like that."

"You won't?"

"Well." He releases me. He glances at Jesse. "I would do it." At least he's being honest. "But only if there was no other way. Your happiness is my top priority. It always has been." He presses a kiss to my forehead. "But I also pay attention to issues of right and wrong in a way my own father never did."

My stomach rumbles.

"For now, perhaps you join us and eat. I've tried a new dish this morning. One I'm sure you'll hate. Let me be the first to warn you away from something the British chefs call 'haggis.'"

I laugh.

Ra laughs, too. "I suspect they knew I would hate it."

Jesse joins us. "I suspect they did. The Brits have a strange sense of humor."

"Do they eat a lot of foods that should be tossed in the rubbish pile?" Ra asks.

"Not too many, thankfully," I say.

"That's good."

John settles in next to us. "We have a lot of things to discuss."

The Prime Minister crosses the room, her heels clicking on the tile floor. "He's correct. We have a lot of things to deal with. First of all, and perhaps most concerning, the newly created Ministry of Magical Matters is receiving new reports every hour of concerned citizens whose powers have returned, but their wives', their daughters', or their mothers' powers have not."

Ra's brow furrows. "It is concerning. I have not yet heard from Bastet—or Anat. That is also surprising. I expected them to be the first to report."

"You think the two are connected?" I ask.

"Anat would have found me already, were her powers intact."

And if a three-thousand-year-old Assimilator can't siphon, what happens? "Will she die? If, like the others, she has no powers?"

"This is abnormal, then?" the Prime Minister asks.

"During my time, men and women possessed the same powers," Ra says. "They had the same likelihood of strength and the same abilities." He shakes his head. "It's not good that even though Sekhmet dismantled Rra and Ā, the powers of the women she freed have not returned."

"What does it mean?" The Prime Minister is way out of her depth, clearly.

She's certainly not alone. "I wish I knew," I say. "I don't even recall what happened or who created the prison world to begin with." I slap the side of my head. "That memory still hasn't been dislodged. I wish it would just hurry up and resurface already."

Ra places a hand on mine, stilling it. "Our minds generally have a good reason for delaying the release of certain memories. Perhaps it will take time for you to process all that happened. Give yourself that time."

"But we need answers." I stand up. "Maybe we can call the leadership of the Followers of Isis. They might know something." I wonder what Duncan's thinking, what he's planning. "That also might let us know whether we should prepare for an attack."

Ra snorts. "Those babies don't know their backside from their front." He shakes his head. "Calling them would be beyond futile. And any offensive they attempt will be easily quelled. No, we will seek answers on our own, as my lieutenants return to me, and as you recover your memories. All will be well. You'll see."

That kind of confidence, that kind of capable knowhow, is exactly what I'm lacking.

The Prime Minister scribbles something on a notepad. "Alright, then." She taps her lip with her pen. "Is this an acceptable time to discuss the upcoming coronation?"

I choke on my orange juice. "Corowhat? I thought I was simply being named the new Super Prime Minister."

"Coronation is the word they use when they name a new ruler," Ra says. "And it comes with a headpiece, I believe."

Jesse laughs again.

"I think now that you're here, Dad, you should take my place." I glance at the Prime Minister, who's frowning.

"That's not the path upon which we agreed," she says. "In fact—"

"It's an upgrade," I say, "believe me." I can sense an exit just out of reach. If I press a bit harder, I can duck out permanently.

"I'm not sure that's true," Ra says. "In fact, I think it's quite wrong. In case it's not immediately clear to you, I'm merely an Assimilator. My daughter Sekhmet, or Alora Benson as you know her, possesses the power of each magic of this world. She is an elemental, of the Fire Called variety. She's a telekinetic, a Lifter, and quite a powerful one. And she's also a shifter. Her form is that of a lioness, and not only that, but she's a supra alpha."

"Which means?" The prime minister is taking notes. Notes.

"It means that if she chose to change your mind, she could do so. Easily." His look can only be described as bemused.

"That's not quite true," I say. "But the point is that the most powerful and rare of all those abilities is assimilation, and my father is quite a bit more skilled than I am in every way. You'd be much better off with—"

"She's being far too modest. She's quite capable of eliminating the free will of every person in the palace, should she choose."

The prime minister's face drains of all natural color, making her bright red lips look like they're hanging off her mouth like a holiday ornament.

"Which is exactly why you'd be better off with Ra as your new ruler, don't you think?" I grab a croissant and stand up. "I'll let you all discuss it while I take a little walk." No one moves to stop me as I dart out the door.

But Jesse follows me out.

"That was a ridiculous morning," he says.

He can say that again.

"I'm not sure what's worse. Dad outing you, or honey trapping John into thinking he needs to be experimented on."

I can't help my laughter.

Jesse frowns. "I'm pretty funny, but that wasn't a joke."

"I don't think 'honey trapping' means what you think it does."

His eyebrows draw together. "Luring him into—"

"It's when you lure someone with romantic means. Was Dad seducing John?" I can't help my giggles. Ra is many things, but the thought of him trying to seduce, well, anyone is just. . . I laugh more.

Jesse rolls his eyes. "Fine. Maybe my urban slang game is weak, but I agree that there are a lot of problematic things about 'Daddy.'"

I push through the door and step into the courtyard, gulping in huge breaths of fresh, brisk air. "What does that mean?"

"Ra's not wrong. You're more powerful even than he is. Are you sure you want him to take charge? He's not an easy person to dislodge."

"You think I shouldn't let him take over?" I frown. "Isn't that what you want, too? To be free of all of this? To be able to live without people telling us what to do all the time?"

His eyes are sad. "I think that ship has sailed."

Is he right? Do we have no chance at a normal life? Am I delusional? My shoulders slump.

"I know we've done a lot of running, but you're not the kind of person to hide, not really. You've done it because you were outgunned, but you hated it every time. Life forced you into that corner. But now life has given you a way to become the person you were always meant to become. I think you should take it."

10

ANCIENT EGYPT

Alexander's coming for Memphis. His army is not far from the edges of the city. He finally took Tyre—just as Isis said he would, which means he's never been defeated.

And now he's here.

Dad looks pissed. He's pacing back and forth, running his hand over his beard like he does when he's livid.

"We agreed on this, Dad. We've been preparing. We're ready."

"Ready to surrender," he says. "No, worse. To pretend to be *defeated*."

I laugh. It goes against every part of Dad's nature to lose. Especially to Isis. "I know," I say, "but that's only because you're looking at it wrong. Morons will think you've been defeated. Ignorant idiots."

"The whole world will think that!" He practically bellows.

"Not the people who matter."

He pauses. "What?"

"Anyone who really knows what happened will

know you were behind it all along. You tricked them. You were 'defeated' only because it suited *your* purpose. Don't forget that."

He nods slightly. "That's true."

"Of course it is. Since when have titans been concerned about the opinions of minnows?"

Shu breezes through the doorway into Dad's room. "It's time."

"They won't engage before tomorrow," I say. "There's no rush."

Shu's eyes flash.

Dad's shoulders straighten. "That was not what we agreed," Dad nearly shouts. "You said—"

"Oh, fine." I stand up and Lift my trunk without thinking. "Fine."

"We'll join you in a day or two," Ra says, much calmer now that I'm not challenging him. "And you'll travel with Bastet and Anat, as agreed."

"Fine," I say. "Fine."

Shu smiles. "I expected a much larger argument this time."

I roll my eyes.

"What? No demands that we keep your bird with us?"

I straighten. If I don't hit this perfectly, they'll figure me out. "Has it occurred to either of you that, while this was my idea, I don't actually relish the idea of watching my home be pillaged and taken by invaders? That perhaps this isn't exactly a dream for me, either? But the world can't be wrapped in silk and put on a shelf. Life is change, and danger, and risk. I think this will be what's best for all of us."

"But if it's not, you can restore all of this with the snap of your stupidly powerful fingers," Shu mocks.

"What must that be like?" His sideways smile is irritated, but not really jealous.

Sometimes I hate thinking about the things I can do. It's why I'm more comfortable hiding.

To avoid having to make any more conversation, I shift. My paws make no sound as I race down the hall, ignoring Shu's and Dad's shouts, my trunk trailing behind me, the tug of my Lifting barely registering for something so small.

Bastet falls into step next to me by the time I reach the courtyard.

Slow down, cub.

I transfer my weight to the pads of my feet and stop immediately. *Ready to leave? I can Lift your belongings.*

The laughter that fills my mind is refreshing. Bastet has never cared for things. She's a Render in her heart of hearts, and lions don't care about belongings.

Right. Of course you don't have a bag.

She lopes along next to me until we reach the place where the others are gathered. Most of the servants with us have been with my father for over a hundred years. They've been exactly the same as they are now for my entire life, and they're ridiculously loyal to my dad. "Sekhmet," Anat says.

I shift back into human form without thinking, Bastet loping off to sweep the perimeter like always.

Anat's not much of a warrior—she prefers to handle the diplomatic tasks for Dad. It made her the perfect person to leave with me and Bastet, but she also hates being left out. I'm counting on that. "Did you hear that Ptah is leaving today too?"

She scrunches her nose. She'd much rather be handling our establishment in India than babysitting me. She's never said it, but I'm sure I'm correct.

"I hope he can manage the delicate balance between being polite and ceding control."

"Ptah is a blockhead," she says.

"Well, he's not always the most. . .carefully considered." I shrug. "In the end, it probably doesn't really matter if we all secure our own rooms. We can look for new lodgings later."

Anat tsks. "I will *not* share with Bastet." She shakes her head. "She shreds everything." She drops to a whisper. "And she smells like rotting meat."

I suppress my laugh. "Not quite rotting, but aged, yes."

Anat shudders.

"Maybe you should go with Ptah," I say.

A tiny wrinkle appears between her eyebrows.

"Or, probably not. I mean, Dad did *order* you to stay with me."

She quirks one eyebrow. "He didn't order me." She purses her lips. She has always voluntarily followed my dad, like most of his supporters, and he never tells her what she *must* do. He doesn't need to—his very wish is their command. But unlike the others, sometimes it rankles with Anat, when her desires aren't in line with his.

"Men don't always know what's best for them."

"You can say that again." She rolls her eyes. "And Ptah is the worst of all. I can't believe Ra chose him to select our future accommodations."

"He didn't," I remind her. "Ptah volunteered."

The lines around her eyes and mouth when she grimaces are just as deep as I need them to be. "That's true."

"Had you volunteered, Dad would probably have leapt on it."

"But you need at least two people to watch your back." She shakes her head.

"What if I change my appearance?" I wave a hand over my face, adopting the persona I worked on yesterday, a simple servant in a linen shift, my hair tied back in a dirty knot. Dirt's smeared on one of my cheeks and embedded under my fingernails. There's a simple rope belt tied around my waist. "No one would even know who I was."

Her eyes widen. "Your skills have come a long way. That's spectacular."

"Thanks."

"The student becomes the master." She circles me. "Why can't I sense your weaving?"

I smile, biting my thin lips. "It's something I've been working on—one of our greatest weaknesses has always been that other Assims can sense our magic. But when I found that Gordian knot, the Assim who made it had inverted the weave, so that not only could it not be sensed, it pulled energy from anyone who tried to undo it and funneled it to power the spell."

She reaches for me with one delicate finger. "So you're not only disguised. If you happened to stumble upon another Assimilator who might want to unwind your disguise, you're also booby trapped." She whistles. "It's unbelievable." Her eyes lift to mine. "Have you shown your father yet?"

I shake my head. I haven't shown anyone. I wasn't even positive it would work until this moment. I was too afraid that if I did, Dad would realize that I came up with the whole thing to address Isis recognizing my cat form. Not that anyone knows about that—I didn't even tell Shu.

Still, I clearly don't handle a guilty conscience very well.

She blinks a few times and then straightens her shoulders. "Well, if you don't think it would leave you at risk, I think I should go with Ptah—make sure he's doing his job well. If things go according to plan, we could be in these new accommodations for quite some time while we decide our next steps. It would be a travesty if they weren't comfortable."

"Absolutely." I lean a little closer. "Can you make sure they're near water?"

"I will." She beams. "Although, I'm sure that Khnum can whip up a smallish lake or a stream if that proves difficult."

"It's not quite the same," I say. "It takes months for the local flora and fauna to adapt."

She laughs. "Alright, I'll be sure it's waterfront, whatever we choose. Tell Ra we'll send word via Hutchai. He's the fastest Wind Called who didn't march out to war."

"Of course."

She presses a kiss to my forehead in the same place Dad always does. It hits me then, how lucky I've been to have Anat. After Hathor left, she never wavered. She didn't try to presume, she never stepped into any role that I didn't press upon her, but she's been what I needed all the time. And now I'm lying to her. Tears well up in my eyes.

"Oh, Sekhmet, if you'd rather I stay—"

I hug her. "No, I'm glad you're in charge of finding us a new home. I'm just emotional about leaving this one, that's all." The next words are a whisper. "And I'm glad I have you."

At least that's not a lie. As if she can sense the truth in my words, there are answering tears in her eyes when she releases me. "Your room will be right in front of a lake or stream, I vow it."

I laugh. "Deal."

After she leaves, it's time for the hard part. Bastet has returned, and it's time to leave. "I need a moment," I say, "to say goodbye."

She never changed out of her lion form, preferring to travel on her own power. She blinks and turns toward the others, issuing orders no one can hear but those she's ordering. Servants load up and prepare. She's going to be both easier and harder to fool—she relies so heavily on her sense of smell and instinct that she won't require conversation. That's good.

But she's more attuned to my normal twitches and actions. Even in this form, she could smell me and never balked at my new form. That's the gist of the problem.

I have to do this *perfectly* or I'll crash and burn. I duck into the cold cellar, searching for something, anything that might work. It needs to be on the larger end—powerful enough to sustain days of action—but weak enough in smell that Bastet won't identify it.

I close my eyes and reach out. The rat won't work. She'd smell that right off. The beetle is too small and far too weak. The birds—she'd sense their flighty nature. No, I need something close to what I already am. Something feline. I reach further, searching for a cat-affiliated energy.

And then I find it, clear on the other side of the palace, hidden in the upper limbs of a tall tree.

A caracal.

It's clean and relatively low in scent, but the smell it has is close enough to leonine. I tug it toward me, a little guilty about using my supra nature. But I won't harm it—it'll be fine when I'm through. Its unease is clear as it approaches, head down, eyes darting right and left. It stops at my feet, curling into a ball. I run my hand down its back and then rest it on its head, my fingers just between its tall, tuft-tipped ears. "Alright, Slink, I think that's what I'll name you. I need a favor." I release my compulsion and stare Slink in the eyes. "Can you help me? Will you?"

She tenses, and I worry she'll sprint away. If she does, I'll call her back, however guilty I'll feel, but she doesn't. She leans against my hand, purring slightly. Most cats can sense my inner lion and naturally want to obey it. "Good girl. What I need is for you to help me break away from my family for a few days. Can you do that?"

She licks my finger, her tongue rough but calm.

And then I get to work. It takes more power than I've ever used before, more energy flowing, flowing, flowing, but when I'm done, even I struggle to believe that I've accomplished it.

I'm standing right in front of myself.

It's an exact replica of me, from my hair down to my scraped toe, wrapped in strappy sandals. I circle, and Slink starts to crouch. I inhale and exhale, shifting things a bit so that's not her first instinct. She's alpha. She challenges, not submits. She stands her ground—she doesn't hide. I layer another round of instinct on top of her natural urges, making my actions her default. I provide a whole set of conversation topics and feelings, and then last, I imbue her with my memories, the skeleton of things I know that make her *real*.

When I step back, she blinks. "Who are you?" Her voice sounds exactly right, but it's strange to hear it the way that I am.

I almost forgot that I'm still wearing the servant guise. "Me? No one. Beg your pardon, Most Divine. I have work to return to doing. And I think Bastet and the others are waiting for you—they're ready to depart."

I hang back while she moves toward them, dropping in to follow her, er, myself, lightly. She walks like me. She swings her arms like me. She even smells like me, I think. Even though I've been practicing, even though it's been my plan for weeks, I'm kind of amazed that I was able to pull it off.

Of course, now she's meeting Bastet, and that's the real test.

But my nanny doesn't give this new version of me a second glance. She merely bounds to the front while not-Sekhmet approaches my horse. He dances sideways, but that's not too abnormal for him. She grabs his reins and swings up to his back smoothly, and he settles down. Thank goodness.

And then they leave without me.

I can hardly believe it.

But I don't waste any time. I change my appearance yet again—this time taking the appearance of Hephaestion. I'm not sure why, except it feels daring. Luckily, no one here knows what he looks like. Since I know the placement of the guards and the location of Dad's and Shu's attack, it's simple to sneak out the back and shift into my lion form to run the rest of the way around back of Alexander's force. The worst part of my plan is when I'm caught and forced to *encourage* a soldier to forget me. It happens twice. Both times are awful. I'm not asking them to do anything they shouldn't—Alexander won't mind my presence—but it still feels *wrong*.

Aside from that, it's easy, easier than I thought it could possibly be, but it still takes all night. By the time the sun's rays are finally sprouting on the horizon, I've reached the edge of the camp. I shift back into human form behind a thick bush, still wearing Alexander's best friend's face, and approach the perimeter of the camp.

I take one moment to check in on not-Sekhmet—still sleeping, the lazy cat. Then I stride past the exterior sentries. The men startle and salute, and then, as I pass more of them, they startle and salute again, but no one stops me. No one challenges me.

I keep expecting to see Shu or Dad or Anat around every corner. If I hadn't been forced to leave a double of myself to satisfy everyone, I'd have sent a bird along with Shu to make sure that things are all proceeding as expected. But without that as a possibility, I'm forced to pray for a good outcome.

I hate being forced to hope for good things. It feels so naive.

"Hephaestion?" The tone with which the man says my name (that isn't really my name) alerts me. Something's off.

"Yes?"

"I thought you were with Alexander?" The soldier blinks. "In fact, I could swear—"

I smooth his mind, removing thoughts of me with Alexander, and replace them with the idea that I told him I'm on my way there. Ugh. That's three times. Thankfully, modifying his memory also tells me where to go. Around the corner and down the central path in camp is the largest tent—Alexander's. It's bright blue. That dye must have been hard to come by.

Either that or Isis magicked it.

Even so, I can't smooth everyone's memory as I walk, so I duck my head for the rest of the way, hoping Bucephalus isn't near. He'd be sure to notice if I modify anyone else in his vicinity. I'm nearly to the front of the tent when Hephaestion himself barrels out of the front, his eyes widening as he sees me. "What—"

I bring my index finger to my lips. "Shh."

He grins and laughs. "I'm on my way to bring lunch. We're nearly done planning the assault." He glances to his side at the guards, staring at us in obvious confusion.

"If Bucephalus isn't close, I can take care of them."

Hephaestion chuckles. "He's not here. He went—never mind. You don't care. Go ahead." He shakes his head. "I'll still order food, but I'll tell him. . . I'm not sure. You'll think of something, I guess."

After removing the memory of two Hephaestions meeting from the guards' minds, I duck inside.

"Did you sprint?" Alexander barks. "Or did you forget something? Because I'm starving. At least send one of the guards."

"I already did," I say.

He grunts and turns back to the map.

"I'm not sure why you're so worried about our approach. You know as well as I do that we're going to defeat them."

Alexander's head snaps up. "How do I know that?"

I tilt my head. "I mean, Sekhmet said—"

He straightens. "She said what? She ran out of here like a bull charging, and we haven't seen her since."

I sputter. "She said that you need to defeat her father. She said you need to free them."

"She's not free as long as she's with him!" Alexander hurls something across the room, something that barely misses my head. It's a pot of some kind, and it shatters against one of the tent poles.

I stumble backward. "I'm your friend. Sheesh."

Alexander freezes. "You're my. . . *friend?*"

I cast about for what part of that statement could be wrong.

Alexander walks toward me.

I shift, moving backwards. "Are we not friends?"

He smiles, stalking me now. "In all the time I've known Hephaestion, he's never called himself my friend. My enemy in wrestling as children, my competitor, and then later, my commander. My soldier. My most loyal companion. But never my *friend*."

I gulp. "I felt like it was time."

Alexander laughs then. "I'm embarrassed it took me so long to realize." He grabs my arms. "But please, please drop this bizarre guise." He shudders. "It's disturbing to be so insanely attracted to my closest *friend*."

I laugh, and the sound is strange, masculine, and foreign. "I don't know what you mean."

He kisses me then, and my disguise melts away, heat and desire and almost-pain replacing it. My arms wind around him, needing more than he can give, needing a future we can't share. But I forget it then, the fear, the doubt, the impossible situation we're in, and I kiss him back.

My lips move against his. It's such a simple thing, gross even, if you think about it, to press your mouth to someone else's. But I can't think about anything right now. I'm too busy feeling *everything*. His hand on my back, pressing me closer, his fingers digging into my hair, his breath mixing with mine. My heart hammering inside my chest.

When he shoves me sideways and we fall together against his blankets, it feels *right*. It feels like the first full breath on an icy winter morning. Like my toes in the sun-warmed sand on the edge of the ocean. Like a perfect bite of a firm but juicy fig, sour and sweet and juicy all at once.

A moan escapes my mouth and Alexander roars, calling to me somehow. He unbuckles his sword belt, flinging it aside, and drops above me, his hands bracing on either side of my body. The heat from his body rolls over me, and I shiver.

"Should I stop?" His whisper against my ear ignites something new inside of me, something primal.

This time, the roar comes from me, the shift pressing against me from deep inside. But I stop it—I have no idea how Alexander would react to fur rolling over my skin. Probably not well. I shake my head back and forth slowly.

"Your eyes," he says reverently. "They're slitted."

Cat irises. That's what he's seeing. I wait for revulsion.

Instead he smiles and covers my mouth with his. "My lioness." His hand slides my shift from my shoulder, his hand replacing it, his skin pressing against mine. And everywhere he touches ignites, in the best way possible. I arch my body upward against him, loving the feel of his weight on top of me.

"Don't stop," I whisper against his mouth. "Please don't stop."

Thoughts and warnings crowd into my brain, but I shove them away. Nothing in the world makes sense if this doesn't make sense. I want to be with Alexander more than I want anything else. I *need* him to possess me.

A tent flap opens, flooding the room with unwelcome sunlight.

"Er, I guess I'll go?" Hephaestion asks.

Alexander's muscles tighten. He shakes his head like a dog that's drying off. "No, wait." He leaps back from me. He drags in a labored breath. "Stay here. Bring us food. We need to eat and talk."

Like a fog has lifted, I realize what we were doing—where we were headed.

Nowhere good.

My body disagrees pretty vehemently. I ache. I yearn for Alexander to return. My heart pounds and my body throbs, but he's right. My father. His mother. I shiver and sit up. "Food. Talking. Good idea."

Hephaestion's mouth twitches with unexpressed laughter, but he says nothing as he sets a tray of food on the ground next to Alexander. "If I'd known, I might have brought oysters. . ."

The time, when Alexander throws something, it's a dagger, and it sinks into Hephaestion's shoulder. "Oww!" He swears loudly. "Are you insane?"

"Don't take it personally. He was kissing you a minute ago," I say.

Hephaestion yanks the dagger out and drops it on the ground. "That's disgusting. I'd rather kiss a pig." He kicks the dagger and stalks out. "You're lucky there's a pair of healers right outside, or I'd be a lot less forgiving, you moody son of a gourd."

"How dare you compliment my mother like that," Alexander says.

I roll my eyes.

"Why are you here?" Alexander asks. "I should have started there." He rips into a loaf of bread and tosses another to me.

I think he started in exactly the right place, and judging from the way he's eyeing me, he agrees. But we both know better than to head down that path again, alone inside his tent. We can't count on Hephaestion to save us again. "I'm not totally sure," I confess. "And it wasn't easy to pull off. My dad has no idea I'm here."

He grunts. "He'd be upset?"

I shrug. "Yes."

"You may not know why you're here," Alexander says, "but I'm not as conflicted as you." He drops the end of the bread on the tray. "I've been thinking about this a lot. What I'd say, if I saw you again. What I wish I'd done in the past."

"Oh?"

He scoots closer and takes my hand. "Yes. Will you listen? Not stop me or interrupt?"

I gulp.

"No promises." He smirks. "That's the Sekhmet I know."

I shake my head. "No, that's not it. It's that—"

He presses a finger to my lips. Even that contact makes my pulse pick up. "Listen. Please."

I nod.

"I tried to tell you something before, but in a symbolically perfect way, my mother barged in and destroyed you, or, er, your dragonfly-cat. My entire life, she's ruined all my happiness. I always make excuses for her. I always try and figure out how to make her happy, and she has had her share of misery that she didn't cause, but she doesn't ever do what she must to escape it. She's never improved her situation, and that's on her."

"Okay, but you said my dad was more evil than I knew."

He lifts one eyebrow. "I said no interrupting."

"I wasn't interrupting. I was letting you know I'm listening."

He catches my hand between his. "Before Mother destroyed you, I was going to make a big mistake. In my desperation, I was going to tell a *cat* how I felt about you."

My heart stops in my chest.

"I was terrified I'd never see you again. I knew in my heart I needed to wait for you to sit across from me to tell you this." He stares into my eyes for one second. Then another. His blue eyes have never been this bright. The muscles in his jaw have never been quite so taut. "Sekhmet, you change everything in my life. You turn misery to joy. You transform darkness to light. You flip despair on its head and create excitement, animation, and hope."

I open my mouth, but he shakes his head, smiling broadly.

He pulls me closer, wrapping an arm around me and pressing a kiss to my temple. "I told you that I didn't believe in love and you laughed in my idiotic face. You must have known then that I'd fall for you—just as I have. You're all I think about. You're all I care about. I love you, Sekhmet, daughter of Ra. Gods forgive me, I love you more than heaven and hell and everything in between."

11

ANCIENT EGYPT

Part of me wishes I was a cat and my response could be a meow.

I swallow.

Then I lick my lips.

And then, blessedly, Hephaestion ducks back inside. "Alright. I've been healed. And I came back to say—"

Alexander's head whips around and he glares pointedly at his friend.

"You're going to throw the knife at my face this time, aren't you?"

I giggle.

"You should consider that I make your tempestuous girlfriend laugh. That's a thing you want to keep around. Right?"

"What do you need?" Alexander asks.

"I thought you might like to know that instead of arranging themselves and waiting like we expected, Ra's—" he coughs. "Er, Darius' army is advancing even now. They'll be upon us within an hour or two, I imagine."

Alexander's eyes widen and his grip on my hand loosens. "Why?" He turns to me. "Is he—"

"My dad doesn't like waiting. I was surprised he let you engage first the last time, but I'm not shocked that he's moving first now."

Alexander jumps to his feet, all the longing and desperation in his eyes gone, replaced with resolve. "So be it."

I stand too. "I'm coming."

Out of the corner of my eye, I notice Hephaestion's jaw drop.

"Absolutely not," Alexander says.

"My father keeps me behind him at all times," I say. "He's always done that, kept me back from any fights, safely ensconced between a handful of his warriors, while he handles any conflict himself." I don't bother explaining how that makes me feel.

I think Alexander already knows.

He grits his teeth. "I hate the idea of you riding out there—in the path of arrows, swords, snapping fangs and tearing claws."

"I have claws of my own." I push the shift through, only on my right hand, watching as my hand shifts into a paw.

"You can't come as a lioness." Hephaestion looks horrified. "Surely your people would recognize you."

I suppose he's right. I let go of the shift and my hand returns. "I'll go disguised, then," I say. "Even without claws, I'm not without protection."

"You'll fight for our side?" Alexander lifts both eyebrows.

"I'll do what I can to prevent the carnage on both sides," I say. "Is that acceptable?"

"You can't limit carnage in war," he says. "War *is* carnage."

"The whole thing is my fault," I say. "Perhaps I should simply end it."

"Is that what you want?" Hephaestion asks at the same time as Alexander says, "It's not your fault. If anything, it's mine. My mother's revenge and my ambition—"

"We could do this all day." Hephaestion shakes his head. "How about we agree that it's *both* your faults and accept that either way, the fight that's been coming for quite some time now looms before us."

"Always so pragmatic," Alexander says. "Even when you're covered in blood from a dagger your companion threw at you."

"You've been violent as long as I've known you," Hephaestion says. "I'm just lucky that we have healers around. Lots of healers."

Alexander argues with me a little more, but his heart isn't in it. By the time the two men have buckled their armor in place, he has agreed that I can come along. "Not as someone threatening. As a young, innocent flag bearer."

"Or better yet, you could be a cat or something," Hephaestion says. "Like last time. Then you'd be safe, but you could still see what's going on."

"Who's going to keep you safe if I'm harmless?" I cross my arms.

Hephaestion splutters. "I keep myself safe."

"From errant arrows? From swords in the back?" I lift one eyebrow.

"There are healers when things go wrong," he says.

"The same is true for me."

"It's like he wasn't even listening when you argued with me," Alexander says.

It's irritating that everyone wants me to hang back, but it's probably also something that's been drilled into them since birth. Protect the women, protect the children.

Part of me doesn't want to pretend to be a flag bearer. Part of me wants to *do* something. Stand up and change the world—show everyone that I don't need anyone to keep me safe but myself. But then I remember that the threat here is my own father and brother, and I resolve to keep my head down and my mouth shut so I can see whether our plan works, whether Alexander will keep his word and vanquish Darius. . .

So that Ra and I can leave.

Before I know it, we're riding out on a huge open field outside of Memphis, the field where Dad's and Shu's army is arrayed to face us. A bigger army even than the tremendous one that Alexander brought, all the warriors drawn out in a long line.

Dad never lets me go with Am-Heh or Bastet or any of the others. Shu never lets me accompany him, either. Excepting the last battle where I came as a hawk, I've never been here before: perched on a jumpy mare, breathing in the anticipation, the nervous energy, and the smell of fear that precedes a pitched battle.

"So you've got your troops grouped," I say. "Renders in four groups—cats, dogs, falcons, and reptiles."

"And the Reapers are broken into two," Hephaestion says.

"The Lifters spread in bunches," Alexander says.

"What about the combination fighting you were teaching the last time I visited?" I don't see elementals mixed with the others.

"It's harder than I expected it would be to integrate them. Trust is earned, I suppose." Alexander shrugs. "We're working on it."

"The elementals are in the smallest pods of all,"

Hephaestion explains. "They're interspersed and taking commands from the Lifter captains. It's the closest we could get to integrated units."

I think about the shattered sheep heads and shudder.

Alexander shifts and Bucephalus edges toward me carefully. "You can still go back," he says softly. "You don't have to stay for this."

"It's very strange watching you be so solicitous to the flag bearer," Hephaestion says. "People are confused."

He's not wrong. People all around us are shooting strange looks our way as Alexander looks fondly at an adolescent boy holding a flag for Isis. Dad would hate my being here so much, even though it makes Alexander look crazy. That thought firms my resolve. The only way I can be sure things will go well is if I can see what happens with my own eyes. If that means I have to witness the destruction I'm also causing, then that's what it means.

"It's not your fault, you know," Alexander says. "None of this is. I'd have come after you and your father even if I'd never met you, I'd just have done it for all the wrong reasons. And the same people would have died, and then your dad would have struck me down as well."

"And probably, eventually, your mother."

"I've often wondered why he didn't just kill her," Alexander says.

"I wish I knew what hold she has on him."

"They have a complex history," he says. "You should ask him about it one day soon."

Maybe I will. But before I can say that, trumpets sound. Riders begin toward us. Not one or two—not a message or a parlay. No, Dad's dispatched the cavalry.

And right behind them, his own Render unit, led by Anubis, races forward in their animal forms—enormous and terrifying wolves. They snap and snarl so loudly I can hear them from here. Horus dips and dives above them, spears and arrows and projectiles at the ready.

Alexander's eyes practically gleam when he signals his troops. They surge forward as well, rushing outward with seemingly no fear, ready to clash with Dad's. At least Shu's not one of the shock troops. He's hanging back by Dad. The warriors collide with snaps, with snarls, with clash of metal on metal, and the tearing sound of flesh and bone on teeth and claws.

I cringe.

Alexander and Hephaestion leap to action, racing forward as well, Alexander urging Bucephalus to move toward the front. I can't hang back like I said I would. I know why they want me to, but I can't do it.

Arrows glance my way, but I shift them aside easily, my eyes casting hazel light all around me. Someone further away locks on to me, curious why a flag bearer would be a Lifter, perhaps, and focuses on me. An Ice Called, it appears, judging from the ice spear that manifests in his hands. It distracts me from the battle at large, and that feels like a good thing. As he races toward me, his eyes intent, his spear lifted, a great sorrow overwhelms me. I could easily kill him. With one small tug, his light, his energy, and his intrinsic power would become mine. I could tuck it into the reservoir in my ring, or the one hanging on a chain around my neck.

I'm sure Dad's doing that very thing, pulling energy from those soldiers who pose a threat to the men and women he cherishes most. He's playing his part—

instead of siphoning every opponent, he's dutifully siphoning only those who are most threatening.

It makes me wonder where Isis is—I should have asked. Like Anat, like every Assim other than my dad and me, she's not well suited to battle. She must touch someone in order to steal their energy. She can't pull it from a distance, which makes her vulnerable. But I'd still expect her to be close, casting protection spells on her blessed son, her final hope for revenge.

Finally, the man hurls his spear—watching in satisfaction as it barrels toward me. I wait until the last minute before I siphon the magic that created it, reducing it to a cloud of mist just before it connects with my body. The man's eyes bulge, his face flushing, and he begins to run toward me, seemingly unconcerned by the fighting taking place all around us.

He pulls a dagger from his boot and flings it my direction. He knows I can Lift. Why he would persist in using projectiles, I don't know. I Lift it and send it back toward him. He leaps aside just in time, the dagger embedding itself in the dirt behind him with a thunk. A desperate woman snatches it up and plunges it into the side of a wolf that's snapping right in her face.

The man keeps coming, drawing near enough that I can see the freckles on the bridge of his nose, and the bald patch underneath his carefully combed hair. I see wrinkles at the edges of his eyes.

I don't want to kill him.

But when he pulls out another dagger and leaps toward me, I see no other way. I knock another stray arrow aside without thinking, and then, though I hate to do it, I tug his energy out and away, tucking it into my ring.

He sinks mid-leap, shriveling and collapsing.

I hate the look of an assimilated human. They become a husk of the person they were. Their total mass doesn't change, but they shrink anyway. The weight of a soul forever gone. I force myself to look around at the fighting surrounding me. It's everywhere. Renders attacking Reapers. Lifters and Wind Called. Fire and Ice Called. People killing people everywhere I look. It's the most depressing, the most horrifying sight I've ever witnessed. The smells, the sounds, the sensations, they crowd in on me, as though I'm somehow, inadvertently tugging them toward me, feeling what they feel.

Power hums inside my chest. My hands shake. I want to step forward. I want to intervene. The power inside each of the people around me thrums, like the vibrations of an individually plucked strand of twisted cable, times thousands. It begs for me to yank it and end this fruitless, pointless onslaught. It could end so quickly, and their lives would at least have some meaning, could be used for something else that would benefit the world.

I finally understand why Ra does it. When people are executed, he siphons them, because at least their energy isn't wasted.

I begin harvesting the dying, the wounded who are so miserable, and suffering so deeply that their souls are stuttering. When the light of their life force begins to wobble and shake, I suck it up, one after another. I end their pain and ease their transition to the hereafter, tucking the light from their souls into my necklace or my ring, flooding my own reservoirs. It feels greedy, but the alternative is letting them just. . .dissipate.

Anger rises up inside of me at the senseless loss, and I'm not sure how much more I can take without doing something, without stopping it, when I hear shouts and follow the sound. To Alexander and Hephaestion. Bucephalus rears, and they race forward, plunging through the gathered troops, ignoring the battle raging around them. The only reason they'd do that is if they found Ra.

I glance at the sky—nearly sunset. It's time.

I urge my mare forward, and when she balks, I push, shifting her will to force her to go. She races willingly then, her fear removed as cleanly as a damp rag removes cobwebs. She punches through groups of Renders with a bit of telekinetic help, and races past enemy troops. I discourage them from following us with just a bit of supra power. It takes a bit of time, but we catch Alexander just as he's closing on Ra and Shu and Am-Heh.

"Halt!" Alexander shouts. "Darius, you coward, face me."

Dad turns around and for a moment, I expect his eyes as they scan past me to stop, outraged, and call me to his side. But he doesn't do that, of course. He sees only a young boy, holding aloft a flag marked for Isis' son.

"I'm no coward," Dad says calmly. "But this isn't a good time for me. Perhaps try me again in half an hour or so."

"I think not." Alexander urges Bucephalus forward. "Face me now."

"You need your friend to fight me?" Dad asks, glaring at Bucephalus. "You can't beat me without his support?"

Alexander leaps from Bucephalus' back and shakes his hand backward, telling his mount to stay back. "Of course not."

Once Bucephalus has retreated, Dad breathes more

easily—I can see it, even if no one else can. Supras, myself excluded I think, make him nervous still, even after all this time. Dad draws his sword. "Winner takes Egypt?"

"I think I'll take Egypt either way."

Dad lunges for him, his blade slicing downward with terrible speed. "Dead people take no prisoners."

Alexander is smiling. "You'd do well to remember that, old man. I think you're closer to verifying that statement than I am."

For a moment, the only sounds come from the blades meeting and labored breathing. Both men are adept swordsmen, and that really says something for Alexander. My dad has had centuries upon centuries to perfect his skills.

"You're not bad with a blade," Dad says. It's a high compliment from him.

Alexander feints and brings his blade up quickly, nicking Dad's arm. "We don't have to be enemies, you know."

Dad laughs. "Is that so?"

"Your fight with my mother can remain between the two of you. I have no quarrel with you, personally."

"Then why have you come into my home and killed my people?"

"To satisfy my mother, but now, if I defeat you today, that's done. She'll have taken her pound of flesh. She'll have gotten her revenge. Ousting you from your home is enough. I can make her forgive you."

Ra's laugh is loud, but also chilling. "Anyone who fancies he can force Isis to do anything is a fool—a dangerously optimistic fool."

"Why haven't you killed her?"

Dad swings down hard, and Alexander blocks him, the clanging of their blades filling the clearing. "You don't destroy a rainbow. You don't shatter stained glass. You don't desecrate a holy place."

"You're comparing my mother to a rainbow?" Alexander pauses, meeting Dad's gaze. "Have you met her?"

Dad laughs.

"You like her, still." This time the surprise in his voice isn't feigned.

"Like is the wrong word," Dad says. "I don't like her at all. In fact, I strongly dislike her, but I also respect what she is. Because of that, I know that there's no place in this world for a peace between us. Her hatred of me is eternal and unyielding. I don't even blame her."

I definitely need to ask my dad some questions.

I'm just not sure he'll tell me the truth.

But this time, when Dad's blade spins toward Alexander, he pulls his back, leaving his throat exposed.

I gasp.

I'm not the only one.

Ra's blade freezes one inch away from decapitating Alexander and an involuntary cry escapes. Hephaestion glares. Shu turns my way, his face full of curiosity.

"Why not just kill me?" Alexander says.

"Because I fear. . ." Dad trails off.

"You fear what?"

"He thinks my sister loves you," Shu says.

Dad chokes.

I expect Dad to argue. Or Alexander to say that they're crazy.

Instead Alexander plunges his sword into Dad's right side and twists. "Then I'll kill you instead, *Darius*. We each have our parts to play."

"She may love you, but she can't ever be with you," Dad whispers, coughing up blood.

I slide off my mare, desperate to reach Dad's side, but before I've gone a single step, Imhotep is beside him. Of course he is. It's all part of the act. Dad's supposed to 'die'—that was the bargain.

"You've seen and witnessed," Alexander says.

Bucephalus nods, his great black horse eyes solemn. Hephaestion presses his fist to his chest. "Seen and witnessed."

Alexander yanks the sword out of Dad's chest. "The world's an ever-changing place. Perhaps, even if it's unlikely, there may yet one day be a place for us."

"Perhaps," Dad says. "But probably not."

Alexander calls his troops back and Shu tells our troops to retreat, and then to surrender. But before he goes, he looks at me once, pointedly, his lip twitching.

He knows.

The second they've withdrawn, I race to Alexander's side. "I can't stay. Shu suspects, and he and Dad will be headed for our rendezvous point immediately."

He doesn't argue with me. He doesn't try to convince me to stay. But he does ask me one question. "Is it true?" He doesn't have to explain what he's asking.

"Yes," I whisper.

He kisses me then, blood-spattered, sweaty, and defeated, even in victory. His eyes when he finally releases me, looking down on me from above, are sad. Profoundly sad. Like he finally understands the depressing truths of the universe. "It changes nothing."

I swing back up on my borrowed mare and race away, tears streaming down my face the entire ride.

"You were there, weren't you?" Shu's voice is low, and he's waited until no one else is around.

"You heard Bastet," I say. "I was with her the entire time."

He shakes his head. "I saw you, I know I did."

"Was that before or after you told Dad that I loved Alexander?"

He hisses and his eyes narrow. "I knew it. The flag boy, right? Why would they bring a flag bearer?"

"Oh please, there were dozens of soldiers there. I could have been any of them."

"But you weren't. When you gasped and leapt from your horse the second Apophis stabbed Father. . ." He whistles. "But how? What did you have to do to convince Bastet to lie?"

I grab his arm and drag him away from Dad and the others. "Lower your voice."

"Oh, what's with the secrecy? Father knows you—"

I slap my hand over his mouth. "Dad may suspect, thanks to your uninformed blabbing on the battlefield, but he doesn't *know* anything, as I haven't even decided how I feel about things myself. And beyond that, Dad certainly doesn't know that *I* know anything at all. So stop it with the secret spilling already."

"We've left that life behind," Shu says. "Since you didn't stay, I think it's safe to assume that no matter how you feel, it's over."

"You don't have to look so delighted about it," I snap.

"What makes you think I'm happy?" He shakes his head. "I think you *should* tell Father how you feel. Defy him if he disagrees and live your own life."

"You think that will go well?" My eyebrows shoot up. "Really?"

"Not at all," Shu says, "but it would be interesting."

"Are you telling me that this isn't interesting enough for you?" I gesture around at our new accommodations. Anat really outdid herself. The palace in Babylon is enormous, and now, as Nidin-Bel's guests, we've been given an entire wing of it to ourselves.

"It's new to you," Shu says, "but I've been here before. Give it a few months, and you'll be as bored with this new place as you were in Memphis. I have a few years on you, and they've taught me one thing. Location doesn't matter nearly as much as the people you're with. If you're not with the person you love, you'll hate anywhere you are."

"Oh, please. Do you know how many places there are to see around here? How many things to do and new cultures to experience? We aren't governing anymore," I say. "We can move on whenever we'd like. That's the whole point!"

"I guess we'll find out soon enough." He looks too tired to argue further. But by the time dinner comes, he's smiling and laughing right along with everyone else.

No matter what Shu may have said, no matter what Dad suspects, and no matter what daft things Alexander may be hoping for, this life is better than the one we left, and I don't regret my path, even if sometimes I dream of a different future.

❧ 12 ❧

EARTH

Jesse and I moved a lot over the past few years. One of the things I noticed was that a new city doesn't really feel quite right until you've found a place to live. To feel like you live somewhere, you need a place to leave your belongings. A place to drop your guard. A place you'll return over and over. I think it's because, as humans, we need a fixed point in space that is ours.

We orient everything else relative to it.

Things in Houston were near or far, relative to our tiny apartment. They were convenient or inconvenient, based entirely on their relative distance from our *home*. The apartment we lived in wasn't expensive. It wasn't very comfortable, and it certainly wasn't nicely furnished. That didn't matter much, because it was *ours*. I could have a terrible day at work, and Jesse could have a miserable one too, and we knew we just had to stick it out until we got home. It was a place we could *breathe*. We kicked our shoes off, we showered the miserable day away, and we reset.

I would have told you that it was something about

our belongings or an innate feeling of location that grounded me.

But when Jesse died—when my entire world cracked open—I didn't care about going back to that place. It didn't matter anymore—it wasn't home without him. That's when I realized it wasn't the place that mattered or my 'home' that anchored me. I never really oriented my life around a geographic location.

It was my brother all along.

It's the memories of a shared space and the promise of a future with a person who matters that made that crappy little apartment with its shabby carpet and scuffed linoleum *home*.

And ever since I ripped Jesse's Terra energy away and shoved him onto Earth—ever since that very moment, I haven't felt quite right. I haven't felt *anchored* in space or time. No amount of new stuff can help, and even life in a palace with servants can't repair the injury. But now Ra has healed him, and my brother is back, retrieving his memories slowly.

So why don't I feel anchored? Why does the world still feel like shifting sand beneath my feet?

"Alora?"

I start at the sound of my name. "Yes?"

"You haven't eaten anything." Jesse's voice is full of concern. It's familiar. And he's right.

I look down at the French toast I've massacred, swimming in a pool of syrup. Huh. I usually devour anything placed in front of me. I shrug. "Not hungry, I guess."

"You haven't been eating very well for a while." His voice is low, urgent. "Do you want something else? Eggs? A smoothie? I really think they'll bring you anything at all."

I'm sure they will. Even though I finally convinced

both Ra and the British government that he was a better selection for their new ruler, they still treat me like I'm royalty. Probably because Dad insists on it. "I'm really not very hungry." I stand up abruptly, causing my chair legs to scrape jarringly against the marble floor.

Jesse stuffs another bite of steak in his mouth. He hasn't had trouble adjusting to being able to eat whatever he wants whenever he wants it, that's for sure. "Alright. What are we doing today?"

He's followed me around like a puppy ever since I stepped back. He watches me like he thinks I'll break if he blinks. It would probably be annoying if it was anyone else, but it's Jesse. "Not sure. I guess I'll go see if Mehen needs me to do anything."

I hated being stuck in meetings from dawn until long after dusk. I hated all the decisions I had to make. I hated the people calling me Most Divine, which Dad has almost entirely been able to stop, thank goodness. But now that it's all gone, passed to Ra, my days are surprisingly empty. "I kind of don't know what to do."

John breezes through the doorway. "I like this smaller room."

More of Dad's lieutenants show up every day, and now they occupy the better part of the Morning Room. It means we've been relegated to the sitting room in front of my queen's bedchamber, which Dad insisted I keep, in spite of assuming my leadership role.

John, of course, is one of Dad's newest lieutenants, and absolutely bursting with pride to have been chosen. He's as annoyingly giddy to serve my father as everyone else.

"You could actually have breakfast with us, if you wanted," I say. "You know, if you wanted to see me at all."

I'm beginning to wonder if he does. I immediately feel petty for thinking it. John has defended me at every single turn—and we definitely share chemistry—but since Ra returned, he's much more attentive to him than to me.

Which is understandable, I suppose, but it's an adjustment.

"Between training with Am-Heh and fulfilling my new duties for Ra, I can't really afford to miss the morning briefing. I'm so far behind the rest of them."

"I'd think you'd be ahead," Jesse says. "You do know the difference between an iPhone and a flat, polished piece of glass. And you can, you know, speak English."

"The way Ra assimilates information and then inserts it into their minds." John shakes his head, his eyes full of awe. "It's one of the most amazing things, even now that I've seen it over and over. It kind of levels the playing field for the lieutenants who were struggling with modernization."

"Yes, Ra is almost like the sun, moon, and stars in human form," I say.

Jesse snickers. "If you love him so much—"

John's lip twitches. "Don't. You know it's not like that. I don't worship him. It's just that, the things he can do, the way he completely enchants everyone he meets, overcoming all their reservations and concerns—"

"He uses magic, John." My voice is flatter than I wish. It's not that I begrudge my father for his vast knowledge and careful use of his unfathomable power. I really don't. From what I recall, and from my experiences here, he only uses those things to improve the world. He's not a villain.

But.

For someone who hates supras, he certainly skirts

the edges of overwriting people's free will himself sometimes, artificially enhancing their faith in him and suppressing their fears. It feels. . .I don't know. It feels a little dodgy, to be honest, even if he's preventing mass panic and rebellion that would only result in a stupid number of casualties.

"Have you had any more dreams?" John's eyes are irritatingly hopeful. "I mean, not to press you."

"No," Jesse says. "Daddy wouldn't like anyone to press her."

I can't blame him for the slight hostility. Since his return, Ra has made it clear that I'm his daughter in every sense and that Jesse is his son, but he's also made it clear that Jesse's not quite as beloved. It's nothing he's said or done, of course, but I always come first. It annoys me, so I'm sure that Jesse feels a little passed over.

Which pisses me off even more.

"It's just that we still can't work out quite why the female shifters and Assimilators—"

"By which you mean Anat," I say. As far as I know, they haven't located her yet either, and Dad's actually panicking about that a little. The other female Assimilators are either hiding well, or no female Assimilators have recovered their powers either.

"Doesn't not knowing what's wrong bother you?" John frowns. "It's like when Ra showed up, you checked out. You don't even *try* anymore."

As much as his zeal and desperation to become more powerful in order to be 'worthy' of me annoys me, he's got a valid point. It felt like everything began and ended with me before, and now that Dad's here, I did kind of give up.

To be honest, it feels nice to do nothing at all.

"I wish I had something to offer, but I haven't

dreamed of the past in days. No new memories here." I tap my head. Something about the dream of the conquering of Egypt *broke* me or something. I woke up afterward sobbing, and I haven't dreamt of Egypt since.

Every time I close my eyes now, dreams of Kahn and Alexander and Jesse and Ra and John all tangle together in a terrifying jumble. I wake in a cold sweat every time, sheets tangled around my legs and arms. It has me going to bed too late and waking far too early.

"Can we talk about these communities that are forming?" Jesse asks. "I don't like them—it feels like the whole world is reordering itself."

Ra's presence in the doorway surprises me, which is hard to do these days. I felt someone coming, of course, but he's usually preceded by a veritable army of clerks and warriors. "It's natural for new groups to align. People who felt disconnected and were searching for their true meaning are finally discovering what they've been missing. They're finding their purpose in this strangely changed world. It's natural for them to want to band together with other people with whom they share a special bond."

"But they had bonds that mattered before," I argue. "Bonds they chose. Friendships, schoolmates, family. They're forsaking those in order to forge new ones."

Mehen and Am-Heh shove past Ra and take up positions on either side of the one window, apparently identifying it as the point of vulnerability in the room.

"If you were receiving reports as I am, you'd know that many of those chosen bonds from before were still in alignment." Ra tilts his head. "Earth elementals married one another more often than not. Feline shifters opened yoga studios together. Fire elementals started businesses as performers working with flames, or running funeral parlors specializing in incineration.

Even without knowing why, these people often chose occupations and formed families that corresponded with their respective affinities. Now that they're out on display, so to speak, they're stronger than ever. Trying to halt that kind of change would be like trying to hold back the tides." He pauses. "Utterly futile."

"And these new communities will be stronger," Mehen says. "They won't betray one another at the first sign of trouble." His English is now perfect, thanks to Ra's intervention. I know it's a wonder that Ra can process so much information and share it with his people. It's been absolutely vital to a successful integration of his people here in the UK, and in the modern world in general, but it's still surreal. I really ought to be doing like John—mirroring him.

But it rankles having to ask him to teach me things I've already learned. If I'm patient, as I gain my memories, I regain my abilities as well. Even though not all of them seem to be entirely intact. Since remembering my personal affinity, I've tried to make a few constructs. Anything larger than a sparrow has been too difficult to maintain and collapsed almost immediately.

"You'll be relieved to know that according to the Minister of Magical Matters, our efforts to register the British Citizens' powers has been well received," Am-Heh says. "We're now reporting that almost 70% of citizens have voluntarily filed paperwork showing their magical abilities and consenting to future testing and power optimization training. Obviously the citizens don't share your concerns about these new groups. They're eager to be able to search for healers, or elementals, etcetera." Am-Heh looks up from his phone and shrugs. "All these new gadgets make it so easy to spread the word and organize the details."

Am-Heh has an iPhone, and I'm not sure I've ever seen anything more bizarre than watching him scrolling his feed on Facebook. At the same time, it's also somehow strangely comforting. Even people over two thousand years old can't seem to withstand the draw of friend updates and celebrated bragging. This new version of him puts some space between my memories of ancient Egypt and the present time.

It has occurred to me that perhaps I'm not allowing the old memories to resurface—I feel increasingly guilty about the betrayal of Ra I sense coming. And though I long for Kahn—er, for Alexander—it's confusing—I also thank my lucky stars that I sent him away. After all, he's the reason I betrayed my own father, I'm virtually certain.

But I can't undo the past.

"Listen, I didn't want to interrupt your breakfast." Ra's eyes scan the table, stopping on my completely untouched plate. "Because apparently you aren't eating well." His eyes reflect his concern. "But I wanted you to hear something from me." He sighs. "Isis appears to be militarizing."

It's like the words don't make sense. "You're saying that the Followers of Isis are preparing to attack us?" I shake my head. "What makes you think that?"

"As you know, we currently only rule here in the United Kingdom. Per your request, we have not extended our reach. You assured me the other countries have governments in place and were largely at peace."

"Hang on. I just said that it didn't seem like we really ought to start barging in with existing governments and—"

His tone is soft. "I'm not criticizing." He smiles. "But the United Kingdom monitors troop movements, and it seems the Isis leadership had no such qualms about allowing other countries to rule themselves. They've seized control of at least fifteen other nations, including the United States and Mexico, the European Union, and upon my departure, Egypt, which I find ironic."

I sit down, bracing my arms on the table. "Okay, so what do we—"

Ra drops a firm hand on my shoulder. "You don't need to worry about it. You said you had no interest in ruling, and I'm not asking you to change that. If you want to be involved, you are of course very welcome, but I only wanted to inform you. I didn't want news of it to catch you off guard." He smiles. "I'm not concerned, nor am I surprised. But if they prepare to take action against us, against the home you've chosen. . ."

"You'll be forced to act."

He shrugs. "Even so."

That's reasonable, of course. I wish I knew why, with Terra gone, Isis is still aiming for us. They know Ra is back, but Terra is gone. What do they think needs to be done? All they're doing is poking a bear. Actually, more like a dragon.

Dad's finger drops gently onto the wrinkle between my eyes, smoothing it. "Cub, you don't need to worry. It's not concerning to me. It's not a real threat, trust me."

I swallow and nod. "Alright."

"Why don't you do something fun today?" John suggests. "You could—"

"We could go see Big Ben," Jesse says. "I've been wanting to see it—or maybe the Tower Bridge."

The idea of going to see tourist attractions, like the world hasn't turned upside down, like we ever could have come here under normal circumstances, is almost laughable. And then I think about it. Maybe that's what I need, something laughable. Something fun. So many things have changed. So many things can't ever be undone. But Jesse and I could spend the day together, doing *nothing* of consequence. We could pretend our parents didn't die and we weren't tossed into the system. That he wasn't killed, and that I didn't haul him here to find a rock that might keep his leaking soul from bleeding out before our ancient father could come and seal up the hole.

My laughter shocks everyone in the room. Except Jesse. His smile reflects mine. He gets it. "Yes. Let's do it. You guys stay here and work out how to deal with invading armies and power anomalies and supply chains. We're going for a walk where we'll pretend nothing has changed and we're here to get a Big Ben clock and a Tower of London statue."

Ra smiles. "Yes. Good idea."

Which is how Jesse and I waltz out the door, arm in arm, with a backpack full of water bottles and a few packets of crisps on a glorious fall day. The brisk breeze smells like hope. The streaming sunlight, occasionally hidden behind clouds, reminds me that even amidst the sorrow, there's joy too.

When I see M&Ms on a street vendor's cart, I buy four packages.

By the time Big Ben comes into view up ahead, I've stopped worrying about Isis. I'm not thinking about the new groups or what they mean. I'm not worried about the goods that Britain needs that come from countries Isis controls. I'm not worrying about what caused me to turn against my own father and lock him away.

I feel free.

"Do you ever worry that maybe Ra missed something? That maybe I'm not really fine?" Jesse's words are a hot poker to my stomach.

I stop mid-step. "Do you feel ill? Or weak?"

He shakes his head, his color good and his smile crooked. "Not at all. I have no reason to suspect he's incorrect. But."

I stare into his deep blue eyes. "But what?"

He shrugs. "You said you can see souls, but you haven't looked at mine since Ra healed me."

I can't quite swallow past the lump in my throat.

"Is there a reason?"

I shrug. "No, but I'm no healer, and I'm basically a baby when it comes to crafting spells with assimilated power. I'm remembering things I once knew, but it's not the same. It's hazy and confusing. I guess I'm worried that I won't know what I'm seeing or that even if I do, I won't be able to—" I gulp.

"You won't be able to face it if he's wrong?"

Maybe that's what's felt off. I don't entirely believe the miracle.

"You can't accept happiness, because you've never known it." Jesse starts to walk again, towing me along behind him.

"I've known happiness," I say. "With Mom and Dad when we were small, we were happy." Before they died.

"But not in a long time."

I can't even argue with that. "I have accepted it. Ra fixed you—just like I hoped he would."

Jesse snorts. "I certainly feel fine." He jogs forward and leaps up and to the side, clicking his heels together. Not that it makes a sound, since he's wearing sneakers.

Still, the movement brings a smile to my face.

"And look." His eyes light up and he scoops up a bundle of rocks from the side of the path, Lifting them in a complicated pattern in front of us, the large rocks weaving in and out in a basketweave while the small rocks fly around them in electron-like orbits. "I've been practicing with Mehen, and I'm getting pretty good. Maybe not 'ancient times' good, but passable, even by Mehen's exacting standards."

"You've been Lifting every day?"

Jesse nods.

That actually makes me feel better. The more energy he used, the more quickly he collapsed before. It's been more than a week, and he's still here. Still fine. Strong, even. I try to let go of the lingering fear, but I'm not sure I can. "I'll probably always worry about you," I say. "But I'm trying."

"It'll take time," he says. "Like all trauma. You can do your best, but your body still fears." He slings an arm around my shoulders. "Luckily, we have plenty of time now."

"How do you know so much about trauma and healing?" I don't roll my eyes at him, but it takes effort. It's almost too cute. Jesse the counselor.

"Ra told me that," he says. "He said eventually, once you're ready, you'll let go of your fear. You won't need me as much." He snorts. "That hurt, a little."

I wonder whether Ra's jealous of my bond with Jesse—but I don't think he is. He never minded how close I was to Shu.

"Hey lady," a voice calls. "We have the best prices on Big Ben clocks here. And a buy one get one free sale."

I duck my head and walk faster.

"Lady! Lady!" The desperation tugs at something inside of me. How badly must this man need money to be hounding people who are clearly ignoring him.

I glance over my shoulder, stumble over the uneven pavement, and very nearly faceplant.

The man hawking two for one tourist crap is Kahn.

Alexander the Great reborn. In an apron. Trying to sell me souvenirs.

He darts out on the sidewalk and offers me his hand. The world doesn't glow golden. The bizarre light is gone. But our connection is stronger. Because I now know where it came from. From a past neither of us knew or remembered. From a love we shared twenty-five hundred years ago.

A love that might have changed the world.

"Have you lost your mind?" Jesse hisses. Then he shoves us inside, raising his voice to say, "I'd love to find a great clock. Is it really buy one get one?" The second we're inside the shop, he's hissing again. "There's no way we aren't being followed. I'd guess you have about thirty seconds before someone barges in here, checking to make sure you're okay."

I blink. Is he right? "Why are you here?"

"I never should have let you kick me out," Kahn says.

The words I've been longing to hear for every moment since he left.

"But that's not why I'm back."

Jesse frowns. "Spit it out, man."

"I assume you know that the female shifters can't shift—they're still powerless."

I nod.

"I came to tell you why." He pauses. "Like Ra, Isis survived, and she's awake."

❧ 13 ❧

EARTH

Jesse was right.

Not ten seconds after Kahn drops that bomb on us, Horus bursts through the shop door, followed immediately by Am-Heh.

I throw my hands up. "It's okay. He's a friend, guys, I swear."

Of course, it would have been a little smoother if Kahn's eyes hadn't immediately lit up, the decorative knives on the back shelf of the shop unsheathing themselves and hovering in the air, sharp sides facing out.

"Oh, for Pete's sake," Jesse says.

"Who's Pete?" Horus asks. The wind that always seems to circulate when he's around tugs on my hair and billows up the front of my blouse.

I'd laugh if they didn't all look ready to kill each other. "Let me take this opportunity to introduce you both to my *friend*, Kahn."

"We've met," Am-Heh says. "In fact, I was there when he left you." He narrows his eyes.

"And I know him fairly well," Horus says, his voice

gruff. "His real name is Apophis." His nostrils flare, but he inclines his head.

I shake my head. "But that's the thing. He isn't Apophis. He was reborn, just like me, only he doesn't have any memories from—"

Kahn clears his throat. I meet his eyes, his sky blue, intense, gorgeous, distracting eyes. "Actually. . ."

The bottom falls out of my stomach. "Actually what?"

"After I learned the information I just shared with you, a few other things happened." His lip curls in exactly the same way it did when he was Alexander, and I notice something else I was too rushed to see before. He has a sword belted at his hip. I haven't seen him wear a sword since we were on Terra, but this particular sword is familiar. He's wearing Alexander's sword. "A few old memories have started to return, and Isis decided I deserved a few relics from the past."

Something about the way he says that sends thrills shooting up my spine. I open my mouth, but no words emerge.

"This is awkward," Jesse says.

"It doesn't need to be," Kahn says. The bright blue light flooding the little shop winks out and all the knives drop, their tips sinking into the laminate of the shop. A strangled cry from the back tells me that someone isn't too happy about the damage to the merchandise or the floors.

Now that Kahn has backed off, Am-Heh relaxes too, and the wind whipping through my hair dies down to nothing but a chilly breeze.

"What do you plan to do with him?" Horus asks.

We're lucky that Ra sent two of my favorite people to trail us. "He's free to go. He came to share information with me, and I have no intention of repaying him by hauling him back—"

"I'd like to come with you," Kahn says, "if you'll allow it. If I'd been thinking straight, I'd never have left your side." He drops his voice until it's the barest whisper. "That's where I belong. It's where I've always belonged."

My heart lurches. My hands shake. I . . .I want him by my side, but can I trust him? He just told me his *mother* is back, and he remembers her. She's raising an army to fight against us. Is there any chance I'm being manipulated? Dad certainly won't like it.

"Well, I, for one, am glad to see you." Jesse hugs Kahn, awkwardly patting his back.

"By the time Ra is done interrogating you, you might wish you'd escaped when you had the chance," Am-Heh says.

"Is it just me, or has Am-Heh's English improved by a magnitude of ten?" Kahn asks. "Which is great, but how?"

"Ra's as powerful as we were led to believe," I say. "I haven't gotten the hang of it yet, but he can use siphoned energy to assimilate information into a form that people can digest rapidly. He's done it for all of his commanders. It's been extremely helpful with the language stuff."

"Which is almost surely why she can speak all the languages," Jesse says. "Some kind of assimilation-of-critical-information-for-the-architect spell."

"You still don't remember what happened?" Kahn asks.

I shake my head.

"What do you recall?"

I can't quite meet his eyes, so I stare at my feet instead. My sneakers squeak against the laminate as I shuffle them. "I regained most of my childhood memories." I glance up to see his reaction.

He bites his lip, his nostrils flaring. "And what about the knot?"

I inhale sharply. "What do you remember about the knot?"

The smile that curls his lips is devilish. "Everything."

A thrill races through my entire body, and I shiver.

His smile deepens.

"What am I missing here?" Jesse asks.

Without freeing my eyes from his, Kahn asks, "Jesse hasn't recalled anything else, yet?"

I shake my head. "Earth memories, but nothing from Egypt. Not yet, anyway."

"He looks healthy enough."

"I'm surprised you even noticed," Jesse says, "with the way you're *undressing my sister with your eyes*. Right in front of me."

"Be grateful it's just with my eyes."

That was 100% Alexander, and something electric passes between Kahn and me.

As if he realizes it wasn't something he'd normally say, Kahn's cheeks flush bright red and his head snaps toward Jesse. "Sorry. I really am happy you're okay. I'm glad that it appears Ra has lived up to the hype."

"At least jokes pull you two out of your fated-mates-haze, or whatever. I'll be sure to remember that." Jesse points sideways. "What about ancient lieutenants that report to your dad?" He glares at me. "Do they factor into our decision making? Or are we still ignoring them?"

"I'm sure your father would like to speak to Apophis," Horus says. "Especially since he doesn't seem to object to coming with us peacefully."

"Did Dad really hate him so much?" I watch Horus' and Am-Heh's faces when I ask the question.

Am-Heh averts his gaze.

Horus' eyes widen sorrowfully. "It's complicated. I believe he'll behave calmly in this new world."

Oh good. He likely won't try to gut Kahn right off the bat. How wonderful.

"Alright, well, let's go." I turn back toward Kahn. "If you're sure."

"As sure as I've ever been," he says.

"For one of the cockiest guys I've met on either world, that's saying something," Jesse says. "Now if we can keep anyone from spearing you. . ."

"I doubt John will be happy to see me either," Kahn says.

"Or Mehen," I say.

The walk back is a little awkward, with Horus and Am-Heh overreacting to every move Kahn makes, but we hadn't come very far, so it's quick. I wondered whether Dad had sent more than just Horus and Am-Heh to trail me, but clearly he didn't. When we approach the gates to the palace, they swing open immediately, but the guards look shocked that we have a visitor.

I log him in the register and march past, clearly heading for the main entrance.

"Most Divine—er—Your Majes—" the guard looks practically green.

"Yes?"

"If you're looking for your father, he and Sir Rochester went with Lord Mehen to the back gardens to practice." He coughs. "To practice their forms, they said."

A huge explosion behind the palace draws my immediate attention. "What in the world was that?"

He swallows. "I believe that's the sound made by the forms practice."

I break into a jog and round the side of the palace, pushing past the guards posted there without stopping. "What's going on?" I'm mostly asking myself, since the booms are growing louder as we approach. I can barely hear myself think, much less string together some sort of line of questioning for the poor guards cringing and jolting outside the gate.

When we finally pass through and round the bend toward the palace maze and flower gardens, a giant explosion about fifty feet above the ground that looks like napalm and black cats had a baby halts our movement quickly enough.

"Yes!" Am-Heh calls from behind me, as if he expected to witness this very thing. "Much better. That was really targeted without sacrificing power."

The man he's talking to spins around, a huge smile on his face.

It's John.

The second he sees me, his smile broadens. "Alora! I thought you were gone all day! I wanted to surprise you, but now you're here, I can't wait."

Did he create that enormous explosion? Is he using some kind of new weaponry? A bomb? A grenade? Or is it some new Fire Called trick?

"I've seen that before," Kahn says.

"Excuse me?" It's too many things at once.

"Your father helped me break through the blockage on my power," John shouts, jogging toward me. "Apparently I've had the ability all along, but I didn't even know it." He shakes his head as if he can hardly believe what he's saying.

"I can make explosions like that," Kahn whispers. "And so can any Fire Called and Lifter team working together." I remember Alexander's experiments at pairing off the various troops—looking for what they could do together instead of apart.

"Turns out, I'm both a Lifter *and* I'm Fire Called."

Dad was right. "But then, why weren't you on Terra?" I ask. "It makes no sense."

"The structure of Terra was complicated," Ra says, approaching slowly from the same place John was standing. "It drew power from the very people it restrained. I mentioned before that I thought he might have more strength than he could access because, like you, his life force is brighter. It's thicker and more vibrant than most people's. I noticed the anomaly the second I evaluated his heart—"

"Wait," I say. "Why did you poke around at his heart in the first place? You don't think I'm a good judge of character?"

"Will you really chastise me for evaluating my daughter's suitor?" Dad asks.

I suppose not.

"I can't explain how he could have an ability that didn't manifest, or how he didn't throw part of his energy onto Terra, but my best guess is that *someone* suppressed his ability to keep him out."

Who would do that? Or, more importantly, who *could* do that? "We all think I created Terra, right?"

Dad shrugs. "We've thought it was possible. Who else would have the strength? But just before Terra was created, I felt a vortex of energy, sucking, sucking, sucking, unlike anything I had ever before seen or felt. I gathered all my closest companions and enclosed us in a bubble of magic, drawing on everything I had in my reserves to keep us safe. That's how we were preserved instead of simply aging and dying—my protection slowly fed each of my companions energy to keep them alive. Had the energy run out before Terra was unraveled. . ."

They'd all have died. I wish I knew who did it in the first place. I wish I knew so many things.

"I'm sure I didn't keep him out, and who else could possibly have—"

"It must have been Isis," Kahn says. "Who else could have done it? I'm not sure *why* she'd do it, but it had to have been her."

John's voice is high, nearly shrill. "What are you doing here?"

"He came back," I say. "He had some important information for us."

"Isis is alive," Ra says quietly. "Isn't she? That's why Kahn's positive that she is the one who kept John out of Terra and also covered up his extra ability?"

My jaw drops, some of my anger over his role in this business with John evaporating. "How could you possibly know that?" I totally wouldn't be surprised if he pulled a rabbit from a hat right now, and he's not even wearing a hat.

Ra shrugs. "It's the only thing that explains why the female shifters haven't regained their powers—she is still alive, and she's the one stealing from them."

"Yes," Kahn says. "She is alive, and she's the reason they can't shift. She's holding onto their abilities some-how, and the power she can pull from her link to them is nearly unfathomable."

Billions of females who can't shift. She's siphoning all that power and she can use it for anything she wants. What a nightmare.

"It's everything she's ever wanted." Ra's face still looks terribly sad.

"And it's very, very bad for us," Mehen says.

"He can't be here." Am-Heh points at Kahn. "He's working for her—he must be."

Mehen's mouth twists. "I told you he was her son. Even now, he's her creature."

"He isn't—he came to help us," I say.

"You're saying he knows nothing of his past life?" Ra asks.

"No, I'm not saying that. I'm saying he chooses to stand by me this time around." But it's about time I figure out what exactly did happen before. "I'm done sitting around waiting for what my brain decides to share. Just tell me what happened, and how Terra was created in the first place."

Ra gestures toward the edge of the garden, and I follow him, stomping with each step. I guess I am still a little mad—about their reaction to Kahn's arrival, about him monkeying with John's brain and abilities, and about my total blank where understanding and memory should be.

No one else makes any move to trail along, which is kind of a relief. I can't be nearly as irrational and angry as I mean to be when other people are hanging on every word.

"What exactly have you remembered so far?" Ra asks.

"I know I betrayed you and that I fell for Alexander. But the last memory I have, I had left him for you. We had just arrived in Babylon, and you and Ptah were pretty cozy with the ruler there. Our accommodations seemed pretty nice for a temporary stay, which made me nervous."

"There were many things to be seen of the world, even from there. You hadn't seen much up to that point."

"Did we actually travel?"

His smile is familiar—the smile he gave me when I was very small, when he was filled with love and also with sympathy for me. Like when I tried to run and fell on my face, or when I tried to shape a very simple spell and botched it badly. "Of course we did."

"Then you did as you promised." I sigh. "I'm the only one who didn't, I guess."

"You never betrayed me, cub. You followed your heart, which is what I taught you to do. It's what I wanted for you, when I was being rational and not emotional."

Something I didn't realize was constricting inside of me snaps, and I gulp in huge breaths. "Wait—I didn't turn on you?"

"I'm the one who let you down." He points at a stone bench.

I sit up much straighter. "What did you do?"

He sighs. "I'll tell you everything I know, if you're positive you want to hear it." He meets my eyes, and his are resolved. Pained, but strong.

"What do you mean by that?"

"I think you're like a person recovering from a terrible trauma, or worse, a soul wound. You've been given a lot of power, but you've also endured a lot of pain."

"But you saved Jesse," I say.

He stares at me silently for a long moment, but finally he says, "His health was not your only injury. Back in Egypt you dealt with a lot, and then the creation of Terra was mind-bogglingly complex. Difficult. Dangerous. Painful. I believe it roped you into something huge—something we still don't understand. Obviously Isis was involved, and I think she knows more than either you or I, even once your memories are fully restored. I could tell you every single thing I know, and I will if you insist upon it, but I think you're remembering things at a pace your mind can handle. You may not have gone through many rehabilitations or recoveries yet, but when you're as old as I am, and you've endured a lot of pain, you gain a healthy respect for healing at a reasonable speed."

"You heard Kahn, though! Isis is alive, and she has all this power, and she's preparing to attack. We don't have time to wait."

He laughs. "Isis." He shakes his head. "I didn't tell you everything when you were young. Perhaps I should have. I withheld information then for *me*, not for your benefit. That was one of my selfishnesses that might have harmed us both."

"Tell me that now, at least."

"Isis and Anat are sisters," he says. "Twins, in fact."

"Whoa," I say. "Anat?"

He nods. "When I found them, they were being used by a supra. I'd been through that myself and felt empathy for them—when I freed them, they were damaged, but grateful." His eyes lose their focus, clearly remembering memories with meaning to him. "Beyond grateful. They both grew to love me, but Anat's love was pure, that of a child for a parent or a servant that truly loves her master. She wanted only to serve me, and through me, the rest of the world. She wanted to improve things for others. She longed to protect the powerless. Caring for her and accepting her service was as easy as breathing."

"But not Isis?"

Dad shakes his head. "Nothing with Isis was ever easy." He chuckles. "She was a tempest in a teapot, to use a modern phrase I particularly like. She was never settled. Never calm. She wanted and wanted and wanted more." He stands up. "Isis. . ."

"You had a relationship with her and downplayed it to me." That much I know from my memories with Alexander.

Dad startles. "I did, yes."

"Alexander told me that much, in my memories."

"So my refusal to be transparent *did* factor into your decisions."

I shrug. "I'm not sure, but I know that your story and his didn't quite jive."

He mouths the word *jive* under his breath and frowns.

"It means they didn't really line up."

He nods. "Alright, well, I'm sorry for that. I didn't want to admit that we had a relationship, especially after all the things she did. I'm sorry for leaving out important details."

"You told me she was impregnated by your friend." My stomach turns. "Please tell me that wasn't a lie." Because if Alexander's my brother. . .

Dad laughs. "Apophis is certainly not my son, if that's your concern."

I draw in a ragged breath.

"But it's only because, in spite of her repeated begging, I flat out refused to create a child with her, or with any Assimilator."

Oh.

"I'd had dozens of Assimilator children, as I told you. None of them were healthy. None of them were viable, and they all had to be destroyed, some earlier than others."

They all became power-crazed and he had to kill them himself, his own children. "Surely she could understand your reasons."

"She knew I'd experimented in the past. She was convinced that it would be different with her. She became obsessed with the idea that our child would be fine. No, better than fine. That our child would be special, miraculous, more powerful than any other." Dad's voice is pained. "I knew that wasn't possible. I knew any child of mine, born to another Assimilator, would be an abomination."

"Which is why you refused."

"You can't force a pregnancy with an Assimilator father."

Eww, gross. So much more than I wanted to know. "Got it. Let's move along."

He clears his throat. "Eventually, she grew upset. Very upset. She left me in favor of my best friend—a man she didn't even like. She did it specifically to hurt me. He was a Lifter named Osiris, even stronger than Mehen. After she became pregnant, she told him she could never be at rest, never feel safe, while I was alive. She sent my own best friend to kill me." This time his voice sounds terribly guilty. "I nearly let him finish me. I was so tired, so terribly disillusioned with everything. In the end, I wasn't ready to die. I killed my best friend, and I hated myself for it. I think that's why I did it." He shakes his head. "I should never have done what I did—I knew the chances that the child would be just like mine were quite high. Casting spells on an assimilator in the womb." He shakes his head. "It never ends well."

"But Apophis was fine."

His smile is wry. "Fate doesn't take kindly to humans who think they know everything. In my attempt at revenge, I couldn't help but try to improve one last time. I knew I wouldn't be the one stuck cleaning up the mess, I wouldn't be the one punished, so I gambled one more time. This time, I changed something critical. I harvested pure, clean elemental powers and fed those into the baby while she was asleep. A spell-induced sleep, of course."

"Did you regret creating such a powerful child?"

He snorts. "I should have, I suppose. I ought to have been angry with myself for giving her another weapon to sharpen and hurl at me." He closes his eyes. "But actually, it made me wonder. Was it a mistake of me to turn her down? Was I wrong? Did I shatter my life—kill my best friend, destroy Isis, all because of my own past failures?"

"Did you experiment on Shu?"

"What?" His eyes widen. "No. I didn't. Even with my changes, Apophis should have been so over-powered that he had to be put down after what I did." Dad's voice is fraught, as emotional as I've ever heard it. "As an unborn child, he absorbed my spell and it changed him—that's the only explanation I could think of."

"But then—"

He nods. "After Apophis, her desire for a child like me, a powerful Assimilator who could defeat me only grew. I think she would have forgiven me, and that she sent Hathor as a way to reconnect. But. . ."

"What?"

"I couldn't forgive her for what she made me do to Osiris—and what she manipulated me into doing to their child. In my rage and pain, I wanted to be punished. I wanted to feel physical pain that matched my emotional anguish. That's part of the reason I fell deeply in love with her appointed punisher—the one sent to hurt me in any way possible."

"You fell for Mother."

"The news that Hathor betrayed her stung," Dad says. "But when Isis heard we were having a child? That's when she began raising armies of her own to attack us. Which really means that *I* broke her. Her plans shifted. After that, she wanted to become like me herself. After all, if I could change a child, she could change herself, or so she believed."

And now she very nearly has what she wanted all this time.

"I can tell you exactly what I know about how close she came," he says. "I can tell you what happened and how I let you down, but I think it might be better for you if you remember those things for yourself." His hand squeezes my knee. "I've messed up before, as you've heard. I've rushed things and pushed and forced. I've fought my way through a lot of problems. But where you're concerned, I'd rather give you time to remember at your own pace. Isis was my fault, and I think I can protect you from her while you heal from the damage."

"But can you keep the world safe?"

"She's not as interested in burning things down as she is in defeating me. She'll want to shock me with the knowledge she's alive, and she'll want to tell me about her newfound, limitless powers herself." He chuckles. "She also won't want anyone else to realize and publicize that she's stealing her power from the shifter women—she'll be working on explanations that vindicate her in the public image."

"You don't think that maybe she's changed in the past few thousand years?"

He shakes his head. "Not in the things that matter, and I don't want a repeat of the past."

"Then why are you tinkering with John's power?" I don't bother hiding my anger.

"That's different," he says. "I'm not giving him anything he doesn't already have." His voice drops to a whisper. "And I'm doing it for you. He's trying to level up in order to be worthy of you."

"Like I care how powerful he is."

Ra's forehead wrinkles as his eyebrows shoot up. "Don't you?" He glances pointedly at Kahn—the most powerful man alive, other than Ra.

"That's different," I say. "There's some kind of weird connection between us—like our souls remember being in love before."

Ra's nostrils flare. "Be careful there. You may learn things that change your mind."

I want to just make him tell me. I want to know— but he's right. I'd only be getting his side of the story. And if I've learned anything in the past few weeks, it's that everyone has an angle. I don't know that my brain is really protecting me. That seems naively optimistic somehow, in a way I don't expect from a five-thousand-year-old person, but I do know that what I *remember* isn't always quite as simple as new information. It has dynamic context. Now if I can just figure out how to reactivate the memories and speed them up. . .

Ra bobs his head toward the group we just left, refocusing my attention. Probably because John and Kahn are shouting at one another. His words are resigned, fatherly. Annoying. "I'm definitely not going to be your biggest problem with welcoming him back."

✿ 14 ✿

ANCIENT EGYPT

"It's spectacular," Shu says. Surprisingly, he sounds like he means it.

The new rooftops Ptah engineered are pretty amazing, and the stained glass is almost unbelievable. Babylon was a decent-sized city when we arrived with nice enough buildings, but now it's practically breathtaking.

"The people here might not be quite as polished as those we left behind." Ptah sniffs. "But they're much more willing to integrate with us and they welcome our help, which makes doing things that require Lifters and fire elementals to work together much simpler."

"I can't figure out *why* you've spent so much time on it," I say. "Since we're leaving next week or the week after."

Ptah's nostrils flare. "I'm not sure that's been decided." He shrugs. "And anyway, not everything we do needs to benefit us in the moment. Even if we do leave, I'll have created a legacy, a work of art that will awe people for centuries, perhaps millennia to come."

Glory seeker extraordinaire, that's Ptah. "Right.

Well, I think it *is* decided." I push past him and nearly jog to the main courtyard where Dad's waiting for me to start dinner. I both hear and sense Shu behind me—probably just as eager to escape Ptah as I am. "Can you believe him? Saying it's not *decided*?" I snort.

"Well."

I spin on my heel.

Shu nearly plows into me. "Whoa, there."

"What does that mean? 'Well' what?"

"Only that Father was saying he was glad we had a new home base," Shu says. "He may not have been encouraging Ptah to go crazy redoing the palace, but he's not exactly stopping him."

"We didn't leave Egypt behind just to redo a new palace here," I say. "We wanted to explore. To see the world."

"Right," Shu says. "But we've been on two exploratory trips and it's all jungle, jungle, and hey! More jungle."

My jaw drops. "Jungle? I mean, I'll admit that there were a lot of overgrown areas, but there were also animals and cultures and even foods that we'd never seen before."

"It's not exactly comfortable, traveling without the amenities we're accustomed to having," Shu says.

"Wait, are you part of the group that wants to, like, put down roots here and just make a new Memphis?" I shake my head. "I thought we were going to take a short break here, which has already grown quite long, and then launch for totally new places, free of the threat that someone will trail us."

Shu's nose scrunches. "What are you thinking you'll find?"

I blink. "I can't possibly know that until we find it, obviously."

"So you thought we'd just ride and ride and ride forever?"

"I thought we'd travel until we reached water, build some boats, and keep on going."

"Don't you think that no matter where we go, it'll be more of the same?"

"The beauty in the world is largely created by us," a deep voice behind us says. Dad.

I spin around, feeling a little betrayed. "So we aren't leaving in a week?" It feels like. . .like I'm lost. Like I was lied to.

"We can absolutely leave in a week," Dad says. "And we will, if you really have your heart set on it." His forced cheer makes it clear that *he* doesn't want to go anywhere.

"But you would rather stay here, now that Isis thinks you're dead and isn't incessantly sending armies to attack you."

"We can travel as much as you'd like," Dad says. "But it makes sense that we should have a new home base, doesn't it?"

"What if rumors reach Isis?" I ask. "We aren't very far away yet, and she'll just start sending armies all over again." Alexander might even come. That's the biggest reason why we need to keep moving. I shove the thought of him down as deep as I can. I haven't seen him in a long time, but not long enough—I still think about him every day. His lips. His shoulders. His flashing eyes.

Dad sighs. "Isis believes I died. You made sure of that—her own son told her I was dead at his hand."

I still feel strange talking about that, even though I shouldn't. It's not like I betrayed Dad. I left with him, and I really did set the whole thing up so we could escape Isis and her constant and apparently never-ending rage. But I think about Alexander too often. I'm practically pining, if I'm being honest. Only my love for Dad has kept me here, making another, bigger version of our palaces in Egypt.

The one thing I can't disagree with is the misery of traveling. Bugs. Miserable accommodations. Bizarre food I didn't expect to hate as much as I do. Lousy weather. People I don't know, and consequently don't care very much about. And every new place we've been has had so many problems—so much misery. It has felt selfish not to stick around long enough to try and fix some of the major problems we've encountered.

But if we don't move on soon, I don't trust myself not to try and figure out how to travel back.

Back to Egypt.

Back East.

Back to Alexander.

And I won't be able to leave him again. I did the right thing and chose Dad over him, so it's just better if we move along while I still remember all the reasons why. "I'm not going to stick around and tempt fate. You and Ptah can stay here, but I'm going to leave next week as planned." I fold my arms across my chest. "I want to see the world." And hopefully there's more to see than we've seen so far. Hopefully there's something to justify my stubborn insistence that we move along.

"I think a few of the lieutenants may decide to stay here and fortify Babylon. Lay down a few roots," Dad says.

"Which is totally fine." I do *not* say that I desperately hope Ptah is among them. I can't hear him talk about his plans for cornices or balustrades for another single second. If anything, my patience with him has only grown shorter since meeting Alexander and fleeing Egypt. Every time he pries his eyes away from a building and looks at me with those longing, puppy-dog eyes, I want to kick him.

Deep down, I might be a bad person.

Dad finally moves toward the banquet tables, signaling the servants to start bringing dinner. It's far too much food, as always. At least everything we don't eat will be passed along to the schools and orphanages we've set up. I hate the idea of so much food waste, and I hate the idea of kids being hungry even more. I can't fix every problem in the world, but so many of the ones around me have solutions if we'll take the time to think them through. Which is another argument for staying here, I know. We can't teach or heal or build anything if we're always moving around.

I take the seat next to Dad, the solid wooden legs scraping against the stone floor. Shu settles on the other side of me, and Dad's lieutenants filter in, taking up seats around us. As always, platters begin arriving in the center of the table first, fanning out around us. Heaping piles of roasted beef, cured ham, whole spitted birds, glistening. Local root vegetables, artfully cooked, mashed, and garnished. Fresh fruits I've never seen, brought in from far-flung places. Even desserts, dripping with honey and covered with rich, sweetened cream.

As lavish as this meal is, it's typical fare for us. I take a few small portions from various platters and lean back in my seat. How can Dad want to do the exact same thing here that we did before? I thought he actually wanted to see people and places that are completely opposite of the norm. Although, perhaps once you've lived a few thousand years, nothing really seems new.

The former ruler of Babylon, Nidin-Bel, has graciously welcomed us here, and he doesn't even seem upset that we've totally usurped his power, reducing him to a glorified events manager. Every night, he grins and tells us about the entertainment he's lined up. And every night, he and his wife and children sit on the edges of the celebration, eating after we are done and watching us carefully to make sure we're happy. It's like he was forced to invite a dragon into his home and now he's stuck hoping we don't reduce anything to smoking ash.

He does a marvelous job hiding his contempt or frustration or whatever he feels, and I've seen his heart myself—he doesn't appear to be harboring any ill intent. He's dressed in what I've decided is his favorite robe tonight, a bright red fabric, heavily embroidered with gold and inlaid with agates, cabochon rubies, and emeralds. "Tonight, we have a real treat. A combined act, showcasing the grace and power of our equine friends alongside the faith and courage of their riders. And after the show, most of the animals performing tonight will be for sale—for the right price." He bows and claps his hands together, his forced smile showing some of the strain I know he must be feeling.

When he takes his seat on the edge of the long table, everyone's already paying attention. But when the enormous drums at the far side of the room start beating a slow, staccato beat, everyone sits up a little straighter still. Boom, boom, wham. Boom, boom, wham. Smaller drums start up next, and I can't even tell who's playing them. They must be hiding behind the courtyard walls.

My heart rate picks up, along with the rhythm of the drums. This is clearly a spectacle meant to entertain, but it's also an audition of sorts. We can purchase the horses, which means they're not Reapers in their animal shape—this entire thing will be done on actual horses.

A dozen snowy horses and a dozen ebony ones dart across the courtyard from opposite directions, riderless, not even wearing bridles. Their cadences are synced, their heads arched in just the same way. Even their manes all fall on the same side, and that's not something nature decides. Someone curated these twenty-four horses very carefully.

I glance around for the people who must have set this up.

My dad does the same thing.

Surely this is exactly the reason we ought to continue to travel, to experience exciting and new things like this.

The horses trot perfectly in line, the black and the white, and then spread slightly, and pass one another, weaving around and through in perfect harmony. I almost can't believe my eyes.

As they circle back around, still formed into perfect rows of black and white, riders in bright red pants and short, silver-embroidered shirts leap from behind pots and benches. A dozen male riders find black horses, and a dozen female riders secure the white with only a hand to their noses. They mount smoothly, in unison, and none of them so much as start or stumble. I can't help myself—I begin searching for the animal I'd like to buy. An outlier in some way. A larger or stronger animal, or one that's more majestic. Anyone who puts together this kind of show deserves a reward. If it were me, I wouldn't want to part with any of them, but if they're for sale. . .maybe they need the money.

The horses speed up, their hooves flashing and clacking against the stone floor. The riders clutch their mounts' manes as reins, directing them where to go, and soon they're weaving in and out in a pattern that's hard to follow. The people performing all have dark, nearly black hair that billows out behind them, brown or black eyes that flash, and quick and sure hands, guiding their animals flawlessly.

Then, all at once, they stop.

It's utterly silent until they wheel around and race toward our tables, hooves pounding, eyes wild. My heart leaps to my throat, and I suppress an urge to leap from my chair and race away. But at the last second, the horses rear backward, their front hooves suspended gracefully in the air only a few feet from us.

It's one of those moments that stretches, like the first moments after waking, or the space of time when you know you're falling and aren't sure how badly the landing will hurt.

Two dozen stunning, perfectly balanced horses, a dozen flawlessly athletic riders, no gimmicks or tricks, just practiced, beautifully executed symmetry.

I'm speechless.

Until the hooves begin to descend on the horse in front of me, and I look at the perfectly formed black horse's face.

It's a face I know.

Most of the animals will be for sale.

The words crackle through my mind like a lash.

They put together such a beautiful group of animals that I almost didn't notice. The black horse in front of me isn't stronger or more powerful than the others, and his coloring is exactly the same as the rest—flawless. But his eyes are different. More intelligent. More aware.

The horse in front of me is no animal.

It's Bucephalus.

Alexander's second most trusted companion.

There's no way he's for sale, which means his presence here signals something else. An attack? A message? I study the faces of every rider, but I recognize none of them. Not a nose, not the eyes, or even a jawline I've seen before. The horses back up slowly, in a straight line, and then they all bow, their front legs dropping to the hard stone in front of them, their riders sliding off to do the same.

Dad cheers, and so does everyone else present.

I wasn't the only one who was eyeing which horse I'd like. The second our host stands up, people start talking.

"Which animals are for sale?" Mehen asks.

"I'd like one of the white ones," Shu says.

"I prefer black." Dad's half smile is a pretty ringing endorsement.

"So do I," Anat says.

As the horses trot away, Dad's supporters grow more concerned. "I thought they were for sale," Am-Heh shouts. "Aren't they?"

"They'll be available at Shadrick's caravan," Nidin says. "Just outside of town."

Which means we'll have to travel out there to have a chance of buying them. Smart. Or it would be, if this wasn't some kind of ambush. I'm about to say something when movement on my far right periphery catches my eye.

Hephaestion.

He brings his index finger to his lips, the universal motion for silence. It certainly validates my belief that Bucephalus was one of the horses, and my heart lurches in my chest at what that might mean.

But do I trust him?

Alexander must be here.

For me.

I can hardly breathe, much less think straight.

"Let's go." Shu stuffs a chunk of bread into his mouth and stands up. "I mean, have you ever wanted to buy a horse more than you do right now?" He smiles. "Be honest."

"Race you there," Am-Heh says.

Within minutes, everyone's headed for the road out of town, their belt pouches bulging. "You're not coming?" Dad asks.

"I do want a white one," I say, "to match Shu." I feign a grimace. "But I think I ate too much. My stomach hurts."

I know very well that Imhotep is already on his way to the horse trader's caravan. Dad's eyes widen. "I'll summon Imhotep and—"

"Please don't," I say. "I'm not ill. I just overate. I'll lie down for a bit, and by the time you return with my new horse, I'll be ready to meet her."

"A mare, then?" Dad asks. "That's what you'd like?"

I shrug. "I don't care, actually. But my other mount's a gelding, so I thought a mare might be a good change of pace, if there are any left."

We both know that Dad will be given first pick. He nods and follows the others out.

It's hard to walk slowly out of the courtyard and around the corner that leads to my room when what I really want to do is sprint in the direction of Hephaestion. But he finds me anyway, the second I round the corner. "Sekhmet." His voice is soft, and a little nervous. It surprises me—he always seems so self-assured, just like his master.

My eyes widen when I turn and take him in. I hadn't noticed anything but his face the last time, but now I see what he's wearing and how he's styled his hair. It's held back in a severe queue against the back of his head, and his skin is darkened. He's wearing the roughspun linen of slaves, and he's barefoot, his feet dirty and calloused. When you don't have an Assimilator to disguise you, you have to get creative yourself.

And it's riskier.

It was bold for him to come. Dad must have seen him, as well as most of his warriors. But would they even give him a second glance, dressed as he is? I doubt it. If I hadn't just seen Bucephalus, I probably wouldn't have spotted him either. Or if I'm being honest with myself, if I hadn't been looking for any possible sign of Alexander for the last year, I still wouldn't have.

"Why have you come?" I ask softly. "Is Alexander okay?"

Hephaestion smirks. "Define 'okay.'"

That makes my heart flip. "Did something happen?"

He quirks one eyebrow. "*Someone* happened."

Jealous rage pulses through me, until I realize he means me. All that anger twists around until it becomes pleasure, joy, and elation instead. Even a year after I last saw him, he still misses me? Could it possibly be as much as I miss him?

"Does he have a message for me?" I glance back at the doorway into the courtyard. "That was some show you put on to sneak in here."

"Not a message, no," a deep voice says from the darkness behind Hephaestion.

My lungs stop working. My knees become wobbly.

Alexander's here.

If my dad knew, he would kill him. It feels like time suspends. I can hear each beat of my heart in my ears. I sense the individual things in the space around me, reaching out for the shape of him, the feel of him. The one person I've longed to see more than any other.

The world snaps back into action, but at double its usual speed. I race toward his voice, my eyes and my arms searching in the near dark where the torches have been snuffed. I can sense him, but until my eyes adjust, I can't see him.

Alexander, my Alexander.

Broad shoulders, cascading hair, and a rich, clean robe. He's not hiding like Hephaestion. Dad would know him immediately.

I grab his upper arm forcefully, prepared to hustle him away to my room where he'll be safe, where no one will find him, where he won't be in danger. But I'm distracted by the bulky muscle contracting under my fingers. I drag in a tortured breath. What's wrong with me?

I've missed him.

I want him.

My world isn't right without him.

I've been drowning out here alone.

Because. . .

I love him.

Lucky for me, my mouth isn't working well enough to say any of those horrifyingly vulnerable things. "Come with me," I finally manage to choke out.

He comes, Hephaestion's bare footsteps trailing us almost silently. "You're lucky all my dad's supporters just high-tailed it for the edge of town." As I say the words, I realize it wasn't luck. Alexander makes his own luck.

He stops. Tugging on his arm is like shoving the leg of an elephant: pointless. I turn around to encourage him along. His eyes meet mine and every thought in my brain dissolves like sugar in water. Like butter over a hot fire. Gone forever.

"I'm lucky you smiled when you saw me," he says.

"I'm lucky you didn't tell your father when you recognized Bucephalus. I'm lucky for a great many things, but your family and friends' departure wasn't luck. I've been planning this moment for a while."

His head shifts toward me, his mouth only inches away, but I can't surrender. Not quite yet. Something terrifying has occurred to me. "You don't mean them harm, do you?"

His laughter is blue skies after a storm. It's the first breath after a long swim. It's the warmth of the sun on my skin after a long winter. It's everything I've longed for, everything I've pretended I didn't need.

"That's not an answer," I say, doggedly.

His lips move toward me again, stopping just a hair's breadth from mine. "I don't mean them any harm, no."

I sigh, and he moves then, and I don't even try to stop him. His lips press into mine—no, they take mine. It's not pleasant and welcoming. It's possessive and demanding.

And it's exactly what I've needed. Exactly what I've imagined. Exactly what I've longed for.

Hephaestion clears his throat. "I wouldn't normally suggest this, but, you were moving to her room, I believe."

Right. We're standing in a hallway, totally out in the open. I gulp and step back from Alexander, but it's hard. Harder than it should be. "My room, yes." I move quickly this time, not bothering to grab his hand. Alexander and Hephaestion both follow.

Heads turn, eyes making note of Ra's daughter, dragging someone with her. I pause long enough to make him over—changing his appearance to match that of Shu, and changing Hephaestion to match Ptah.

They're with me often enough. No one will even take note of it.

Hephaestion turns his hands over slowly, marveling at the difference.

Alexander grasps my hand. "Who did you make me? Who would everyone expect you to take to your room?"

"You're Shu," I say. "But don't worry. I'll release it once we're not in the open. Trust me—it's safer this way."

Alexander arches one eyebrow. "Should I read anything into the fact that you made Hephaestion, who is also following you to your room, into someone handsome, while you made me into your brother?"

I laugh. "I like Shu quite a bit more than *him*." I shake my head. "Ptah has been following me around, badgering me about design questions for years. Don't read into it."

"Fair enough," he says.

We move a little more slowly, camouflaged, without the terror that spurred me on before, speed that probably only increased the likelihood that I would draw attention to us. "You didn't seem to like being disguised," I say. "Does your mom not do that to you?"

He shakes his head. "I've never allowed her to, not since I was quite young."

Interesting.

We finally reach the door to my room, and I draw up short, suddenly shy for some reason. "Uh, so, these are my quarters."

Alexander smiles.

"Why are you here, exactly?"

"I think you know why," he says.

"Nothing has changed," I whisper. "Your mother, my father." I shrug. "It's pointless."

"And has that kept you from thinking of me?" Alexander's words are loaded, and he knows it. He must already know my answer by my reaction to his presence here. By my desire to keep him safe.

I don't want to say it. If I keep my feelings hidden, they'll go away. Eventually, they *will* go away. I shrug again.

"Tell me to leave and I will."

"That's a lie," Hephaestion says. "He's been absolutely single-minded over the past year. First, he meant to draw you back to us, but when that didn't work, taking every outlying area, he switched tactics and began searching. Once he figured out where you were —you don't want to know how much he spent on spies to do it—he began shaping a new plan. This one."

Alexander's jaw drops.

Hephaestion doesn't even look chagrined. "Look, being coy clearly isn't helping you."

I love Alexander's best friend. Or maybe I'm just buzzing from the things he's said, the thought that Alexander has been as heartsick as I have. "I can't believe Bucephalus agreed to put on that show," I say. "He let other people ride him. And surely he forced all those horses to behave as they did."

"It was his idea," Hephaestion says. "None of us like Alexander when he's this mopey. He's insufferable, truly."

Alexander's fist connects with Hephaestion's jaw with a crack. Of course, it looks like Shu just punched Ptah, which is also somewhat enjoyable to watch.

Suddenly the two of them are brawling on the floor, Hephaestion getting in a surprising number of solid shots. But after a moment, I'm a little bored by it. If I wasn't watching a facsimile of my brother pounding on my would-be-fiancé, it might be better. I could probably watch Alexander fight all day, my eyes focused on his muscles bunching and relaxing, but I can't change them back, not out here. So I open the door and walk through, closing it behind me and muffling the sounds of masculinity gone mad.

Less than thirty seconds later, the sounds of fighting abate.

The tentative knock on my door is kind of cute, like watching a little boy with his head down, preparing to apologize.

"Sekhmet," Alexander hisses. "Open the door."

"Are you done?" I lean my head against the solid wood. "Because I don't like tantrums."

"We're done," Hephaestion says. "Sorry."

I imagine Alexander's friends and supporters who know about me haven't exactly been very supportive, by and large. It's probably obnoxious to watch him fixated on something we all know he can't have.

And that's the gist of the problem. No matter which way we turn it, Alexander and I can't be together. It makes this something of an exercise in futility.

Or self torture. Take your pick.

Apparently a glutton for punishment, I open the door. As they walk through the doorway, I drop their disguises. "What exactly is your plan?"

The right side of Alexander's jaw is swollen, and there's a small cut over his left eye, but he's smiling at me. "I didn't have one that went further than seeing you."

Hephaestion groans.

When Alexander kisses me again, I forget about everything else. This seems like a pretty decent plan, honestly. His arms circle my waist, and he backs me up until my back bumps up against the wall. Then he pulls away slightly, braces his hands on either side of my face, and reaches toward me with his index finger, tracing the curve of my nose, the line of my temple, the angle where my chin meets my jaw. "You are perfect. Even more perfect than the last time I saw you."

"Stop," I say. "You have to stop."

"I can't," he whispers. "I can't stop thinking about you. Wishing you were with me."

"But nothing has changed," I say. "I love my dad. I love my brother. Your mother—"

"You can be anyone," he says. "You can look like anything at all. Have you considered that?"

"Your mother would know," I say.

"You'll think of a way around that." He brushes his mouth against mine again. "I came here with one thought in my head. One goal in mind." He shifts again, his mouth so close to mine that we're almost one person, joined at the lips. "Marry me, Sekhmet. Join *me*. Make *me* your family. I promise, I'll never let you down."

I freeze. "But you said—you said you didn't believe in love."

"I changed my position on that a long time ago," he says. "You already knew that."

"Marry you?" I shake my head. "It's not possible."

"Why not?"

I can't think with him this close, with his hand stroking my hair. With his breath mixing with mine. With his words against my skin. "My dad will kill you, for one," I say. "It would be a short marriage."

"I'll take that risk."

I shove him. "I won't, you big idiot."

He grins this time, which makes no sense. "I'm telling you no, and you're smiling?"

Hephaestion chuckles. "I told you that you had no chance, but I do like her."

I forgot he was here.

Apparently Alexander did too. "What are you doing there, just watching us? It's creepy. Go find a corner and, I don't know, read a book."

Hephaestion scowls, and I worry they'll start punching each other again. "Fine." He walks away, ducking into my water closet. I'm sure he'll figure out what it is and come shooting back out any moment.

But I don't notice whether he does, since Alexander immediately demands my attention again. "Think it through. You already come visit me from time to time."

I arch one eyebrow.

"Introduce me to your dad—say I'm whoever you'd like. Then announce we're getting married. I can visit here. You can come visit me, too."

"And tell your mother, what? That I'm whom?"

He shrugs. "I. Don't. Care."

"My mother is one of your mother's friends. Have you thought of that?" I throw my hands up in the air. "Unlike you, I have thought past seeing you."

He's grinning again.

"What?"

His grin widens. "You've been searching for a solution too." He corners me again, his hand brushing hair from my face. "You've been thinking of me."

I ball my hand into a fist and punch his chest. It hurts. "Of course I have."

He kisses me again, his lips firm but soft. His chest broad and warm. His hands strong and sure. His right hand cups my jaw and shifts it upward, opening my mouth to him. He kisses me again, but demands more.

He's not going to let me ride away this time, I realize. He's not going to surrender.

I Lift him backward, giving us some space. "No matter what we do, we set ourselves on a collision course with misery," I say. "I've thought about this at least as much as you have." Heat rises in my cheeks. "But there isn't a way for us to be together that doesn't involve someone dying."

"If my mother ever tried to harm you, I'd kill her myself." He moves toward me again, but I Bind him in place.

That would ruin us. He may not see it, but we can't have a marriage, a partnership, a lifetime commitment, that starts or ends or survives something like that. No matter how complicated their relationship, Isis is his mother. Ra is my father. "We were doomed before we were born," I whisper.

"We haven't even tried," Alexander says. "And I'm done fighting fate." He flexes his strength, busting my Binding, and walks toward me. "Your father will fix things. Or my mother will forgive him. Or something will change, because it has to." He swallows, his Adam's apple shifting. "I love you, Sekhmet, and I'm done ignoring it. I'm Alexander, son of Isis. I don't surrender. Ever."

He's right, of course, he never surrenders. He's a warrior and that's his way.

"Would you fight me?" I tilt my head up, daring him to cross that line. "If I ask you to go?"

The muscles in his jaw work.

I sense them, horses and riders in a group, moving back toward the palace. "Your plan is coming to fruition," I say. "I feel my dad and my brother and the others returning."

His eyes widen. "You can sense out that far?"

I shrug. "My dad will kill you," I say. "He'll think you're a threat to me, no matter what you say."

"I'll never be your enemy," Alexander says. "Not in any world. Not in any time or place. I'll always do whatever is best for you." He takes my hand. "I just wish you'd see that too, that you'd trust me."

"My dad—"

"I haven't wanted to bring this up," Alexander says. "I don't want to be *that* guy, but Ra is not who he pretends to be. He hasn't been honest with you. If you look beneath the surface, you'll find out he's hiding things from you, things you won't like."

For the first time since we met, I wonder. Alexander feels something for me, I can tell. No one can fake that well. But is there any chance that Isis sent him? Could he be here to turn me against my own dad? Could all this be part of some kind of long-term plan?

Because I'm the only person on Earth who has the power to kill Dad, well and truly. I'm probably the only person who could ever take him down.

And for the first time since we met, I doubt Alexander.

It's ironic that my doubt in him was created by his attempt to make me doubt Dad.

But it's still true.

"I can't come with you," I say. "I don't think I ever will."

"Then ask him," Alexander says. "I'll go." He calls for Hephaestion. "I'll leave, and I won't pursue you right away. But first, promise me this. Ask him about your birth and your powers. Ask him for the truth of that, and truth of what happened with my mother."

My doubt twists and turns inside of me, desperate to determine up from down. Desperate to know what's real and what's lie. Terrified about what it all means.

But after one last hug, one last desperate embrace, Alexander and Hephaestion dash out, declining any further disguises. And I'm left to wonder.

Moments after they leave, someone reaches my door. I can sense who it is, of course.

Dad.

I open the door.

"Do you feel better?" His eyes are full of concern.

I nod. "Thanks."

"I found you the perfect mare. Pure white with bright blue eyes." His smile breaks my heart.

"Dad, we need to talk."

His lips part, just a bit, and he inhales. "Is everything alright?"

I choke on a sob. "Not really."

He drops an arm over my shoulder. "Tell me." He walks into my room, leading me toward a chair. "But sit. Be calm."

"I need to tell you something," I say.

"You met Alexander," he says. "And you fell in love with him."

I kept waiting on him to bring it up, to ask me, but he never did. I can barely bring myself to meet his eyes, but finally I do, and I nod. "How long have you known?" I already know the truth, but I can't admit it. It's easier if he tells me.

"I knew something was strange when he spent so much time searching for a Neser." His eyes sparkle. "Did you think I'd forgotten what the Fire Called refer to you as? That I'd be that lax?" He shakes his head. "My memory is perfect when it comes to you."

I should have known.

"But when you asked to return to check on him again. . ." He shakes his head. "I was almost certain something had transpired. I couldn't know what he felt, of course, or how deep your curiosity ran, so I let you go. You should know that when you returned, Tefnut refused to tell me a thing." He laughs. "You never have trouble creating loyal supporters. I'm proud of that, you know."

"Did Shu—"

"Your brother would slit my throat and watch me die if you asked him to do it." Dad's not even a bit angry. He's proud. "He never told me a single thing. Not with a look, not with a misplaced word. But when I met Alexander, I knew. He wanted me to like him. That's when I knew he loved you, and based on your desire to come with us into battle, I guessed how you felt too."

"You never said a word," I say.

"I've always let you come to me in your own time," he says.

"I have a question for you," I say.

He shrugs. "I don't know how Isis will respond to the same news."

But for once, Dad was wrong about what I wanted to know. I hope it's not a sign that my love for Alexander is already driving us apart. "Okay, but when you told me the truth so many years ago, after Mother left, did you tell me everything? Or did you hold some things back?"

Dad's eyes widen, and his breaths come faster. "Everything about what?"

"Was I really just a happy accident?" I finally force myself to ask. "Or did you make me into who I am?"

Could I be the monster Mother insisted I was when she left?

❧ 15 ❧

EARTH

If Ra's right and I woke up because I'm not quite ready to know the answers I asked about, then I hate my brain. Why in the world would I wake up right then? I need those answers. I close my eyes in the near dark and will myself to go back to sleep. I mean, seriously? I finally recover some of my old memories, but the memory ends before the most important moment?

Well. Maybe not the *most* important moment.

My lips feel swollen from those kisses with Alexander, and they were only a memory.

But I did need that information.

Ra looked guilty. No, more than that, he looked downright *troubled* when I asked him whether he had cast a spell to make me who I am. That's not very promising. Neither is the concept that my brain is shielding me from a truth I already know but can't accept. What awful thing might he have done? What kind of spell must he have used?

Am I the monster I feared I was? Am I so terrible,

so ghastly, that my own mother felt compelled to leave me?

I think about Kahn, of his beauty and grace. I think about my memories of Alexander and the things he could do. Nothing about him repulsed me. Nothing about him made me shudder. And Ra confessed that he altered Kahn, er, Alexander, but I don't find him monstrous. Why, then, does the prospect of the same thing done to me leave me at once angry and scared?

This is all so confusing.

But I can't imagine Ra, his eyes full of sorrow when he discussed the children he had to kill, gambling with my safety. No, whatever he hasn't yet told me, it can't be that bad.

Right?

I finally give in and kick the blankets off. I'm not going back to sleep. Whatever information Ra may have been about to confess or deny, I'm not going to find out by reliving that moment.

Which means I may as well get going for the day. I'm more relieved than ever that Ra is back, and he can handle all the preparations for Isis' army, but I'm still worried. She controls more governments than I want to consider, and she's channeling the power of the majority of the women who are *alive*. I can't even think about what she might do with that. As much as I'd like to let Ra just handle everything, I know he's going to need my help.

I was hoping to remember exactly how Terra was made so that I could comprehend what went into the spell in the first place, but even without that memory, I should be helping. Usually when I wake up, there are people hovering outside waiting to clean or bring me food. It's kind of annoying, but I didn't realize how much I've relied upon the frenetic energy of the palace.

With no other duties or tasks pressing on me, I shower and get myself ready for the day. That's when I realize that I haven't paid nearly enough attention to the layout of this place and, more specifically, where anyone else is located. When I open my door and step into a long, empty hallway, I have no idea where to go. Jesse's next door to me and I can sense his quiet, still presence in the bed. I'm sure he'd be fine with it, but I don't want to wake him. I want him to get as much sleep as possible. I know he looks fine, but I still worry.

Which means I don't really have any idea of where to go. The Morning Room? Turn around and go back inside my room until someone shows up?

As if my thoughts summoned him, someone tall and athletic is walking toward me at the end of the hallway. It's strange how quickly my awareness of the weight of things around me has caught up to what it was in Ancient Egypt. It's as if the return of my memories is restoring my abilities as well.

"Alora?" John's voice, even from several paces away, sends a little thrill through me, and the hairs on my arms rise.

"I couldn't sleep."

"Me either," he says. "But probably for different reasons." He beams. "I could sense you moving around, and I even knew you were in the hall, alone."

Kahn's back, and John figured out that he has a whole new power yesterday. With the announcement of Isis being alive, all his thunder was kind of stolen, but it's still borderline unbelievable news.

I'm a lousy friend, and if I'm still his girlfriend, I'm a terrible one. We're in a confusing place, for sure.

He wraps his arms around me and squeezes. While moments ago I was lamenting the lack of people milling about, I'm now relieved that we have the hallway to ourselves. "I'm sorry I didn't get a chance to talk to you yesterday. It was a lot to take in."

"I think discovering that a millennia-old Assimilator is alive and well and plotting the demise of the world takes precedence." His voice is low, and I can both hear it and feel it rumbling in his chest against my ear.

I look upward, meeting his eyes. "Even when the world's crumbling around us—actually, no. *Especially* when the world is crumbling around us, I care about *you* and about how you're feeling. Are you alright?"

"I'm fine. You, on the other hand." He inhales slowly. "Your soulmate has returned, which means there's an awkward conversation looming in our future."

I should argue with him, but I can't find the energy or the words. "All the memories I'm regaining are really confusing—"

He squeezes me closer. "It was always a long shot between you and me." His grin is lopsided, his eyes almost playful. "I'm the guy who dates someone way above him on a rebound."

"John, you were there for me when the world was falling apart. You were there for me on Erra, too. We have a connection—"

His smile is sad, now. "Alora, I've given it a lot of thought. I could be the guy who complains and makes himself into a pain, but it would be pointless, and I'd hate myself for it." He shrugs. "I've decided instead to be grateful for the time we had."

"It's not like that," I say.

"Yeah, I'm not even a proper rebound. I'm just unworthy."

I close my eyes and breathe him in. His smell is

familiar, comforting even. Piney, bright, and clean. "You're not unworthy, John. You've never been unworthy."

A squeak behind us steals our attention. A maid with wide eyes shoves a broom behind her, like it's a dirty secret we shouldn't see. I suppress a laugh. It's not funny that we've made her uncomfortable with our canoodling in the middle of the hallway.

"We still need to talk," I say. "Can we—"

"Sure." John steps toward my room, and the maid squeaks again.

Because of course, she was here to clean my room. I sigh. The sun's barely peeking over the horizon. We can talk, work through this, and I'll still have plenty of time to help Dad with another day of saving mankind from a power-hungry sociopath.

"Your room," I say. "Let's just go there."

"Sounds good to me." He smirks. He just can't help himself. What an idiot. That's one of the things I've always liked about John, though. His insouciance, his playfulness—he's a little like Jesse. I doubt he'd appreciate being compared to my brother, but the similarities are there nonetheless.

I roll my eyes and push past him before I realize I have no idea where his room actually is. Most everyone comes to me. Alora from last month would hate who I've become. A pampered, self-centered diva with two guys who like her. Maybe before my shower, I should give myself a little slap.

John's smirking—not sure whether it's at me, or at himself—when we turn the corner and duck down a smaller hallway. He reaches his room and pushes yet another solid wooden door open. I'll give the British royalty this: they build nice residences.

"How do you feel about having a second power?" I

need a few minutes to figure out what I want to say to him about Kahn. I can't lie—he doesn't deserve that, and I don't want it—but I really care about John too. If it weren't for all these old memories with Alexander, I don't know what I'd be feeling right now.

John closes the door behind me and leans against it. "Okay."

I'm not sure whether he's saying that he's okay with it, or if he's calling me out on changing the subject. Could this conversation be any more awkward?

He closes the space between us and puts a hand on my shoulder. "I care about you, Alora, a great deal, and I have for some time now, but I think all of this stuff —" He waves his hand around. "Ra returning, the collapsing worlds, you being asked to rule, and my new power." He shakes his head. "It's a lot to take in, and I've wondered myself whether some of my feelings for you were based on, I don't know. This isn't the right word, really, but, like, awe, maybe? You're like a comet streaking toward Earth. I know you'll smash me, but I can't stop standing and staring, gape-mouthed."

He thinks that I'm like a comet? "I can barely find time to shower," I say. "I have no idea what to do, ever. I'm a disaster."

He laughs. "Well, if you're a disaster, sign me up to join the HazMat team." His smile fades. "Look, I think what I'm saying is that even without having had some kind of additional lifetime to spend with you, even with only our shared memories from Erra, I think I get what's happening with you, at least a little bit. I was overwhelmed just processing the lightning fast changes in the world and the memories I regained when Erra collapsed. I can't imagine if I was remembering an entirely different lifetime on top of Erra, and for you, Terra, and your history in Egypt." He sighs. "I've never wanted to pressure you. I've never wanted to force you to do or feel anything that doesn't bring you peace, safety, and joy."

He turns around and crosses the room, his movements forced. "So like I said before, back in that ridiculous outpost in the middle of nowhere." He sighs, and his next words feel forced, but still true. "I'm your friend first and always."

"My friend who now has a lot more firepower."

He grins. "Alright, you are acting like I might be traumatized, but—" He shakes his head, his smile somehow growing. "Jesse may not have been like this, but it's most little boys' dream to—"

"To have superpowers." His smile is infectious, and even in this awkward moment, I find myself smiling back. "I remember."

He sits on the edge of his bed. "I care for you, Alora. I won't say I love you, because that sounds aggressive somehow, but it's probably still true. Even so, I don't expect anything from you. Even if you and I —" He gestures between us. "If nothing else ever happens there, it's okay. You've made me a better man, a stronger man, and a more noble man."

"You are a good man," I say. "One of the best I've ever met. I'm honored to be your friend. And you're pretty easy on the eyes."

He laughs. "As far as breakups go, this one has been decent."

My shoulders slump. "I don't want to break up," I say. "It's just that I don't know what I want."

"Which is essentially the same thing." His eyes are kind. I wish they weren't so kind. I wish he wasn't so understanding. It would be easier if he was a villain.

But he's not wrong. If I'm not head over heels for him like he seems to be for me, then it's not right.

"How did you and Ra figure out that you might be able to do more than Call Fire? I mean, it's not like you were locked into any other world, and Terra should have come first, or at least it did for me and Kahn."

"I know you're suspicious that your dad and I hatched some kind of evil plan or that he cast some terrible spell, but it wasn't like that. It's more like, I asked Ra to help me fulfill my potential, and Am-Heh offered to help me maximize my capacity."

I stand up, full of nervous energy. He's right—I am worried that Ra somehow caused this. I'm worried that he's still experimenting. The timing is undeniably strange. I circle the room, my hand trailing over the mostly bare dresser.

"Alora, all I can say is that one moment I was working on improving my blasts, which you should probably be doing too. You force a sustained burst of flame directly at a single item. It's an extremely effective offensive attack." He shakes his head as if to refocus. "Am-Heh was showing me how to deepen the push so that my flame was even hotter than I thought possible, and then the very next second, it felt like. . ." He pauses, his eyes focusing inward. "It was like a net or something that had been placed around my chest pulled tight." He meets my eyes and shrugs. "I know that sounds confusing, but I can't explain it better than that. I had this constricted feeling, and then BAM. It disappeared, and the rebound of power knocked me clean off my feet. I practically incinerated the entire Royal Stable."

That would have been bad. I shudder.

"Ra and Am-Heh both rushed over to try and help me calm down. They told me to breathe, and after inhaling and exhaling slowly, I managed to stop shaking. And when I could think straight again. . ." He shrugs again. "I could sense things in a way I never could before. I could feel something inside of me flex, vibrate almost, and whenever I focused on an object in front of me, I can't explain it very well, but I suspect you'll *get* it. It felt like I had a third arm, and when I used it, things just moved."

Lifting. He's describing the feeling of being able to Lift. "You couldn't feel that before? Not at all?"

He shakes his head. "Not at all."

That makes no sense. I resume my drifting, pacing in a circle, trailing my hand over things.

WHAM.

I knock a metal picture frame off the end table and it falls face down on the wooden floor. I'm such an idiot when I'm distracted. "I'm so sorry," I say, thinking that it might not even be his. It's not like we've been here long enough to do much decorating, and none of us brought many belongings.

But if it *is* his, it's probably pretty important.

I crouch down to pick it up, but before I can, John's hand blocks mine. His fingers close over the small pewter frame slowly, almost reverently. He turns it over, and I feel something akin to what he just described—not the constriction, but it feels, when I look at the image in the frame, like the air has been knocked out of me.

"Where did you get that photo?" I can't breathe. I can't think. My hand trembles where it's extended, inches from the photograph underneath the cracked glass.

John's eyes as they turn toward me are confused. "I've always had this."

"You've always had a photograph of *Isis*?" She's wearing normal clothing. A yellow sweater. Dark jeans. Her hair is pulled back into a ponytail, but everything else is the same. The same midnight blue eyes. The raven hair. The knowing glance. It's all her.

"This isn't Isis." John tilts his head, his tone cautious. "This is the only photo I brought with me of my mother."

❀ 16 ❀

EARTH

There's no way this is right. Isis cannot be John's mother.

Because Isis is Kahn's mother.

Also, John's mother died. Years ago.

"I don't understand." No other words come to mind. It's like I'm fumbling with frozen fingers to catch a glass orb, waiting for it to shatter.

"This is my mother," he says slowly, as if I've had some kind of mental break. "It can't be Isis."

I glance down at the photograph again, uncertainty creeping in to replace my shock. "I must be mistaken."

John laughs. "You probably shouldn't have woken up so early. You need more sleep."

He's not wrong there. I need to sleep more so I can get answers about what happened, and probably also so that my brain can function properly. There's no way John's mother can be a woman who must have been trapped. . .somewhere. Right? She must have been trapped, probably with the Assimilators. Or would she have been free for some reason? I wasn't free. Kahn

234

wasn't free. It stands to reason that she would be stuck somewhere, too.

"Your mother," I say. "Your dad said she Wasted on Erra *before* she died on Earth? Right? The dreamers said that's how it happened."

John nods. "You were there when he said it." He presses a hand to my forehead. "Are you feeling alright?"

I touch the broken glass fragment partially obscuring the smile of the woman in the photo. "This woman looks *exactly* like Alexander the Great's mother did in my memories. I mean, it could be a coincidence, but it's a strange one. Kahn's your cousin, right?"

"Right." John frowns.

"But what if. . ."

He shakes his head. "No, there's no way that my mother really is Isis." But even as he says the words, I can see that he's wondering. Uncertainty is creeping in for him, too.

"Ra said the power of Lifting was somehow suppressed—hidden, intentionally by someone. At the time, Kahn said the only person it could have been hidden by would be Isis. It didn't make sense for her to have anything to do with you, but if her son was born with more than one power, or if she *created* a son with multiple powers, like Ra created Apophis. . ."

"This can't be right," John says.

"But what if it is? What if she didn't Waste on Erra. What if she Woke and then broke free from Erra? What if, like me, she could follow the path to Earth, and she never went back. That could have set the entire mechanism to unraveling. And if she did change you somehow, she might not want anyone else to know. Or if she changed you *after* you were already born. . ."

"I would never have been on Terra in the first

place." John's eyes are wide with horror. He shakes his head. "It can't be true. It's too insane. But maybe we should show this photograph to Ra to be extra positive."

I wish I wasn't so confused about my father. Sometimes he seems like a great guy, and other times he's confessing that he cast spells on unborn children in order to get revenge on his ex. But even with the confusing inconsistencies, John's right about this. Ra's our best resource on Isis.

Or maybe Kahn is better. He's regaining the same memories that I am.

"You're thinking of asking Kahn about it," John says.

I jump. "Uh, yeah." How'd he know?

"You get this weird, faraway look in your eyes whenever you think about him."

I stiffen. "That's ridiculous."

His lip twists, but it's with humor, not with bitterness. "I agree."

I straighten and brush off my pants, as if a little lint is my problem. "Are you ready to go now? Or do you need time to think about it?"

John crosses the room and opens the door. "Ra is always in the breakfast room by six a.m. sharp. I don't need time to think. I'm virtually certain it's all a misunderstanding."

Virtually certain.

"Unless you need time," he says. "And if you do, we can wait."

A surge of emotion floods my chest. Lately, it feels like I'm either treading water or I'm racing at a dead sprint and there's nothing in between. It's silly to get emotional about him asking me if I'm alright, but it's more than just the simple offer. It's the way John always puts me first. The way he always protects me, even at the expense of his own needs. "Thank you."

"Even if you and Kahn find eternal bliss," John says. "I'll always take care of you. Friends first." His smile is so kind that looking directly at it hurts.

I nod my head and duck out. And when we march into the breakfast room, every head turns to look at us.

Ra's utterly calm and self-assured, as always. Mehen stands, pressing his fist to his heart. He's taken to doing that every time he sees me. Since he's not calling me Most Divine anymore, I haven't had the heart to stop it. Am-Heh grins broadly and salutes. Imhotep inclines his head.

John clears his throat. Which probably means he has no idea what to say—how to bridge the gap between the current conversation and our question.

"Hi." I'm not sure what to say either. My stomach feels too unsettled to eat, so I can't delay under the pretense of nourishment.

"You should eat something," Ra says. "You look much too thin."

It turns out that even with an unsettled stomach, I can't resist delaying just a bit.

And he's not entirely wrong about me losing weight. Between the dead sprinting and the treading water, I either don't have time to eat, or I don't have an appetite. I force my legs to work again, jolting and jerking my way across the pristine parquet floor to the long table loaded with breakfast foods. I've piled my plate about three inches high before I realize I haven't been paying any attention to what I was scooping.

"You don't even like oatmeal, do you?" John's voice is soft, but I can hear him perfectly from where he's now standing near my elbow.

I've ladled oatmeal on top of something that looks

like chunks of roasted potatoes and baked beans. Why the heck do they have this stuff out for breakfast? And what are the weird-looking black wafers?

John takes the plate and sets it in a clear spot on the buffet table. "How about you sit down, and I'll grab you a few things."

Does he think I'm a mental patient?

Ra stands and pulls out a chair for me.

It's kind of starting to annoy me. "I'm fine, everyone. I don't know why you're acting like I'm crazy."

My ancient father presses a kiss to my forehead. "It's been a very difficult few weeks, and you haven't been sleeping well. John tells me you have some news for us." He lifts both eyebrows as he takes his seat again.

"News?" Kahn's eyes scan the room as he walks through the door. I wonder if the palace is a shock to him. It's certainly a major level up from our accommodations before.

Jesse's right behind him, looking fresh, healthy, and strong. Although there is a chunk of hair that's sticking up funny.

I stand up, cross the room, and brush it down. "If you let that dry, it'll stick up all day."

"Thanks." Jesse's eyes widen a bit as he looks around. "Is the news bad? What's going on? Has Isis attacked?"

"Nothing like that," I say. "But we do have a question for Kahn and Ra." I glance at John and bob my head up and down slightly.

"For both of us?" Kahn frowns. "Really?"

John extends his hand, but not quite far enough that either Ra or Kahn could reach out and take the picture frame. He's probably unconsciously still protective of his mother, or at least her memory, and who can blame him? I was devastated when I learned that someone I loved might be an evil villain. Actually, I'm still not entirely sure he isn't. With every new memory, every new revelation, I find myself waiting for the boot to drop—I wait to discover Ra *is* the bad guy after all.

"How do you have a photograph of Isis?" Kahn asks, and then he does a double take. His eyes widen, his brows draw together, and his whole body curls toward the photo frame. "Wait." He swallows slowly. "I've only seen Isis from a recorded image—I didn't mention that I'm the rebirth of her son. I bolted the second I heard she was alive and that she had control of the women who can't shift. I still can't believe they believe she'll surrender her link to that power once the threat of Ra is gone." His breathing's uneven.

"You said you're getting your memories back, some of them," I whisper.

He nods.

"Do you remember Isis—when she was your mother?"

He nods again.

"And." I gently take the photo from John, whose face is almost completely white. "Is this her? Do you know why John has this photo?"

"But that's Aunt—" Kahn swallows. "It's John's mother."

"And your Dad's sister," I say.

Kahn nods again, like speaking is too hard right now.

Every single person in the entire room is staring at him. Or peering over his shoulder to try and see the photograph. But not Ra. He looks. . .thoughtful.

"Dad?" I ask. "Why aren't you more upset?"

"I should've known." He shrugs. "John's new ability,

the discovery of which coincides with the return of
Isis?"

A small sound like a whimper escapes John.

"Your mother is Isis?" Kahn hands the photograph
back to John. "I can't believe my aunt was Isis all
along." His nose scrunches up. "But then why didn't
she give birth to me? Why is she my aunt instead?"

"We don't understand how the rebirth worked in
the first place," Ra says. "I suspect it's a byproduct of
the spell that created Terra. It must have somehow
sucked Isis and Apophis and Sekhmet into the spell
and then spit you back out recently."

John looks dazed.

Dad softens his voice. "She may not have known
who she was until very recently. She may never have
known that Kahn was her son from two millennia ago,
and she may have had no idea who she was in a prior
life. Alora didn't recall any of it until very recently."

"Okay." John does not look alright. He looks shell-
shocked, which he should. This whole thing is insane.
This woman has, not one, but *two sons* right here in this
room and instead of reaching out for them, instead of
trying to find them or protect them or *being any kind of
a mother*, she's making threats and planning to murder
my family.

"I hate her," I say. "And I hate this." I wave my
hands around, my fury snowballing. "I hate not
knowing anything, and not being sure what's the right
thing to do. I hate that she *stole* these women's powers.
And most of all, I hate that she's burning things down
when she should be building them up."

"Alora," Ra says. His voice is soft, but urgent.

"What?"

"The palace walls are shaking." Kahn's looking at
me like everyone looked at me when I covered my

plate with oatmeal. "Maybe it's time to calm down a hair."

I sense it then, the entire building, the *push* of frustration that made me reach out for something to shake, something to destroy, something to shred. "I don't want to calm down. I'm sick of being calm. I'm sick of being pushed around."

"Alora," John says.

Everyone keeps saying my name, like calling for me will fix something.

"Alora," Jesse says.

His voice grounds me. It reminds me that we can survive this. If I can save my brother from death, if that kind of wrong can be made right, then maybe we can still fix the other things that have gone belly up. And more importantly, my anger right now is a threat to everyone here, including all the people I love. I need to keep them safe, so I need to stop freaking out. "You're right, J." I close my eyes and I let go of my rage. I let go of my frustration at the futility of everything and release my grip on the building that surrounds all of us.

The walls stop trembling.

The foundation creaks a little, so I Bind the rubble underneath back into place. The noises finally stop, thankfully, but everyone's still looking at me with concern. With fear. Or perhaps with pity.

I think pity is the worst.

Except Jesse. He's looking at me with love. He wraps an arm around me and I rest my head against his shoulder.

"I can't keep doing this," I say. "I can't keep sitting around while waves of bizarre connection that I don't comprehend crash over us. Am I the only one who's sick of it?" How does John feel? His whole life must seem like a lie. Boy, can I relate to that sentiment. "I want to go on the offensive," I say, finally. "I think we should take the fight to her."

"I agree," Jesse says. "Before she has time to hurt anyone else, before she can cast more spells, before she can sacrifice more people on the altar of her ego, we need to do something."

Ra looks from Jesse to me and back again. "I'm not sure this is very helpful. It's almost like an echo chamber."

"What?" He's making no sense.

"We need to talk," he says. "Just you and me." He glances at Jesse pointedly.

"He's your son," I say. "He loves you, too."

"That's what we need to talk about."

Oh, please. What's he saying now?

"Would you come with me?" Ra's voice is gentle. His eyes entreat me to agree.

I don't have the energy to argue, not right now. "Okay."

But we don't just walk into the next room like I expect. We walk down the hall, through the back hallway, and down the back stairs into the formal palace garden. The air's brisk and I rub my arms before I remember how to heat the space around me. Am-Heh has spent a bit of time teaching me basics, and I'm remembering more and more of what I knew. I can't decide whether that's exciting or horrifying.

Probably both, like every aspect of my life.

Ra sits on a bench—the same bench we spoke on last night, actually. He pats the spot next to him. After I sit, he reaches down and digs his fingers into the dirt. I'm not sure what I expected him to do, but this was not it. He wriggles his fingers around and around and finally brings his hand back up before straightening with a calm expression.

He's holding a worm.

A wriggly, disgusting, brown earthworm.

"Uh, are we going fishing? Because I veto."

He tilts his head. "Fishing?"

"What's the worm for, Dad?" Sometimes you just have to ask the obvious questions when your dad is thousands of years old and doesn't catch context clues.

"I'm going to try and do something that doesn't come easily to me." The stones in his vambrace flare briefly as he tugs a bit of power from each, and I notice one of them is missing.

"What happened to that stone?" I point at the empty space where one had clearly been set into the front of his right vambrace. "You only have five, but there's a setting for a sixth."

"Let's not get distracted right this moment." He flattens his palm, the movement causing the worm to wriggle even more vigorously.

I try not to cringe.

"I'm not very gifted with constructs, but if I focus, I should be able to turn this into—"

"Oh, I *am* good with them." I hold out my hand. "I could make it into a bird. Or a butterfly. A mouse?"

Ra shakes his head. "That's precisely my point. You're quite good at constructs. From the time you were very small, only weeks after I taught you to bleed power from the scorpions, you learned to shape raw energy into creations, as you called them. You made butterflies from ants. You crafted mice from spiders and worms. You even made a pet monkey from a beetle. He followed you around everywhere for weeks."

"I'm not sure what this has to do with Isis—"

"That's why you should try *listening* for once." His

words are curt, but his tone and eyes are kind. "Your mind is so sharp, it's always dancing ahead. It has always been like that, and usually I love it. But in this instance. . ." He sighs. "I thought that, given time, you would realize it for yourself. I'm beginning to wonder whether you'll ignore the truth forever."

"Ignore what?" Fear tickles the edges of my consciousness. It makes my fingers curl into fists. It clenches like sickness in my belly. And a chill creeps across my back and wraps its tendrils around my head and my heart. "What am I ignoring?"

He said we needed to talk about Jesse—and he implied that he's not his son, which is just strange. And now he's talking about *me,* about my constructs, and not about Jesse at all.

"You told me about what happened the night you finally busted through the barrier that trapped all of mankind on Terra. It was also the night you accessed your powers for the first time on Earth."

My heart doesn't beat. My lungs don't inflate. My eyes can't blink.

I want to throw my hands over my ears and hum.

Maybe it's too late for any of that.

I'm aces at constructs, and he says there's something I'm ignoring because I can't face it.

And now.

He's talking about the night that. . .the night that Jesse died.

"No," I say.

"Alora," he says.

I shake my head. I stand up, my limbs finally working again. "No." I back up a step. "Jesse has been regaining his memories, even memories from his time here on Earth."

"Is he?" Ra's eyes are sad. "Has he remembered anything that *you* didn't also remember?"

I wrack my brain, desperate. But the memories Jesse shared were all things we did together. "Maybe he only told me about the ones he knew I'd also remember. Maybe he was sharing them to bring me joy and peace."

Ra doesn't speak. He simply looks at me.

"We aren't an echo chamber," I insist doggedly. "He argues with me. He insisted that I couldn't keep feeding energy into him."

"Have you ever been conflicted about something?" He raises both eyebrows. "Did it feel almost like arguing with yourself?"

No, it didn't. No, it's not like I'd have erased my own memory . . . In a rush of relief, I remember that— "I saw his soul." I cross my arms. "That's conclusive proof that he's real."

"You use something to create a base for each one of your constructs," Ra says. "A worm or a mouse or a bird, for small things."

"You're saying I saw the soul of some bug and not Jesse?" That sounds insane. I'd have noticed.

"I'm saying you saw what you needed to see, just as your mind created what you needed to create in order for you to continue to function, in order for you to cope with the grief."

"You don't think anyone would have noticed, if that was true?" I shake my head. "It can't be true. Jesse's alive. I brought him back, and you healed him."

Even in all the memories of my life as Sekhmet, I've never seen Ra look so wrecked. "The only thing I've ever wanted on this earth is to keep you safe and protect you from harm. I wish I could protect you from this. I would give everything, including my life, if I could have healed him."

"You did heal him." Even to my ears, the words sound flat and desperate.

"Imhotep can do amazing things." Ra stands. "I've seen him bring men back from the brink of death."

What he's saying is insane. No one could create a construct of an actual person. My memory of replicating myself comes to mind, and I reject it. If I'd done what he's saying, I would know. My whole body is shaking violently, and I back up another step. "Stop talking."

"Alora, I know you don't want to deal with this, but with Isis back, we've run out of time. You have to face the truth." A tear rolls down Ra's cheek. "I loved Shu, maybe not as much as you, but you have to believe I was delighted when I thought I'd be able to see him again, that I'd be able to embrace him once more. I truly wish I could."

"NO!" I fling him backward as forcefully as I can, and I watch in horrified fascination as his body flattens against the hard ground, his head cracking loudly against a landscaping rock. "Don't say another word." I drop my face into my hands.

Somehow, miraculously, probably thanks to some kind of spell, Ra is fine. He stands up and brushes leafy detritus from his pants. "Alora."

Why does he keep repeating my name? "I want to see Jesse. I want to see my brother, right now." I hold out my hands, and realize they're wet. Why are my hands wet? A tear rolls down my face and lands on the ground.

I didn't even realize I was crying.

With both hands, I swipe the tears away, rapidly.

"I'm not sad. I'm not angry. I'm fine," I insist, "because Jesse is also *fine*."

"I can do many things, Alora. I can stop marauding armies. I can use the energy I took from them to work marvelous wonders. I can practically turn back the hands of time, reversing the impact of aging. I can remake the appearance of things, not as an illusion, but as actual fact. I can seal cracks in the foundations of buildings. I can pull precious metals and gems from the earth. I can rejuvenate flagging animals, and I can craft spells that do even more amazing things. But there's one thing I've been asked to do countless times in the past few thousand years, and I'm just as unable to do it now as I was as a child."

"Dad, I'm begging you." I'm sobbing now. Great, heaving sobs wrack my body. "Don't say it."

"I can't heal someone who has died, Alora. I can't bring anyone *back* from death to life." His voice drops to the barest whisper, but I still hear it. I still hear every single word. "You couldn't save Jesse, because from the moment his soul left his body, he was already gone."

"He was alive on Terra," I say, doggedly.

"He wasn't ever alive on Terra. The Jesse who existed on Terra was always a bundle of energy. Memories, thoughts, and feelings, yes, those returned to their rightful bodies as their control of their own magic returned. You destroyed the restrictions and freed those people, but Jesse's energy had no anchor to return to."

I don't want to think about it, but I remember it now. That miserable night, the worst of my life, in my desperation, I pulled energy and tiny bright souls away from Terra, and they peeled away from me and shot down to their bodies as I approached Earth.

But Jesse's energy didn't have a body to find. It stayed with me. It took a massive amount of power, of magic, to force what I thought was his soul to Earth. I wasn't sure I'd be able to survive the trip.

"Are you saying that I didn't save him, but that I *created* a new facsimile of him?" I don't see how that could be possible. "I couldn't have done that. I remember how to create constructs now, thanks to my memories as Sekhmet, but I knew nothing about that then." But I can't make decent constructs now. I remember *how*, but they don't last. They crumble, in the same way they did in the past. . .if I already had another one in use.

No. I refuse to believe it. It can't be true. I'd know. I'd be able to sense it.

"Call for Jesse."

"He'll never hear me from here," I say. "Because he's *not* a construct. He's a real person. A person I saved. A person who thinks and talks and eats and lives. A person you healed."

"Call for him," Ra urges, still inexplicably calm, still unbearably gentle.

Before I make a sound, Jesse pops out of the back door, a perplexed expression on his familiar and utterly perfect face. "Alora? Did you need me?"

My heart cracks inside my chest then. Splits wide open. "No."

"You need to look at his heart," Ra says.

"I've done that," I practically shout, triumphant. "His soul was as beautifully bright as I knew it would be!"

"This time," Ra says, "you have to look and you have to *see*." His mouth twists. "You have to accept what you want to deny."

"The soul I saw had to be his. It was brilliant and

bright." But part of me wonders why Jesse isn't inter-jecting. Why isn't he demanding to know what's going on?

"Hey, what in the world is going on?" Jesse asks.

The crack in my heart widens.

"Look," Ra says, "and accept the truth."

I don't want to do it. I want to prove him wrong, but I'm afraid. Could this all have been a delusion? Could I be so pathetic that I created a fake brother to love? It sounds so *insane*. It sounds so desperate.

Tears stream unchecked down my cheeks as I turn to face my brother—my beloved, funny, brilliant, generous, snarky, selfless brother. The one person in all this world I trust with my entire heart and my entire soul.

The one person I would do *anything* to save.

And I force myself to *look*.

The soul inside of him is as bright and lovely as I remember.

For one short second, hope flares.

But then I broaden my scope, and I see what's there instead of what I want to see.

It's not really Jesse's soul.

Inside his body, inside the construct I created to house the energy signature in Terra that was tied to my brother, is a black and white dog.

The crevice in my heart cracks wide open and I drop to my knees. I have to release that poor creature. I'm so ashamed. Everything I've worked for, everything I've fought for, everything I've cared about, it's all been a lie. Now that I'm seeing the truth, I know what Ra did as well. His 'healing' consisted of prying off one of his full reservoir stones and inserting it into my construct's chest, linked with a small spell that siphons power as needed to fuel the walking, talking facsimile of my brother.

"Why didn't you tell me before?" I can barely speak. "Why did you lie?" I know it's not Ra's fault. I know it's mine, but I can't take the blame. I need someone else to be at fault. My anger needs an outlet.

"You weren't ready," he says.

"I was never going to be ready," I say.

"You're stronger than you know," Ra says. "Shu knew that better than anyone. He has always known just how brightly you shine. He's always seen you for who and what you are, and he's always been proud of you, of your goodness, and of your strength. Wherever we go when this life is over, he's there now, watching you and loving you still. That I promise."

But words can't fix what I feel. Nothing can.

Jesse's arms wrap around me and I realize that his presence, real or not, is the only thing that can help me. He's always been the only person who can heal me. "It's okay, Alora. I'm here. I'm not going anywhere."

Except now I realize that he's just saying the things that I want him to say. He's saying the things that my version of Jesse would say, probably, but there's no way to know how Jesse would truly act.

And that's exactly the problem.

I may have known my brother better than anyone else on Earth. In the short time I knew him on Terra, I may have even known him better than anyone else there, too, but I only knew one version of him. I only knew one sliver of who he was and how he loved. And no matter what I knew about him, the thing that made Jesse into Jesse, his choices, his free will, his agency, his ability to grow, that's all gone forever.

Which is why, no matter how convincing it looks or sounds or feels, this version of Jesse will always be lacking. Even so, the thought of letting it go pains me. Like losing my teddy bear when I was four at Mom and Dad's funeral. Like leaving behind all my belongings, meager as they were, when we fled the group home. I know they can't help me, but parting still hurts.

I hug almost-Jesse one last time. I know it's not really him, but it's *part* of him. It's the part I knew. It's the part I loved. It's the part that loved me most clearly. It's a better goodbye than most people get. "I will always love you," I say.

"I know that," Jesse says. "It's the one thing I know for sure."

I hope that's true. I hope wherever he is, he does know how much I love him and how much he's brightened my life. He has shaped and guided me in every single moment. He's made me better than I ever could have been without him. And in that moment, I realize the one thing that might keep me going, that might bind the broken shards of my heart back into something capable of muscling on after he's truly gone.

My brother would not want me to fall apart.

He wouldn't want me to give up. He would tell me to let him go and keep growing and learning and changing. He showed that with his last action—he gave his life to save mine, which means it's my job not to waste that sacrifice.

"I'm sorry, J. You deserved better. If I had Woken sooner, or if I had been stronger. . ." I clutch him to my chest one last time, and then, before he can say another not-quite-real word, I unravel the construct. Thread by thread, one warp and one weft at a time, I siphon the energy of Jesse into the reservoir stones Ra gave me until all that's left in front of me is a shaggy black and white dog, smiling up at me with an expression that is painfully similar to one Jesse would have made. Eager, happy, and loving. I can't help wondering whether this sweet dog is now infused with Jesse's energy, or whether he was always like this.

"Is everyone okay?" John's standing on the steps of the back door, Kahn beside him.

"Yes," I say, shocked to my core that it's true. "Dad was right. I did know the truth all along."

"Is that Suerte?" John drops to one knee and pats his thighs. "Suerte. Come here, boy."

The dog next to me perks up, his ears lifting and his eyes tracking toward John's voice. Then he sails past me, racing toward John. When he reaches John's side, he licks and licks and licks everything he can reach. Hands, face, legs.

"Okay, alright, that's enough. Good boy." John's eyes are searching. "What's he doing here?"

"How do you know him?"

"That's my neighbor's dog," John says. "I watch him when she's out of town."

Of course he is. I needed a life around which to shape my construct, and the larger and more robust the base creature, the better. I snatched the closest life in being that I could find. "I'm afraid you'll have to call that poor woman and explain. If it helps, it really was a matter of life and death." My voice hitches then, and I realize it was actually just a matter of death, and my own inability to accept it. "I hope she hasn't been too devastated that he was missing."

"She was an older lady, and she always joked that I should keep him. She regretted buying such an energetic, bouncy dog. She'll probably be grateful for the break." John's smile is kind. "But I don't understand how he wound up here."

As if he can sense my distress, as if my feelings are now coded into his doggy DNA, Suerte sprints back across the grass and jumps up on me, both his paws planted near my shoulders. And then he licks my face, replacing my involuntary tears with slobber. I swear, Suerte looks like he's smirking about it.

I do think Ra got one other thing right. As I throw a stick for Suerte and watch him bring it back, I believe that Jesse really is somewhere, watching me.

And I think he's smiling.

❧ 17 ❧

ANCIENT EGYPT

"Are you sure you want to do this?" Shu's eyes are so very blue, and utterly concerned.

"I'm sure." I lash the large bag on the sheepskin pad strapped to Dove's back. The irony isn't lost on me—I'm loading up the horse Dad just bought me. . .so that I can leave him.

"You're upset. You might change your mind—"

"And if I do, I know the way to return." Or, at least Shu does.

I'm pretty sure.

I release the bag and step back. Dove nuzzles my hand, always hoping for a treat. "He *created* me, Shu, and then he lied to me about it."

"In his defense, he was trying to help you." He pauses so I'm forced to meet his gaze. "You aren't a monster, but you're worried that you are now that you know." He frowns. "You don't think Alexander's a terrible person, clearly, or we wouldn't be going to see him right now."

"It's a double standard," I say. "I acknowledge that."

"Mother left you because of it." Shu's eyes are full

of empathy, understanding, and love. He's not mad enough, not by half.

"Just like Alexander, I had no choice," I say. "My whole life would have been different if I'd been born like you. Like I should have been born, and he took that away from me."

"Most people would say he gave you a great gift," Shu says.

I leap up onto Dove's back. "I'm not most people." I wheel her around and urge her to move. She's the best horse I've ever owned, and she loves to run. That's especially perfect right now.

It takes my irritating brother almost ten minutes to catch me.

"You're a brat." He's winded and puffing. "And I need a better horse if you're going to pull that nonsense very often."

"Good luck finding one like this."

"Yeah, *Dad* really outdid himself."

I grit my teeth, pulling Dove back to a walk.

Shu sighs melodramatically with relief. "Thank goodness. That fire behind us must have finally been extinguished."

"I can't listen to him make any more excuses," I say. "Everything he says makes me more angry."

"So he cast a spell on you," Shu says. "He casts a lot of spells."

I yank too hard on Dove's reins when I ask her to stop, so I pat her neck by way of apology. It's not her fault my dad's a supervillain. "What's Dad's greatest misery? The worst thing he ever endured?"

Shu blinks.

"His father, the evil, the terrible, the horrific supra alpha kept him in a box. He treated him like. . .I don't know what gets treated that badly. It's a miracle he turned into the compassionate, generous ruler that he did. I get it." I inhale and exhale to give Shu time to make this connection. "But the worst part about what his dad did was what?"

Shu's brow furrows. "Well, he killed a lot of people and took things from him. He made Dad keep him and his supporters young and strong enough to keep doing it."

"No, that's not the worst part, at least, not to me."

He doesn't get it. I was hoping he would.

"Dad's father took away Dad's choices. He couldn't even fight against him. It's the reason he hates supras. It's the reason he's so distrustful of most Renders. Because he values his free will." I resist the urge to take off at a gallop again. At some point, I have to make Shu understand why I'm so hurt.

"You're upset that Dad did the same thing to you, before you were even born. That you had no say in it."

"Exactly."

"But there are plenty of things we have no power to control," Shu says. "Dad gave you much more power, and the ability to control almost anything at all, if it really was his spell that made you what you are."

My fists tighten on my reins. "You're so aggravating —saying the ends justify the means. Do you really not see?"

"I get what you're saying," Shu says. "But I think that, to Dad, he was protecting you from the very thing that made him vulnerable. He wanted you to have *more* power and control, not less."

"*He* wanted. Not me, him. And while we're on this topic, he killed one hundred people to harvest the power for that spell, Shu. One hundred people *died* to make me into what I am. What about their choices?"

"I don't really want to point this out, but they all

chose to sacrifice their lives willingly, remember? That was a big part of the deal. If Dad had used the energy from one hundred people he executed, the energy wouldn't have been the same. So if we're talking about free will, they had it. They wanted to be a part of making someone exceptional, someone who was nearly all-powerful."

The ground around us starts to shake.

"Mehen would remind you to breathe in and out deeply, if he were here," Shu says.

As if that stupid observation will be less annoying than just telling me himself. I know what happens when I get agitated. I wreck things. "This is a prime example of the kind of thing I shouldn't have to deal with. You're a powerful Lifter, one of the best, but you can't topple a mountain. No one should be able to do that."

"I'm not arguing with you," Shu says. "You must have mistaken me for another brother, a stupid one, who likes to rile you up and get kicked around." He slides off his horse and leads him close enough to put his hand on my boot. "You love Father. I know that, because if you didn't, you wouldn't feel so betrayed."

"You can love someone and not want anything to do with them."

"He's done a lot of things wrong in his absurdly long life," Shu says. "He's the first one to admit that he's probably morally grey at best."

"If you don't want me to kick you around, you should stop defending him."

"I'll never be the kind of person who just blindly agrees with you. It's not who I am. I love you more than anyone, but you need someone to tell you the truth. Leaving Father, well, it's dramatic and it shows him how upset you are. That's fine, but those people made their *choice*. You can't say it's all about choices and then be upset that you don't approve of the one they made."

I stare straight ahead, refusing to look into his pleading eyes.

"Father has done some bad things, but he's been a very good ruler. He's ensured peace and prosperity and relative equality for most of the people he's ruled. He's probably done more good than bad, on balance, and the people recognize that."

"That's not why he cast that spell on me," I say. "He did it because he was lonely and wanted someone who was like him."

Shu throws his hands up in the air. "True. He's a selfish tyrant. Does that make you happy?"

I finally look at him. "Why aren't you more angry? Don't tell me you don't look at me differently now. A hundred people *died* so that I could be *special*. That's messed up."

"I agree with you. I'd never have done it." Shu shifts his horse back a bit so he can't bite Dove. "But I haven't lived through what he has. I haven't been forced to kill my own children. I didn't lose a girlfriend because I wouldn't have any more children. And I didn't watch that girlfriend do what I had failed to do—turning an Assimilator into something more stable."

"He didn't do that to me, though, did he?"

"Just think about what I'm saying," he says. "It's going to be a miserable ride if you insist on fixating on this madness the entire time."

"It's not madness," I say.

"It kind of is. Our father hates Alexander's mother. They're mortal enemies. The spell cast on him is the *reason* our father did what he did to you, the thing that has you so upset, and now you're going to use it. . ." He freezes. "Oh."

"What?"

"You've been pining." He smiles. "I finally get it."

"Get what?"

"You've been pining for years now. You've been dreaming of him and thinking about him. You blush whenever his name comes up. You've been dying for any reason to be with the dashing, the handsome, and the compelling Alexander."

"Shut your mouth." I shift in my seat, and Dove starts moving again. I hold her to a walk. I'm not trying to escape—I just need him to stop talking.

Shu's on his horse in the blink of an eye, racing after me. "You couldn't go to him—there was no way. Any way you looked at it, doing that would be betraying our father, the person you love most. But now. . ."

He stops talking and just rides.

I try to forget what he's said. I intentionally don't connect the dots.

They have nothing to do with the facts. Dad lied to me. He cast a spell on me. He needed pure magic, not energy harvested from criminals and villains. He needed the kind of power that turned his reservoirs bright white, not pulsing red. And when his acolytes discovered his need, they rushed to offer their lives. After all, the opportunity to be a part of something huge, the chance to create a new god? What believer wouldn't leap to his death for that chance?

He should never have taken advantage of them. He should never have done what he did. My rage is justified. It's right. It's pure. Mother left when she discovered that he had changed me, shaped me into something I never should have become. I truly mourn the loss of the life I should have had, a life where I would've fit in. Dad should have known that creating someone like him, someone who's like no one else, was a terrible thing to do. He'd already been lonely for centuries.

My fury is justified.

But I can't quite dislodge Shu's words. Am I as angry as I am because it lets me finally have what I want? Is my rage the excuse I was seeking to do what I've wanted to do? To go to Alexander? To finally be with Alexander?

The birds hoot and whistle and call. Small animals move through the treetops and scurry through the underbrush. As we leave the forest, deer with strange horns bound away in herds. Hawks wheel overhead, their cries plaintive, their eyes sharp.

I think about all of those things. I obsess about anything other than the one thing to which my brother has irritatingly drawn my attention. Am I using Dad's past bad actions to justify my own?

"So what if I am?" I shrug. "Dad's the reason I can't be with Alexander. Dad may as well be the reason I finally can."

"Is that how you want things to be?" Shu's voice isn't judgmental. It's concerned.

"I don't want anything to be like this. I want the world to go back to how it was, but we don't always get what we want."

"No." He can't argue with that. In the end, we often do not get the very thing we want with all our hearts.

"When we reach the great Alexander, what are you going to do? March up to his throne and drag him to your side? Are you going to propose to him?" Shu's voice is different now. Frustratingly playful.

"Of course not."

"No?"

"That's not how we are."

"How are you?" His lips twitch.

I Lift a dozen pebbles and fling them at him in quick succession. "You're the worst brother of all time."

"I'm the best."

"The worst. You should be supporting me. You should be giving me advice. Instead you're pestering me and arguing with me and mocking me."

"I'm doing what you need instead of what you want, like I always do."

His words strike me then, like a splash of cold water against my face. He's right. He has always done everything I need. Dad's spell on me changed more than just my life. It drastically altered Shu's. He should have been the most beloved. He should have been Dad's heir, as his son and the firstborn child of his true love.

But I drove a wedge between Mother and Dad. I supplanted Shu's place. I took all their attention and most of Dad's love. Shu should hate me.

"Why do you love me?" I expect him to crack a joke. Or brush me off. Or roll his eyes.

I do not expect him to sound utterly sincere. "Why do people love rainbows? Why do they love the first snowfall? Why do they love the grace and beauty of a perfectly proportioned horse, racing across a field?" He smiles at me. "I love you for all of those reasons and more. You're a good person, right down to your very center. You love boldly and always have. You care fiercely and always will. You make everyone around you better and stronger, and you have loved me in the very same way."

"If I stay with Alexander, I won't see Dad often, if

at all." My eyes brim with tears. My throat closes off and makes it almost impossible to speak. "Will you stay with me? Or go back to him?"

"How can you even ask that?"

"I'm sorry," I say. "I'm not trying to pressure you. I know Dad has given you purpose, and that you have an important role with his—"

He laughs. "You're not pressuring me, but I figured you already knew the answer to that." He tilts his head, the corner of his mouth turning up. "You're not just my sister, you're my best friend. One day, some woman will sweep me off my feet and I'll forget all about you, but until then, you're stuck with me."

My heart brightens then, and I didn't realize how badly I needed something good.

Shu doesn't bring up Dad for the next three days. Not once. It's like he wanted to make sure I had considered everything, that I had all the facts straight, and then he was content to let me do whatever I wanted. When he's not telling me an outlandish story or making something mundane into a joke, I think about the things he said. I think about Dad's actions. Dad's motivations.

And although it takes me several days, I forgive him.

It's not easy. It's not simple. I may not have completely let go of the pain, or of my fear that I'm not something that should exist, but my anger melts away. After any reckoning has been completed, I may be an abomination as Mother said, but I had nothing to do with it, and I can't change it. Since I already exist, my only option is to do the best I can in the situations in which I'm placed.

Which feels a lot harder when we finally reach the Euphrates. Once we cross, we'll be on the skirts of

Thapsacus, which is (according to our best information) Alexander's current location.

"He wasn't kidding about not giving up, was he?" Shu's hard to impress, but bringing an army of 30,000 militia and 10,000 mounted cavalry to pick a fight with a girl's dad is apparently enough to do it.

"He wasn't, no." I can't bring myself to lie and say that I'm unmoved, either. He got what he wanted when we met, accomplished the task his mom set for him, and still he's bringing this enormous force to bear, insisting on pursuing me in spite of all the obstacles. He's here in spite of the very powerful people he knows will likely stand in his way. And so far, he's done it in a way that won't cause me distress or grief.

Not intentionally, anyway.

"So what kind of spectacularly beautiful disguise do you have worked up this time?" Shu slides off his horse.

"We should cross here," I say.

"Why?"

"I'll Bind us a visible bridge to cross so that it doesn't spook the horses, and that's best done out of view. But also." I grin.

"Oh, no. Do I even want to ask?"

"I had an idea. It's the only way I can think of that he'll never realize it's me."

Shu's eyes widen. "You want to see how he behaves when he doesn't realize you're around?"

It sounds kind of distrustful when he puts it that way. "I thought I knew Dad. I thought I knew Mother." I'm learning that the only thing I really do know is that I don't know anything at all.

"Alexander isn't Ra, and he's certainly not Hathor," Shu says.

I shrug. "What can I say? Before I commit to *be* with him, before I agree to walk away from my entire life, I want to know how he acts when he doesn't know anyone's watching."

"He's Alexander the Great. Someone's always watching."

That's precisely the point. Unlike most people, we will face an extraordinary amount of scrutiny and unlimited options.

"You could send a construct," Shu says. "You could spy on him any number of ways that would be less difficult."

"I'm not spying on him," I lie.

My brother knows that I am, though. He always knows. "Every single time, he spots you right away." Shu smirks. "What makes you think this will be any different?"

"Because I've been watching, and I've noticed something. No one pays any attention to eunuchs."

※ 18 ※

ANCIENT EGYPT

This feels. . .strange. I've changed my appearance before, on so many instances I've probably lost track of them all. I'm as good at it as Ra, and almost as good as Anat. But in all those times, I've never changed my gender for more than a brief moment. It feels. . .dissonant. Like my outside *really* doesn't match my inside. At least I won't be this way for very long.

We make a pen for our horses before heading into town. I spend a little more time than I intended making it, but I really don't want to lose Dove. She's been just as wonderful as I had hoped.

No one gives us a second glance on our way through the gates of Thapsacus. It makes sense. We're just a guard (I matched Shu's clothing to that of the gate guards) escorting a servant back to the mansion at the center of town. One of the good things about having *such* a large military force is that no one can keep track of everyone. Unfamiliar faces are everywhere. Tents sprawl outward from the small but established settlement like mushrooms that have sprung up in damp soil. Several hawks wheel in lazy circles overhead, hoping to snag any wildlife that's been displaced by the increased human activity, probably.

"You have the letter?" I ask.

"No." Shu rolls his eyes. "I dropped it in the last hundred yards."

I shouldn't be this nervous.

"Remember to speak in Greek."

"Terribly accented Greek for you," he says. "You're supposed to have been captured in Persia, remember?"

I swallow. He doesn't remind me to speak with a deep voice, but he doesn't have to. There's an obnoxious reminder dangling between my legs. Ugh. It shifts with every step, and I keep wanting to shove it out of the way. How do men ever run?

Eventually we reach the entrance to the largest building in town—easy to find since we can both sense most everything around us. There are, of course, guards at the entrance, which is precisely the purpose of the letter. It takes them a moment, but after reading it twice, or perhaps once very slowly, the guards wave us through.

"Accompany the eunuch to the steward, second door on the left, and then report to the Marshall to receive your assignment. He's in the last room on the right."

The eunuch. Like that's all I am. Not a person, not a man, defined only by what I lack. I've never thought about it until this very moment, but it's kind of terrible. The practice of making men into eunuchs is awful enough, but the treatment afterward is almost worse. I should do something about it.

Shu nods, drawing my attention, and I realize that I didn't even ask him if he was okay with pretending to be one of Alexander's new officers, sent as a reinforcement from Macedonia. He didn't complain about my failure to give him a choice, even after I made such a big deal about it. I have a good brother. Better than I deserve.

Moments later, I'm bowing stiffly in front of the steward, and Shu's leaving and it's all happening so fast. I stare dumbly at the door as it closes, wondering if this was a huge mistake. I'm alone in a place I don't know, surrounded by people I don't know, all so that I can do what? Spy on Alexander?

Is my lack of trust in my father causing me to distrust everyone?

"You've been in service for years?" The steward, surprisingly, is a woman. Her dark eyes look me over critically, starting with my head and ending with my feet. She doesn't wait for an answer. "And what's your affinity?"

Does she mean my power?

"Answer."

"I'm Earth Called," I say. "I am excellent at growing nutritious vegetables and roots."

She sighs. "Useless. I doubt we'll be here long enough to grow anything at all. And you certainly don't look very strong."

"When I'm not tending the garden, I mostly clean things," I say. "At the last palace, I cleaned the quarters of the queen herself."

"Yes, well, I doubt that either Sophene or Armenia are on par with our standards." She frowns. "I won't be placing you in charge of a task as critical as cleaning the royal quarters for a very long time." She puts her hands on her hips. "But I might let you empty and clean the royal chamberpot. How's that for glamour? You're quite proud of yourself, and precocious for a eunuch. Did no one teach you to keep your eyes lowered?" She narrows her eyes. "I expect you to learn that quickly."

I nod and stare at my roughly finished brown boots. "Yes, your . . . Er," I switch to Persian. I can't think of many honorifics in Greek. "Your esteemed personage." I don't know what to call her. How stupid of me.

"You will not use Persian here, not while Alexander rules. Turn around."

Turn around? Why? Her eyes widen alarmingly, so after a brief pause, I comply.

"Bow your head."

I do that too, but I'm not sure why until I reach out with my senses and realize she's grabbed a whip.

It takes every ounce of my resolve not to cry out in pain when she lashes my back. Even through my rough-spun tunic, the injury stings fiercely. Apparently for the crime of using what she believes to be my native tongue, one lash is not enough. But after the third, I'm about ready to Bind her to the ground and show her how it feels to be punished when she clears her throat. "I trust that will help you remember. You may call me Aghaye, but that will be the only Persian term you're allowed to use. We only allow it because so many of the people in this town don't speak Greek at all. Is that clear?"

I nod.

"You've arrived at a good time. We lost one of our best workers yesterday. You'll clean the chamber pots of every bedroom in the building, starting next to me, and ending with His Esteemed Majesty, Alexander the Great."

If the whip wasn't enough to convince me that I made a mistake, the next few hours absolutely are. I've never fully appreciated the work that's done by people who don't have the same powers as me. I'm *dying* to

Lift the contents of these filthy pots away and not go anywhere near them with my fingers, but masquerading as an Earth Called means that I can't.

My back smarts enough that I finally duck into an alcove and shift into lion form to heal the swollen and angry skin. When I shift back, I smell just as bad as I did before. I'm about one chamber pot away from chopping my filthy hands right off, when I hear it.

Alexander's voice.

And the tinkling sound of a woman's voice, laughing. I poke my head around the corner, desperate to catch a glimpse.

Her arm rests on his, her eyes alight with mirth as she laughs again at something he's saying.

I'm seized with an utterly irrational desire to turn her inside out, dumping her internal organs all over the floor. It would be so easy, like peeling an overripe banana. I barely remember that I can't do that—indeed I can't say anything at all. This exact scenario is the reason I came in a disguise. If I wreck it by disclosing my identity, all that excrement I just eliminated was a complete waste.

Of course, a glop of filth falls from the pot I'm holding to land on my foot.

I shudder.

The movement draws Alexander's eye and I almost duck back behind the wall. But then I remember that I not only don't look like myself, I look like a *man*. It's hard, but I force myself to drop my eyes immediately.

"We're done in there," the woman says. "You can clean it up now." She waves her hand at me, and I swear, everything around me turns reddish. Intelligence gathering? Forget it. I'm going to kill her.

But then I remember that I'm a servant. Ordering me around is literally what everyone is supposed to do.

I bow my head and wait for them to walk down the hall before I slink into Alexander's room. Women's clothing is strewn all over the antechamber, and someone clearly slept on the couch recently. Blankets are piled up in a wad near one edge.

My emotions completely shift when I see that. With all these rooms, there's only one reason a woman would sleep on the couch of Alexander's antechamber. I don't want to kill her. I want to strangle Alexander. How could he have lied to me so spectacularly? Did he like me at all? Was our connection truly so very one-sided? My mouth is dry. My breathing's ragged, and there's absolutely no chance I'm going to empty a chamber pot from this room. They can drown in their filth for all I care. I pivot on my heel and practically race out the door.

And crash right into the high and mighty Aghaye herself. "Oof."

"Where in all of blasted Persia do you think you're going?" Her lips are pressed into a hard, tight line. She's clearly wishing she had her whip in her hand.

But I don't care anymore. I'm done bowing and gritting my teeth and dumping buckets of sewage. I open my mouth to tell her where she can go when she throws her hands up into the air.

"Forget that. Now that you've finished, you need to get yourself cleaned up immediately. The Great and Noble Alexander has requested a formal dinner with entertainment. We're short staffed, and everyone will have to help serve."

The one thing I want more than to escape is to wreak a little vengeance. It's probably the worst idea I've ever had, but I can't quite pass up my chance to show Alexander that I know he's a rat in a rather public way. "Yes, great Aghaye. I do as I am bid." Now all I need to do is get close enough to reveal who I am —and then leave. And never return.

Cleaning up apparently involves scrubbing myself with a rag from a bucket. The same bucket of water that was already used by three other eunuchs. It makes sense that I'd go last, having recently handled chamber pots, but it takes a lot of the wind out of my sails, knowing I'll be arriving as a foul-smelling servant who's little better than a slave.

By the time I reach the great hall, the location of the fête, I'm even able to admit to myself that I'm desperately hoping for some kind of explanation. The further it gets from the incident, the more the details grow fuzzy, and the more feelings I recall of the time we've spent together. Alexander's expression when he discovers it's me each time. His desperation to see me a week ago in Babylon.

Why did he lie about all of that?

Unless his mother does know Dad is still alive.

And Alexander wants to capture me as a bargaining chip to use to kill my father, once and for all.

Shu marches into the room with a line of other guards, his eyes meeting mine immediately. I can tell by the set of his jaw that he's heard Alexander has a female visitor. His eyes dart toward the door and back at me, clearly suggesting that we leave. I'll be going soon, I imagine, but not until I'm entirely certain nothing could have been misconstrued. Am I desperate to need more proof? Stupid? Greedy for punishment?

Maybe.

But I feel too much for him, and I've gone through too much, even in our brief encounters, to simply walk away. So I wait. And wait. No one eats a single roll. No one drinks a single sip. We all wait silently for the honored guests. Even if he hadn't been with another woman, I'd be a little put out with him for making us all wait so long. What on earth could be keeping him?

When he finally breezes through the door with the woman still on his arm, her cheeks pink, her eyes bright, I'm gripped with the same rage as before.

"I still can't believe how that felt!" She beams at him. "How could any other man ever measure up to you, after something like that?"

My hands ball into fists at my side. What more evidence did I want? Do I really need to watch him kiss her? What's wrong with me? I wanted to expose him in public, but now that I'm in the same room as him all the rage inside of me is gone. Melted away. I don't want to yell at him or out him or make him gnash his teeth. I just want to curl up into a ball and die. Or cry. Or cry and then die.

I'm a mess.

They stroll to the front of the room and jaunt up the steps to the raised table clearly prepared for two. The woman sits down right away, but Alexander turns to face the gathering. "Friends, guests, welcome. Eat with us until you can't eat any more, and then we'll enjoy a show." He sits, and suddenly, I'm being jabbed.

"Wine, idiot. You're new, but you're not deaf. Take a flagon of wine."

Which of course, if I were really who I'm supposed to be, I would have known to do. I almost Lift it, but I catch myself just in time and heft it with my actual arms instead. It weighs a lot more than I expected, and the only way I can carry it is to lurch along oafishly.

Surprisingly, Alexander waves the first round away. "We lost track of time and made you all wait. Please, you drink first."

But that also means that the other servants are already pouring for everyone, except Alexander and the *woman*. I grit my teeth and climb the steps to the raised platform. "Ah, you're new," Alexander says, looking up at me. "Thank you."

He thanks the servants everyone else abuses? Of course he does. It makes it a lot harder to hate him, even if he has been lying to me and possibly trying to lure me out in order to defeat my father. No wonder I don't know what I want or how to act. He's as inconsistent as my feelings.

By the time I finish pouring his wine and move to the woman's chalice, my hands are trembling. I can't tell whether it's from nerves, anger, or muscle fatigue. I'm not used to this much demanding physical labor. I need to Lift less and use my physical body more, clearly. Ugh. Telekinetic problems. Or perhaps my emotions have sapped my energy. Either way, I'm barely hanging on to the pitcher. I manage to pour it into her cup, thankfully.

"That's enough," the woman says. Her expression is pleasant, and she certainly smells much better than I do. She isn't thanking me precisely, but she's much more polite than everyone else I've encountered, including the other servants.

When I try to angle the heavy ceramic flagon backward to stop the flow, my arm shakes and wine spills out and all over the table, dripping down on her robes. I stumble backward, focusing all my attention on righting the flagon before more wine dumps out.

A strong hand on my shoulder stabilizes me. "Easy there. Don't fall over."

Alexander's eyes are open and kind. He even offers me, the clumsy one at whom everyone else is glaring, a half smile. "No harm done."

To my great dismay, the woman isn't even irrational or rude. "I imagine that's quite heavy, and you've already done a lot of work today. Wasn't it you cleaning Alexander's room earlier?"

No chance they won't know who's to blame for the very full chamber pots. Good.

"You should sit down and take a break." She smiles. "Long enough to calm your nerves, in any case."

I hate how beautiful she is. I hate her high cheekbones, her delicate features, and the graceful line of her collarbone. I also despise her sky blue eyes and her golden hair, which are as classically Greek as I will never be.

I should have known that someone raised to appreciate the Greek standard of beauty wouldn't really be attracted to someone who looks like me. I'm far too Egyptian.

"Do you need a hand?" Alexander tilts his head.

Because I'm still not moving, like a complete imbecile. I shake my head, reminding myself to respond in broken Greek. "No. Please enjoy with your girlfriend."

Alexander's lips press together in humor. His eyes dance. "My girlfriend? Perhaps your comprehension of Greek is not very good. This isn't my girlfriend. It's my sister, Thessalonike. She came to see her husband, my companion Cassander, but I sent him on an errand, so the task of keeping her occupied falls to my very inept hands."

"Your sister." My heart stalls. My hands shake, more wine sloshing over the side. She's not his girlfriend. He hasn't been flirting with her. He didn't lie to me? Guilt rushes in. How could I have doubted him so easily?

This time, when Alexander's hand braces my shoulder, his eyes meet mine. And his widen. "You thought she was my girlfriend, and that. . .*distressed you*?" Now his mouth widens in a broad smile. "You were so upset you were shaking." He looks at me more closely, and then the corner of his mouth smiles. "You looked absolutely flummoxed in the hallway when we first saw you."

"Not at all, Your Majesty," I say.

His voice drops to a whisper. "Bravo. You've outdone yourself this time." He steps closer, his hand dropping to my waist. "But then, I thought I'd failed. I didn't think you'd ever come find me." His head lowers toward mine. He's going to kiss me.

In front of a room full of people.

His lips meet mine boldly, eagerly, and I kiss him back. Before I'm reminded that I'm not myself. I'm a man. I groan.

He releases me, startling a bit. "Oh, right."

Every single person in the room is staring at us with complete and total shock. Alexander the Great, the Magnificent, the Conqueror, just kissed a servant. And not any servant—a eunuch. Even his sister stares at us gape-mouthed. I'm utterly shocked that he was so sure, so positive it was me, that he kissed a man in view of every one of his biggest supporters.

"Does this mean that you've come to answer my question?" He doesn't seem to care who's watching. I suppose that's one benefit of being a supreme ruler. "Does that mean that you'll marry me?"

His sister gasps. "Alexander. You mustn't jest like this. It's too much."

I tap into my reservoir and shed the disguise as though it was a second skin. "It does." I can't quite prevent my own smile.

He spins me around, lifting me up high in the air before setting me back down. "This is the happiest day of my life."

"That wasn't the day you met me?" I arch one eyebrow.

"You told me that day that I only care about the thrill of the chase. You thought that my admiration for you was a passing fancy."

I shake my head. "I'm confused a lot, your Esteemed Highness. What can I say?"

"You can say 'I love you,' and mean it. You can say, 'Yes, Alexander, I'd be delighted to marry you' so I don't worry that I've misunderstood something. Then you can promise me that you won't disappear tomorrow."

"There are a great many things I don't know," I say. "But I think I can safely say that I won't leave tomorrow. In fact, if I have my way, we'll never be apart again."

"It's not exactly what I told you to say, but close enough." He spins around and faces the people who still can't seem to speak or look away. "I'd like to introduce you to my fiancée, the stunning, the magnificent, the deliciously beautiful—"

As much as I'd love to hear him say my name, I can't risk word of his marriage to me reaching Isis. "Roxana of Sogdia."

Alexander barely misses a beat. "I am still learning the proper inflection of her name, so pardon me. Yes, my stunning bride, Roxana of Sogdia."

If I expected everyone to start speaking now that they realize I'm a woman after all, I'd have been disappointed. But I don't feel sad or upset at all, because in that moment, Alexander kisses me again, and I forget everything but the feel of his arms around me.

❧ 19 ❧

ANCIENT EGYPT

"Was this a mistake?" I've lost all perspective. It's hard to know whether you're making the right choice when you want something so very badly. "We can turn around." I close my eyes, trusting Dove to pick a safe path during my moment of panic.

"We've been through this," Alexander's voice is soft. "Shu believes he's sincere, and I agree. After talking to you about the things he's done, and even knowing there may be more revelations ahead of us, everyone agrees that above all other things, your father loves you. If you're going to marry someone he hates, you ought to at least invite him to the ceremony."

Dove stumbles and my panic momentarily balloons. Are we about to fall? Am I going to have a split lip or a broken arm on my wedding day? I open my eyes, but it was nothing. An awkwardly-shaped rock. A dip in the hard packed dirt of the, well, sort of the road to Babylon. "That's exactly what worries me." I sigh. "We aren't just inviting him. We're letting him *throw* the wedding. I'm trusting the man who lied to me with the organization of the entire thing."

"You can't get married without your family," Shu says.

He's right—it's more than just Dad. His lieutenants are my family. Bastet, Anat, Mehen, Am-Heh, Tefnut, Imhotep, Horus, Anubis—and many more. They all want to see me wed, even if they dislike the person I'm marrying. "They better be supportive."

"I'll be okay with Ptah hating me," Alexander says. "It sucks to lose."

He's been cracking jokes about him ever since Shu told him Dad tried to set us up.

I laugh. "As if he was ever a real option."

"Even Ptah is helping out. I hear he's making the wedding altar and bower," Shu says. "They're all trying."

Which is why we're going. I'm just hoping it's not a big mistake.

"What about your mother?" I ask. "Are you going to be upset that she missed it?"

Alexander's sigh is so gusty that it startles Dove. Bucephalus, of course, doesn't miss a beat. Then again, he's surely following the conversation. To Dove, it's all just noise. I'm a little surprised that Alexander rides him, but Bucephalus insists that he prefers his animal form and is happy to serve. It is one more layer of protection should anyone attack.

And who am I to argue? I want to keep Alexander safe more than anyone.

"So that's a yes? You're upset?" I knew it.

He laughs, and this time Dove dances sideways. She should be used to it by now. Alexander does everything big. "I've told you half a dozen times. My mother's relationship with me has always been complicated. She loves me, but she can't help trying to control me. She'd gain no joy from attending my wedding to her enemy's child, especially since I swore to her that my future father-in-law was dead."

I still feel guilty about that. I asked him when we had only just met to lie to his own mother.

And he did it.

"I chose you then, you know." He smiles. "Up until then, no one mattered more to me than my mother."

Bucephalus neighs.

Alexander pats his neck. "Except my devoted friends, of course." He shifts Bucephalus a bit closer to me. "But from the moment we met, I've known that you would change everything, and you did. My life is so much better with you in it. I don't lament the path I've taken to get here. And I won't regret that my mother can't attend our wedding. It's her own fault."

"But surely we can't keep my identity hidden forever."

"We aren't." He grins. "You're Roxana, remember? Daughter of one of my regionally appointed satraps."

"I'm a nobody," I say.

"Let's hope she buys it," Shu says.

"I don't care whether she buys it or not." Alexander's shoulders straighten. "I won't even tell her it's happened until it's done. Besides, she's too busy enjoying her new position as queen of the world back in Greece. She won't bother to come here, halfway to the end of the world, to see what new lands I'm conquering. Trust me."

I hope he's right. Because if she did show up, things could get much worse. Dad has made it clear he can't or won't kill her, and of course I don't want him to either. I can't even imagine how bad it would make things between me and Alexander if my father killed his mother.

At least our ride into Babylon is uneventful. When we ride through the main gates—I knew Dad had basically taken over when we arrived, but I had no idea he would go so far for my wedding. The buildings that comprise the town of Babylon are beautiful. Domed ceilings. Stained glass. Works of unbelievable beauty created by combining telekinetic, elemental, and even a bit of assimilator powers.

But the Earth elementals outdid themselves dressing everything up to a whole new level.

Roses cascade along each of the stone fences.

Lilies bloom profusely in perfectly symmetrical clusters under every window.

Flowering vines, blossoming trees, and brightly colored shrubs frame up every formerly bare section of the route to the palace in ways I never thought possible. Butterflies and birds flit and call and swoop in and out of the landscaping. To crown it all, as we reach the entrance to the palace itself, a dozen swans float in the central fountain, their snowy wings and graceful necks even more notable for their rarity here.

My father steps out from behind the palace doorway and raises his hands. "Alexander the Majestic, Alexander the Powerful, Alexander, son of Isis, welcome to Babylon. It is my absolute joy to host the wedding between you and my beloved daughter, Sekhmet."

It's a lovely speech, but only two things really matter. First, his smile is genuine. And second, he called my fiancé Alexander, as I asked. Apophis was the name his mother gave him. Alexander is the name he chose for himself when she made him masquerade as a child of Philip of Macedon. Dad has never referred to him as Alexander, and the fact that he's willing to do that, that he's willing to accept Alexander on his own terms, means he's willing to accept my choices too.

I slide from Dove's back and run to him.

When Dad's arms go around me, an audience of people I hadn't even noticed were present cheer, loudly. "I'm so glad you're home." He holds me longer than he ever has, but it's still not quite long enough. "I hope this is the wedding of your dreams."

I hear the subtext. He's still not sure about Alexander, but he's willing to hope.

"The ceremony will be simple, as you asked," he says.

We insisted that we keep it to no more than fifty people, including Alexander's closest friends and Dad's. Even the thought of that many people knowing the truth terrifies me to my very core. If any of them betray us. . .I can't think about it. I won't. We know and love them all. None of them will tell Isis.

The next few moments are a blur of activity. It's my own fault. I was so nervous about this whole thing that I insisted on having the ceremony the day we arrived. Anat has prepared my wedding robes, and they're more beautiful than I expected they would be. I would have chosen golden or purple fabric, or perhaps a vivid red.

Shockingly, she chose white. If she'd told me that, I'd have objected, but looking at it now—it's pure, perfect, and utterly impractical. The smallest speck of dirt or dust will show immediately. But maybe that's what makes it so perfect? A marriage is something that must be practical and real and that lasts.

A wedding is different, though. It's a beautiful, perfect, shining moment in time where we take a bit to contemplate the future we have chosen to spend together.

Instead of being boring and clean and flat like I'd have expected of white, this shade is full of dimension. It looks as if every color of the rainbow shimmers from its depths. Everyone knows that black represents all the colors mixed and that white is the absence thereof, but looking at this rich, buttery fabric, I'd almost believe the opposite is true.

"I would never have imagined this color would be so beautiful," I say.

"It's simple—the gown isn't meant to be the highlight of this moment, you are. You don't need much to showcase your unicity. You're stunning in your own right. I wanted something that showed both how good you are and how powerful. I hope this does that."

She wraps the fabric around me artfully, sweeping it sideways and then twisting it around and pinning it in place with a bright blue gem.

"What's that?" I shake my head. "It's not mine."

"It is now," she says. "You're supposed to get married with something old and something new. I've given you one of each."

"You didn't need to do all this." My lower lip wobbles.

"You're joining yourself to another person to create your own family." Tears well in her eyes. "You should have your mother with you." Her delicate brows pull together. "Ra says he confessed that Isis is my sister. The very person who deceived your mother and turned her against you is my twin." She wipes her eyes. "I'm sorry there wasn't a better person to help you."

I hug her, crushing the delicate white fabric between us. "You're a better mother than Hathor, and you chose to take care of me. That makes you *more* special to me."

She breaks down and bawls then. Perfect, pristine,

always-put-together Anat cries like her heart is breaking.

"He's a good person," I say.

She breathes in and out several times and crushes my hand with hers. "He's my nephew, you know."

I hadn't even thought of that. "That's. . .wonderful." So he does have some family here, even if he didn't realize it.

She tells me about everything I've missed in the month I've been gone while she does my hair. It takes much longer than I expected, but when she's finished, my hair looks marvelous.

"This looks absolutely perfect," she says, but then she frowns. "Did you realize you have a blemish here?" She touches the side of my nose. Trust Anat to notice that I've got a zit on my wedding day.

"It's all the sweaty riding," I say. "Sometimes there's not much you can do about it."

Her lips curl up. "There's always something *we* can do."

Duh.

I spin sideways and approach the polished bronze plate Anat has on her wall. For a moment, I don't recognize the woman standing in front of me. With a floor-length white robe, draped perfectly over my body, I look more like Anat than myself. My hair adds to the effect, with cascading curls that ripple and shine. Compared to all that, I doubt anyone will notice the small spot, but I suppose I'll know it's there. I lean close enough to see it and pull on my reservoir, but more than one reverberates with energy. The blue stone Anat gave me is also a reservoir, and I was so preoccupied that I didn't even notice. Its capacity is much smaller, but it's there nonetheless.

A place to store energy is the most important thing

an Assimilator can own—it allows us to cast spells without having to siphon.

"That was my very first stone," Anat says. "And I want you to have it so that you'll always know you're loved by more than just Shu and Ra."

This time it's my eyes that fill with tears.

"Enough of this," she says.

"Not quite." Dad's standing in the doorway, as reserved and understated as ever. "I need to talk to my daughter for a moment."

"Of course," Anat says.

Anat leaves, but Dad's still standing in the doorway. He must be *nervous*. That's a first, but then again, the last time I saw him, I was so angry I could barely form words and all of the ones I could form emerged as shouts.

"I'm still upset that you worked a spell on me." I can barely force the words out. "And that you lied about it."

He swallows.

"However, Shu has been a pretty consistent advocate of yours. He insists that there's nothing wrong with me, and that while what you did was probably not morally sound, I turned out alright. He also says that you lied because you were afraid of losing me, and that I can't fault you for that."

Dad's mouth opens and my anger rushes back. I don't think I can stand it if he starts making more excuses.

"What do you want?" My hands clench at my sides.

I've never seen his eyes—anyone's eyes—look quite so broken.

"I didn't lie because I was afraid of losing you." Dad sighs. "I was afraid *for* you, that you might believe what Isis convinced your mother is true, that you're not good because of what I did." There are lines around his eyes, like my departure has aged him. I know he could erase them, but he hasn't done it.

"Sit down." I gesture to the chairs in the sitting area of my room, and he sits. I remain standing, because I have things to say, now that he's here. "You don't get to pull at my heartstrings with all this mopey, sad, decrepit stuff." I cross my arms. "I know you're still Ra, energy vampire, destroyer of worlds, eater of souls, god of the sun. You still command power beyond what anyone else on earth does, so don't pretend to be all weak and old."

He laughs. "Sometimes you really remind me of your mother." But he's not sad when he says it. His eyes sparkle, almost like he misses her. I haven't spent much time thinking about it, but I'll bet he does. He still says she was the love of his life.

"I don't really remember her anymore," I say. "I mean, little things here and there, impressions, but not a lot of details."

"She should never have left you. It was the biggest mistake of her life."

"Not leaving you?" My mouth curls up on one side.

He shrugs. "If I were her, I'd probably never have liked me in the first place."

"Dad, I hope it wasn't a mistake for me to come here." I sit next to him. "You're not going to ruin this wedding, right?"

He takes my hand and traces the back of my fingers. "Your hand was so small when you were born that it could barely wrap around my smallest finger."

"That's not an answer," I press.

He drops my hand and turns to face me. "You'll have no cause to regret coming here, I swear on my love for you."

"What do you need to say, then?"

His brows draw together, and he breathes in and out several times as if steeling himself for something he has dreaded. "I just want to be positive that you're *sure* about this."

I groan. "Dad."

"No, you're misunderstanding what I'm saying. I'm not arguing with you or trying to dissuade you." He pats my hand. "You didn't talk to me about him, and Shu assures me you've met him several times. I suppose I know the times. You didn't hide that you were going to see him, for the most part, but I didn't understand how involved you were or how vested. I didn't know how deeply you'd connected."

"What are you saying, then?"

"You care for him, and he cares for you, that much is clear." He pauses. "But I've cared for a great many people over the years and—"

"I'm not you."

"I completely understand that, and your feelings run deep. I'm not arguing with that, but are you *positive* you want to marry him? Are you *positive* that he's the right man for you? You haven't spent much time with him."

"You said you and mother fell in love while she was torturing you—and that took place over a short period."

"That's true," he says. "But we had both lived quite a long life, and we knew what we wanted."

"Neither Alexander nor I have ever loved anyone before," I say. "That means everyone thinks we don't know our own minds."

He shrugs.

"It's not just physical attraction that draws me to

him, or the excitement of being around someone noto-rious, or powerful, or handsome."

"Could it be the pull of the forbidden? Because there's no way that his mother will ever—"

I shake my head. "That's actually been our biggest issue. I would have told you about him long ago if Isis hadn't been his mother."

"And I would have been happy for you, but I can't say I'm delighted that your future spouse's mother is probably the one person on earth most likely to try and kill you."

"Is there any chance that you might patch things up with her?" I wave my hands. "Not romantically, but just so that you could be in the same room?"

"She lied to me, tried to manipulate me, turned my best friend against me, and sent him after me, forcing me to kill him. After all of that, she sent a continual round of armies against me, all because I refused to have children with her and then had them with someone else." His chuckle is mirthless. "I don't see us making peace any time soon."

He doesn't say he can't forgive her.

"Look, if you're absolutely positive that this is what you want, and if you understand that you are *always* welcome with me, no matter what happens, no matter when, I'll support you wholeheartedly."

The tendrils of doubt and anxiety that had wrapped themselves around my heart die, freeing me to breathe again. "I am. I haven't lived long, but no matter how long you live, loving someone is always a leap of faith, and I believe Alexander will catch me."

Dad studies my face for a moment and nods. "Then I should let you know about the gift I've prepared for your wedding."

"But this whole thing—" I gesture around. "It's already too much."

"It was nothing at all," he says. "As I'm sure you already know, I didn't do any of it. Anat coordinated wardrobe and decorations. Food was handled by Imhotep. Mehen managed security. Am-Heh coordinated lodgings, and Tefnut handled anything we forgot. Innumerable other people were giddy to step in and lend a hand."

"Please tell me that they don't all know—"

"None but the individuals you named know who Alexander really is."

I breathe a heavy sigh of relief.

"But none of those things constitute a suitable gift from the God of the Sun for his daughter's wedding." He smirks.

"What does?" Now I'm intrigued.

"It's more a sequence of gifts, really." He waves around. "You said you wanted to travel. You and I both know that at some point, Isis is going to hear from someone that you're more than the daughter of a regional satrap, or she's going to stumble out here and discover who you are herself, so I'm giving you an extended alibi. You could even call it a honeymoon."

I don't understand.

"I've coordinated a mock battle at a place called Gaugamela, complete with paid off scribes and scholars who will tell the tale of Alexander's conquest far and wide. The great Alexander has won yet another prize, that of the entire Persian Empire. Our people will move along, and you will live in Babylon for a while. Once Isis grows insistent, Alexander will move on to the next place we've gone, and so on, and so on, so you can put her off indefinitely as he expands the reach of his empire."

"Dad, how could that—"

"You don't understand Isis. As long as Alexander is adding to her glory, as long as he's doing her bidding, she won't suspect a thing. So you'll keep 'conquering' new places, and she'll hang back in Greece or Egypt where she won't be inconvenienced."

"And Alexander and I can avoid any kind of confrontation."

"You can also see me as often as you'd like." His voice is soft, his eyes downcast. "Or not, as you choose."

I slide closer and hug him then, and his big arms wrap around me immediately.

"I'm so sorry, cub. Sorry that I let you down. And more than anything else, I'm sorry that I lied."

"It's alright," I say. And I mostly mean it.

Not long afterward, I walk with my dad around the corner, my hand on his arm. People are already gathered when we move into the transformed courtyard. Birds call and swoop overhead. Swallows. Hawks. Jays. Even parrots. The fabulous decorations of the Earth Called cover every arbor, archway, and nook. Flowers of all kinds bloom, with butterflies and bees buzzing around them.

"Sekhmet." Alexander's voice is soft, but it's clear, even over the sounds of the wildlife around us.

The people we've invited line the walkway on both sides, Alexander's friends mixing with ours. All Dad's commanders are present, as well as a few of his house servants. Imhotep. Ammit. Horus. Tefnut. Anubis. Ptah. Bastet. Am-Heh. Anat. Even Mehen, his arms crossed and his eyes flashing. Clearly he's not excited about the wedding, but when he meets my eyes, even he forces a smile.

Alexander's closest friends are present too, from

Hephaestion and Bucephalus to Cassander, his wife, Alexander's half-sister Thessalonike, Antigonus, Seleucus, and his dear friend Ptolemy. Even his old teacher, Aristotle, has traveled all this way to witness his marriage to the daughter of his worst enemy.

Finally, after what feels like far too long, I'm standing by Alexander's side. The embroidery on his robes, the heft of his exposed biceps, the curl in his hair, the beautiful straps of his new sandals, it's all perfect. But I can't really look anywhere but at the serene, perfect sky blue of his eyes.

"You're sure your dad is willing to officiate?" Alexander scrunches his nose. "Because if not—"

"He's happy for us," I say.

"One parent out of four," he jokes, "is better than none, I guess."

It hits me then, how sad this whole thing is. Our closest friends are here, and my father and brother and half-sister, but Alexander's mother can't even find out we've married, or she'll try to kill me. I wonder whether he's had someone sit him down and ask whether he's totally sure, like my dad did with me.

I was a little irritated with my dad, but he was watching out for me. I'd hate to have Alexander resent me down the road—the long road we'll have to travel just to get space from his insane mother.

My dad climbs the steps until he's standing half a dozen feet away, but directly in front of us. "As most of you likely already know, marriage is when two people choose to join themselves together as one. They become a family, standing together against the world, often raising children together. There are plenty of circumstances in which the couple being married isn't in love." He pauses and looks from Alexander to me, holding each of our gazes. "This isn't one of those.

Against all odds, against all reason, these two people love one another enough that they're choosing to join. It makes me wonder, skeptic though I am, about the existence of fate."

I swallow. Hard. Dad's actually saying interesting things, but something else matters more. I whisper, "Are you positive this is what you want?"

Alexander's head shifts slightly, his hiss even softer than mine. "Are you kidding?"

"If any part of you is unsure—"

His laughter is as beautiful as it ever is.

"Is there something I should know?" Dad doesn't look amused. Suddenly I feel four years old.

Alexander doesn't, apparently. "It's not customary for the groom to speak during a wedding ceremony," he says, "but I think you'll agree this isn't a normal situation."

Dad's grudging nod gives me hope. Perhaps he's starting to see what I love so much.

Alexander turns to face the gathered crowd, but his eyes are all on me. "My beautiful bride just asked me if this is really what I want. I imagine she's not the only one to wonder, given that my mother is most notably not present and we've sworn you all to secrecy about the ceremony." He sighs. "It feels like it was a very long time ago, but it's been less than three years since I met this woman for the first time, in Gordion. Not long after, I met her there again, and I told her boldly that marriage was not for me." He laughs. "Fate likes to make us into fools."

This time I laugh, too. It's surely true.

"We were both acutely aware each time we met that we could never fall in love or get married or have a family. It could never be the two of us against the world, because the world was already split into two great powers and we were on opposite sides. Neither of us had any interest in betraying our generals, so. . ." He throws his hands up in the air. "It was doomed from the start."

Everyone falls silent.

"A wedding of the daughter of Ra, a marriage of the son of Isis, either of those things would normally warrant huge, epic events, celebrated across city and state boundaries, fêted for days. Tributes would be sent from all foreign rulers." His voice drops and softens. "Instead, we're here with only our most trusted allies." He chuckles. "Is it any wonder that my bride is a bit unsure of me?" He reaches into his pocket and fumbles around briefly until he finally produces a beautiful, vibrant red stone the size of a plum. "This was my mother's most prized possession. She has a long story about where she found it, but if I had to guess, I'd say she stole it from Ra." He glances at my dad, who can't stop staring at his hand. "I had a replica made from a smaller receptacle that I disguised to take the place of this one. I'm not sure quite how long it will take her to recognize that the real one is gone, but eventually her search will lead to me."

I don't understand.

"This gift is my present to my bride on our wedding day. It's a gift fit for someone as powerful as her, but it's also symbolic. Neither of us would change sides, so we could never come together. Until today."

What is he saying?

His voice this time is only for me. "When my mother discovers what we've done, I stand with you, always with you, always by your side." He bows his head and then straightens with a smile.

The man who set out to conquer the world was conquered instead—by me.

"I can't imagine anything I say would be better than that," Ra says. "So, by the power that was inexplicably given to me, by my authority as a ruler of men, I hereby join this man and this woman together in marriage and wish them all the blessings of Earth on their union."

The weight of the rock in my hand is heavy, and I know Alexander's change of heart isn't enough to protect us from future conflict and pain. But when Alexander kisses me, I forget my worries and my fears and I sink into the joy of the moment. When you're not sure how much time you'll have, you must appreciate every bit of it.

EARTH

Grief isn't like a road, stretching out before you, inviting you to walk a long and straight path until you've reached your destination. It's more like the ocean: vast, limitless, full of darkness and evil creatures waiting to eat you alive. It crashes over you in waves, each of them desperately trying to drown you.

The only way to get through it is to paddle your way to the surface over and over and over.

Unless you decide it's too hard.

The thought of giving up, giving in, always beckons. The fastest and easiest way to end the pain. The only thing that guarantees I won't have to keep paddling, keep sputtering, and keep coming up desperate for air over and over.

Jesse has been gone for weeks, now. I should be far past denial and anger, and well on my way through depression or maybe even bargaining.

Except I got stuck on denial, for way too long. I wonder how many people, in my place, would have stayed in denial. I wish I had been there a little longer.

There's a beauty in believing something is good, even if it's predicated on a lie. Isn't that the whole premise of diet food? Of slimming mirrors? Or what about all the face creams and beauty products that people buy? They pay good money for those things because they're supposed to fix their problems. They'll make us thin and beautiful and young.

We all want a chance to turn back the clock.

Except the clock can't be reversed.

The dead can't be healed.

My brother is dead and gone and no amount of denial or bargaining or rage can change that fact.

Another wave crashes over me, and I'm not sure I even want to paddle. Isis is coming with an army to destroy us. She's currently holding the power of billions of women in her metaphorical hands, so I should care about things, about life and living and moral imperatives.

I may be the only one who can fix the world's problems.

But I'm tired of having to fix things.

The one thing I needed someone to repair couldn't be fixed.

My brother's life was the cost of awakening my powers so I could save a bunch of people who probably didn't deserve his sacrifice. People who mistreated us. People who are greedy and selfish and ignorant. People I don't even know and never will.

Jesse would tell me that my obligation to do the right thing isn't eliminated because the people who need my help aren't worthy. He would say that if I'm the only one who can stop a great evil, then it becomes my responsibility, no matter the cost. But, oh, the cost. Another wave crashes over me.

I think about his lopsided smile. His squinty eyes.

His silly, self-deprecating humor. I think about how he could look at a computer program and somehow comprehend what was going on, and not only that. He drilled down to the problem with it and fixed it. I think about the times we sat and laughed in the theater at bad plots, or marveled at the beautifully woven stories. We liked them all, because our enjoyment of those movies came not from the filmmaker, but from our own experiences and our shared history.

A history I now share with no one.

I'm reliving memories only *I* have.

The one person who always protected me did what he always did, and I failed to protect him when it mattered the most.

Someone's pounding on the door again.

I ignore it for a while.

Something's jammed into the lock and the door's thrust open.

I Lift to slam it shut and then I Bind it in place. "Go away."

"Alora." John's voice pleads with me. He has come by the most. "You need to eat something, at least."

"Go. Away."

"You were doing fine before," he says. "What happened?"

I ignore him.

Finally he listens. He leaves.

Someone taps on the window next. Are they kidding?

"Sekhmet," Ra says. "Please let me in."

I don't even want to know how he's knocking on my third floor window. I'm guessing a wind elemental is involved. "Go away."

"Alora," he says. "I'm sorry for using the wrong name. Please talk to me."

He's sorry for using the wrong name? It's a blatant manipulation. He's trying to gently remind me I'm not alone, and that we have a shared history. The fact that he thinks I wouldn't immediately spot his attempt shows how little he knows *me*, Alora Benson. I'm not his daughter, the optimistic princess who was raised with a silver chamber pot. I'm not the naive little girl who hoped for the best in everything and everyone.

She would likely already be leading the charge to save the world.

Too bad for Ra. He's stuck with the broken, jaded, foster-home facsimile of her. I'm not saving anyone. I can't even save myself. I'm broken beyond repair.

Huh. Maybe I am smack in the middle of depression after all.

"Alora," Kahn says.

I ignore him too.

"Alora, I've remembered more things. Please let me in."

Nice try, buddy.

"I remembered our wedding," he says. "And the night after."

My heart thunders in my ears. Is he serious, or is he lying? Ra could have told him we got married. He could be making this up to get inside and plead with me to strap on my armor to fight Isis. "What did you give me as a wedding gift?" It's the first time I've said anything but 'go away.'

"My mother's largest receptacle stone."

He did remember.

Or Ra could have told him that, too. "What was Shu wearing?"

"I don't recall. I wasn't looking at him."

He's probably lying. "What color were my robes?"

"White, but not a flat white. It had silver and gold

and other colors woven into the fabric. Made with magic, probably, but no magic I'd seen before."

I sit up in bed, the fury of the ocean waves receding slightly. "What do you want?"

"I want to see you," he says. "Once I'm sure you're alright, I'll leave you alone, I swear it."

My legs shake and nearly buckle when I stand, but I make it to the door, barely. My hand trembles as I turn the knob.

The second I see his face, I know he wasn't lying. He does remember, and just like me, he's different in the present than he was then. More uptight, more tightly wound, and a little bit broken. Modern day Earth has been easier in some ways, but harder in many others. Instead of knowing his mother, Kahn lost his parents quite young. Instead of being celebrated, or being taught how to use his powers, he didn't even know he had half of them.

And instead of meeting me with an army at his back, he locked me in a holding cell, concerned I was going to destroy the entire world.

But even still.

There is no world in which we are enemies.

For the first time, possibly ever, I believe those words. Ra may let me down or manipulate me. Everyone else has some kind of agenda, some kind of angle that affects how we interact, but not Kahn. When I told him that if he stuck to what he believed, he would lose me over it, he walked away. Alexander might have stayed by my side no matter what.

Kahn won't go against what he believes just because I demand it.

I thought that was bad, that John was right for following me, but now I see how wrong I was. I need someone with principles, someone who will tell me the truth, no matter what I want. But someone who is never, ever my enemy. Someone who will never let anything come between us.

I need someone like Jesse. I need an anchor, because right now, I'm capsized. The whole world is upside down.

He reaches for me and I collapse in his arms, sobbing on his shoulder. His arms encircle me, tightening exactly the right amount. I don't feel trapped, but I know he's there. For the first time since I admitted that Jesse was gone, I don't feel so utterly bereft.

"Can I ask what set this off?" His voice is muffled a bit by my hair. "You seemed fine right after you found out. I mean, maybe not fine, but you were playing fetch with, er, with the dog. . ."

I played with the dog I inadvertently stole. Everyone thought I was handling the news well, and then when I went to bed, I refused to come out again. I've been hiding in my room ever since like a complete lunatic, refusing any food or conversation.

Ignoring the existence and threat posed by a power-hungry nut job who's already halfway to world domination.

"Every single time I go to sleep, I remember things. Memories from my past life, same as you." I lift my face upward so he can see me. I must look absolutely horrifying.

"You're with Shu, and then you wake up, and he's still gone."

He understands. He may be the only one who really can. "It's like I'm me, but I'm not me. When I'm asleep, when I'm in the memory, I'm not conflicted. I'm this girl who didn't have a traumatic upbringing."

Kahn's eyebrows draw together in a frown. He

brushes my hair back from my face and tucks it behind my ear. "I do know just what you mean. My parents died in a tragic accident that I sort of caused, and I was woken and thrown into a world I hated. Even on Terra, my parents died when I was young, leaving me an orphan. It shapes you—someone might even argue it warped me." His smirk warms my heart. "But you're wrong about one thing." His hand trails down the side of my face, his fingers brushing against my jaw.

An electric current runs through me from my face right down to my toes. My lips part. My scalp tingles. My pulse pounds. All I want is for him to kiss me.

"Don't you want to know what you got wrong?"

Not really. I just want him. I lean toward him, my eyes intent on his mouth.

He lifts my chin upward.

Yes, kiss me. Kiss me!

But he doesn't. He waits until my eyes find his. "You aren't a monster, Alora. You're the furthest thing from it that I've ever seen. You're fiercely loyal. You're unbearably brave. You're brilliant and caring. And you're relentless in pursing your goals. I love all those things about you."

For a moment, it feels like my two lives tangle, and I fall against him, our lips finally making contact. Our bodies press together from chest to knee, and his hands press us tighter still. His mouth claims me, insistent and bold.

My dream ended after the wedding ceremony, but I can imagine what happened next. And if I keep going, soon I won't need to hypothesize. I leap upward, and he catches me, my legs wrapping around his waist. His ferocity only increases as he stumbles sideways. I realize in a haze that we're moving toward my bed.

Yes.

I want this.

I want him.

I need to feel something good, something bright, something joyful.

And Alexander always brings me joy.

But the word strikes me wrong: Alexander.

This isn't Alexander, and I'm not Sekhmet. We didn't just get married. We're not in Asia. We're in England, and this is Kahn. My brother didn't just drink the night away at my wedding.

He's dead.

Just as my back sinks onto the cushion of my mattress, I stiffen. I shouldn't be doing this. I'm just trying to numb my mind from the pain, and I like Kahn too much to use him like that. He's not a vat of ramen noodles, or a sappy romantic comedy on Netflix I can binge.

He should be enjoyed.

Savored.

Loved for who and what he is and the connection we have.

This is *wrong*.

He senses that something has changed and releases me, stepping back. "You okay?"

Tears roll down my face—one second after he was kissing me, I'm bawling like an insane woman. He settles next to me and gathers me against his chest. "Alora, it's alright."

"It will never be alright," I manage to say through fitful sobs.

"No, you misunderstand me. I'm not saying *you* should be okay. I'm saying it's alright that you aren't. I'm here for whatever you need, however long you need it."

I relax against him, spent, my tears turning his shirt

damp. I manage to suppress the grief wracking my body and almost eliminate the tears. They're barely leaking down my face when I say, "Can you tell everyone—"

When someone interrupts me by knocking, loudly, we both respond at the same time. "Go away," Kahn says. "Go away," I say as well. And we smile. There's absurdity all around me right now, even in the grief. Even in the misery.

"I'd love to leave you alone," Mehen says, "but this can't wait."

"What is it?" Kahn asks.

"Isis has some demands, but she won't make them until Alora joins us."

There really is no day so bad that it can't get worse.

"There's my other son," Isis says, when Kahn and I walk into the main conference room.

Her face on an 80-inch plasma screen is way, way too big, but she looks almost exactly as I remember her from my memory as a cat in Alexander's tent. Gorgeous, horrifying, diabolical, and far too *present* for just one person, especially since she's not even physically here.

Of course, the fact that her face is almost three feet tall isn't helping me see her as ordinary.

"I am not your son," Kahn says.

"You might be more my son than he is." Isis' smile is bemused, like she's enjoying some kind of witty repartee with an old friend. "You knew the real me, and we had decades together, whereas my time with John was cut so short. I didn't even realize who I was when I was raising him, or I'd have done a much better job."

John flinches, and I worry about how conflicted he must feel right now. The mother he loved utterly and completely is standing in front of him. Sort of.

As the villain.

Ra even looks conflicted—he's always been kind of a mess where Isis is concerned. If he'd just killed her when she sent his friend Osiris to eliminate him, none of this would be happening. I wonder if he feels at all culpable for the creation of Terra and all the fallout.

"We'll have plenty of time to catch up later. For now, I'll have to rely on my two handsome boys to convince Ra and his little family of the sincerity of what I'm about to say. As you may have discovered, even with the collapse of Terra, I was able to retain control of the link to the female Renders, Reapers, and Assimilators. For the first time in my life, I'm not limited by needing to physically touch another person in order to siphon energy, and let me tell you, it's *glorious*." She looks directly at Ra and shakes her head. "To think, you've lived like this your entire life. You don't even appreciate what you have."

"That power isn't yours to command," Ra says. "I never stole from anyone. I only took from those who gave it freely, or who posed a direct threat."

"Never?"

Ra scowls. "I may not have begun with such wholesome moral underpinnings, but as I grew, I created them for myself. As you have aged, your moral compass has only become more corrupted. Even so, I didn't expect this from you."

Her smile sends a shiver down my spine. "I'm sure you didn't expect anyone to become your equal." She arches an eyebrow. "Or are you most upset that someone is finally stronger than you?"

"You're leaving all those women vulnerable and unprotected, as you have for the past two plus millennia. You should be ashamed of yourself."

"You sound like my mother. She was always going on and on about how I should feel. I ignored her, too."

Ra narrows his eyes. "Speaking of your family, where's your sister?"

"Ah, darling Anat, your most loyal supporter." She shrugs. "Seeing as she's now tied to me, all her power in my hands—" She wiggles her fingers in front of her face. "I thought it best if she stayed close to my side. You've trained her to be a very good little lapdog."

Ra snarls. My reserved, calm, collected father actually snarls like an animal.

"What do you want?" John's voice is curt, abrasive even.

"Oh, my sweet little John. Tell me you're not angry with me, too."

"Anger doesn't begin to touch what I feel." John's practically shaking with suppressed rage. "Hatred isn't even a strong enough word. You think I would advocate for you? I don't even know you."

"I think that's unfair," she says, "I hadn't regained my memories or my powers while you were small. Thanks to the bungling of stupid Sekhmet, I was stuck in Erra without powers."

"Why Erra?" Ra asks.

Isis' smile is chilling. "You still don't know? She hasn't remembered?" She shakes her head. "She thrust me into the mechanism—bound somehow to the structure itself. I floated there, in limbo, not aware of who or what I was, until I was reborn, my soul connected to a place from which I could never Wake on Earth. It was diabolical, really."

"But you're free now," Ra says.

"I couldn't free myself from there until *this one*—" She points at me. "—experienced some kind of trauma on Earth. For some reason, perhaps because it shifted the internal spell mechanism, that released me and my memories began to return."

"Are you saying that when I Woke, you were freed?" Jesse's death freed her?

She rolls her eyes. "No, idiot. I'm not sure what it was precisely—I was in a mental hospital at the time. But my husband was obsessed with your brother, sure he would be a powerful Lifter who held the key to deciphering the prophecy. I'm not sure *what* set me free—I know from Devlin's idiotic letters that you were in a group home, and then you ran. That's around the same time my memory returned."

John blinks. "Before that, you didn't know who you were?"

"Of course not," she snaps. "But the memories flooded back as soon as I was released from Erra."

"You could Assimilate then?"

"Of course. And I'm not a terrible mother. I checked in on you from time to time. That's when I gave you the power to Lift as well." She pauses. "You're welcome."

"*You* changed me?" His voice has dropped to barely a whisper. "Why?"

"I was tethered, when I was reborn into *Erra*. A more useless place I can't imagine. Like fools, the elementals split into warring factions. I suppose thanks to my location, you were stuck as an Elemental. But as to why I gave you that power—I wanted to see whether I could still alter the makeup of a person's being with a spell," she says. "I knew making you an Assimilator was a stretch, but your father could Lift." She shrugs. "I figured if I was going to expend all that power to see what I could do, it might as well benefit me."

She experimented on her own son, not to help him, but to test her abilities.

"I realized immediately that if anyone noticed

what I'd done, they'd quickly track it back to me. That's why I suppressed your new ability—put a lid on it, so to speak. At that point, I'd already faked my own death. I couldn't have them realizing who I really was, not before Terra was unwound by the stupid Warden."

"You let everyone think you had died." John shakes his head. "I still don't understand why."

"The woman I was *did* die, John. The mother you knew was weak. She was a victim. When my memories returned, I had no need for that false persona." Her shoulders straighten. "Isis has never been a victim, and once I regained knowledge of who and what I was, I turned you into something extraordinary. You should be thanking me."

"You're insane," I say. "You risked his life in order to confirm you were still powerful, without his consent, and then you hid what you did to keep yourself safe. You let him believe his mother had died because it was more convenient for you. What part of that should he be thanking you for?"

Isis' nostrils flare and her eyes widen.

"Mother, why don't you just tell us what you want," Kahn's voice is steady and strong. He distracted her, so she didn't try to do something awful to me. I doubt she could do much through a television screen. I almost wish she'd tried.

"Don't you have some questions for me, too, my darling Apophis?"

He shakes his head. "I'm not Apophis, I'm Kahn. I've led a completely different life, and I have no desire to deny who I've become in the here and now."

"A completely different life you say. . .and yet you're standing right next to Sekhmet, even in this lifetime. Don't you find that curious?" She lifts her eyebrows.

"Don't you find it *strange* how many things have happened in a similar way?"

John grunts. "What *I* find strange is you, acting like you mean anything to any of us. You said it yourself. My mother died—you are not her. You're a problem to be solved, an error to be righted. You're a blight. Tell us what you want, so we can end this call."

She laughs, long and strong. "I admire your spirit, my sweet John, but there's no way to defeat me. I'm much stronger than the conflicted and confused teenager with you. I'm stronger than the old, wizened Ra who came to support her as well."

She might be right. She created Terra, and she controls the women who fueled it. Which means. . .can she recreate it? It's the very thing the Followers of Isis wanted all along.

In the past two thousand years, what has been improved by our inability to use our powers? Women have been subjugated and abused. Terrible men with and without powers have mistreated one another and women and children alike. The entire premise on which the creation of Terra was predicated was a lie. And we bought it, hook, line, and sinker.

And the woman who created that false construct is right here, threatening us all over again.

"Isis, please tell us what you want," Ra says. He sounds tired. More tired than I've ever heard him sound.

"It's cute that you keep calling it what I *want*. What I want is to have my two sons by my side. What I want is to have subjects who adore me, who serve for the joy of giving me what I desire." She shrugs. "I may never have any of that, but I've grown accustomed to not having what I want. But what I *demand* is the complete and total surrender of Ra and his daughter Sekhmet, or

Alora, or whatever name she goes by these days. Once you've both been executed, then I can worry about what I want."

John's fists clench. The muscle in Kahn's jaw works. Ra's eyes flash. Mehen and Am-Heh and Ammit shout various swear words in Egyptian. If she were here physically, they'd be attacking her—that much is clear. Obviously no one thinks that our deaths are a great option. But I'm wondering why she thinks we might accept that demand.

"What are you offering in exchange?" I ask. "Because you're asking for the death of the two people most able to enforce the terms of any bargain we make."

Her eyes meet mine and she smiles. "So this new Sekhmet has thoughts and opinions of her own."

"I've always had my own thoughts and opinions," I say, "but I'm not surprised that you never paid attention to them."

"What I'm offering is quite simple. Starting twenty-four hours from now, at six in the evening my time, which is ten a.m. for you in London, I will kill a hundred thousand people. I will start in Seattle, where I'm currently located, and continue to eliminate people in one-hundred-thousand-person batches until the entire population is gone. When you surrender, I'll stop. It's that simple. The math works like this." She lifts her right hand. "Two lives." She lifts her left hand. "Or several billion."

"You can't kill people so easily," Ra says. "You don't have the same power Sekhmet and I have, even with your theft from all those women."

"Is that so?" Isis sighs. "I wondered whether a demonstration would be necessary. Well, just remember that you asked me to do it." She closes her eyes and exhales briefly. She frowns, and then she grits her teeth, and then she opens them again. "It's that simple for me. The only hard part is pinpointing the exact geographic area where the people are located. That has taken some getting used to."

"You're telling me that you just. . .did what?" I ask. "Killed people in Seattle?"

"Don't be ridiculous," Isis says. "How would you verify that? No, I'm starting here with my demonstration because it's close, and because you probably knew people here. Our records show you lived here for years as a child."

I blink.

"What I just did, as easily as closing my eyes and focusing, was kill eighty thousand or so women in London. *That* you can verify."

"You what?" Mehen's eyes bulge.

"You asked me to show you why you should consider my offer," Isis says, her face a model of innocence. "I didn't have much choice."

"Your link to those women may allow you to drain them," Ra says, "but every time you do that, you weaken yourself in the long run. All we have to do is sit and wait while you eliminate every single person providing you with power."

"Eighty thousand, or even several million deaths, won't make much difference to me," she says. "If it comes to that, I'll travel all the way to London and kill everyone between you and me until I'm finally able to end you. I'm quite sure I can do it, once we're in the same location. The real question is how messy you'd like to make things before you die."

"And if I said I'd do it, but I had conditions?" I ask.

Again, nearly everyone in the room has an opinion

about that. I tune them out, but it's hard to hear over their shouts and screams.

"What specifically did you want from me?" Isis lifts one eyebrow. "I'm a reasonable lady."

All other evidence to the contrary. "I haven't agreed," I say. "And I'm not able to speak for my father in any case. But if we both travel to Seattle, I'd like the killing to be placed on hold the second we agree. It's not a quick trip to make, and I don't fancy the thought of people dying every hour while we make it. Secondly, I don't think we could surrender to someone who still has the power to tyrannize the entire world. You'd have to cede control of the billions of women you're holding hostage for us to even consider it."

She laughs. "The second I did that, you'd end me."

"Let's say we could work out a solution to that dilemma," I say. "Would you agree to it, if you were certain that we would die? Would you give up your control over every Reaper, Render, and Assimilator?"

The room falls silent while we wait for her response. "It's a difficult thing you ask," she says. "You worry about my tyranny, but I've never been a tyrant. In each circumstance when I've ruled, I've been fair and generous. But I'd be surrendering my power in exchange for a freedom from the fear that has always hounded my steps. That of your father, finally coming to destroy me. Am I more motivated by my underlying and long-held desire? Or by my fear?" She taps her lip, but finally, she shrugs. "Yes. If I could trust that you'd do as you promised, if I could be sure of your deaths, I would agree to release my hold on the women of Earth in exchange for the easy and clean death, in front of my very eyes, of Sekhmet and Ra."

"I think we all know what we need to know," I say.

"Thanks for calling." I Lift the remote for the transmission and press End Call. The screen goes black.

If I thought there was pandemonium before, I was wrong. What ensues after I cut the feed is sheer and complete madness. Mehen's shouting sets it in motion, but the local British leadership, who were standing at the back, and all of Dad's commanders, and also all my allies, from Martin to Thomas, from Henry to Rosalinde, whom I didn't even realize were present, are all shouting at one another.

I do what any reasonable Lifter would do and Bind their mouths shut. "While I appreciate the value and experience each of you provide, I think you'll agree that this is a decision that my father and I must ultimately make."

The bright red faces and the gesturing hands tell me that they don't agree at all. I'm past the point of caring. The local leaders chose us to rule. My friends should support my decision, as it's my life at stake, and my father's commanders should trust his judgment.

It's really only Kahn and, to a certain extent, John, whom I feel deserve a say, sort of, since it's their mother making the demands. And also, they love me. Or, I believe they do.

Regardless, the first person I need to talk to is my dad. So I Lift the people in the room all at once, and I float them out the door, one at a time, setting them down outside. Once the last two, Kahn and John, are removed from the room, I release them all.

And Bind the door shut.

Mehen and Kahn both try valiantly to get around my work, and although they're both quite skilled, they're no match for me in sheer power.

"That was quite a show of force," Dad says. "Against our allies, no less."

"We have a chance to end this," I say. "All of it. We have one chance to free the world and return things to the way they should be."

Dad says nothing.

"What do you think we should do?"

"It's clear what you think," he says, "and if she would be satisfied with only me, I would agree with you." He shrugs. "I would trade myself to her, even without your conditions."

I sense a 'but' coming.

"However."

Close enough.

"What I will not support is her demand that you die." He frowns. "I wish you hadn't ended the call so abruptly."

I shrug. "She won't accept you alone. You know that as well as I do."

"I won't accept your death." He crosses his arms. "It appears we're at an impasse."

Someone bangs on the door. Dad looks at me and frowns. "I thought that you—"

"This is someone new—not any of the people who were inside during the call."

"Your Most Divine," the person on the other side of the door shouts. "Most Divine!"

"Yes?" Ra asks.

I wonder whether he hates being called divine. It's so absurd.

"I hate to bother you—and I can see that you wish to be alone."

I almost laugh. What was his first sign? The Bound door? Or the dozens of people I locked outside?

"We're receiving reports of sudden heart attacks— hundreds of them already. People all over the city are just dropping dead. And they're all women."

Rage pulses through me.

"We didn't think she was bluffing anyway," Dad says.

I suppose not.

"Thank you," I say. "We know about that, and we're pursuing a solution. Unfortunately, there's very little we can do about those who have already died."

His gulp is so loud I can hear it on this side of the door.

"What do I tell the media who are calling about it?"

"Tell them we're under attack," Dad says.

"No," I say. "That will terrify people. An attack they can't defend against? An enemy halfway around the world?" It's hard enough that they don't have powers in a new world where everyone seems to be able to do something amazing. It's terrifying already. The last thing we need is rioting in the streets.

What's the least harmful thing they could believe, or perhaps the least distressing? "Tell them it's a side effect of the destruction of Rra, and that we are working to restore their powers and keep them all safe. Tell them we're aware of what's happening and are actively working to rectify it."

"Yes, Most Divine."

I sense it when he walks away.

"I know that she's distressed you with her talk of killing millions, but she's too sensible to kill off her own source of power for very long," Dad says.

"You really think we should wait it out?" I can't believe what I'm hearing. "You think we should let her kill all those people?"

"You take too much on yourself. She's the one doing it, not you." Ra shrugs. "I've come to understand, over a very long life, that we can only take responsibility for the things that we do, not for bad decisions made by others."

"But we have a way to stop it." I can't believe what he's saying. "Right now, my aunt Trina is merrily going about her business. She's probably at work, crunching the numbers she always crunches, or whatever it is that accountants do all day. She has no idea that tomorrow some lunatic will kill her."

"Only if she happens to be a Render or a Reaper," Dad says. "Which I suppose she could be, since she's not biologically related to you."

"I'm a Render," I say. "Even if she was related to me, she could be in a group of women who die." I pull my phone out of my pocket, relieved I grabbed it before leaving my room. "I should call her and warn her, at least. I can do that much. If I beg, she might leave."

I don't have her number saved, but a quick web search reveals the name of her company and its phone number. I press Call.

Dad reaches for my arm. "Don't call her. She doesn't deserve your help."

I can't believe he'd say that. "Every single person there deserves my help."

"She mistreated you," he says. "Badly."

"I was an unwanted obligation thrust upon her—"

"Kissinger Lebowitz," a receptionist says. "How may I direct your call?"

"Trina Benson," I say. "This is her niece." If Dad thinks she's so unworthy, he can't object to this test. If she takes my call, I'll tell her to get away from Seattle. If she declines it, she won't get a warning.

"You haven't heard?" The receptionist's voice sounds strange, almost like she pities me.

Am I too late? Did she already start killing people

around Seattle? If so, why is this woman calmly taking phone calls?

"Trina Benson was murdered," she says, "rather gruesomely."

What? I hate that my feelings are mixed about that. Ra wasn't wrong about how badly she treated me, and how hard she made my life. I hate her for abandoning Jesse and me to the state after her brother died. But she was dealing with her own grief, and I try not to be angry about it.

"Oh. Okay." I hang up.

Ra's face is stricken, when I turn again to face him. Like he already knows what I'm going to say. "She's dead." He's not surprised in the least.

"How do you already know that?"

A terrible pounding starts at the back of my head, like tiny men are taking turns banging on it with a sledgehammer. The bad news keeps piling up, and I'm beginning to think that some of this is Ra's fault.

"I killed her," he says simply.

In the same tone he might use to say, "we need eggs from the store." Or "we should go see the new super-hero movie." Not that he'd ever say any of that.

"You *killed* her?"

He sniffs and then he swallows, but he never looks away from my eyes. "After I awoke, I made it my study to discover the life you'd led here, without me."

A terribly uneasy feeling starts in my stomach.

"I found that your life had been far worse than unsatisfactory. It became quite clear why you clung to Shu so tightly. He was the only person in your life you could rely upon. He was the only person in your life who loved you, and who was loyal to you."

He's right, of course. "But you killed her?" The words don't feel real, somehow, like this is some kind of dream. Like nothing that's happening is *really* happening.

"Since you're asking, I'll confess. I killed her. I also killed the men who caused the accident that resulted in your adoptive parents' deaths. I restrained myself from killing your biological father, as I wasn't sure whether his death would minimize your trauma from his terrible parenting or exacerbate it. And finally, I killed the three boys who accosted you in that group home. All of those people caused you terrible pain, and they deserved to die."

He's still explaining in a tone that he might use to describe how he assembled a desk bought from Ikea. Like it's somewhat fascinating, but not at all morally horrifying.

In that moment, something becomes crystal clear to me.

My father is a monster.

As his creation, I probably am too.

"If I ask you to honor Isis' request and travel to Seattle—if I ask you to die with me, would you do it?"

He may have casually mentioned killing all those people who harmed me, but he's not casual now. His eyes are intent, his body taut, and his face is deadly earnest when he says, "Yes. If you ask that of me, I will do it. I have always given you everything you asked. And I always will, right to the end."

"Then I'm asking you." There have been so many things in my life I don't know the answer to, so many things I don't understand. But this one thing makes perfect sense. If giving our lives can spare even a hundred others, we should do it. It's basic math.

But in this case, it's even more of a landslide decision. If the sacrifice of two monsters will declaw another, and spare countless lives in the same event?

It's the right decision, hands down. Jesse would tell me to do it. I know he would.

"I have only one condition," Ra says.

I prepare for something that will obviate our plan to die, something that will undermine the entire thing.

"I want you to sleep on the decision. You heard Isis. She'll wait for us if necessary, holding off on any killing while we travel. I will spend the entire time you're sleeping looking for a solution to the issue of holding her to her vow to release the women she's controlling."

"It's a deal." Not a good one, but the right one. Sometimes that's the best thing on the table.

22

ANCIENT EGYPT

"Alexander!" I hope he can still hear me. He just left, but hopefully hasn't gone too far. I shout again, even louder. "Alexander!! Come quick!"

A half a moment later, he darts back into our bedroom, his eyes wide, scanning the room for danger. "What's wrong?"

I smile. "Nothing's wrong." My hand's on my belly. "But I think something is right." I wave him over.

His concern melts into irritation. "You know I don't want to go. I'd rather stay here with you, but the rumor is that Mother—"

I snatch his hand and press it to my belly. "I felt the baby kick. Not from inside my stomach, but right here." I bump on my belly again, like I did before. "I'm not totally positive, but I think the kick was a reaction to me sort of squashing him."

"Don't risk harming him." His eyes are riveted to my stomach, still wide, but this time with wonder.

I laugh. "Not a chance, but be still for a moment."

A minute passes by, and then another. But finally, there it is. His foot, I know, since I can sense him, presses against our hands. Alexander can sense him too, but this is different somehow, feeling the external evidence that he's growing stronger.

"He's going to be extraordinary," he says. "Just like his mother." He presses a kiss to my forehead.

I lean toward him, inhaling his scent. It's hard every time he leaves. I hate knowing he's going to be gone, but it feels harder now that I'm pregnant.

"Perhaps we tell her," I say.

He doesn't have to ask what I mean.

"It's been seven years." I look into his eyes. "I'm tired of all the traveling, and even worse, the lying."

"If anything, Mother's grown worse. She's snappy, she's demanding, and she's—"

"She's downright irritable all the time," a woman's voice says from the doorway.

It's a familiar voice, but I haven't heard it in the past two decades or more.

Alexander stiffens beside me. "Hathor. I had no idea you were coming."

"No, I guess you didn't," she says, "or I imagine your wife would have disguised herself to look like Roxana, like she did the last time Isis sent me with a message." My mother's eyes aren't angry, and they aren't unkind. They are, however, profoundly sad. "I suppose that's my fault."

"It is," Alexander says. "And I think you'll understand when I tell you that we can't possibly allow you to leave, now that you came unannounced and saw things you should never have seen."

"I have no desire to leave," Hathor says. "All I want to do is apologize to my daughter." Her eyes widen. "A grandchild?"

Her words couldn't be more surprising. "Apologize?"

"I'm afraid that when I left—" She throws her hands into the air. "Must we do this like this?"

I'm lounging on a settee, with Kahn leaning over me, his hands still contoured to my belly.

"I'm pregnant," I confirm. "I have no intention of moving to make this less awkward for you."

Alexander smiles at me broadly. He's always proud of me, even now that I'm pregnant and growly.

"I deserve that, I suppose," Hathor says.

"Say what you have to say," Alexander says.

Hathor crouches beside me, her eyes intent on mine. "Many years ago, Isis discovered me. She had me taught and trained. She helped me learn and grow and become something I might never have become without her help. When she sent me to do a task that I felt was just and right—to kill Ra, the Sun God, the man who had ruined Isis' life—I knew it was something that had to be done. Of course, you know that I fell in love with your father. I betrayed the woman who had taught me."

"I know the story," I say. "A few years and two kids later, you still felt bad about it, clearly."

"Isis had told me terrible things about your father, but I wanted to believe none of them were true. I was naive and hopeful. I thought she would hate me for my decisions, but when I happened upon her years later, she welcomed me. She cried with me over my difficulties and celebrated my success." Hathor pauses, her eyes drifting. "When I discovered that Ra had done the very things she accused him of doing. . .to our daughter. . ." She shakes her head. "Every time I looked at you, I felt like a fool. I had been lied to, I had fallen for his deceptions—I wasn't special like I thought. I had been used for my unique blend of powers. I couldn't stand the idea of staying with him for another second."

"And you didn't," I say.

"You should know that I wanted to take you with me, but I knew he would never allow it. He would have killed me, the woman he professed to love, to keep you by his side. I won't lie and say that didn't upset me deeply as well, the knowledge that my daughter had replaced me in his affections." She shakes her head. "What kind of mother is jealous of her own daughter?"

"Not a good one," Alexander mutters.

"Instead of trying to take you, which I knew I could never do, given your father's power, I tried to wound him instead." She looks down at her feet. "But I'm afraid that my attempts harmed you. I'm truly sorry for causing you to doubt yourself and your own value."

I sit up, dislodging Alexander's hands, but also straightening my shoulders. Showing her that, even though I'm to be a mother soon, I'm every bit as strong as I ever have been. "Enough people loved me, enough people treasured me, that I was able to move past your attempts to injure Dad and me." I pause. "You lost."

Her eyes meet mine again, and this time they're brimming with regret and pain. "I *have* lost, in so many ways. All of my woes are of my own making, but when I heard rumors of Alexander's baby, and rumors that his wife was not who she seemed, instead of reporting them to Isis, I kept them to myself. And when she called for a messenger to summon Alexander to her side, I volunteered."

"Now you'll be able to return to your *mentor*, and deliver the news that her enemy's daughter is wed to her own son. It's everything she's surely dying to know."

"That's not my plan," Hathor says. "Although I do still believe that your father is less of a hero and more a villain, I'm not here to betray you. I want good things for you, not bad. I do think that Isis would say the same. She might not approve of your connection to Ra, but she loves me in spite of mine."

"Now that you've divorced yourself from him, maybe," I say. "But I don't plan to stop seeing my father. I love him too much. He has flaws, yes, and he's a little overbearing, but he loves me and he protects me, always. That means that, no matter what, I'm an enemy to Isis, by the lines she has drawn herself."

Alexander stands. "I'm going to tell Hephaestion that you're here and rework our plans accordingly. I need to ascertain how you outstripped our information channels."

"May I stay with my daughter?" Hathor asks.

"That's entirely up to her," Alexander says. "If you knew her at all, you'd know that she makes all her own decisions, as well as most of mine." He's smiling when he walks through the doorway. Hephaestion's working with some new soldiers in the front courtyard, just outside my window.

No matter what excuse he gives, my sweet husband is really just giving me some space. Not so much that he won't hear me if I call for him, but enough that our interaction won't be distracted by him. It's tragic that he feels the need to keep me safe from my own mother.

His gentle reminder that Hathor doesn't know me wasn't even a jab at her, like she probably assumes. It was a reminder to me that I don't know her and that I shouldn't trust her.

As if I needed that.

"What do you really want?" I ask.

"To know you," she says. "To meet my grandson, and to be around my son again."

"You could always have seen Shu." I shrug. "You don't need me for that."

"Ah, but I do. When I sent for him after I left, he told me he won't so much as even write me until I make things right with you. In my attempt to wound your father, I lost both my children."

He never even told me that he cut her off, which is so *Shu* of him. "It must have hurt to lose the connection to the child you didn't despise," I say.

"I've never despised you." She drops to her knees. "It may take some time for you to forgive me, but I will do whatever it takes, even if you want me to walk away from Isis. Even if you want me to. . ."

"To what?" I arch one eyebrow. This should be good.

"To apologize to your father." The words seem practically ripped from her mouth.

"Let's not go crazy," I say. "No one expects miracles." But I feel myself softening, far sooner than I really should. Alexander's right. I don't know her at all. She left me when I needed her, and at best, she used me as a pawn to harm my father, if, as she insists, she didn't actually believe the words she spoke. At worst, she's lying, and she's here at Isis' insistence.

"Maybe we should take things one day at a time," I say. "You can stay here for a bit and get to know me some. I won't ask you to make any sweeping apologies to anyone, and you won't fault me for not trusting you."

"It's more than I hoped for, more than I had any reason to expect."

"Sekhmet!" Hephaestion almost never calls for me. What could he need?

Hathor's already standing. I struggle to my feet as quickly as I can and push past her. His call came from the front courtyard, where Alexander was headed.

No other sound emerges, no other shouts or cries, and I reach out with my senses. Two figures are lying prone on the ground, and one more is standing. They're all large. Before I have time to puzzle out anything else, I round the bend and see everything.

Alexander and Hephaestion are both on the ground, surrounded by growing pools of blood, their heads separated from their bodies.

For a moment, I can't move. I can't breathe. I can't tear my eyes away. I only stare, stupidly, at my husband and at his best friend, who just a moment before was calling my name. I finally cast about for the third person, shocked to see him floating away. Clearly the work of a Wind Called, or perhaps a group of them.

What really floors me is that the person floating away is Shu.

His robes are soaked in blood.

He's smiling at me as he escapes, after killing my husband.

After destroying my life.

He's nearly gone by the time my brain kicks in and I realize it can't possibly be Shu. He would never, not in a lifetime, not in an eternity, have done something like this to me.

It must be a disguise.

I reach for it, for him, and I wrap my whole brain around his or her appearance and then I *peel* as hard and as fast as I can. Shu's face, Shu's body, sloughs away, and just like that, I'm staring at a startled Mehen. My father's right hand. His closest companion. His personal bodyguard.

I start shouting then, for healers, for anyone who can help me, but I know it's already too late. You can't heal decapitation.

My father sent Mehen to kill Alexander, and Hephaestion was collateral damage.

It cuts me like a knife to the heart, like a burning poker to my belly, but I can't deny the truth: my father has betrayed me.

I sense my mother's presence at my back.

Her apology no longer warms my heart.

Nothing will warm my heart ever again, or that's how it feels. I ought to find out why. I ought to discover the motives, the reason my father would act *now*, after years of peace. Why would he send Mehen to kill Alexander? He should know that I'd discover him.

But even as the questions form in my brain, they're destroyed by an all-consuming rage. A fury that seems to grow and grow and grow, eclipsing anything else I feel or think or know. A fury fed by my pain, my loss, and my horror.

The only thing that will stem the tide of my madness is justice. "I want to meet with Isis," I say, softly. "Can you make that happen?"

Mother's startled, but after a moment, she nods. "Yes. I can arrange a meeting for you."

❧ 23 ❧

EARTH

Every single time I think that things can't possibly get worse, they do.

I should have known that something terrible caused me to shield myself from these memories. Ra told me that himself, in fact. He just neglected to mention that the awful thing I wasn't ready to remember was something *he* did.

I wonder whether he would have told me that he killed my husband.

How could I have been so wrong about what I thought I knew? Is my judgment that bad? I thought killing every person who ever mistreated me was bad, but this?

I know Kahn's alive, but that makes me wonder. How can he be? I assumed we'd been drawn into the spell, our souls not dead, yet no longer alive. I thought that we'd somehow been preserved as Ra was, but in a different state, and our souls were simply integrated into new bodies.

But what does it mean that Alexander died, and yet now he's alive again?

It feels like the more I learn, the more I don't understand.

A wave of terrible guilt crashes over me, and again, I consider letting it take me under. Surely my death here would satisfy Isis, if someone just took her my body for proof. First I caused Jesse's death, by being unable to Wake. And now I discover that millennia before, I caused Alexander's too, because I trusted my father.

But why support us and love us for years before killing him? The timing makes no sense.

I'm up and dressing before I can question myself. Because one person has the answers I lack, and he's about to give them to me. When I shoot out the door, I nearly run over Kahn. "You're awake," he says.

As if I'm Sleeping Beauty, and my consciousness is some kind of miracle. "I'm awake." My voice is flat, full of suppressed rage, grief, and self-loathing.

"You're clearly still upset," he says, "and that's why I wanted to talk to you. I know you're sad about Jesse, and I think that may be clouding your judgment."

"My judgment?" My anger should be channeling itself at him. After all, he's trying to reroute me. He's trying to talk me out of surrendering to his mother, just like Ra tried to do before. But this is different.

Kahn's doing it because he loves me.

I thought that was Ra's reason too, but clearly there are plenty of things I don't know about Ra. He lies so well I can't discern between truth and fiction with him.

I can't be mad at Kahn. It's not inside of me, not anymore. Especially now that I remember the years we spent together. He was everything I wanted. He was everything I needed.

We were genuinely happy.

Until Ra wrecked it, and that action caused me to

meet with Isis, and it probably created the entire prison thing to begin with. Ugh. I know I can't blame Ra for my poor decisions, but boy, I want to do just that.

"I need to speak to Ra. Immediately."

Kahn catches my hands. "Alora, listen to me first."

The torrents of emotion inside of me still for one second. With my eyes closed, the images of Alexander, beheaded, flash over and over. But unlike Shu, who's alive in my memories but dead in real life, Alexander's dead in the past but very much alive now.

And he has a request. I can't deny him. "Of course."

"I love you, and so everything I say will be biased by that fact." He sighs. "For probably the first time in my life, I don't want to be unbiased. I think that your father, Ra, or whatever you're calling him right now, is correct. I think that we can't simply give in to Isis' terrorist demands, no matter how much the self-sacrificing part of you wants to do it. She ruined our past life, but we can't let her ruin the present."

I frown. "Isis didn't ruin our past."

It's Kahn's turn to look confused. "I thought—"

"Do you remember dying?"

His eyes widen and he shakes his head.

"What's the last thing you do remember?"

"Shu attacked me," he says, "for no reason. I didn't want to mention it, because I thought it might upset you."

I swallow. "He didn't just attack you," I say. "He killed you." My eyes well with tears. "But it wasn't Shu. It was Mehen."

He absolutely loathes Kahn and always has, possibly because he knew we'd remember what had happened—what he did. It was surely done by order of my father, but he died by Mehen's hand.

"He killed Hephaestion as well."

Kahn's lips twist. Even though they're only memories, they're powerful. I feel it too, like the things I'm remembering happened yesterday.

"I know you want to save me, and I totally get it. I would be doing the same thing if she demanded that you die. But you have to see that, if Ra has found a way, or if I can contrive a way to ensure that Isis will release her powers the second we're dead—" I shake my head, a little frightened at that thought. I clear my throat. "No one should have the power that we have. Me and Ra and even Isis with this spell linking her to all those people, we're all far, far too powerful. It's not right. We should never have existed in the first place."

Kahn pulls me close and wraps his arms around me. "Then I'll die alongside you. I was created in the same way that you were."

"But you're not like me or Isis or Ra," I insist. "You took the spells that Isis cast on you and you changed them into something different. You can do a lot, you can protect and fight and shine, but you can't wreck the entire world."

He has no answer for that. He knows it's true. When I wriggle outside of the safe, comforting circle of his arms, he doesn't stop me from marching down the hallway toward Ra. I'm positive he'll be in the conference room we've used as a command center.

And he is, sitting casually in a chair, as though I'm not here to tell him that it's time to die. As if I don't want him dead myself.

"You slept on it," he says. "How do you feel now?"

Consumed by rage. Convinced that killing him and gutting Isis' power is worth my death. I shouldn't tell him my reasons. I should keep my mouth shut.

But I can't.

"I remembered something."

He frowns. "What? Is it helpful?" He doesn't look afraid at all. Why isn't he nervous that I might finally discover what he did?

"I finally know the truth."

He blinks. "Okay. Is it something we can use?" He must be a sociopath. He's utterly unconcerned.

"I dreamt of the thing you said I wouldn't recall until I was ready."

He stands up. "You remembered making Terra?" Why does he look so hopeful? Could the thousands of years in a prison cell have warped his brain?

"You never cared about me," I say. "You couldn't possibly, not with what you did."

He flinches as if I struck him.

"You lied to me, and you tricked me, and you used me," I say. "But what I can't figure out is *why*. The timing makes no sense."

He swallows. "Why—" He draws in a ragged breath and tries again. "Why do you say that?"

"You killed him," I say. "You murdered Alexander." Tears spring into my eyes and roll down my face. "I was pregnant. Did you know that?" Understanding dawns. "Was that why you did it? You couldn't stand the thought that some new little being might be more powerful than you? My child would be a person you couldn't raise on your lies."

His mouth dangles open, and I've never in my current life or all my memories seen Ra so discomfited. "I—no. I don't understand. I never killed Alexander. We had come to like one another. Respect that we each made you happy in our own way."

"You sent Mehen." I choke again. "To kill my husband, while I was pregnant with a son. I know you're old, but you haven't been slow before now."

He shakes his head and glances at Mehen for confirmation.

Mehen's brows are drawn together, and his shoulders are slumped.

"Do you really not remember?" I shake my head. "I *saw you*," I say. "I pulled the disguise that either Anat or my dad put on you, and when the Wind Called whisked you away from me, I saw your face. I know it was you."

"I've made no secret of my distaste for him," Mehen says.

"You told me to kill him," I shout. "When you first saw him, you tried to kill him."

He crosses his arms. "I never thought Alexander was good enough for you, and after you married him, I didn't like that you were forced to live on the run. I didn't like that you had to lie to the world, masquerading as the daughter of a tribal leader *he* had allegedly conquered."

"You decapitated him." I can barely say the words, even now, even though I know it happened thousands of years ago.

"I did not. I did hate that the Most Divine was forced to live like a nomad, running from *his mother.*" He drops to his knees. "I don't deny trying my hardest when I awoke to separate you from him in this life. I knew you didn't remember who he was and your bond was not based on actual experiences. I hoped to separate the two of you with truthful stories of his heritage and past. But I would *never* have harmed any member of your family, not then, and not now. If you truly believe I did that, you should kill me. I won't resist." He bows down in front of me, pressing his face against the ground as if I might lop his head off, to roll across the polished parquet floor.

"I vow that I never sent Mehen, or anyone else, to harm you or any part of your family," Ra says. "Consider the timing. When you and Isis created Terra, you and Alexander had been living together for some seven years. There was no reason for me to harm him. I knew of your pregnancy and was delighted. I could hardly wait to meet my grandson."

He seems sincere, but how many times has he tricked me?

"Who else could it have been?" I wracked my brain before and came up blank.

"It must have been my mother," Kahn says. "She did it precisely because you would never even consider her as the culprit." He grunts. "She discovered we'd been deceiving her and must have realized what she never had before."

"Huh?" I ask.

"That the one person who could truly defeat Ra was *you*," Kahn says. "And she knew the only way to turn you against Ra was—"

"To kill her own son?" I ask. "That's insane."

But I was just thinking yesterday that she was bonkers. Could it be true? Could I have believed it was my own father and trusted the very person who killed him?

"Hathor arrived moments before it happened," Alexander says. "I remember that part. She apologized to you, and you two were bonding. I was happy for you."

Was she waiting there for me to be vulnerable, so that she could do the very thing I asked? Set up a meeting with Isis? Surely I would have seen it then.

But I was too naive. I was too trusting. I hadn't lived the life I've lived now, full of betrayal and isolation and deceit.

"I'll surrender to her," Dad says. "I'll fly out right now, and she can kill me. It'll be enough. I'm the person she's always wanted to punish."

I shake my head. "It won't work. She has a new target now, one that scares her more than you. The child who can defeat even her own father, the only threat to her hegemony."

Ra and Kahn and Mehen and Am-Heh all look miserable, but no one argues with me. Even with as little as I know of her, I'm aware that Isis will never be satisfied with killing only my father.

"You'll be happy to know that I believe I have a solution to your quandary," Ra says. "If Isis permits Kahn and John to stand on either side of her, with a knife to her throat, and I think she will, since she believes they truly love her, deep down, they can be our surety that she'll release the power of the women bound to her."

"The problem with this plan," Kahn says, "is that she won't release her abilities until you're dead."

Unlike my darling Kahn, I don't see our deaths as much of a problem.

❧ 24 ❧

ANCIENT EGYPT

"Welcome to Macedonia." Isis is wearing the most gorgeous robes I've ever seen, her hair pulled up into a complicated sequence that ripples down around her bare shoulders. She crosses the throne room to greet me. She doesn't even spare a glance for Shu or Hathor who came in behind me. "I won't lie and say that I'm pleased that Hathor kept her knowledge of you from me, but I'm happy that you're here, finally ready to hear the truth about Ra." She reaches her hands out to me, as if we will embrace.

I don't think anything about me could be described as happy right now, and I step backward, bumping into Shu. "I still can't believe what he did."

Isis' face crumples then. She's had a few days to deal with the news about her son, but I can't imagine it's become easier to bear.

Guilt over my cold reaction wars with the desolation that rules my heart and mind. "Were you surprised to hear it?" I hate to prod a grieving mother, but I just can't wrap my head around the timing. Why would Ra kill Alexander now, after years of supporting us?

"Would you be surprised that a snake strikes?" The vitriol in her voice is sharp, fresh. "Or surprised that a mantis would attack the one it loved most dearly?" She shakes her head. "Ra's heinous acts rarely surprise me. What shocked me was discovering that he allowed you to marry and build a life together in the first place. I would never have expected that."

"He seemed genuinely happy for us." I think back to our visits, to the many times we ate dinner together. Alexander *liked* my father. He trusted him, too. That's all my fault—he trusted my father because I trusted him.

Because I'm an idiot.

"But why would he do it now, when I need Alexander more than ever?" I place my hands on my belly, finally showing through my robes. An errant tear runs down my cheek.

"He wants you to need him. He wants you to rely on him, and that will give him access to make changes to your child, probably without your knowledge. It's what he does. He keeps you close, right under his thumb. Ra doesn't share love, not with anyone."

"He's never minded that Shu and I are close."

"Ah, but Shu is also his child. That's not quite the same."

I don't want to talk to her about Ra's children anymore, and Shu looks as uncomfortable as I've ever seen him. He's as shocked and betrayed and upset as I am.

Isis taps her lip with one finger. "I'm sure he thought that this phase with Alexander would pass. He figured he'd support you until the two of you fell out, but having a child, that's permanent." Her mouth is pressed into a hard line, and I remember that she and Ra first argued because he wouldn't have any children. Or at least, not hers.

Hathor stands utterly still and totally silent at my side. I wonder how she feels? Vindicated? Disgusted with me for trusting him? I can't see any emotion in her face at all, not that I'm an expert in reading her moods after more than twenty years spent apart.

"Shu, what do you think?" Isis asks.

"About what?" He didn't want to come here at all. He thought we should confront Dad directly, which I just cannot face.

"Are you angry?"

He sputters. "Am I *angry*?" He shakes his head. "I'm broken. I'm livid. I'm enraged. But I'm not sure what you can possibly do about any of the things I feel."

Isis raises one eyebrow and inclines her head slightly. "Still loyal to him, even now?"

I can't let Isis and Shu get into some kind of fight. Emotions are high for everyone, obviously. "I'm not sure why I wanted to see you," I say. "I suppose after it happened, I wanted to meet Alexander's mother—" I'm halted by tears. For this baby's sake, I need to get it together.

"You poor thing." Isis closes the space between us and wraps her arms around me.

"The hardest part is that it doesn't *feel* like he's dead," I whisper. "My heart should know that he's gone, but whenever I think about him, I feel warmth and comfort. It's only when my brain fully engages that I realize he's never coming back."

"That's normal," Hathor murmurs.

"Is it?" It seems anything but normal to me. Shouldn't my soul know that his is gone?

Isis pats my back. "I felt like Ra was still alive, but I thought it was because I feared to trust my good luck."

I gasp. If there's any chance that. . .

But I saw him. I touched him. There was no spark left by the time the Healers came. There was nothing they could do. My voice cracks as I say, "It's the constant *hope* that keeps resurging for no reason at all that's making me crazy."

"You probably won't feel better until you *do* something," Hathor says.

"But what should I do?" I feel so upended. Like a capsized boat, floating upside down. Like every single day is another chance to drown in sorrow and disappointment and unending grief.

"I haven't known Ra was yet alive for very long," Isis says, "but I had decades before Alexander told me he was gone to plan ways to counter his seemingly limitless power."

Counter? What's she saying?

"None of them were very feasible, given my own limited strength and resources." Isis is measuring her words carefully, but I'm not sure why.

"What do you mean, 'counter' his power?" Shu asks.

Isis looks at me, not Shu, when she answers. "If a scorpion stung you, what would you do?" She takes a few steps toward an alcove at the corner of the room and sits. She points at the bench next to her.

I follow her over, Shu and Hathor trailing us. "I'd seek a Healer, I imagine, or if I couldn't find one, I'd shift." Somewhat reluctantly, I sit.

"Would you let the scorpion go?"

"Did I startle it?" I'm confused. "Did I attack it first, prompting its aggression?"

"It was hiding in your room. Perhaps it was in a

basket you used to store your robes. When you reached inside, it struck you."

I shake my head. "I'm not sure. I might kill it out of instinct."

"Would you feel better, knowing that you'd killed the creature that wounded you?"

I shrug. "I'm not sure. I've always been able to sense things like that, so I've never been struck by surprise. I always know when something lurks."

Except Mehen, waiting to kill Alexander. If I hadn't been so distracted by Hathor, I might have been able to do something.

Isis glances skyward. "It must be amazing to have so much power. The ability to Lift and the senses that accompany it, the strength of the Fire Called, the ability to transform into a creature that can tear skin from bone and heal yourself from most injuries in a trice. And most of all, the ability to assimilate from a distance." She sighs. "How about this, then? Imagine your child has already been born. How would you react if a scorpion struck him or her? What would you do to it?"

"If it struck my son, I'd kill it, if only to keep it from striking again."

Isis smiles from ear to ear, and I realize her point.

"You think my father needs to die?" Even saying the words is hard. It's like my brain can't quite comprehend what he did, so it can't process any action that I should take in retaliation.

She shrugs. "It would be the simplest solution, but even you must agree that he must be contained."

Last month, I would have defended him. Last year I would have attacked her to keep him safe. But now? I can't argue with her, not on any of her points.

"To protect your child and anyone else you love,

you have to do something. Anyone else he sees as a threat to the relationship he has with you is at risk."

"He would never harm me or my child," I say. But even as I say the words, I wonder if I'm actually positive. I still can't believe that Mehen would harm anyone I cared about, even if my dad ordered him to do it. I've known him since I was born. He's always cared for me. He's always defended me.

I thought he loved me.

Maybe I don't know anything at all.

"You can never be quite sure what he will do. Ra was abused as a child, for almost a century. Did he tell you that?"

She knew him quite well. Alarmingly well.

"Anyone who is loved by Ra eventually becomes corrupted, as his father twisted everything that matters inside of him. It's the nature of warped love. It warps everything around it. That's why I left, and it's why your mother left. It's the only way to escape his influence, but that may not always be the case. With your help, we could create a world that's free from that curse."

"What could we possibly do? He can siphon anyone within a several-mile radius. Any army we sent, any attempt we made, they would all end in disaster. We would only be killing anyone who agreed to help us."

"I think I owe you the credit for my most promising idea," Isis says.

"Huh? How could you owe me for it?"

"My son told me that the Gordian knot repelled any attempt to touch it, sucking the power of the object into itself."

I blink.

"I was so curious that I asked him to bring me the remains, which he did."

"Okay."

"It took me months of study of the magical residues to recognize the spell as a siphon trap." She bobs her head. "I knew the Assimilator who helped him must have been tremendously powerful, but he insisted when I asked that no one helped him. I should have known then." She shakes her head. "I attributed it to fate, without a better explanation. I thought that he was meant to do what he did. Or I thought that perhaps he used his elemental powers to counteract it. I was so relieved that he survived that I didn't apply enough logic to the situation, clearly."

"I don't understand how—"

"The weave on that siphon trap was inverted," Isis' voice is low, forcing me to lean closer so I can hear her properly. "You figured out that it was inverted, and you had no choice but to apply brute strength to invert it." She lifts her eyebrows, and I realize she's guessing.

"Yes," I say. "That's exactly what happened."

"That was quite a leap of faith," she says. "Only someone very confident in their absolute power could have done something like that."

"I had a full reservoir, of course."

"Of course." Her eyes widen. "Speaking of, did Alexander happen to—"

"He did." I wince. "On our wedding day he gave me yours." I hate that I have to do this, but I can't really do otherwise. I reach underneath my robes and tug the chain upward, finally revealing the enormous reservoir Alexander gave me on the day he told me that he chose *me*. Over all others. On the day I doomed him to die, apparently. I unclasp the chain and extend my hand toward her. "I'm sorry. He was trying to show me that he cared for me above all others." I close my eyes, waiting for her to take it.

She never does.

"He stole it from you," I say.

This time, Isis has tears in her eyes. "He found it for me in the first place. Did he tell you that?" She shakes her head. "You keep that. He gave it to you as a gift."

That surprises me, and I realize that she's been hard for so long that she's forgotten how to be soft. Losing her son isn't helping with that, I imagine.

"When I realized you could invert a weave if you flipped it hard enough. . ." She turns on her bench and calls out loudly. "Agnija. Come."

A woman peels away from the guards posted near the door. She is so tall, so strong, that I had mistaken her for one of them, but she's holding no weapons as she approaches and bows.

"Are you absolutely sure you're alright with this?" Isis asks, gently. More gently than anything I've heard her say until now.

"Of course, Your Highness. I serve gladly, joyfully."

Isis turns back toward me. "I'm going to show you something. I stumbled upon it by accident after seeing that siphon trap." Isis stands up and places her hands on the crown of Agnija's dark head. "You need to watch my weaving, or you'll never understand."

At first I can't tell what she's doing, but then I see it and I'm drawn closer against my will. She's using energy from her reservoir to crack the lid on Agnija's, well, her inner soul-energy for lack of a better word. Instead of siphoning her, she's. . . I squint. She's. . . "What are you doing?"

"I'm inverting her powers." Then she does just that, somehow isolating the source of Agnija's Reaper abilities—she can shift into a squirrel; strange for such a large and imposing woman—and then inverting it. When she stops, Agnija sighs with contentment.

"What happened?" I ask.

"Agnija, approach this woman here." Isis gestures toward me. "Take her hand."

The woman stands and walks toward me, seemingly unharmed.

"Wait," Isis says. "First, let me ask you to do something else."

Agnija stops, willing eyes turned on Isis. "Anything."

"Try to shift for me."

She frowns. Her hands clench at her sides, and I see fear in her eyes. "I cannot."

Isis smiles. "As it should be. Thank you."

The poor woman frowns, but continues toward me, reaching to take my hand. Some instinct inside of me wants to recoil from her, but I force myself to stay steady. When her hand touches me, it's the same feeling I had when I touched the siphon trap. The sucking, twisting vortex of hunger pulls on me, voracious.

It takes a great yank on my reservoir to dispel it, and it sends poor Agnija skidding backward. Not one second later, she shifts into a squirrel and scurries away.

My heart races, and I'm a bit horrified, realizing that someone must have died to create the spell protecting that Gordian knot, but I don't see how that will help us with Ra. I'm about to say just that when Isis beams at me. "That's how we can contain your father."

"I don't understand what just happened," Shu says. "Can you tell me?"

He's clearly asking me, but Isis isn't about to pass the glory of this discovery to anyone else. "I realized that when you invert the powers at the center of who an individual is, it creates a power vacuum that will steal any amount of strength from anyone it approaches until their central selves are returned to normal."

And that's when it hits me, what she wants to do. "You want to invert a few dozen people and send them to Ra, like animals prepared to attack," I say.

Her smile is positively triumphant. "Not a dozen. Not even two dozen. One hundred women, all powerful, all willing. Twenty-five Reapers. Twenty-five Renders. Twenty-five Elementals. Twenty Lifters and five Assimilators."

"You don't need me for that," I say. "You could do it yourself."

She shakes her head. "I'm not strong enough. The first time I tried it, I almost couldn't invert the person's powers. I nearly died for my efforts. That's why I demonstrated with a squirrel. Anyone more dominant and I can't complete the process."

"You think you really need that many people to defeat my father?"

"I know I do," she says. "I've found the method and I've found the willing accomplices, but you're the only one strong enough to slay the scorpion."

No matter how much it hurts to destroy a beautifully evil creature, you do it, to keep the future safe. I rest my hands on either side of my belly, cradling our dear sweet son, the only part of Alexander I have left. "What do I need to do?"

"For tonight, rest," Isis says. "I shouldn't have met with you the second you arrived. Hathor can show you and Shu to your rooms. They're adjoining. I hoped it would make you more comfortable. We can begin tomorrow."

"I'd rather start now," I say. "I'm no more or less tired than I'll be tomorrow, and I want to get this over with." Before I lose my resolve. Before I can't bring myself to set the trap that will slay the scorpion after all.

"So be it," Isis says. "Eat something while I gather my volunteers."

I can barely bring myself to eat a little bread and some dates. Most women have nausea near the beginning of pregnancy, but mine started after Alexander died. It nearly put me off food entirely. The only time I feel the baby moving now is right after I eat, so I force food down at regular intervals for his sake.

True to her word, Isis gathers people immediately, and as she mentioned, they're all women. They're also all wearing white robes.

"Are you sure about all this?" Shu asks. "She seems a little off."

I laugh. "I'm definitely a little off. Losing the person you love most will do that to you." I close my eyes and drop my head onto my forearms where they're resting on the table.

He rubs my lower back. "We can leave right now, if you don't want to do this."

"She's not going to stop," I say, "not now that she knows."

His voice is the barest whisper. "Father has never been willing to do it, but you could kill her easily."

"Kill her?" I shake my head. "She's grieving a son. I'd have to be a monster to kill her."

He shrugs. "Do you really think Dad deserves to die?"

I wish I knew. Some moments I'm positive. Others, when I think about my childhood, my heart contracts at the thought. "I don't know anything."

"Before you sign his death order, maybe you should work that out."

Except that a wave of grief crashes over me in that moment and I do know. "I'm positive that she's right," I say. "I'm just too emotional about everything right now and it's making me erratic, but when I stop thinking about how much Dad has done for me, I know what I have to do." He has too much power. Just like me.

The truly noble act would be to rid the world of both of us. We're anomalies who should never have been born in the first place. There can be no balance when the power spectrum is so uneven. I shove that thought away for now. If I'm thinking it, Shu won't be far behind, and I can't have him realizing what I'm contemplating.

He's the only one I trust to care for my child when I'm gone.

"Are you ready?" Isis asks.

I turn around to face the main room, no longer able to hide in my corner, and I'm overwhelmed at the sheer number of women Isis has brought. They look so similar, and also each unique. Their hair color ranges from the deepest black to the brightest red to the most shining gold and even the purest white. Their faces are young and fresh, mature and competent, and old and wizened. Their features span the same spectrum. Some are breathtakingly beautiful, some are downright homely. But their countenances, like their robes, are all exactly the same. Bright, peaceful, and determined.

"I dressed them alike so that you will remember that while they are all different, we are united in purpose, to rid the world of an evil that has plagued it for millennia." Isis inclines her head slightly, and every single one of them bows.

"Do you all come here of your own free will and choice?" I ask.

"We do." They all chant those two words at the same time, with the same inflection, like. . .like they're connected somehow. It's a little creepy.

But the dread that has pooled at the bottom of my belly for days, ever since Alexander died, starts to drain away as I realize—I'm doing something. Finally. After doing nothing but wallow in despair and grief and denial, I'm finally taking action. "What do you need me to do?"

"You need to invert their powers without turning them loose. You'll have to braid them all together to create one united trap that your father can't overpower, even with the magic stored in his many reservoirs," she says. "It feels a little different for each discipline, for the shifters, the telekinetics, and the elementals. I've never inverted an Assimilator, so I'm not sure what to expect."

I frown. "Perhaps we should leave them out." I cross my arms. "It's not like we need this many. As long as they don't approach en masse, all dressed exactly the same, he won't see a sole woman as a threat until it's too late."

Isis smiles. "I've been studying this for quite some time. If we try and fail, the punishment he will rain down upon us. . ." She shakes her head. "We need the full hundred."

Arguing with her will just delay things.

"Has Isis explained to all of you why you're here?"

They bow their heads again. "She has." Again, they say it all together, in the same tone and cadence. "Are they already linked?" I can't help the vague feeling of unease creeping up my spine.

"We are not, lady," the woman closest to me says.

She has nut-brown hair and dark, deep brown eyes. "We have chosen this, and we know our purpose."

"You understand that it's risky?"

The woman bows her head and crosses her arms over her chest. Her words are clear and crisp. "It's an honor to die in the service of what is right."

An honor to die? "Hopefully that's not necessary." It's not like Agnija died. . .

"As the great creator wills it," she says, with a pleasant smile on her face.

Well, clearly Isis didn't hide the risks from them if they're ready to *die*. "I suppose I'll start with you, then," I say. "What's your power?"

The woman gestures behind her. "We are Lifters, lady."

I think about what I saw Isis do, and I delicately weave a small, thin ribbon of power and wedge it between the woman's soul and her light force energy, pushing to pop them apart. It's as simple as cracking an almond or prying loose the lid of a box that's stuck.

Inverting her power is a bit trickier, as her soul doesn't want to be separated from her ability. I wrestle with it for a moment, the woman grimacing, before Isis says, "Think of reaching to the bottom and then tugging it outward."

There is no bottom, not really, but I sense what she means more than understanding her words, and I reach inward and then snap back out.

And it works.

The hard part is not releasing the inversion. I almost do before Isis reminds me. "Don't let go. You'll need to connect them at the end, remember?"

Right. After the first one, it's easier. I do all the telekinetics before beginning the elementals. It becomes harder to hold onto them with each new inversion I add. I wipe away the sweat beading on my brow.

"Are you alright?" Shu asks. "I don't like this. It feels strange. Why are all these women here? Why did they offer to do this? Shouldn't they be afraid of Ra? Or at least nervous to be sent to destroy him?"

"Stop distracting her," Isis says.

"It's okay," I say. "It's tiring, yes, but it's become simpler now that I know what I'm doing." Figuring out how to do the Reapers and Renders was the easiest of all, because I saw Isis do it already. Oddly, the entrance point for the seam between their soul and their heart energy is in their stomach. There may be a joke in that somewhere, once I'm ready to make jokes again.

Of course, now that I've thought about it, it feels like I'll never make a joke again.

I'm drawing pretty heavily on my reservoir as I invert the last Render, and without any warning, my knees give out. Shu lunges for me, but he stumbles. In the end, it's Isis who catches me before my backside hits the hard floor. Her arms slide underneath my armpits and she lifts me upward.

"I'm sorry," I say. "I didn't think about how tiring this would be."

"I knew it would be hard." Isis' eyes are full of concern. "There's no shame in needing assistance."

Shu scowls as he climbs to his feet again, brushing his pants off. "What did I trip over?" He looks around. "There's nothing here."

"Sometimes we all trip over our own feet," Isis says. "No shame in that either."

"Thank you," I say.

She releases me, but one of the guards brings me a wooden chair. I gratefully sit, even though it feels a little disrespectful in front of all these women standing perfectly still. Other than the five Assimilators I haven't yet inverted, none of them so much as shifted their gaze when I nearly fell.

"Are they alright?" I ask.

"They're suspended right now," Isis says. "With their souls flayed open like that, they can't think or move or struggle. It's a very vulnerable position, so we should hurry."

I'm so exhausted by the time I reach for the first Assimilator that I nearly cry. But I can't sob right now. There are moments in life where you're allowed to be weak, when you're allowed to wallow and complain. This isn't one of those times. Strength and tenacity are what we need right now. I dig deep and pull on my reservoir again, this time fashioning more of a dagger than a ribbon.

Even so, when I try to pry the first willing volunteer's heart energy from her soul, she snaps back. It's a reflex, I'm sure. Her face contorts and she cries out. "No!"

"Are you alright? Do you want out of this?"

She drops to her knees. "I do not, my lady. I absolutely do want to help. I'm so sorry. The will is strong, but I worry that my heart is stronger still."

As long as she's sure, I won't hold back. This time, I plunge the dagger of magic into the place between her soul and her powers and don't hold back. It slides far and deep, and I have to push harder than I've ever pushed to invert it. When I do, the entire taut mass of souls I'm holding vibrates, like a plucked string.

"Are you okay?" Isis is much closer than I realized, standing just behind my chair.

"I am."

"Can you do the last four?" Her voice quivers, like

she's worried about me. Or perhaps she's concerned about the well-being of her grandson.

"I can, yes." I inhale deeply and then dive into the second. I don't stop until I have only one left. She's the strongest, I think, and I'm so very tired.

I was exhausted, body and soul, when I arrived, and this task has felt endless. I'm slumped in my chair, struggling to stay upright, but I have only one more to go. I fashion one last bit of magic, strong and sharp, and I press fast and strong to separate the final woman and invert her powers, creating my one-hundredth siphon trap of the day.

"Now you must braid the connections together," Isis says. "Once you've released the mass of them, they'll come back to themselves, but they'll be connected. As soon as he reaches for one of them, they'll all pull until he can't fight any longer."

I sense the individual behind every single strand, every single connection to a real, living, breathing woman who has volunteered to risk herself for this endeavor.

"These women represent the strongest, the brightest, the best of their kind," Isis says. "Together, nothing can stop them."

I begin to braid the filaments together carefully, much as Mehen always taught me to entwine objects when I was learning to Lift. That thought sends a twinge of sorrow through my own heart. I still can't believe that he would ever betray me, that he would wound me like he did.

Finally, the filaments are all braided together, and I try to release them.

But it doesn't work.

They're stuck to me, vibrating, twirling, and pulsing. Entirely attached. "I can't seem to release them."

"What?" Isis asks.

"I bound them together, as you said, but now. . ." I shake my hands in the air to show what I mean. "They're stuck."

She frowns. "They won't wake up until they're released."

"I understand," I say, "but I can't let them go. It's like trying to release a sticker brush. They won't come off."

Isis peers at the women, trying to understand what I'm struggling with.

"Have you ever had this issue?"

She shakes her head. "But I've never done this with more than three."

I turn to face her fully. "Three?" How could she have assembled a hundred for me when she's never tried it with more than *three*? My back aches. My neck is screaming. My head throbs in time with my pulse. I should've asked more questions.

I should never have listened to her.

"It's alright," she says. "Pass them to me. I'll figure it out. Maybe it's your exhaustion, which is totally understandable. We can't leave you like this. It might not be good for the baby."

I hadn't even contemplated him. Of course it can't be. "Okay."

She weaves something so quickly that I can't follow quite what it is and sends a filament of a spell toward me. It's so delicate, so complex, and so elegant that I want to study it. "What are you doing?"

"I hear from your mother that your affinity is constructs," Isis says. "My sister Anat is adept with appearance modification, as you have great cause to know."

She's talking about Mehen looking exactly like Shu, of course. At that thought, I feel very near collapse.

"My affinity is spellcraft, specifically the creation of new, complex spells. I'm able to create things so delicate, so complicated, that no one of my strength level has ever seen the like. It's how I was able to puzzle out the siphon trap from the mere residue. It's how I was able to develop this idea in the first place. But in this instance, it's also how I was able to begin this spell to extricate you from the interwoven bindings. It's also how you can trust that I'll be able to release them again." She smiles at me reassuringly. "I'm also not as exhausted as you."

When her spell reaches me, wrapping its delicate tendrils around the filaments of energy that are desperate to squirm away but reluctant to release me, I let go.

And her spell traps each and every inverted weave, tugging them toward her inexorably.

I breathe a sigh of relief as the last filament leaves me and transfers to her, tugging as it goes, a little uncomfortably. I cry out, but Isis is too busy to notice.

Only then do I wonder where Shu has gone. He was constantly at my back for most of this ordeal, but now, even though I'm in obvious discomfort, he's not checking on me. Come to think of it, he's been silent for quite some time. It's hard to even turn my head, I'm so tired, but I force my body to comply.

Even circling entirely around, I don't see Shu, but I do watch in complete awe as a complex spiderweb pattern of energy that has been laced through the ceiling, the tapestries, and even the rugs, lifts away from the room around us and drops into Isis's outstretched arms, twisting around the bound filaments.

"What are you doing?" I ask.

She ignores me, too caught up in her work.

But that small tugging sensation strengthens, and I moan. Something's not right. I look downward, to the source of the discomfort.

A filament spirals outward, from my belly, toward Isis. She's somehow captured and inverted the energy of my unborn child. It's hard, but I stagger to my feet. "Isis! You must stop. We've somehow accidentally inverted my baby."

She turns toward me again, looking nothing like the woman who has been speaking to me for the last few hours. Her face is triumphant, eager, and maniacal. "It wasn't an accident."

"What?"

"Don't you see?"

I shake my head.

"Your father isn't the only threat. You're all threats, of varying degrees."

Her words make no sense.

"The only way I'll ever truly rule is if I'm the only person with magic, the only one who has power. For thousands of years, your father has been like a dragon in the face of gnats." She cackles. "Now I'll be the dragon. You'll all bow."

"But you can't take everyone's magic," I say. "That's insane."

"You've done the hard part for me," she says. "You were probably the only person on Earth who could do it, and for that, you have my eternal thanks."

I follow the filaments she took from me, and I realize she used them to do much, much more. The women seemed off because they *were* off. She had somehow linked them to others like them. She had brought in one hundred women, who were all tied to other women. When I inverted them, it grew harder, because that inversion stole the power of all to whom they were linked, including their sons, their husbands, their fathers.

"But you can't do that," I say. "Even I could never—"

"You've never given yourself enough credit," she says. "Your power is unfathomable, almost. But you're right that you wouldn't have thought of this. You're too naive and wholesome to even *want* something like this." She points at the women, prone on the floor. "They gathered their relatives themselves. I collected the women who had been abused, neglected, and mistreated. The women whose children had suffered. When I asked them to gather for me, they leapt at the chance. They performed a simple ritual, at my request, and bound many, many more women to themselves than I had any hope they would. If you've ever seen a tornado form, you know that in the beginning a lot of force and torque is required, but after that, it's self-sustaining, sucking things into its center with its own inertia."

I watch, interpreting the delicate, perfectly formed threads of magic as she speaks, and I see it then, the avalanche of power pouring down the filaments toward her. Siphoned from the traps I created that set it into motion, each pull bringing in another person, and another.

"This wasn't about Ra."

She shrugs. "Of course it is. His power was natural, given by the gods. It was always his, so he took it for granted. But mine was hard won. He gave me the idea, and without him, I would never have known for what I yearned. Soon now, the tornado will encompass him as well, and then." She closes her eyes. "That will be glorious."

The tugging on my belly tightens, causing more pain. "This is *wrong*. How can you think it's glorious? You're injuring your own grandchild."

She laughs then. "I can Lift, Sekhmet." Her eyes light up, and benches in the corner rise into the air, spinning around her rapidly. "I can shift." Her eyes flash golden and she falls forward, her face lengthening, her legs bending backward. Suddenly a hyena rises in her place and she shrieks.

The pain in my belly is unbearable. "But when you kill them, you'll lose all that power."

She shifts back in a blink. "I won't kill them, you simpleton. I could never do that for precisely the reason you've given. I'll lose everything if I do."

And suddenly, my purpose becomes crystal clear. I've always wondered why, if there are gods in heaven, if there is a creator in this world, I was given so much *more* than everyone else. I've felt guilt over it, and fear at what I can do. But if there was ever a time not to hold back, it's now.

I shift then, sinking into the strength of my furry, muscle-bound body, and I lunge for her, Lifting objects out of my way. Once I'm close enough, I leap for her throat, my mouth wide open.

She hurls things at me that I block easily, and I'm inches from ripping her voice box out when she finally flings a fireball at me, burning the entire side of my body.

I don't care.

My entire attack was a distraction, meant to create an opportunity. She may have skill with spellcraft, and she may have been planning this for some time, but no one does overwhelming force quite as well as I do, even when I'm tired. The sword of raw power I had been secretly crafting slams into her like a sledgehammer, shattering her hold on the spiraling tornado of siphon trap energy. I wrench it away easily, like stealing a ball of yarn from a surprised kitten.

The power flowing through it hits me like a tidal wave, and I stagger backward.

"No!" Isis shouts, as she comes for me.

Without her recent acquisition of powers, she doesn't stand a chance.

"Now!" she screams, her voice hoarse. "Right now! Do it!"

Do what? The siphon traps continue to pull, dragging new souls in at a horrifying rate, from farther and farther away, just as she said they would. It takes every ounce of my energy to keep control of them, but when I turn around to see what she's shrieking about, my heart stops.

Dead in my chest.

Not a single beat.

Two men are holding Shu and Alexander, both of them with swords in hand, pressing the blades against their throats.

"Kill them," she says.

And I realize her end game—she disguised her assassins as Mehen, and then put another layer over the top so that I could discover the plot she wanted me to discover. She didn't kill Alexander either, and if it had even occurred to me that he might not be who he appeared to be. . . I mourned the death of someone who had been magicked to look like Alexander. Not my husband himself.

I want to save them, but I know there's no hope. Even as I stumble toward them, even as I reach out to Lift the men away, the swords separate their heads from their bodies.

But their souls were caught up first, as are the

guards', in the whirling tornado around me, and I realize that although their bodies were dying, their souls are yet alive. They try to join the shining throng, the massive power that Isis assembled for herself, but I can't let them.

The soul of my unborn child is already gone, lost to the whirlwind, but these two I hold out separate. They are mine.

My heart cracks down the middle. I can barely stay upright. But I can't lose them too, my most beloved lights in the darkness. I twist their souls around my own heart, keeping them bound to me.

I can't set things right. I don't know how.

I can't stop the separation of souls from powers. I don't know how to do that either.

But I can ensure that Isis isn't controlling this. . .whatever it is. I can ensure that their powers have somewhere to go, somewhere they won't be used for evil.

I think about the sights Alexander, and Ra, and Shu saw with me over the past eight years, and I start to *create* as many vast, endless constructs as I have the power to create. One is all mountains and streams and valleys, bounded on all sides by an ocean. I spin the Lifters off as they arrive and send them there.

I parse another, larger land into quarters. One full of water for the creation of ice. One barren and rocky, and bounded by spewing mountains, a land of fire and ash. Another with endless lakes, high mountains, and craggy peaks for those who fly and blow. And finally, a land of loamy, welcoming earth. A place for plants and lush greenery to flourish.

Next I embark on the most ambitious creation yet. A vast expanse of land, full of lowlands and grasslands, sweeping mountains, and vast, untouched jungle. A place for animals to prowl and hunt and hide. High, bright skies through which birds can fly and dive. Bright, unsoiled oceans in which marine life can dart and soar.

Finally, I create a small, enclosed space with extra energy funneled into the walls on which they can feed, to keep my dear, misunderstood, rare Assimilators safe and comfortable.

As I'm putting the finishing touches on the last world, a great light whirls toward me. I know it's Ra. The father I wrongfully tried to kill. The man who would do anything, lose anything, give everything to save me. "I'm so sorry," I whisper. "I didn't know." I brush my finger against his light, infusing it with all the spare energy I have left, confident that he'll use it wisely, to keep safe as long as possible.

And then I fiercely yank the one remaining light, the one holdout, into the whirlwind, and I tether it to the worlds I've created.

I cradle the last two souls that are with me, my dearest, most beloved brother, and the imperfect, brash, adventurous other side of my soul next to my own heart.

And I let go.

❊ 25 ❊

DREAM

She Who Mauls.
Mistress of Dread.
The Powerful and Mighty Destroyer.
She Before Whom All Tremble and Despair.

Those are my titles. They're the names by which I have been known in this life or in the one that came before. Of course those are the titles I've had: I'm a monster. I should never have been born. If Ra hadn't broken natural laws, I never would have been.

I caused the end of one world already.

And now I'm wrecking what survived.

I thought that Ra and I should surrender. I got on the plane bound for Seattle to offer myself to Isis. I've finally recalled exactly what happened, and only one thing I know has changed. I still have to die. So does my father.

And somehow, we have to take Isis with us.

"Alora," a voice calls, but the world is nothing but blackness and misery.

"Wake up, Alora, please," the same voice says. The voice is tears and sorrow and regret.

"Come on. We don't have long." He's sad, the voice. He's worried. That makes me want to open my eyes, but it's so hard. The darkness is so deep, so oppressive, and so heavy.

"Please, Alora. It's Jesse. Wake up."

Jesse.

I know that name.

He's my brother.

"Alora, you know the prophecy. You remember it. You have to wake up so we can talk about it."

The prophecy? It comes to me then, in a rush.

With the women it began, with the birth of the Warden it will end. She who can bridge the divide will rend the prison walls, rescuing the wartorn. They will fall, one after another, each in turn. The Telekinetics, the Elementals, the Renders and Reapers, and the Assimilators. In time, the prison walls will disintegrate until the world becomes whole again.

That part is done. I tore the prison apart, but the world isn't whole yet. Which means, my job as Warden isn't complete. What did the rest of it say?

The Earth will come unbound, and if the Warden fails, will be ripped apart.

It's come true. The Earth did come unbound, but it's not free. And Isis is planning to do just that: rip the world apart in order to rule it.

The storm will rage against her, but with a great sacrifice, and with the strength of her balance, all will fall and be remade.

The strength of my balance. Oh, no. No. It must mean Jesse. He was always the only thing that kept me sane, the only person who cared about me through it all. He was the great sacrifice I didn't even realize had already been made.

None can stand against her wrath, and none can endure without her compassion. Salvation comes from her hand, but at the end of all things, the world will only be healed when she is reunited with the OathMaker and the mistake is undone, the crime forgiven.

Who is the OathMaker? Does it mean Ra? Does it mean Isis? Could it be Kahn? I hate how stupidly vague it is. It only makes sense once I've already done something. Why are prophecies so useless?

"It's not vague," Jesse says. "Ra made you a promise. He told you he had not changed you, that he had not altered who you were. That was a lie."

But how could that mistake be undone? How could he—he confessed, I realize. He can't change who I *am*, but he can admit what he did was wrong.

Which means, for me to heal the world, I have to forgive him. Even now, anger about what he did and how he lied to me about it pulses inside of me. Who knows what kind of peaceful, wonderful life I might have had if he hadn't done what he did?

Jesse might never have died.

"I also might never have lived," Jesse says. "I'm the rebirth of Shu, and had you not been who you were, you couldn't have saved me so that I could return."

But you're not back. You're gone. That loss hits me all over again, like a blow to the head. Like an avalanche trying to crush me.

"You're forgetting the last part."

Only she can choose. Only she can restore. Only she can forgive. But she can't do it alone.

I can *only* do it alone. You're gone!

"I am here. Open your eyes to see me."

I struggle. I writhe. And finally, I force my eyes to open. But it's bright, so very bright. The light comes from all around me, blinding me, piercing me with shafts of pure pain.

"It's rare," he says, "for us to be granted permission

to see the living." He's kneeling in front of me, clasping my hands between his own. "I had to beg for quite a long time."

I drag my poor, maladjusted eyes upward until they meet his deep blue ones. And then he smiles and all the misery, all the pain, it's totally worth it. "You died." My voice, when I finally find it, is dusty and broken. My words sound more like a wheeze than an actual statement, but it's nice to be forming them instead of merely *thinking* at him.

"I did." But he doesn't look sad. He doesn't look broken. "You already know this, Alora. Death is not the end."

Elation surges inside my chest. "Then I'll join you! We can be together again."

"Not yet." But his eyes aren't sad. "I know it's hard. I know you feel alone." He squeezes my hands tightly. A single tear runs down his face. "Your pain hurts me, too, but it's the only pain I feel in this place—the pain of knowing that you're hurting."

"If there's no pain here," I say, "then why can't I join you? I have a plan—it will fix the mistake made when I was created, and we'll be together again."

He smiles again. "That's why they let me see you." He brushes my hair back from my eyes. "It's not time for you to die, Alora. Your creation was never a mistake."

I blink, still not adjusting to the light. So much light.

"It's bright here all the time. But after you die, your body's better and stronger. You're prepared for it."

I gulp. "Can't someone else do what I need to do? I'm tired, and Jesse, I'm bad. I deserve to die. Trust me."

He gathers me in his arms then, like he'd gather a

child. I'm reminded of the times he held me when he was Shu. Of the times he rocked me to sleep and told me stories. "That's my message for you, Alora. I know it's confusing on Earth, but your main doubt comes down to this: how can there be a God and still be so much suffering?"

"Sometimes it feels like there's more pain than joy. And so many people are born evil. How can that be, if there is a God?"

Jesse shakes his head. "You weren't born evil. Neither was Ra. No one is born *evil*. Evil is manmade. It comes from greed, regardless of our powers, regardless of our country, regardless of our beliefs. It comes when we don't guard well enough against the bad, when we don't cling to good. Evil is easy. Evil is constant. And the answer is that banishing evil won't help." He purses his lips. "How can I explain this?"

"Why won't it help?"

"Good only exists because of bad. Hot only exists because of cold."

"That's confusing."

"Believe me, I know, and with your poor, imperfect, limited human brain, it's even harder to make sense of it. Eventually you'll get an upgrade, but until then, listen closely. The universe is created upon principles of balance. As evil rises, good is sent to beat it back. The world is less about what we have and more about what we do. We grow and change based on our actions. Our grandfather chose to do a lot of evil and in so doing, he became a very strong force of bad in the world. Dad wasn't lying about that. Dad was sent, and endured great pain in order to defeat him. His actions restored balance to the world and allowed people the choice of whether to grow in goodness or in evil. Dad knew right from wrong and created peace and prosperity precisely because he had suffered from their lack."

"But his children—"

"Their lives, and even their deaths, were not a punishment. It happened because of those children's choices. Sometimes when we're not raised in adversity, we don't learn the critical importance of choosing good. Those children all had the same choices to make as you and as our father. They could choose to do good or to do bad, but as they chose evil, it demanded more and more. They became power starved because evil actions never bring true joy, only more hunger."

I almost understand.

"But if Dad and I can destroy Isis together, if we can defeat her, even if it kills us—"

"It's not your time to die," Jesse says again. "You have a lot of good to do and a lot of balance to restore before you rest."

But I don't want to do it without Jesse. The prophecy says I'm not alone. "Why?" I start to cry, great heaving sobs wracking my body. "I don't want to be alone. You're explaining things to me now, just like you always have. I *need* you. Tell them that I'll stay, and I'll fight, and I'll do good—but only if you come back." I cross my arms and set my jaw.

Jesse laughs, and the sound is like Christmas and Fourth of July and Easter morning all at once. It's everything good and happy and right in the world. "Only you would try to bargain with God, even as I'm revealing the secrets of the universe." He cradles my cheek with his hand. "I can't return. It doesn't work that way."

My heart breaks all over again. Why does it hurt this badly every single time?

"You will want to stay, you'll want to live on and

fight without me, once you accept that you *are* good. You were created just as you are, a bright, beautiful soul, ready to shine light on the world. You cling to me because you think I'm the only one who can love you." His eyes are unbearably kind. "But that's never been true. You've always had infinite worth—you're not a monster. You're a miracle, and I'm not the only one who sees it."

My heart expands. It has been too much, too many losses, too many wounds. "I'm not sure—"

"You aren't alone. You're surrounded by people who love you," he says. "And you'll always have the memories of our time together. Like the Christmas when we woke up at three in the morning and rearranged all the toys that the charities brought, taking the best ones for ourselves."

"I took the slinky," I say, "not because I wanted one, but because I knew how badly Lex wanted it. I didn't want him to have anything that he wanted. How is that the action of a miracle?"

Jesse snorts. "Religion often teaches that things are black and white, but God doesn't care about belongings or toys. He cares about justice and equity and mercy and the light in our souls."

"So stealing Lex's toy so that he would be sad, how was that light?"

Jesse laughs. "Lex deserved not to be rewarded for the terrible things he had said and done. It was justice that he not reap a reward. I, on the other hand, took the mega-sized box of dominoes because I really thought they'd be fun. Instead, we spent hours and hours and hours setting up a course—"

"And when Dr. Bowers opened the door," I say, "they all fell down in three seconds."

He smiles with real recollection, and my heart

hurts. I wish I could stay here with him, or keep him with me to make more memories. I don't want the story we've had to be our entire story. It's the finality of our last page, of *The End* that hurts the most.

"We're out of time," Jesse says. "But one last thing to remember. Our time together was a gift. Your time with Kahn and the return of your memories, they were all gifts. Each minute we have on Earth is a chance for us to learn and grow and love. Don't waste those moments. Honor each and every one, for me."

And then he's gone, and the blackness encompasses me again.

Only this time, it doesn't feel quite so heavy. It doesn't feel quite so oppressive. Because as hard as it is for me to do, I believe him. Whatever I may have been called before, I have a job to do, and I will restore balance and be everything that the world needs.

Even if I can't see him again, I know he's watching me now. And I will make Jesse proud, even though it's apparently not supposed to be the last thing I do.

The drop in altitude from the plane's landing wakes me up. One glance out the window shows me that the ground beneath us is quickly approaching.

"Oh." I look around, half expecting to see Jesse. But it's not Jesse sitting next to me. It's Kahn. "We're in Seattle?"

He nods.

"I remembered it all." I swallow. "I did create Terra. It was my fault."

Kahn sighs. "You keep insisting that you are a terrible person, but—"

"You're right," I say. "It's hard for me to accept, especially because I know the mistakes I've made, and there have been a lot."

"But they've all been from trusting the wrong people, not from being a bad person yourself."

He's right. How often do the people around us comprehend the very thing that we haven't been able to grasp about ourselves? "I saw what happened, and then afterward. . ."

The plane jounces and jerks its way down the runway, slowing quickly. It's so loud that I almost want to cover my ears.

"After what?" Kahn practically shouts.

"I should have woken up, but I didn't." I can't say this above a whisper. We're not alone on the plane. "I saw Jesse."

He's unnaturally still, his eyes concerned.

"Not, like, fake Jesse." I shouldn't have told him. I can't tell anyone. It was too private.

"I believe you."

My heart expands. "You do?"

"How many inexplicable, bizarre, unbelievable things have we seen together?" His eyes meet mine, and a zing flies through me. He shivers at the same time.

"Through time and space," I say.

"Through countless difficulties," he says.

"There's no world in which we are enemies," I whisper.

He kisses me then. It's quick, but thorough, his mouth covering mine, his heart bolstering the pep talk Jesse just gave me. I'm a good person. I'm worthy of love, even an epic one like this. I could kiss him forever, but there's no time. Even now, the plane's stopping. I need to come up with a plan. I need to tell my dad. I pull away.

"Your mother killed you," I say. "Just as we thought. Just as Dad said."

"Dad?" Kahn asks. "We're back to calling him that?" He looks bemused.

"Dad?" I unbuckle and stand. "Dad?!"

Two rows back, he stands up. "I'm here, cub." His eyes are kind, and as open and welcoming as they've always been. In that moment, all my doubts, all my fears, and all my uncertainty disappears. Even without trying to, his soul shines through to my view. It's bright, it's clear, and it's beautiful. There are two dark strands hidden among hundreds of shining ones. I wonder if even my soul is that bright.

He may hold a grudge, and he may be ruthless when someone he loves is threatened, but apparently that's not unredeemable. In spite of everyone trying to convince me otherwise, he's exactly the man I hoped, the father I longed for but never had.

"I don't want us to die," I say. "Jesse doesn't want us to die." I can't believe I said that out loud. Everyone will think I'm insane.

"Of course he doesn't." Dad smiles. "He always saw you for what you really are. It was only you who couldn't see."

"What can we do?" I look down at Kahn. "Maybe John and Kahn should stay here, since she's their mother."

"She's not my mother," Kahn says. "I hate her."

"Me either," John says. "Anyone who would abandon me, anyone who would lie to me like that, anyone who would use me to get what she wants is no mother of mine."

"We're agreed," Ra says.

"You're not alone," Martin says. "We're all with you."

Mehen. Am-Heh. Imhotep. Ammit. Tefnut. Anubis. Henry. Rosalinde. Thomas. Even Ptah. They all came. Kahn and John are both smiling at me. They all have faith that I'll come up with something.

And I have no idea what to do.

I just know what Isis has done. Before I could release the energy from Rra and Ā, she gathered the filaments like she always planned to do and tethered them to herself. It's how she can cut cords and kill their linked souls or she can draw power from them just as she tied the women's powers together in the first place. I didn't realize I was dooming all women to be powerless when I rolled them in to the formation of Terra, but Isis knew. The tornado sucked all the souls in, but only the females were bound.

It was why they could feel a connection to the prison world, why they could dream of it, but also why they were powerless. Now the same power siphon is binding them down while Isis steals and steals and steals from them.

I have to cut those cords without killing their souls.

"We need to do this right, or a lot of people are going to die."

"I'll kill her," John says. "Even if I die doing it. I won't regret it."

"I have a better idea," Ra says.

Maybe he understands why John's plan won't work. "I'm all ears," I say.

He frowns, and so do the other ancient commanders. He has a pretty good grasp of English, but sometimes colloquialisms still trip him up.

"I'm listening," I clarify. "Go ahead."

"She thinks we're surrendering," he says. "She's agreed to having her sons on either side of her while we voluntarily offer ourselves up. She'll want to make a big show of it."

"Okay."

"So let's do that," he says. "But John and Kahn slit her throat the second you signal, instead of waiting for her to surrender her control after we've died, obviously."

"I don't know for sure what will happen to the souls

bound to her if she dies," I say, "but I'm pretty sure they'll all die as well."

"We have to somehow unwind that link before we kill her?" Mehen asks.

I nod.

There's a banging on the door of the jet that must be from one of Isis' men.

We're out of time.

When the flight crew opens the door, I'm somewhat surprised to see Duncan on the other side. I suppose I shouldn't be, but I am all the same.

"I'm sorry," he says.

I don't even need to ask for clarification. I know why he's sorry. Clearly he chose poorly with imperfect knowledge and information. "It's alright," I say. "I've picked the wrong person to back several times." I'm surprised to find that I mean it. All my anger at him is gone. He was a lousy father, and he didn't fix things when he had a chance, but it doesn't matter.

I have an excellent dad.

He was just a stand-in. It's not like placeholders are really expected to do much. When I push past him, I don't even feel upset. I have bigger fish to filet and then fry until they're blackened.

Assuming Isis doesn't massacre us first.

"Wait for the rest of us." Kahn jogs down behind me, John on his heels.

"Or more prudently, wait for those of us who are skilled." Am-Heh jostles past John and slides into place on my right side on the ground.

"I've remembered more than you ever knew, old man," Kahn says.

He might even be right about that. I do wait, though, until everyone has disembarked and gathered around me. "We don't really have a plan, right?" John whispers. "We're kind of winging it?"

"The plan is, try to keep anyone from dying while we kill her," Henry hisses. "Right?"

"Hush," I say.

Isis sent a group of ten guards to escort us from the landing strip to the inside of the small airport. Anubis snarls a bit when one of them ushers us together, and I swear I see much sharper incisors than he should have flash in the incandescent light, but for the most part, we're model citizens. We march along between the guards, all of us probably scrambling for any idea we can use to force Isis to release her loaded gun.

Problem is, I keep coming up blank.

How can we take her down without killing billions of innocent people? These women have already been subjected and abused. While he was throwing out truth bombs, why didn't Jesse toss me a bone about that?

And then I realize I may already know. I did it the last time.

I distracted her, and I took them.

We need a distraction large enough that I can snatch the threads back without somehow creating another whirling, bucking energy tornado. Simple, right? If they're inverted still, taking them in one fell swoop will probably cause a similar problem. It didn't happen when Isis seized them because she was already connected, clearly. When I held her for last, along with Alexander and Shu, we somehow wound up being sucked into the mechanism and spit out on the back end as things began to unravel.

And here we are.

"You came." Isis sounds exactly the same as she did in my memory, after she was done pretending. A little unhinged, a little power mad.

"Of course we did," I say, channeling my inner guilt and self-loathing. Up until recently, I didn't even have to work hard to summon it. "I said we would."

"Where's Anat?" Dad asks.

"Where's Anat?" Isis shakes her head. "The first time we're in the same room together, after thousands of years apart, and you ask about my sister?"

"Please tell me you didn't harm her."

"You always loved her more," Isis says. "Not enough, obviously. Not the way either of us deserved to be loved, but unlike me, she was okay with scraps." She bites her lip. "Well, I always was stronger. I did what was best for her. I'm keeping her safe, away from you, away from this, until you've been eliminated. Then I'll free her."

I hope Anat is okay, but we have bigger matters at hand than even the life of one single woman. Bastet's missing too, but I'll search for her after we've eliminated Isis. Time to get things back on track. "Isis," I call out. "Are you prepared to honor your end of the bargain? Once we're dead, will you actually free everyone? Anat? Bastet? Every single woman whose powers you've hijacked?"

"I see that my beautiful boys have come to hold me to my word." She frowns. "But why did you bring so many others?"

Mehen crosses his right arm over his heart like he's about to recite the pledge, except his fist is closed. "If our Master dies, we die with him."

"That's cute," she says, "and of course, it's also delusionally insane, but if that's what you want." She lifts her right hand and a group of soldiers peel away from the wall, circling around behind us.

"Where are we going?" I ask, hoping to buy a little more time to think.

"If I've learned anything from watching modern television programs," Isis says, "it's that monologuing is the worst thing a villain can do."

"You admit that you're the villain?" Dad asks.

"You think I am." She shrugs. "You know better than anyone that the real villain is the one who loses. The winner writes the story any way they want, like you did after murdering your own father."

Dad's eyes flash.

"Do it." Isis steps closer to him. "Attack me, I dare you. I've been *dying* to inflict a little punishment on all these pathetic, trembling humans. They don't even know how to *be* anymore. They can't spend a single second alone with their thoughts. They whine and whinge about every minor inconvenience, so bored with the plenty and ease of their lives. Their lack of purpose leads them to create problems for themselves."

"They've been separated from who they really are for so long," I say, "that they've forgotten the truth. They've forgotten that they have intrinsic value that isn't tied to what they have or what they can do." I forgot the same thing. It's not part of our culture or our history any more.

If I survive this, I need to change that.

There are so many things we need to change.

"You're as insufferable and introspective as ever," Isis says. "At least this time I'm not forced to fake-cry in order to get your help. I can do anything that needs to be done all on my own." Power swells around her and I realize she's just pulled on her connection to her tethered lives, tapping into them like I might have guzzled a Slurpee—greedily, with no thought for the impact on the people at all.

But she's doing it for a purpose. Dad must be able

to see it too, as she forms the magical sword she's going to use to slay us.

I still haven't thought of a single way to distract her. It's not like I can lunge at her again. She's stationed male guards, presumably trained to fight, up and down on either side of the room, ready to leap in front of any of us that might attack. Even if I do distract her, I'm not sure how to free those souls without causing another siphon tornado and resetting a smaller, weaker version of Terra.

A memory surfaces then, of the day Jesse and I spent setting up all those dominos. Everyone at the group home went to a fancy dinner on Christmas Day, paid for by a wealthy family who felt guilty that they had so much, I think. But Lex had told Dr. Bower another lie, and my punishment was missing the dinner.

Jesse, like always, chose to stay at the home with me.

"I'd rather eat cold ham sandwiches with you than steak and baked potatoes with those jerks," he'd said.

Although, when we made the sandwiches and I snatched the last bit of mustard, he grumbled. "Remind me again why I'm stuck eating this dry junk?"

I offered him my sandwich, but he declined.

Jesse had always loved dominoes and had quite a few, but with the new box he'd received, we had a spectacular amount. We spent the next six hours setting up the most epic domino course either of us could have imagined. "Alright," he had said. "Let's start right here." He pointed at the domino at the very top of an old built-in bookcase, almost entirely devoid of any actual books. "It's high enough that everything should go down."

But before either of us could bump it, the front

door opened, and Dr. Bower swung it a little too far. The edge of the door hit the dominoes and that was that.

Every last domino went down from that one simple hit.

Maybe Jesse was sending me a message after all.

I suddenly know what I need to do, if only I can distract her long enough to do it.

"Dad," I whisper.

Mehen, Am-Heh, and Henry all hear me, judging by the way they twitch. I'm worried that a few of the guards may have, too.

"I need help," I whisper. "A distraction," I say in Egyptian, hoping the guards won't understand.

Unfortunately, Mehen, and Am-Heh all understand me as well. Before Dad can do anything at all, they leap forward. Twin pillars of fire shoot from Am-Heh's palms, incinerating everything in their path.

Isis leaps aside just in time, fury suffusing her features.

Mehen flings the guards aside like rag dolls, seizing every bit of detritus from all corners of the airport lobby and hurling them at her.

She blocks them easily, but her anger only grows.

And Henry, who may not have understood what I said, but who quickly figured it out, inclines his head slightly toward me and then lunges for Isis, attacking her just as I did so long ago, headlong and unafraid.

The power swords Isis shaped for Dad and me find new homes, one of them splitting in two, with one half sailing easily into Am-Heh's chest, and the other half finding a home by severing Mehen's head from his body. It's not lost on me that it's the exact wound Isis made me believe he had dealt to Alexander. Another blast of energy enters Henry's body, lighting him up like a lantern until he explodes in a shattering spray of light and gore.

But instead of mourning them, instead of allowing his pain and sorrow to cloud his judgment, Dad moves immediately toward Isis, wrapping his arms around her. "It was always going to end this way," he says. "I knew it, and so did you."

She doesn't even struggle against him, with all her vast power. She closes her eyes, almost peacefully. Was she waiting on Dad all along?

No.

He's siphoning her—he's buying me the time I need. Time to kick the dominoes, to start the collapse that will end everything.

I reach out carefully and extricate just one filament, one single fiber, a bright one, but not one of the bright-est. I separate one ordinary soul. Someone's mother. Someone's daughter. Someone's friend.

Instead of yanking it to me, I flip the soul back-ward, righting it at last, ending the siphon trap. Righting the great wrong I created when I listened to Isis in the first place.

And like dominoes, all the other connected fila-ments snap inward, flipping back into their rightful shapes. They free themselves, one by one, from their connection to Isis. They go down just like those domi-noes, as Jesse must have known they would, and as they float away, as they free themselves, Isis slumps smaller and duller, slowly lessening.

Dad needs to release her. "Let go!" I shout. "I've done it."

But he doesn't let go. His arms stay circled around her.

"Dad! You have to let go!" I shout at the top of my lungs. "Please! Don't wait."

"You always were the best thing I ever did, the best part of my life. You are still my greatest joy."

Why hasn't he released her? "Dad, drop her, now!"

He shakes his head. "It's too late for that."

When I *look*, I see why. His soul is already connected to hers—he used his own soul to weigh her down, to keep her from fighting me.

"The link to those souls she stole has been sustaining her," he says. "When it's gone, we'll both die."

He's not surprised. He knew what would happen, and he did it anyway.

"Please listen." I can't lose anyone else.

But Jesse's words come back to me, and I realize that, like Dad, he knew. Just as he mentioned the dominoes to prepare me, he also warned me about this.

But if Dad and I can destroy Isis together, if we can defeat her, even if it kills us— I said.

He cut me off. *It's not your time to die. You have a lot of good to do, a lot of balance to restore before you can rest.*

I said Dad and I could work together. He gently told me that *I* had a lot of work yet to do. He didn't mention Dad. I should have noticed that he didn't mention Dad. I only just realized how good he was. I only recently forgave him. I jog toward him, desperate to fix this.

"It's his choice." Kahn doesn't stop me, but his words hang in the air between us.

I've grown enough to listen to my family and friends. In possibly the most un-Alora-like thing I've ever done, I do nothing. I let him make his sacrifice. "I love you, Dad," I say.

And then I watch him die, that the world might live.

27

EARTH

"The Prime Minister's on the phone again," Kahn says.

"Tell her I'm busy," I say.

"She says that she already knows it's a bad time, but it's urgent."

The Prime Minister is one of the most charismatic women I've ever met. The people of Great Britain, and probably half the world, are in love with her.

She's a daily burr in my side. "Fine." I extend my hand.

Kahn puts the cell phone in it. "I'll get the bags."

I brace myself as I answer. "Hello?"

"Most Divine!" Amelia, thankfully, now calls me that as a joke. "First of all, let me just say how delighted I am to hear that you're finally in labor."

"How do you even know?" I ask. "The contractions began less than an hour ago."

"Anat told me when I called, but she said she couldn't talk—she was on a ferry."

I'm relieved to hear she caught it. Actually, I wouldn't be surprised if they held it for her. She's a bit of a celebrity around here, as my liaison to the UK. "I'll let her know you're looking for her as soon as she arrives. Is that all you need?"

Amelia sighs. "She knows I need to talk to her. The thing is, the Elementals have decided—"

"Amelia, I'm sure she'll call you. . ." I've learned to be a little better about letting people put out their own fires. Amelia's hard to shake, like a koala stuck to someone's leg in those gifs, but not quite as cute. She is capable, however, and she'll figure this out herself, if she can't badger one of us into stepping in for her.

"When you decided to live in Ireland, I told you it was a mistake. Now that you're finally having the baby, I wanted to mention how superior our hospitals are in England. They're staffed only by the highest level Healers. I would be happy to send a jet for you right now."

Because flying while in labor would be a great plan? If my opinion of her competency was based on this conversation, I'd wonder how Amelia manages to run the country. "Imhotep manages our local hospital. Are you implying that he's not competent?"

I can almost hear her gritting her teeth. I know what she wants—the headline.

"Amelia, I'm not going to answer any calls for the next week. And if you reach out for any reason other than impending nuclear war, I won't step in to help with the next round of trade negotiations."

She hangs up.

It's a delicate balance, maintaining peace without actually ruling anyone.

Except for the Irish.

When Kahn and I came here to help mediate a long-standing dispute in leadership between Ireland and England, we fell in love. The rolling green hills. The fences made out of bushes. The fluffy white sheep.

The beautiful, lyrical accents. The gruff, red-bearded men. Actually, I might like the bearded men more than Kahn. Either way, when we arrived, we'd just discovered I was pregnant, and it felt like the perfect place to start a family and build a home.

But when we asked for permission to relocate, the Irish struck a hard bargain. They wanted Northern Ireland rejoined with Ireland, and they wanted Kahn and me to rule. I absolutely refused to accept the title of queen, empress, monarch, or pharaoh.

As if.

It took a lot of back and forth, but we finally settled on being called the Governor and Governess of Ireland. It sounds suitably regal without despotic undertones, or that's my hope. And of course, Ireland is now entirely and completely free of English rule. The separation caused a reasonable amount of discontent, but not many people feel like questioning me these days, and sometimes that's actually nice.

In the end, even the hassle of ruling an island felt like a fair trade—we have an actual home.

"Did you call Imhotep?" Rosalinde has insisted on sleeping in the same house as me for the last four weeks. I'm not quite sure why. If there's a problem, I can probably shift and fix it.

Or I could weave a little energy patch. Thanks to Anat's help, I can heal most anything that isn't already dead. (Been there, tried that, not making that mistake again.)

"Does he need me to call?" I sigh. "I feel like he's been living at the hospital. He's certainly sent me daily, sometimes hourly texts, with images of the room he's prepared for us."

"Rooms." Kahn drops the bags on the ground and sighs with exasperation.

"You could Lift those, you know," I say.

"Honestly, it feels good to use my actual body sometimes."

I step toward him. "You can say that again."

His eyes meet mine and he grins the wolfish, hungry smile that he only shares with me. "Alright, I will." He stalks toward me, his eyes intent on my face. He may not be a shifter, but sometimes he moves like a restless animal. "I don't hate your actual body, either." His hand grabs the base of my neck and tugs me closer.

"Oh my gosh!" Rosalinde covers her eyes. "What is wrong with the two of you?"

Kahn's head's lowering toward mine when another contraction hits and my hands clench into fists.

"Okay, okay, hospital it is." Kahn Lifts the bags this time, towing them along behind us. He drapes one arm around my lower back as if he worries I might collapse.

"Wait!" Bastet runs down the hall like she's fleeing a bonfire.

"What's wrong?" I don't see anything burning, or anyone attacking. I don't even sense anyone near the house.

"I finished it just in time." She's holding something bulky in her hands. It looks like. . .

"Is that a blanket?" It looks like it was made by a child.

"This is what grandmas here do for their grandchildren," she says. "I've been doing some research, now that I have a computer."

She's had a laptop for six months. She still struggles to open Chrome. I'll have to check her search history to prepare myself for future surprises. "Your research led you to make us a gigantic yarn ball?"

Kahn squeezes my hand a little too hard.

"That's a joke," I say. "What a lovely blanket." Which is an absolute lie.

She releases most of it, and it unfurls, if that word can be used for the irregular, far-too-large, knotty mess of purple and green and pink.

"We're having a boy," I say.

"I know that." Bastet frowns. "And now he won't be cold at all, even in this miserably frigid place." She extends her hand.

Thankfully, Kahn takes it. "We love it. Thank you so much."

"You should really thank *I Love Yarn*, on YourTube."

"I'm pretty sure it's called YouTube," I say.

"Right." Bastet's got a bag over her shoulder, and she points at the door. "We better hurry, or you'll drop your litter on the floor."

What a wonderful image. I doubt anyone else at the hospital will have a three-thousand-year-old Lioness Warlord at their bedside when they give birth.

Their loss.

Bastet and Rosalinde duck out the door, probably to bring the car around. I'm glad that Bastet doesn't have a driver's license, but she's been bugging me more and more often about getting one. I'm running out of excuses to put her off, but the idea of her behind the wheel of a car terrifies me.

"Anat's coming?" Kahn asks.

"She's on the ferry, I think."

"Did you invite anyone else?" He's trying to stuff the blanket into one of the bags, but as soon as he gets the majority of it in, a side part pops out.

I Lift the rest and tuck it inside.

"Thanks."

"Only Martin," I say. "He's already there, waiting."

"He's been at that hotel nearby for two weeks. I still don't know why he didn't stay with us," Kahn says.

"He didn't want to stress us out," I say.

"We've had Healers basically crawling all over us for the last few weeks." Kahn's lips twist.

"Hey." I run my fingers over the fine lines at the sides of his eyes. He's stressed. Even with all the Healers prowling the premises, this pregnancy has been hard on him.

And on me.

We both remember the last one.

"What do you think happened to our son?" His voice is soft.

I don't even have to ask which son he's talking about, because I've wondered the same thing myself a million times. "I'm not sure."

"Do you think—" He presses a hand against my belly. "Did he die?"

"He might have." Saying the words feels so final. We've lost so many people—too many. Dad and Jesse, Mehen and Am-Heh, Henry and countless others— gone forever. "But I like to hope that his soul went into Terra like everyone else, and he was spun out to live his life somewhere."

Kahn doesn't point out that all the other souls had bodies already on Earth, whereas Alexander and I were sucked into Terra and didn't emerge until we were reborn. I try not to think about those details.

"We're going to have a smooth delivery and a healthy son," I say.

"No invading army. No insane, power-hungry parents trying to take over the world." He grins. "Having a baby these days will be a piece of cake."

Anat's waiting at the hospital when we arrive,

tapping her stiletto-heeled foot. "You took forever. I was worried there were problems."

"We're all fine," I say.

For a few days after we finally ended the threat of Isis—technically, after Dad finally ended the threat—Anat was in some kind of coma. I was so shook by everything that happened that I didn't even think to try funneling energy into her. After I did, she revived quickly. She was essentially starved, and I let her suffer.

Even after she woke, it took her nearly a week to come to terms with Dad's sacrifice. I thought she might mourn the loss of her sister, but she kept insisting, "She ceased to be my sister long ago."

I'm not sure whether that's really true, but for now she's blocking any pain that loss causes her. I can't blame her for finding peace any way that she can.

Standing in front of the local hospital, she looks every inch the modern aristocrat. The British government gave her a title, the Duchess of Kendal, in exchange for her services to them in navigating the magical side of this new world. She wanted something far enough to give me and Kahn our space, but close enough to pop over at a moment's notice. She's struck a great balance so far. Bastet won't leave my side, but Anat comes running at the slightest suggestion, leaving us alone otherwise.

"Labor's going to work the same as it always has," Imhotep explains, as he greets us all at the door. "Your body will prepare for the ejection of the child—"

"Ejection?" Kahn's face reflects the horror in his tone.

"It's time for him to survive on his own," Imhotep says.

We settle in our rooms quickly, but then nothing changes. My contractions are irregular and relatively mild. At first, everyone's very excited, attentive, and energetic. But after about three hours, Bastet shifts and takes a nap in the corner. Martin starts playing some kind of numbers game on his phone. Anat starts changing small things about her appearance in the mirror—a terrible habit she's had for centuries, apparently. Imhotep leaves to see other patients.

"Should I be worried?" I ask.

Rosalinde shakes her head. "Having a baby seems to be a bit like dealing with a government agency. There's a lot of hurry up and wait."

But finally, the contractions grow nearer together. Even Kahn's hand on my back doesn't help, and when Imhotep checks, he declares, "You're ready. It's time for you to push."

You'd think with so much magic in the world, and specifically the amount in this room, there would be a better way to do this, but apparently not. It takes longer than I expected, and I'm fairly sure I've crushed Kahn and Anat's hand bones, but finally, our baby boy enters the world, crying from his first breath.

I send out a group text once he's all cleaned up, and receive dozens of messages of congratulations from all over the world, including a very kind one from John. He was always my friend first, and he and Kahn are much closer now than they ever were as kids. But shortly after that, I discover that having a baby wasn't the hard part. *Worrying* about a baby is so much scarier than giving birth.

"What's wrong?" Anat asks.

"I'm not really sure, but every time I look at him, at his perfect cheeks, at his beautiful eyelashes, at his tiny nose, I get this panicked feeling. What if I can't keep him safe? What if the world hurts him?"

Anat's smile is familiar, gentle, and wise. She takes

him from my arms and cradles him, softly brushing his dark hair with her free hand. "The world will hurt him, and then we will reduce whoever or whatever did to rubble. And we'll incinerate the remains."

Occasionally I forget that she comes from a more horrifying time, and then she says things like that and I remember.

"But there is beauty in the world too, and he will find it." She presses a kiss to his forehead.

"I hope that's true."

"Of course it is," she says. "We will craft the most wonderful life for him."

I trust her on that. She's working on it right now.

Her voice drops to a whisper, clearly addressing the baby. "And don't worry about your head being a little oddly shaped. If it doesn't round out, or if you ever wish you had straighter teeth or brighter eyes, you know who can help, little one. Aunt Anat will—"

"Anat."

Her mouth clicks shut. "You know I would never do anything without your permission."

I do know that. Or at least, I think I do. She stares at that little baby with the same zealous admiration she reserved for my dad. "Thank you for being here—but I don't think of you as an aunt, not really."

Her face turns toward mine. "I know that you've had a terrible run with mothers, and I know my sister was awful, but—"

"I don't see you as an aunt, because you're more like a mother to me."

Her lip trembles. Her eyes well with tears. When she nods, it seems like she's trying to keep from bawling.

"How does Grandma Anat sound to you?"

She hugs me so tightly, I worry that she might be

squishing the baby. Luckily, he's fine. When she passes him back to me, I think about the number of people surrounding and supporting us. Martin, Anat, Bastet, Rosalinde, John, Imhotep, Horus, and so many more.

When I had only Jesse, the loss of him destroyed me. But with a large family, with connections to an entire community of people, sorrow is shared and joy increased. This little boy will be surrounded by many connections, by so much love.

Of course, my moment of peace doesn't last forever. A few hours later, I've officially lost my perspective again.

"He won't wake up to eat," I say. "All he does is sleep."

"Don't worry. He'll wake when he's hungry." Kahn's standing over me, smiling.

"Imhotep said he needs to eat every two to three hours."

"Okay. . ."

"It's been three hours *and eleven minutes*."

He snorts.

I glare at him. "Are you implying our son's health and well-being isn't a priority?"

He gently takes him from me. "You and I have found one another in two different lifetimes. We survived insane parents. We've worked through all kinds of earth-shattering problems."

"And don't forget," I say, "We got our taxes filed on time." Barely. I was a little nervous it wouldn't happen for a while there.

He beams at me. "But our greatest adventures still lie ahead of us, and I'll be by your side for every minute of them. We'll figure it all out, and when we can't work something out on our own, we'll ask for help." He tugs the little blue cap down a little further on baby Jesse's head. "The best news is that our happy ending is just getting started."

I'm reminded by his words just how right Jesse was in that dream. Time is our greatest gift, and thanks to him, I try my hardest never to take it for granted.

<<<<>>>

If you enjoyed that, you should try my Birthright Series. Displaced is FREE on all platforms. You can read a sample chapter if you keep scrolling.

Or, if you've read that, Marked is also FREE. (Scroll on to read the first chapter for free!)

Wait, you read that series too!?! WHAT? Have you tried my romances? Finding Faith is free on all platforms as well.

Or there's also the Birch Creek Ranch Series, which starts with The Bequest.

You can sign up for my newsletter at: www.BridgetEBakerWrites.com, (and get a free book!)

Or you can join my reader group on Facebook at: https://www.facebook.com/groups/750807222376182.

28

SAMPLE CHAPTER OF
MARKED

I'm a big fat coward.

I've known this about myself definitively since one month before my sixth birthday. The night I lost my dad.

Case in point: I'm just shy of seventeen. I've been in love with the same guy for almost three years. Even though I see Wesley a few times a week, I haven't said a word. But tonight I have the perfect opportunity to do what I've always feared to try. Tonight, to celebrate our upcoming Path selections, all the teens in Port Gibson play a stupid, risky game.

Spin the Bottle.

I glance around as I walk toward the campfire in front of me. Only thirty-five kids turned seventeen in the past year, so of course I know them all. My best girl friend, Gemette, waves me over. I try to squash my disappointment at not seeing Wesley. When I played this scene in my brain earlier, I was sitting by him.

"You gonna scowl at the fire all night, Ruby?" Gemette pats a gloved hand on the slab of granite underneath her.

"You couldn't have saved us one of those seats?" I point at the smooth, flat stumps on the other side of the fire. I sit down and shift around, trying to find a flat spot.

"I think what you meant to say was, 'Thanks, Gemette. You're the best.'"

Her straight black hair reflects the campfire flames when she tosses it back over her shoulder. It's against the Council's rules for hair to cover your forehead. Gotta make it easy to see anyone who might be Marked. Except tonight, no one's following the rules. Everyone's wearing their hair down, and Gemette's silky locks frame her face beautifully. I envy her sleek hair almost as much as I covet her curves.

"My bum's already hurting on this," I mutter.

"If you weighed more than eighty-five pounds soaking wet, it wouldn't bother you so much."

Instead of curves, I've got twig arms and a non-existent backside. I shift on the huge slab, trying to find a position that doesn't hurt. I arch one eyebrow, not that she can see it in the dark. "I weigh ninety-two pounds, thank you very much."

Gemette snorts. "That proves my point, you bony butt."

She leans toward the fire and picks up the glass bottle lying on its side. She tosses it a few inches up into the air before catching it again.

"Be careful with that." That bottle's the only reason I'm sitting here, sour-faced, stomach churning.

Slowly the remaining seats around the fire fill up. Wesley shows up last. There aren't any seats left, but before I can convince Gemette to squish over, he grabs a bucket. He turns it upside down and takes a seat a few feet away from everyone else. I guess that's fitting. His dad's the Mayor of Port Gibson and a Counsellor on the CentiCouncil, so Wesley's in charge by default tonight. He'll probably take over for his dad one day, which isn't as glamorous as it sounds since less than two thousand people live here.

He looks around the fire, and his gaze stops on me. He bobs his head in my direction, and I shoot him a smile. I'm glad he can't hear the thundering of my heart.

Although we're all huddled around a campfire, and I've known most of the kids here for years, we maintain carefully measured space between us. Tercera dictates our habits even when we're rebelling. Which we're only doing because it's a tradition.

Maybe Tercera's made cowards of us all.

"Are we starting?" Tom's sitting to my left. His parents are both in Agriculture and he's Pathing there, too. He has broad shoulders and tan skin from working outside most of the day. Gemette likes him, and it's easy to see why. Of course, he's nothing to Wesley.

I glance across the fire in time to see Wesley stand up. He straightens the collar of his coat slowly and methodically, like his dad always does before a town hall meeting. Wesley loves doing impressions, and he's usually convincingly good at them.

"I'd like to take this opportunity to welcome you all to the Last Supper." His voice mimics his father's, and he touches his chin with his right hand in the same way his dad always rubs his beard. Wesley himself is tall and lean with long black hair that he's wearing down, for once. It falls in his eyes in a way I've never seen before, and I feel a little rush. I want to touch it.

Wesley smirks. "I know you may be less than impressed with the culinary offerings for our gathering, but as I always say, Tradition has Value." He cracks a grin then, and everyone laughs. "Seriously though." He drops the impression and returns to his normal voice, which I like way better anyway. "I know the food sucks, but this whole thing started with a bunch of teenagers who were sick of rules and ready to throw caution to the wind for a night."

I look down at the three or four-dozen nondescript metal cans with the tops peeled back, resting on coals. Another few dozen are open but sitting away from the fire. Presumably they contain fruit or something else we won't want to eat hot.

Wesley leans over and snags the first can, his gloves keeping him safe from the heat. "I hope you'll all forgive me, but this was what we could find."

"This is a pretty crummy tradition." Lina reaches down and grabs a can with mittened hands. Her dark brown hair falls in a long, thick braid down her back, like it has every single time I've seen her.

"Traditions matter, even the silly ones. They help pull us together as a community, which is valuable when fear of Tercera yanks communities apart. We're stronger when we aren't alone. Thinking every man should look out for himself hurts all of us." Wesley takes his first bite right before Lina. I grab a can of baked beans.

The food really is as bad as it looks, but at least it's not spoiled.

Wesley talks while we eat.

"As you already know, we come from a variety of backgrounds. Before the Marking, Port Gibson housed approximately the same number of people, but not a single person who lived here before the Marking survived. We cleaned out the homes, burned some to the ground and rebuilt, circled the city with a wall, and made it our own. The Unmarked who live here are Christian, Muslim, atheist, black, white, Hispanic,

Russian, German and Japanese. I could keep going, but I don't need to. Before the Marking, these differences divided humanity. Now, we know that what truly matters is what we all share. We embrace the traditions that bring us all together, because we're more alike than we are unalike."

I swallow the last spoonful of baked beans from my can and set it down on the ground by my feet. I'm almost the last one to finish eating, but several half-full cans are scattered around the campfire. A few people grab a can of fruit. I prefer the stuff my Aunt and I process and can ourselves, so I don't bother.

I rub my hands together briskly. Even in mittens, my fingers feel stiff. It's usually not too cold in Mississippi, even in January, but a late freeze has everyone bundled up. The Last Supper's supposed to be a chance to rebel, but I'm grateful that everyone's as covered as possible. It means I won't look as cowardly for keeping my mittens on. My aunt is Port Gibson's head of the Science Path, so I know all about how Tercera congregates first in the skin cells, even before the Mark has shown up on the forehead in some cases.

The wind moans as it blows through the trees, and we all huddle around the meager fire. Even though the flames have died down to coals in most places, it burns hot. My face roasts while my back freezes. The bottle lies stationary on the weathered flagstones by the fire where Gemette set it, light glinting off of the dingy glass at strange angles.

The quiet conversations die off and the nervous laughter ends. Eyes dart to and fro among the thirty something teenagers gathered.

"So." Evan's voice cracks, and he clears his throat. "Who goes first?"

"Thanks for volunteering," Wesley says.

I suspect no one else asked for just this reason. All eyes turn toward poor, gangly, redheaded Evan.

Evan gawks momentarily. Even though he and I work in Sanitation together, I don't know him well. I haven't been there long enough to guess whether he feels lucky or put upon. He sighs, and then leans forward and tweaks the bottle. It twists sharp and fast and skitters to the right, spinning furiously.

I really hope the bottle doesn't stop on me, and I doubt I'm alone in that thought. Evan's funny in a self-deprecating way, but he isn't smart, and he definitely isn't hot. I bite my lip, worried about what I'll do if it does stop on me.

It slows quickly and finally stops pointing to my left. I sigh in relief, which I belatedly hope no one heard.

Tom gasps, and then in a raspy voice says, "No way. I mean, you're nice and all Evan, but I'm not . . . I don't . . ."

"Yeah, me either. Chill, man." Evan laughs. "So, does it pass to the next person over?" Evan raises his eyebrows and glances at me.

I want to protest, but my throat closes off and I look down at my feet instead.

Evan stands up. "So Ruby . . ."

He may not have saved me a seat, but Wesley jumps in to save me now, thank goodness. "That's not how it works. If you get someone of the same gender, and neither of you . . . well, then your turn passes to him or her. Which means you sit down Evan, and you spin next, Tom."

"Who made these rules?" Evan grumbles as he sits.

Gemette smiles. "They make sense, Evan. I mean, it's not spin the bottle and pick best out of three. Your way, you'd basically pick someone in the circle who's close and kiss whoever you want."

Evan shrugs and glances at me again with a smile. "Sounds pretty okay, actually."

Tom snorts. "I don't hear Ruby complaining about Wesley's rules. I'd say that's your answer, man."

I look back down at my shoes, but not before I see Tom's wink. Jerk. Evan must feel idiotic, and I definitely want to sink into the ground.

I bite my lip again, this time a little harder. Tom's an obviously good-looking guy, but I have no interest in kissing him. I hope his wink was a joke about Evan and not some kind of message.

Cold air blows past me as Tom leans forward to spin the bottle, his body no longer blocking the wind. One thing jumps out at me as he reaches for the glass bottle. In spite of the cold, Tom isn't wearing gloves. He must've taken them off at some point. He's either a daredevil or an idiot. I'm not sure which.

Tom spins the bottle less forcefully than Evan and rocks back and forth as the bottle circles round and round. His eyes focus intently on the spinning glass as if he can somehow control where it stops. I wonder who he's hoping for and look around the circle for clues. Andrea seems particularly bright-eyed. My eyes continue to wander. One gorgeous, deep blue pair of eyes in the circle stares right back at me. Wesley. I've looked at him a lot over the past few years, but this feels different somehow. A spark zooms through me, and I quickly stare at my feet.

No luck for Andrea tonight, or Gemette. The bottle comes to rest on Andrea's best friend, Annelise, instead. She and I were in Science together a long time ago. Her dark brown hair hangs loose, framing high cheekbones and expressive chocolate eyes. She frowns.

Tonight doesn't seem to be going right for anyone so far.

"Now what?" Annelise's voice shakes. "We just kiss, right here in front of everyone?"

"No, of course not," Gemette snaps.

"Who made you the boss?" Evan frowns. Judging by his sulky tone, he's still mad about losing his turn earlier.

"Unfortunately, I'm the boss," Wesley says, "and she's right." He points to a dilapidated shed at the top of the hill. "You two go up there."

"Romantic." Tom rolls his eyes as he stands up. He rubs his bare palms on his pants. Gross. At least I know I'm not the only nervous one here. Tom and Annelise trudge a path through clumps of frozen brown grass toward the rundown tool shed.

What a special memory for their first kiss.

Gemette sighs and I pat her gloved hand with my own. I'd feel worse for her, but Gemette likes every decent looking guy in town, including a few boys a year younger than us. She'll recover from missing out on a special moment with Tom.

I glance again toward Andrea, an acquaintance from my time in Agriculture. She and Tom trained together for years. She may have liked him as long as I've liked Wesley. She looks into the fire while her foot digs a messy hole in the soil. I wonder how I'll feel if Wesley spins and gets Andrea. Or worse, Gemette. I'll have to sit here and twiddle my thumbs while I know he's in there kissing a friend. My stomach lurches. Coming tonight was a stupid idea. I clearly didn't think this through.

No one speaks to distract me from my anxiety. The shed isn't far. We could easily eavesdrop on them if the wind would shriek a little less.

"How long does this take?" Evan asks.

"Who the heck knows?" Gemette points at the bottle. "Impatient for another crack at it?"

Kids around us chuckle.

After another few awkward moments, Gemette grabs the bottle and gives it a twist. "No reason we have to wait on them."

"Sure," Wesley says. "Whoever it lands on can go next."

"Wait," Evan asks, "whoever it lands on goes next as in it's their turn to spin? Or goes next as in Gemette's going to kiss them?"

The bottle stops before anyone can respond, pointing directly at Wesley. His perfectly shaped brows draw together under disheveled black hair. Gorgeous hair. His lips form a perfect "o". His bright blue eyes meet mine again.

My heart races and the baked beans sit like a lump in my belly. I shouldn't have come. Of course Wesley will want to kiss her. Gemette's gorgeous, curvy, and smart. Ugh. Am I going to have to sit here while my best friend kisses the guy I like twenty feet away? This is all my fault. If I'd only told Gemette, she'd beg off.

I bite down a little harder on my lip and taste blood this time. I really need to kick this particular habit, especially with kissing in my future. Maybe. Hopefully. I'm such an idiot.

Wesley clears his throat. "I think I'm going to sit this game out. I'm more of a moderator than a participant."

"No," I blurt out. "You can't. You're here, you're seventeen, you have to participate." What am I doing? Why am I shoving him at my friend? But if I don't make him play, I'm flushing my chance to kiss him down the toilet. I want to cry.

"Well, then I guess it's my turn to spin." His deep voice sounds completely different than any of the other kids here tonight. My stomach ties in knots when I hear him speak, which is ridiculous because I've heard his voice a million times.

I glance at Gemette. She looks disappointed and I want to cry with relief, but I don't blame her. He could've kissed her but didn't pursue it. I imagine most any girl here would be disappointed. He glances up and his eyes lock with mine again. Caught. I start to shiver and try to stop it. This look is different somehow from any before, like something shifted. Wesley clears his throat, looks down at the bottle, gracefully reaches over, and snaps it between his fingers.

It spins evenly, not moving to the right or the left. It spins on and on, and I wonder if it'll ever stop. It slows, whirling a little less with each rotation, the butterflies in my stomach swooping and swirling with each pass.

Until it finally stops. On me.

My eyes snap up reflexively, wide with shock. Wesley doesn't even seem surprised. He simply stands and inclines his head toward the shed.

"Isn't it still..." I clear my throat. "Umm, occupied?"

"We can wait over there." He gestures at the hill to the right of the shed. One side of his mouth lifts in a smile and I feel an answering grin form on my lips. Which makes me think about what we're about to do with our lips.

Swarms and swarms of butterflies flutter in my chest.

"Sure," I say.

I stand up and without even thinking, I wipe my palms on my jeans. They aren't even sweaty and what's more, I'm wearing mittens! I really hope no one noticed. Okay, more specifically, I hope Wesley didn't notice. Gemette holds something out to me when I stand. I can't tell what it is from feel alone thanks to my thick mittens, and in the dark I have to squint to make it out at all. A tube of something. "What—"

"Lip gloss," she whispers. "A gift from my mom. I was going to use it, but looks like you need it more, you lucky, lip-biting brat." She winks.

I'm glad Wesley's still across the fire from me and that it's dark. Maybe he somehow miraculously missed both the palm wipe and her wink.

I walk as slowly as I can toward the old shed, partially to avoid tripping, but also so I won't look overeager. I try to hide my face while I apply the fruit-scented lip-gloss so that Wesley won't notice. It's dark, but I don't want him to be put off by dry, scratchy lips, or worse, dried blood. Gemette's a good friend. I feel guilty for overreacting earlier when I thought she might kiss Wesley. Not super guilty, but you know, a little.

Neither of us speaks a word, but I feel the eyes of the other teens follow us toward the shed. We're only a few crunching steps away when the swinging door flies open and Tom and Annelise barrel out. I jump when it bangs shut behind them.

Tom looks as ruffled as I feel, his eyes darting back and forth. He ducks his head and reaches down to take Annelise's hand. They walk out and away from the fire and the rest of Port Gibson's teens. I can't tell where they're headed, but somewhere far away from here.

"Did you know almost a third of the couples in town trace their start to the Last Supper?" Wesley asks.

"No way."

He shrugs. "We've only been an Unmarked town for seven years, so it's even more impressive. Not all of them are matched up from a bottle spin, but I think the game helps people realize how they feel."

A thrill rushes through me. Does Wesley feel the same as me?

My hand reaches for the door handle and collides en route with his. I'm wearing mittens, of course, and he's wearing shiny, brown gloves, but a thrill runs through me when we touch, even through layers. He doesn't move his hand away, but instead draws my hand in his and pushes the door handle back in one fluid movement. My heart skips a beat and time stops. When the door's completely open, he slowly releases my hand. I lower my eyes and step over the threshold into the rundown little building.

Although there's clearly no power, and consequently neither heat nor an overhead light, the walls at least cut the wind. It's at once both warmer and quieter. Two tall candles burn softly on a pile of rusted metal boxes in the corner. Someone prepared this dump, I realize. I wonder whether it was Wesley. The flames provide enough light that I can see his face. His dark brows are an even more startling contrast to his dark blue eyes than usual, accentuated by his hair falling in his face.

"So," I say. "Here we are."

Wesley looks at me from less than a foot away. The shed's small and crammed full of moldering farm implements. The air around us practically hums, but that isn't new. It's always like the moments right before a lightning storm when he's near. Supercharged almost, like the electrons around my body might fly off at his slightest touch. The difference is that here, away from the town's work projects, away from my family and his, it feels like anything really could happen.

Wesley's so close I can smell him, the same citrusy,

woodsy smell I've secretly savored for years. It's even stronger tonight, like he put on more of whatever it is he usually wears. I breathe deep, and all the memories of him re-imprint on my brain. Scrubbing, sanding, painting, digging, cleaning, hammering. Projects his dad made him attend, but I suffered through to be near him. When I'm with him, I belong somewhere for the first time in a decade.

When we become adults next week, Wesley's mandatory attendance at work projects ends. Wesley steps into his role as an administrator, and I'll become part of Port Gibson's janitorial crew. It's now or never if I want to make any kind of permanent place with Wesley.

I never thought I'd be close to him like this, and I know I may never be again. I lean toward him and tilt my face upward, eyes closed, ready for what comes next. Maybe I'm even a touch impatient. I have waited for this for years.

Except I keep waiting, and then I wait some more.

Not a single thing happens. The trouble with being ridiculously small is that Wesley, who's on the tall side anyway, towers over me. Even with my face angled up, his lips are pretty far away. I can barely make out his expression, but it looks guarded.

Maybe he doesn't know how to do it?

No way. Wesley must know. I mean, it's not hard, right? You just push your lips onto the other person's mouth. Why isn't he doing anything? This is the moment. THE moment!

Until it passes. And then another moment falls on top of it, and another. All passing. Even the butterflies in my stomach get bored and go look for flowers elsewhere.

I'm not sure exactly how much time has elapsed,

but the seconds drag, heavy with my growing frustration. Soon, someone will bang on the door. "You've been in there forever," they'll say. "Make room for the next couple."

I want to smack them in their eager faces.

I know I don't have much time, and I want to say something, anything. I need to tell him how I feel, say the words, take a gamble. But like it always does, my tongue shuts down. My throat closes off. The words stick inside my throat. Why am I such a coward? Our perfect moment withers and dies. Tears well up in my eyes, and I can't breathe.

Wesley isn't similarly affected. He steps back and says, "We don't have to do this, Ruby. It's not safe at all. I don't know why my dad even lets these dinners happen."

"Why'd you spin the bottle in the first place?" I hear the desperation in my voice, but the words pour out in spite of myself. "I know you, and you know me. How's it dangerous for us?"

He takes another step back, his expression registering surprise. "People get Marked, Ruby. It still happens. Every few weeks, in fact. Maybe I'm Marked. You don't know. It happens, even here, even with all our rules. It may take years to die once you're Marked, but it's inevitable."

I roll my eyes. "Well I'm not Marked, if that's what you're worried about." I point at my forehead. "See? Clear."

"We shouldn't be taking these risks." Wesley scowls. "Not now, not right before our real lives begin. This whole thing's supposed to be a time to say goodbye to being a kid, not act like an idiotic five-year-old, breaking rules for no reason."

Our real lives? Maybe he never thought it felt right,

the time we spent, the way we are together. Maybe I never belonged with him at all. "Why'd you even come, then? Why follow me in here if you're not going to kiss me?"

Was he hoping for someone else? Was he stuck with me and looking for any excuse to bolt? Am I Evan in this scenario?

I look up, but I'm too close. The hair cascading over his face obscures my view. I want to touch his hair; I want to kiss him; I want to tell him I love him, and that I always have. My fingers and toes and everything connecting them zings in spite of the bitter cold, in spite of the indifference of his words. Energy spins round and round in my body, a closed circuit with nowhere to go.

"Look, Ruby, I don't know what to say . . . but the thing is . . ." He sounds torn, confused.

Suddenly, I don't want to hear "the thing," whatever it is. I've been talking to Wesley for years, talking and talking, and working alongside him, but I don't want to talk to him anymore. I know what I want and I'll never have a better chance to play things off as part of a game, if he feels like I now suspect he does. The notion of an excuse appeals to my cowardly heart. I can't speak the words, but I won't stand here and do nothing, not anymore, because he's the real life I've longed for.

I stop thinking and step toward him instead. He tries to step back and slams up against the back wall. I quickly take one more step and use my gloved hand to pull his head down to mine. I push my lips against his. In my haste, I push too hard and pull a little too fast. Our teeth smack into each other and my tooth knocks against my own lip, splitting it wide open again.

It's the opposite of magical.

I look up at Wesley instinctively. He has blood on his mouth, but whether it's his, or mine, I can't tell. And if it's not awful enough already, Wesley stiffens from head to toe like I mauled him, like I forced him into something torturous.

A tear rolls down my cheek and I inhale deeply. I won't cry over this. I can't, because there's no way I can play it all off as a game if I bawl my eyes out. I turn away from him. If I can't stop the tears, at least he doesn't need to see them. When did this go so wrong? I should be calm, cool, in control. I need to laugh it all off and tell him friends can't be expected to kiss well. Whoops.

Except my heart won't listen to the screaming from my head. I'm not calm. I'm the opposite of cool. I've lost all control.

He grabs my shoulder and tugs me around. I turn, but my eyes stay glued to the ground, too ashamed to meet his gaze.

"Ruby, look at me."

He puts two gloved fingers under my chin and lifts. His head comes down then, but slowly, too slowly. My heart stops pumping and I worry it might never beat again. His lips brush mine gently, then with more pressure. I ignore the discomfort of my torn lip and lean into him, connected to him in a way I can't explain. I need more air, but I want less, because that means more space between us. If this never ends, maybe it'll erase the moments that preceded it.

Suddenly, he lets me go and steps back. Emptiness fills the space where he stood. I reel again, sucking air in and blowing my breath back out to steady myself.

When I raise my eyes, our gazes lock. All my sorrow from before is gone, replaced with a feeling like I'm flying, soaring, floating on top of the world. His sapphire blue eyes reflect candlelight back at me. He's breathing as deeply as I am; he's as affected as me. I can't look away from his strong, almost hawkish nose, his square jaw, his flashing eyes and thick black lashes. I continue to stare as Wesley reaches up and brushes his unkempt hair away from his eyes.

I almost faint.

Such a simple movement. Small in the grand scheme of things, but also vast, earth shattering, all encompassing. My dreams crumble. My world spins out of control. He moves his hair off his forehead, and suddenly things make sense. His reticence to touch me, his skittishness, but also his quick recovery. Once he knew it was too late, he didn't hesitate to kiss me.

Because we'd already touched.

A tiny rash mars his otherwise perfect forehead. Before the world died, it wouldn't have mattered. Before the Marking, no one would have cared about a few bumps. It would be harmless: acne, a bug bite, or a reaction to hair product. It shouldn't matter that his forehead has a blemish. It shouldn't terrify me, but it does. Because that small rash means Wesley is Marked, and in under three years, he's going to die terribly.

And now, so am I.

You can grab Marked right now.

❦ 29 ❦

SAMPLE CHAPTER OF
DISPLACED

My mom should have killed me the day I was born. In her nearly nine-hundred-year reign as the Empress of the First Family, sparing my life seventeen years ago was her single act of mercy.

Evians around the world refer to me as "Enora's Folly."

It's no wonder I'm fatally flawed, a blemish among the shining population of evians Mom rules. I spent my childhood running away from my twin sister's taunts. Maybe that's why no one on the island can catch me. On days when life feels too heavy and my heart struggles to beat without melancholy, the Kona wind blowing against my face reminds me the world is vast and full of possibility. And on days when I need that wind, but my mom's too busy to run with me, there's always Lark.

"Wait up," she calls from dozens of yards behind me.

I stop at the top of the northeastern cliffs, the highest point on Ni'ihau, and scan the horizon while I wait for her. Dolphins leap energetically in the distance. I've been on this island the majority of my life, yet every single time I stop to take in the lush island of Kauai in the distance, and every time I stand at the highest point of Ni'ihau, the majesty of my surroundings astonishes me. When Lark finally reaches my side, her lungs heave in great, gulping breaths and she bends over double. "We should've taken the horses."

"Are you okay?" I lift one eyebrow.

She waves her hand at me absently and wheezes. "Fine, you idiot. Not all of us are machines. You've got to ease up for the little people."

"You're the one who suggested we take this trail."

"I guess that makes me the idiot." She straightens next to me, her heart rate decelerating back to normal.

"As your best friend, I officially disagree with you." I grin. "You're smart and talented, Lark. People like you. Now repeat that until you believe it."

"Speaking of how much you love me..." Lark won't meet my eye.

"What's up?" I ask.

"I need help."

Most evians don't do favors, not without negotiation and *quid pro quo*, or at least a few moments of analysis to weigh the impact and risk to them. But I'm the broken heir, the defective twin, the one who doesn't view friendship as a commodity like I should.

Which is why I immediately say, "Anything. You already know that."

Lark's voice drops to a whisper. "The intelligence subsection is getting more competitive every year."

She's a year older than me and recently completed her training, which means placement for her first work assignment happens in the next few days.

"Right," I say. "Balth said it's gotten popular." Not that I care, since I'll never be placed anywhere. I'm stuck here forever.

"A few years ago, Mom could've gotten me a spot for sure."

"But now?"

"Well." She clears her throat. "She can't do much now. But if I could defeat a seventh gen in a challenge. . ."

Lark wants to fight me. And more than that, she needs to beat me. Publicly.

"You want to stab me with a sword in front of everyone we know?" That's a pretty big ask. I mean, I heal lightning quick, but it still hurts. Plus, Lark is tenth gen. Losing to her would be a new low, even for me.

"I really don't want to get stuck working for Uncle Max."

"Oh come on. He loves fostering the young minds. He's always talking about it."

"He is." Lark groans. "The idea of restructuring corporations all day long. . ." She closes her eyes. "I'll die of boredom."

Lark has always been melodramatic. "Just submit your DNA and you'll be auto-admitted into intelligence. It's not *that* competitive. I mean, you suck at appearance modification, and your mom is pretty well known, so you'll probably be stuck human side initially, but you can buckle down and practice your modifications and you'll cross over eventually."

"But if I defeat you, I'd be automatically ranked number one in Alamecha's class."

And I'd look pathetic, losing to someone with three generations more genetic deletions. I open my mouth to tell her no, but her quick inhalation stops me. She can test right into a top tier Security placement with a simple blood draw. Usually only candidates below fifteenth gen resort to theatrics like a public challenge. Why would she ask me to destroy my reputation for something she doesn't even need?

"You're absolutely positive you want a Security placement?" I ask.

Her gray eyes widen and her breath hitches again. This request matters to her. She might have even orchestrated this run to ask me without interruption. Heaven knows she never wants to go jogging, so this suggestion came out of the blue. My oldest friend has never asked me for a single thing, not in seventeen years. She probably knows better than anyone else how hard things are for me, and now she's asking me to do something she doesn't really need, knowing Judica will never let me forget my defeat.

Why?

I want to shove the thoughts away and ignore the nigglings at the back of my mind. But I can't. I'm not wired that way, and I keep circling back to the same conclusion. "I can only think of one reason you'd ask me to throw a challenge."

Lark's heart rate spikes and the scent of her perspiration rises, almost as strongly as when she was running full tilt.

Unfortunately, that's the confirmation I need. "You can't do the blood test."

Her nostrils flare. "Of course I can."

She's lying to me, but I hope I'm wrong about why. Because I think she just asked me to commit treason, and she didn't even plan to tell me I was doing it.

Why does she need me to throw a fight? I rarely train in earnest, whereas she spends hours every morning with her mom. Actually, she's rumored to be one of the best fighters on the compound. "Why not simply challenge me?"

Lark's gray eyes widen.

"Come on Lark, you can tell me. What's going on?" Please, please come clean.

"Never mind. It's fine." Lark turns away from me and picks at non-existent lint on her pants.

When I grab her hand, she jumps like I electrocuted her. "Tell me."

She yanks her hand away with wounded eyes. "There's nothing to tell."

"You're half human." My words hang in the air like a cloud of gnats, impeding my vision of the future, clouding my memory of the past, a plague on my heart. I wish I could wave my hand and dissipate the reality of my accusation, but I can't. Only Lark can fix this, by denying my wild claim.

I need her to deny it.

I'm afraid she can't.

When she doesn't say a word, I struggle to breathe. Lark's father must have been human. She's only half evian. Every moment of our seventeen years as best friends shifts, recharacterized by my new knowledge. Her heaving when we run, her training alone, her reticence to travel with me. The ground beneath my feet feels unsteady, like there's been an earthquake.

"Why didn't you tell me?" I whisper. "Why didn't you confess years ago?" The realization that she didn't even tell me now slaps me hard. I had to figure this out, about my own best friend.

A tear streaks down her face and she wipes it away ruthlessly. "What will you do now you know?"

"Look at me."

She doesn't.

"I can't believe you're asking me that right now. I'd

never turn you in. You think I could ever watch your execution? Lark, *look at me*."

Her lower lip wobbles. "I should never have asked in the first place. Mom was right. Why did I try to outsmart you? I'm deficient."

I can't even imagine living with that kind of fear. Why didn't her mother leave with her or adopt her out? The idea of life without Lark shatters my heart into pieces. All this time and she couldn't even risk telling her best friend. That's reason enough for me to throw one fight. No one should live like she's had to live, and if I can create a safer space for her in our world, I'll do it.

This time it's my voice that wobbles. "Your mistake wasn't in asking, it was in withholding the relevant information. Of course I'll do whatever you need. You'll get into Security and select intelligence and then you'll leave." I realize one reason I didn't want to help her before is that her Uncle Max lives here, and I didn't want her to leave.

But she has to go.

If she stays on the island, it's only a matter of time before someone else figures it out. "Then no one will ever know."

She shakes her head. "If you figured out why I asked, someone else might guess too."

"So we stage your challenge. Someone optimistically throws one down on me at least twice a year, you know, seeing as I'm the useless twin. I always turn them down flat, but maybe you'd make me mad enough to accept. Best friends know exactly which buttons to push, right?"

The corner of Lark's mouth turns up slightly. "Even so, Balthasar might figure it out," she says. "During the match I mean. It's dangerous, too dangerous to risk, which is why Mom said not to even ask you." She drops her face into her hands. "Mom's going to kill me when I tell her about all this."

"Tell your mom that you have an ally now." I smile and take her hand in mine. "I may not be *the Heir,* but I'm an heir, and beating me will be enough. Besides, once you're in the field working from the human side, you'll be away from all the evian politics. And working on the human side, you'll be safe."

"That's the plan," she says. "But when Mom finds out you know..."

"So don't tell her."

Lark shakes her head. "I can't lie to my mom. I can't. I lie to everyone else."

Her life has been harder than I ever realized. "How slow are you, exactly?"

Lark balls her fingers into a fist and swings at me. I duck easily. Her reflexes probably put a human to shame, but they're notably slower than mine. Ugh. How will we pull this off?

"I think the only way people won't notice your speed is if I'm truly horrible," I say. "Which shouldn't be too hard. I haven't reached the point of integrating active combat into my training yet, so I'm sure I'll be convincingly terrible."

"You're saying your mom's insistence on training you in old school melodics might save me?" Lark's smile reaches her eyes this time, and when her stormy gray eyes sparkle, I decide we can pull this off.

We don't have a choice.

Grab Displaced right now!

ACKNOWLEDGMENTS

My husband is always acknowledged, and it's still not enough. He does anything and everything to support me. With evert book, I whine the same whines. I whinge the same whinges. I fear the same failure. I doubt my words. I doubt my purpose. I doubt my abilities.

He's always there to tell me it's great, I'm great, keep going, no matter how many times he's said it before. I don't deserve him, but I'm glad I have him all the same.

This series has been the hardest I've ever written. I knew the ending from the very first chapter. I knew it would suck to write, and it would suck to read, and sometimes, by golly, life just sucks.

But I think the beauty in life lies in cherishing the beautiful moments. If they weren't quite so lovely, watching them end wouldn't be quite so sad.

Love the Jesses in your life every single day. Hold them close.

I'm so much luckier than Alora was—I am surrounded by people who love and support me. My children are amazing. My parents are wonderful. My mom, especially, is my biggest cheerleader and always has been. I have extended family and friends (including a very much alive brother and sister, both of whom I adore!) who are there for me, whenever I am down or out (of sorts!)

And I can't conclude this book or this series without extending a huge thank you to my editor Carrie, and to both my cover designers (Christian and Lara!).

Finally, to my readers, you guys have no idea how much your comments, your reviews, and your support mean to me. You guys are the whole reason I keep writing. (It sure ain't the sleepless nights, the characters yelling at me, or the tears shed while writing about highs and lows of FAKE people!!) Thank you for caring about my worlds and my words, and for sharing them with your friends and family. It's the greatest compliment you can pay me, and I'll never not be grateful.

ABOUT THE AUTHOR

Bridget's a lawyer, but does as little legal work as possible. She has five kids and soooo many animals that she loses count.

Horses, dogs, cats, rabbits, and so many chickens. Animals are her great love, after the hubby, the kids, and the books.

She makes cookies waaaaay too often and believes they should be their own food group. In a (possibly misguided) attempt at balancing the scales, she kickboxes daily. So if you don't like her books, maybe don't tell her in person.

Bridget is active on social media, and has a facebook group she comments in often. (Her husband even gets on there sometimes.) Please feel free to join her there: https://www.facebook.com/groups/750807222376182

romance and women's fiction books to keep from confusing Amazon's algorithms!)

The Finding Home Series:

Finding Faith (1)

Finding Cupid (2)

Finding Spring (3)

Finding Liberty (4)

Finding Holly (5)

Finding Home (6)

Finding Balance (7)

Finding Peace (8)

The Finding Home Series Boxset Books 1-3

The Finding Home Series Boxset Books 4-6

The Birch Creek Ranch Series:

The Bequest: November 30, 2021

The Vow: February 15, 2022

The Ranch: (April 15, 2022)

Children's Picture Book

Yuck! What's for Dinner?